D1105124

THIS SIDE OF GLORY

By the Author

DEEP SUMMER

THE HANDSOME ROAD

THIS SIDE OF GLORY

TOMORROW IS FOREVER

Gwen Bristow

_____

This Side of Glory

Buccaneer Books
Cutchogue, New York

International Standard Book Number: 0-89966-026-6

For ordering information, contact:

Buccaneer Books, Inc.
P.O. Box 168
Cutchogue, N.Y. 11935

(631) 734-5724, Fax (631) 734-7920
    www.BuccaneerBooks.com

Foreword

THE HANDSOME ROAD ends in 1882. In the spring of that year the Mississippi River was higher than it had ever been before, and in many places there were devastating floods like the one young Fred Upjohn saw when his levee broke. But the crash of the levees in 1882 had a good result, for it brought about the beginning of the modern efficient national system of flood control. Fred was not the only boy who made up his mind that year that when he grew up he would find some way to boss that river.

This Side of Glory begins thirty years later, in 1912, two years before the start of the First World War. Fred Upjohn has become a levee contractor. These levee builders are men who know the river as they know their own homes. They contract with the national government to build the levees and keep them in repair, so the river, when swollen by the melting snows from the North, will not overflow to wreck the fields. (A levee is an artificial embankment built to reinforce the natural bank of the river.)

Protection of the land along the river was becoming more and more important, for in the main this was cotton land, and cotton was vital to the economy of the United States. At the start of the First World War, nearly nine-tenths of the textiles in the world were made of cotton. Cotton was the largest export of this country; and because it was necessary to people everywhere, cotton had more to do with international finance and politics than any other commodity in the world.

In 1882, Denis Larne II was a young man twenty-two years old, Fred Upjohn was fourteen. In the thirty years since then, Denis and Fred have married and had children of their own. Denis' elder son is Kester Larne, Fred's daughter is Eleanor Upjohn. At the beginning of *This Side of Glory* Kester is twenty-seven years old and Eleanor twenty-two.

Kester and Eleanor grew up only a few miles apart, but their two childhoods were utterly different. The Larnes, the Sheramys, the other proud families who lost so much in the Civil War, rebuilt their life to be as nearly as possible like the old one. Their ways of thinking and doing, their emotional attitudes, were those they had had before. Kester Larne was born of the marriage between Denis Larne II and Lysiane St. Clair. (Lysiane too was descended from one of the families who came to Louisiana at the same time as Philip Larne. In the first chapter of *Deep Summer* you read about Mark Sheramy's calling a greeting from his flatboat to a family named St. Clair, who were bringing their own flatboat down the river.)

Born of these two gentlefolk, Kester has been bred in the old ways. He is a gentleman of beautiful manners, with reverence for the traditions of his ancestors. Kester also has the strength and gallantry of Philip Larne and the force of Judith Sheramy, everything that made it possible for them to hack their civilization out of the wilderness. But in Kester these traits are sleepy, because they have never had to wake up.

Eleanor is different because everything around her has made her different. Her father was no flower of a great family. Fred Upjohn started off with nothing but strength, but he had plenty of that. He married a girl who had no more to start with than himself, and they made their own way; and like many other such parents they gave their children better chances than they had had. Eleanor Upjohn knows about her father's struggle and is proud of it. When she notices people like the Larnes—which she seldom does—she feels neither envy nor admiration. What she does feel is an amused contempt. Until she meets Kester.

The strains represented by Eleanor and Kester have been called the New South and the Old. They are different. But they both have strength.

With Eleanor's type this is the strength of aggressive energy. With Kester's it is the strength of endurance. Both these qualities have value. But either of them, pushed to its limit, changes from good into an absurdity. Eleanor's sort of people, in their eagerness to get things done, will move everything and change everything, forgetting that progress does not always mean progress toward something better. On the other hand, Kester's strength is the sort that made the defenders of Vicksburg in 1863 eat rats and faint with scurvy and still refuse to surrender, long after they knew the battle was lost.

These types of people exist not only in the American South. You can find them in any place where an old order is changing into a new order, which in our time means just about everywhere. They do not agree—they can't—but they need each other.

Again, for those who like to follow the lines of descent, here they are. Those who don't care about ancestors can skip the paragraphs in italics:

Kester and Eleanor are both descendants of Dolores, removed by five generations. Kester is the grandson of Ann Sheramy, who was a great-granddaughter of Dolores; Eleanor is the granddaughter of Corrie May Upjohn, who was also a great-granddaughter of Dolores.

Kester is descended also, through five generations, from Judith and Philip Larne. Here the line of descent has been: Philip, David, Sebastian, Denis I, Denis II, Kester. Through David Larne's wife, Emily Purcell, Kester is also a descendant of Gervaise and Walter Purcell, of Deep Summer.

Deep Summer and *The Handsome Road* told how the two classes, aristocrats and poor white trash, came into being. *This Side of Glory* tells how Kester and Eleanor, born of these divergent groups, met their conflicts and learned to blend the differences between themselves. Doing this, they could leave a better tradition than had been left to either of them.

THE PEOPLE OF THE STORIES

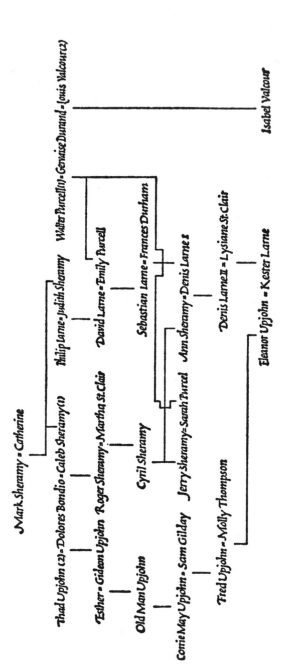

Less important characters have been omitted;
the reader will recognize that such minor figures as Bob Purcell and
Neal Sheramy are descendants of these families.

Chapter One

THE SKY was like thick blue velvet, and the river glittered in the sun. The time was January, 1912. Eleanor Upjohn, who was ten years older than the century, sat before her typewriter in the main tent of the levee camp by the river, answering her father's correspondence. Her father, Fred Upjohn, contractor in charge of the work, was reading and signing the letters while he finished the cigar he smoked after his noon dinner.

Fred and Eleanor were very good friends. They respected each other. Fred had spent thirty years building ramparts to hold the river back from the towns and plantations that bordered it, and when Eleanor came home from college announcing that she had studied stenography in her spare time and wanted to work, Fred welcomed her as his secretary. He had no regard for idleness.

Eleanor could remember him as he had been when she was a little girl, studying in the ring of light made by a kerosene lamp, while her mother, the baby in her arms and the coming baby bulging her apron, urged him to go to bed and at the same time kept bringing coffee to keep him awake. Eleanor was proud of him. From sandbag-toter to the best levee contractor on the Mississippi—not many men could boast such a rise. Today the Upjohns had a home on one of the most beautiful residential streets in New Orleans, and when Fred came upriver to supervise the construction of a levee he lived in spacious comfort.

The very tent they occupied had a look of success. This tent was the main room of the contractor's quarters, and with its companions formed a dwelling as easily lived in as a house. Its floor was made in tongue-and-groove sections three feet long so they could be taken apart and transported when the men moved camp. The four sides consisted of wooden walls three feet high and screen-wire from there to the top, with canvas sides that could be rolled up in good weather or dropped and buckled to the floor in seasons of rain or cold. The room was furnished with a dining-table, chairs, a book-

1

case, a wood-burning stove—the pipe of which went through a metal support in the canvas wall—and the desk at which Eleanor was writing. The bedrooms and kitchen were similarly constructed and separated from one another by canvas-covered boardwalks a yard wide. Eleanor liked working with her father in the levee camps. She was a crisp, competent young person and idleness bored her.

Eleanor was not pretty, but she was beautiful as a steel bridge is beautiful, and gave the same impression of strength and economy of line. Built with the structural excellence of an object fit for its purpose, her body was lean and hard, with long thighs, so that when she stood up she was straight as a spear and when she walked she moved directly and without haste. Her features were far from perfect, the nose too long and the jaw too wide, and there was a stubborn line to her mouth, but its very irregularities made it a striking face, with a look of cool and uncompromising honesty; and she had very fine eyes, dark blue with black lashes and clearly arched black eyebrows. Her hair was dark brown, braided to lie above her forehead like a coronet.

Eleanor never laced—not from scorn of the fashions but because she had found it too hard to breathe in a tight corset —but much outdoor exercise had given her a natural trimness and she looked well in her clothes. She was wearing a tailored shirtwaist of dark blue satin, with a white collar high around her throat, and a blue serge skirt that dropped straight to her insteps; but by a characteristic talent she achieved smartness and freedom at once, so the high collar was starched instead of boned, the belt looked tight only because she had no slouchiness about her waistline, and there was a cleverly concealed pleat below her knees that made walking easy without spoiling the hobble-skirt look. The effect was that of a sheath fitting with hardly a wrinkle over a figure too clean-cut to need any decoration.

The brilliance of the day gave a sparkle even to the interior of the tent. Eleanor wanted to go out. She had been working since six that morning, with only a pause for dinner, and she had a typewriter-cramp between her shoulders. There were only three more letters, and she slit them open quickly. A Senator had written reminding Fred of the national conference on waterways President Taft had summoned for next fall. Fred had already promised to attend the President's conference, so Eleanor dropped the letter into the wastebasket. The next was addressed to herself. Her eyes hastily skimmed the first paragraph. ". . . to impress upon recent graduates of American colleges for women the importance of supporting woman suffrage. . . ." That went into the wastebasket too. As she had never had much difficulty in getting what she wanted and did not particularly care whether other people got what they wanted or not, Eleanor had no interest in causes. The last letter required an answer. She rolled a sheet of paper into the typewriter.

"Nearly done?" Fred asked.

She nodded, her fingers snapping out the lines.

". . . and unless the work should be seriously impeded by bad weather, we are confident that the new levee will be finished by the first of March. Yours very truly, Fred Upjohn, Contractor in Charge."

As she typed his name under the space left for his signature Fred put out his cigar and reached for the pen.

"That's the last," Eleanor exclaimed, "and I'm dead."

"You don't look it," Fred answered without concern. He worked fourteen hours a day when he was building a levee and saw no reason why anybody else should object to doing the same.

Eleanor made a face at him as she put an envelope into the typewriter and wrote the address. "Mr. Kester Larne, Ardeith Plantation, Dalroy, Louisiana."

"What's this an answer to?" Fred inquired.

"Mr. Larne wrote asking when we expected to be finished. He's just hoping we'll be gone when he starts planting his cotton."

"The planters don't think we're a good influence on their laborers," Fred remarked good-humoredly as he wrote his name. "But my men don't make trouble."

Eleanor stood up and stretched. "Is all that cotton land over there Ardeith Plantation?"

He nodded.

"An enormous place. Must be two thousand acres."

"Mortgaged for all it's worth, I expect," he commented indifferently.

"Why do you say that?"

Fred grinned as he got to his feet. "They're that sort, honey, the Larnes. Got ancestors like the plague, too blue-blooded to work or do anything else except drink and chase women and look mournful about the Civil War."

3

Eleanor laughed. She had perched herself on the desk with relaxed enjoyment. "Anyway, the government's giving them a good levee to protect their land."

"Right." Fred started for the door. "I guess I'd better be getting back."

She watched him go out of the tent. He walked with hard, firm strides, like a man who had spent most of his life walking on earth instead of pavements. Here I am, he said with every step, get out of my way. Eleanor smiled as she looked after him. There was nobody else she admired as much as she did her father.

After a moment she slipped off the desk, stretched again, and went into her bedroom-tent for a coat. Throwing it over her arm she climbed the abandoned levee and walked along the crest. The air was almost twinkling; on one side of the levee the black earth was pleading for plows, and on the other side the river was a streak of gold and fire. As she reached a little oak tree that had found a foothold on the old levee Eleanor stopped, leaning back against the trunk to catch her breath and enjoy the dazzle around her.

Below her the river idled past in winter quietness. On the strip of sand between the river and the levee, left uncovered now by the low water, stretched the city of tents where the laborers lived. Three hundred yards ahead of her Eleanor could see the men and the great mule-drawn scoops that were bringing up tons of earth from the borrow-pit and dumping it on the new levee that would replace the one where she stood, which had been battered to uselessness by the high water of many Aprils. Eleanor liked the scene: on one side the quiet fields, on the other the camp, where the pickaninnies played among the tents while their mothers cooked and their fathers worked on the new levee ahead. She knew every look of the river, tawny in the sun and purple at evening and white as magnolias under the moon, shrunken and docile in the fall, wild as a panther in the spring. Born in a camp like this one, she had grown up loving and fearing the river as she might have felt toward a genial monarch who in spite of his kindliness held over his subjects the power of life and death.

From far away she heard a chugging noise. The persistent rhythm of the sound made it clear under the irregular shouts from the workmen. Eleanor turned to look. Along a road for cotton wagons that led through the field came a loud and graceless little automobile, spouting smoke and rattling as it went over the ruts. The car had no top, and as it puffed nearer she could see that there was a hatless man at the wheel, his hair blowing as he drove.

The car groaned to a stop near a scrub pine at the foot of the levee, and without quieting the engine the driver sprang out. She saw that he was young and tall, with hair blown to a froth all over his head. He glanced around, then with a start of evident surprise he caught sight of her. An instant later he was climbing the levee to where she stood.

He looked like a young man who considered the world a delightful place and himself most fortunate to have been born. Nearly a head taller than herself, he was deep-chested and sunburnt, as though he had spent his life outdoors; he would have looked like a Viking except that his hair and eyes were the rich brown of cane syrup fresh from the grinding. His forehead was broad, and his nose faintly arched. He was smiling upon her with admiring deference, the look of the born charmer of women who by habit smiles upon any one of them not positively ugly, as though he is already sure she will like him very much. Usually Eleanor found this sort of approach annoying. But for some reason, with this young man it was rather delightful.

"Please forgive me for intruding," he said, with a slight inclination from the waist as though he had stepped unannounced into her parlor. His voice was deeper than she had expected it to be.

"You were looking for someone?" Eleanor asked in return. She could not help smiling at him.

"No, ma'am," said the audacious young man, "I wasn't. I came out to have a look at the fields, and then I saw you."

Eleanor burst out laughing.

"Do you mind?" he inquired.

"Why should I?" she asked, trying to appear unconscious of his flattering eyes. "The levee belongs to the United States government—as a citizen and taxpayer you have a perfect right to be here." Though her words were commonplace she was surprised to hear how rich and cordial her voice was, as though it had responded without any conscious direction of her own to his assumption that they were going to be friends.

"Good!" he exclaimed. Eleanor was thinking, such a goose. If he behaves like this toward every girl he sees he can't have time to do much else. The young man went on, "We probably

5

have a mutual acquaintance who could introduce us properly, but in the meantime my name is Kester Larne."

"Larne?" repeated Eleanor. "Oh yes, of course! I've just written a letter to you."

"To me?" He looked adorably puzzled. "How could I be so fortunate? If I'd ever seen you before I couldn't possibly have forgotten you."

"Don't be silly," she retorted, but she was still laughing because she could not help it. "My father is in charge of this work and you wrote him asking how soon we'd be finished. I'm his secretary, so I wrote the answer."

"Oh." He nodded.

"You'll be glad to know," she continued, "that we hope to be gone by the first of March." She took a step nearer, sorry for the sudden apology in his face. "Don't think I take it as a personal affront that you wanted to get rid of us! I know levee Negroes are a tough breed. They don't get along with cotton Negroes, and I'm not blaming you a bit."

"What an intelligent girl!" he exclaimed, abruptly radiant. "You're so right. They don't get along, and I *was* hoping the levee would be finished by planting time. But does that mean you'll go, too?"

"Certainly."

He looked disappointed. Then, brightening, he said, "But that's almost two months, anyway. Won't you tell me your name?"

"Eleanor Upjohn."

"Thanks." Kester took off his coat and spread it on the grass. "Will you sit down?"

Liking him more than she would have wanted him to guess, Eleanor indicated the coat over her arm. "I have one."

"Ah, but you must put that on. I wondered when I saw you why you were carrying it. These bright days are deceptive." Without further argument he took the coat from her and held it ready.

Though she was not used to being so guarded, Eleanor obeyed him. He had an endearing way of making her feel frail, and though she told herself it was absurd she found there was something rather pleasant about it. She sat down on his coat and Kester dispersed his big person on the grass beside her. "It's damp," Eleanor warned.

"I never catch cold." Supporting himself on his elbows, he looked up at her. Eleanor was remembering what her father had said about the Larnes. Kester might chase women—if she was any judge he certainly did—but whatever might be true of him he decidedly did not look moth-eaten. In fact, she thought she had never seen a more magnificent physical specimen. "Eleanor," he was saying. "Nice name. Do you like it?"

"All right, except when anybody calls me Nellie."

He gave a low chuckle. "Who would call a girl like you Nellie?"

"Dad, sometimes. He started it when I was a little girl, but it seemed as if every mule in every camp was named Nellie and I got tired being gee'd and whoa'd all day long. I made him quit, but now and then he forgets."

"I never will. I promise."

"Do you know," said Eleanor, "that you've left your engine running?"

Without glancing at the car he asked, "Did you ever have to crank one of those things?"

Lazy, she thought. Extravagant. Maybe dad wasn't so wrong. Aloud she said, "If you don't like to crank why don't you drive a buggy?"

"Because I like automobiles," said Kester. "And I perceive that you are a very dominating young woman."

"I've been told that I am," she returned, smiling.

"I suppose you've also been told that you're very good-looking?"

"No." Eleanor shook her head rebukingly. "I'll accept as much flattery as most girls, Mr. Larne, but I know about my nose, and my square chin—"

"You must have been around college boys who liked them cute and curly. Didn't anybody ever tell you the difference between—" he paused tantalizingly.

"Between—?"

"Well—strawberries and caviar?"

Eleanor glanced down at herself, taken aback, because most of her male acquaintances so far *had* been college boys, and engineers who respected her because she could solve mathematical equations faster than any of them. Kester was considerably older than a sophomore—twenty-six or seven, she thought—and he probably would not be at all interested in her talent as a lightning calculator. But she put a brake on her thoughts. He didn't mean a word he was saying. No man could please a girl so expertly unless he had had abundant practice in doing it. Kester was giving her a teasing scrutiny.

7

"You don't believe me, do you?"

"No," she answered, startled.

"It doesn't matter. Let's take a ride."

"A ride? Where?"

"Anywhere. Come on. Please!" He had scrambled to his feet and was eagerly holding out his hands to help her up.

Eleanor's mind answered before her voice. Her mind said: I suspect that I am being deliberately captivated. I believe this young man is inviting me because he simply cannot endure the thought that any reasonably attractive woman could regard him with indifference. If I knew what was good for me I should say no. And I am going to say yes.

She answered: "I'd like to very much, thank you."

"Fine!" He caught her hands and she stood up. Kester had received her answer with delight; she thought she had never seen so sparkling a personality as his. He was about to start down the levee, when with some difficulty at being practical Eleanor put out a detaining hand.

"Your coat," she reminded him.

Chuckling at her prudence and his own forgetfulness, he picked it up and began to put it on. The coat was crumpled from her having sat on it, yet in spite of his casual appearance Kester had an air of elegance, as unconscious and as evident as the color of his eyes. She tried to define it. Probably it was his self-assurance, the way he moved and spoke as though nothing had ever assailed him. The feudal nobles whose effigies lay on their tombs, their legs crossed as the sign they had been on a Crusade, had even in stone this air of lordship.

They scrambled down the levee slope, Kester holding her hand, and got into his car. Eleanor tucked her skirt around her, for the little car was one of the type that had only an opening in the side in place of a door.

"Hold on," advised Kester. "This road was never meant for the horseless age."

The car began to bump noisily over the ruts. Kester drove out of the cottonfield and into the highway, jolting along at a speed that was unsafe and exciting, and evidently having the time of his life. The dust rose around them and streamed out behind the car like a plume. Eleanor clung to her seat, half frightened and half exhilarated, till at last Kester began to go more slowly. She saw that they had reached a high wrought-iron fence enclosing an estate.

"This is where I live," said Kester. "I thought we'd go in

and have some coffee to clear the dust out of our throats."

"Do you often drive like that?" Eleanor demanded.

"Oh, yes, ma'am, always. You weren't scared, were you? I'm a very good driver."

"Wait a minute," said Eleanor. She reminded him, "I don't know you from Adam. Are you sure you live here?"

She could not help laughing at his look of startled innocence. "Miss Eleanor," he assured her gravely, "I have lived here—I mean my family has lived here—since before the Revolution." He put on the brake and began reaching into his pockets. "I ought to have something with my name on it. Here." He showed her a little silver pocket-knife, and she saw it had "Kester Larne" engraved in tiny letters on the handle. "My mother gave it to me once for my birthday," he continued, "and had my name put on it because I'm always losing things."

"Is your mother at home?" she asked.

"I believe she and my father are out making calls. But the servants are here. So come on in!" he urged. "It's the only place around where we can get any drinkable coffee."

She consented, and Kester started to drive down the avenue.

Eleanor exclaimed with admiration. From the gates two lines of live oaks led to a vast white house, half hidden by the festoons of gray moss hanging from the trees. As they came to the end of the avenue she saw the house, surrounded by a broad veranda with Doric columns reaching to the roof. The front door, which stood open like the gates, was high and wide, and on either side were windows reaching to the floor, with heavy curtains shadowing the rooms within.

As they got out of the car Eleanor stood still a moment, silent before the beauty of the place where Kester lived. The house was very Greek and at the same time very American; evidently it was a remnant of the classic revival that, beginning with the stirrings of democracy that had produced the American and French Revolutions, had gradually changed from an intellectual ideal to an emotional fervor and then to a parlor fashion, producing the Bill of Rights and the guillotine, then the pseudo-Greek costumes of the early eighteen-hundreds, and at last, sweeping into architecture, had studded the newly democratic countries with such richness of pediments, porticoes, columns and acanthus leaves that one could hardly feel right about praying in a church or leaving money in a bank that did not suggest the Acropolis, and rich men felt it their duty to provide that their children should be born in houses that looked like Greek temples. The builder of this house, however, had combined fashion with good taste; its proportions were excellent and its Doric austerity unmarred by any prettifying, and unlike many houses of its period it suggested a cool patrician simplicity. Eleanor turned an appreciative look to Kester.

"I've never seen a more beautiful place," she told him. "Let's go inside."

The main hall was wide and lofty, and near the entrance a spiral staircase curved up to the second floor. On the walls were portraits. At Eleanor's left a man in a white powdered wig looked down upon her, and opposite was a young woman in a high eighteenth-century coiffure against a blue background. Beyond was a woman with black curls on her forehead, dressed in a square-necked gown belted just under her bosom in the style they wore when Napoleon was Emperor of France. Eleanor went in farther, and stood at the foot of the spiral staircase. Above her hung a pair of companion portraits, one of a young man in a gray Confederate uniform, the other of a girl in a blue hoop-skirt; she had evidently stood for her portrait where Eleanor stood now, for her hand rested on the balustrade and the turning steps showed behind her.

Eleanor turned back to Kester. "Tell me about these people," she exclaimed. "Who are they?"

Good-humoredly, Kester complied. The man in the white wig was his great-great-great-grandfather, Philip Larne, who had received the land that was now Ardeith Plantation from George the Third of England as a reward for his soldiering in the French and Indian War. The woman opposite was Philip's wife. They had both come down the river on flatboats in the days when steam was nothing but a vapor that came out of a kettle-spout. The woman in the Empire dress had married into the Larne family about the time of the Louisiana Purchase. The Civil War pair were Kester's grandparents. The young man had been killed during the war, but the girl had lived to be an old lady; Kester could remember her from his childhood. Oh yes, there were other pictures. He'd be glad to show them to her sometime, and the rest of the house if she wanted to see it. It was very large, with many rooms that no longer served any purpose but to wear out brooms. Originally

10

there had been thirty besides the servants' quarters, though some of them had been cut up to make bathrooms and closets. Eleanor went through a doorway at one side of the hall. This room was a library. On the bookshelves modern novels stood alongside bound volumes of *Putnam's Magazine* and *Godey's Lady's Book,* old treatises on cotton-growing, and romances with astonishing names.

"The Curse of Clifton," she read aloud, and chuckled. *"The Ladies' Parlor Annual, 1841*—I've heard of those annuals but I don't believe I've ever seen one before. And who's this alphabetical author, Mrs. E. D. E. N. Southworth?"

"She wrote what they used to call sensation stories, mostly devoted to howling storms and people stabbing each other with jeweled daggers." Kester shook his head. "My family had its good qualities, Miss Eleanor, but they did indulge in some deplorable literature."

Eleanor took down a volume of *Godey's* and turned the leaves, smiling at the stilted phrases that caught her eye and the burdensome gowns of the fashion plates. "There's something very attractive about those times," she remarked. "People seem to have been so sure of themselves. I suppose life was simpler then."

Kester grinned. "I used to read voraciously in here," he said to her. "I've skimmed through dozens of volumes a century or two centuries old, and every one of them laments the simplicity of the age just past and sighs over the complexities of the present."

"Then you don't think nineteenth-century life was easier than ours?"

"The period that included the American Civil War, the Sepoy Rebellion and the siege of Paris? No ma'am, I don't. We think olden times were simple because we know how grandpa's problems were solved, and any problem is simple when you can look up the answer in the back of the book."

They laughed together. Eleanor replaced the volume of *Godey's* and looked around the library again. On the center table was an enormous Bible fastened with metal clasps. She asked him to open it for her. The Bible fell open itself in the middle, where the pages had been left blank for family records, and here were lines in many handwritings, in inks browned with time, recording the births and marriages and deaths of the Larnes. Eleanor read here and there as she turned the pages.

11

"Died, at Ardeith Plantation, September 23, 1810, Philip Larne, native of the colony of South Carolina. . . .

"Married, at Dalroy, Louisiana, April 4, 1833, Sebastian Larne and Frances Durham. . . .

"Married, at Silverwood Plantation, Louisiana, December 6, 1859, Denis Larne and Ann Sheramy. . . .

"Married, at Dalroy, Louisiana, March 21, 1884, Denis Larne II and Lysiane St. Clair."

"They were your parents?" she asked him.

Kester nodded. He seemed amused at her interest, but rather pleased by it too, as though he had taken his home for granted and enjoyed seeing a newcomer's pleasure in it. Eleanor turned the pages again. She came to the records of the births, and near the end she read,

"Born, at Ardeith Plantation, February 18, 1885, Kester Denis Larne, son of Denis Larne II and Lysiane St. Clair."

He had a younger brother and sister. The three births were the last of the records. She lifted her eyes again.

"Isn't it somehow awesome, to see yourself at the end of such a line?"

"Why no. Why should it be?"

"Oh—I mean—doesn't it make you feel like a link in an endless chain?"

"Aren't we all?" asked Kester, laughing a little.

They closed the Bible and went back into the hall. Bending down, Kester showed her the dent of a horseshoe on the bottom step of the spiral staircase. It was clearly marked, though in later years the stairs had been carefully repainted. That had been put there during the invasion of Louisiana in the eighteen-sixties, when a troop of soldiers had ransacked the house and one of them had ridden his horse into the hall.

"It's fascinating as you tell it," said Eleanor. "I studied about all that sort of thing in school, of course, but here it seems so real!"

"Anybody hearing you," he said with amusement, "would think you came from ten thousand miles away."

"I was born in a levee camp in West Feliciana Parish," she returned, "but that's a long way from things like this. Am I tiring you, making you talk so much?"

"Well, ma'am," said Kester. "I *could* do with that coffee."

Eleanor laughed apologetically, and they crossed the hall into the parlor opposite the library. This was the main living-room, and here were deep mahogany sofas, and a great square rosewood piano, and modernity represented by a phonograph. Like the library, this room had a white marble fireplace, but in this one a fire danced behind brass andirons. On the wall hung a bellcord of the sort ladies used to embroider to while away a journey up the river in the old steamboat days.

"Does that still work?" Eleanor asked.

"Why yes." Kester gave it a pull.

A Negro man in a funereal black coat came in answer to the summons. Kester called him Cameo. He ordered coffee, and Cameo approached Eleanor with grave courtesy.

"Rest yo' wrap, miss?" he inquired.

Eleanor gave him her coat. As Cameo went out she observed that the door had a silver knob and silver hinges, shining with the soft glow of time, and she remembered that the door of the library had them too. For a moment she stood still. It was her first glimpse of the dignity of plantation life, and she was conscious of a heightened awareness, as though all her senses had been sharpened to rare appreciation. She began to understand what people might be like when they had lived for generations in this quiet grandeur, their instincts curbed by the standards of their culture till they had no uncertainties, their characters polished by their knowledge in all circumstances of what was expected of them. The house, the staircase, the portraits, the ancient oaks, all suggested the same self-assurance she had observed in Kester. It was easy now to understand it.

Kester had begun to play a ragtime record on the phonograph. He turned it off as Cameo came in and placed a tray with a silver coffee service on a low table in front of the fire. Kester and Eleanor curled up on the floor, facing each other, and Eleanor poured the coffee.

"What a beautiful set this is," she observed, watching the firelight stroke the pot. "It looks like a wedding present."

"I believe it was."

"Your mother's?"

"No, earlier than that. My great-grandmother's, I think— there's a monogram on it."

Eleanor turned the pot to find the initials. "F. D. L.," she read. "Is that Frances Durham?—I saw a line in the big Bible about her wedding. But Kester!" she broke off sharply.

"What is it?"

"It's none of my business," said Eleanor, "but one of your

13

servants has been frightfully careless. Did you know there was a big dent in the side, just over the monogram?"

Kester gave a low chuckle. "We've been meaning to do something about that dent for forty years. That's where a spade struck it when they were digging up the silver after the Civil War."

"Oh yes," Eleanor said softly. She smiled as she watched the firelight flashing into the old depression. There was something touching and authentic about such a flaw, like the little irregularities that distinguish handmade lace from machinery imitations. "I can't tell you how I'm enjoying this!" she exclaimed. "It's so different from anything I've ever seen before. I live in a house in New Orleans that was built nine years ago, and we're always complaining that it isn't modern enough."

"I've often thought it would be mighty convenient to live in a new house," said Kester. "One where the plumbing always works and the attic stairs aren't in danger of dropping on your head. May I have some coffee, please, ma'am?"

She refilled his cup. "If you knew my father," she continued, "you'd understand what I'm trying to tell you. He's so entirely of today. It's the typical American story—a self-made man, so proud of being able to give his children the chances he never had."

"I think I'd have known even if you hadn't told me," Kester said thoughtfully, "that you had a streak of power. You're like your father, aren't you?"

"People say I am. I've been working for him a long time—during the summers while I was at college, and regularly since I finished."

"Where'd you go to college?"

"Barnard. Where did you?"

"Tulane. Did you like college?"

"Not particularly," said Eleanor. "I'm not very bookish, and the other girls seemed—well, so *young*. When you've lived on the river and seen real struggles, men fighting days and nights to keep a flood back, you get used to fundamentals —you can't believe the most important thing on earth is the band of ribbon around your hair. I hope I don't sound like somebody trying to be superior, but do you understand?"

"Yes," he returned seriously. and added, "I've never known a girl like you before. What else about the girls at school?"

14

Eleanor brought her knees up under her chin and wrapped her arms around them. "Well, the way they whispered with such curiosity about things I had taken for granted all my life. Birth and death are always going on in a levee camp, and of course I had known about them, and about the honky-tonk tent and why I mustn't go down there. I don't suppose I was ever very girlish."

"You're not girlish," Kester said, smiling. He was sitting crosslegged on the floor, listening with interest. "Go on. Tell me about a levee camp."

Though she did not often talk so much about herself, she continued. She told him about her cook, whose name was Randa and who had diamonds in her teeth, because Randa's husband was killed in an accident on a levee job and the government paid her compensation; and Randa, afraid some fortune-hunter would try to marry her, devised that means of keeping her wealth to herself. She told him about Jelly Roll, who was the aristocrat of the camp, partly because he earned two dollars and a quarter a day and could afford shirts of flowered percale and partly because he was a genius at his work. Jelly Roll's job was to keep the slope of the levee graded, and as the drivers came up with the scoops he told them where to dump the dirt; though he had only a grade-stake in the middle and a tow-stake on either side to guide him he gave directions so fast that he could direct the dumping of three wheelers at once, and with such accuracy that when the contractor measured the slope it was always right, three-to-one on the inside and four-to-one on the outside. "I like anybody who has a passion for doing his job well, like that," said Eleanor. "That's one reason I admire my father so much. Dad builds the best levees on the river. He's incredibly careful, studying the soil formation and patterning the levee like a fine dress before he moves a spoonful of earth."

"Do you know," said Kester, "I've lived on the river all my life, but you make me feel as if I'm just beginning to learn about it. I've always thought of this country in terms of cotton."

"But you'd have to. After all, that's your business, and building levees isn't. Did you always want to be a planter?"

"Why yes, I always took it for granted that I would be. My brother Sebastian wanted to go into business, so when my

15

father retired he made over the plantation to me, and Sebastian went to New Orleans."

"What does he do?"

"He's a cotton broker." Kester stood up, grinning. "Doing very well at it, I believe. A most excellent young man, the only one of us who is strong-minded enough to make cotton work for him instead of making himself work for cotton."

Kester stood with his elbow on the marble mantel. Her chin on her knees, Eleanor lifted her eyes to look up at him. "You needn't try to be flippant," she said. "I'm beginning to understand you love this place devotedly, and are a little bit ashamed to confess how much it means to you."

He nodded, half proud and half embarrassed. "I do love it, Miss Eleanor. I feel so much a part of it, you see—though not many people can make me own up to it so frankly."

There was a pause. The shadows were beginning to thicken in the corners, but Kester's figure stood out in clear relief as though all the firelight had gathered to meet his glowing vitality. He was right, she thought: he belonged to Ardeith as essentially as the house or the oaks, and it would be impossible to think of him apart from his background. Though he was standing quietly by the fire she was acutely aware of his powerful presence. It was easy to imagine his entering a crowded room and making everybody else in it flatten into unimportance by the mere fact of his being there. Again remembering what her father had said about the Larnes, Eleanor reflected that Fred knew nothing about them and was relegating them to a category, perhaps unfairly; certainly Kester was an attractive young man, who had not only the gift of fascinating but the rarer gift of being fascinated. "I could like him very much," Eleanor said to herself. "In fact, I do."

They both started as they heard a sound of footsteps at the front door.

Eleanor sprang up, feeling suddenly self-conscious, as though she had been interrupted in a moment of intimacy. Kester had turned toward the door. "Is that company?" she asked.

"No, only my mother and father. I'll bring them in."

He crossed the room to meet them, and a moment later Eleanor was being presented to his parents.

The first word that occurred to Eleanor in regard to Mr.

16

and Mrs. Larne was *exquisite*. They looked rather alike: they were both tall and slender and graceful, they both spoke in soft, beautifully modulated voices, they both gave her an impression of perfectly charming uselessness. Mr. Larne insisted that she must have a glass of sherry with them before supper, and when she hesitated, thinking they might prefer to be left alone, he told her with flattering urgency that it was not every day Kester brought in a delightful young lady and he wouldn't think of parting with her yet. Both amused and puzzled, Eleanor sat down again; it was quite impossible to tell whether these people meant what they were saying, but she decided to remain long enough for one glass of sherry and then go. Mrs. Larne gave her big plumed hat to a maid and Cameo brought in a decanter and glasses. Denis Larne II, married to Lysiane St. Clair, she remembered; yes, he did look like a gentleman whose doings would be rightly recorded in the right places. He would know vintages, and fine cigars, and clever lines from the new novels, he would like Debussy and shiver at ragtime, both he and Lysiane had distinction and a quiet air of breeding, but how in the name of heaven had this porcelain pair created Kester?

"You are visiting in the neighborhood, Miss Upjohn?" Denis Larne was asking her as he poured the sherry.

Eleanor recalled her thoughts. "Yes. I live in New Orleans."

"New Orleans, yes. I believe I must be acquainted with your family—the name Upjohn sounds familiar to me, though I'm ashamed to say I can't place it."

"You might have heard of my father. He's the contractor in charge of the new levee just upriver from here."

"Possibly that's it. I hope you like this, Miss Upjohn," he added, offering her a glass.

"How pretty it is!" Eleanor exclaimed. She held up the glass to let the firelight dance through it.

Lysiane smilingly agreed with her. "I've often said I shouldn't care for sherry if I couldn't see it." She glanced at Kester, who had returned to his place by the mantel. "Did we get any letters this afternoon, Kester?"

"Yes, ma'am, several from New Orleans. They look like invitations to Carnival balls."

"It's about time we were going back to New Orleans," Denis remarked at the mention of Carnival.

Eleanor glanced up in surprise. "Don't you live here?"

17

"Father's health isn't of the best," Kester explained to her, "and he and mother have lived in New Orleans since he gave up managing the plantation several years ago. They only came up to Ardeith for Christmas."

"I see. But isn't it lonely in this big house for you?"

"Why no," said Kester, and his mother added,

"My dear, Kester is either out of the house or has it full of people, all the time. He has a passionate fondness for the human race."

"Don't you like people?" Kester asked Eleanor.

"Some of them, of course. But not everybody."

"Oh, I do," said Kester. "Clever people are entertaining and stupid ones give me such a pleasant sense of superiority."

Lysiane laughed at him, and Kester asked,

"Where've you been all afternoon?"

Lysiane puckered her pretty little mouth as if her afternoon had not been entirely blissful. "We made several calls, winding up with Sylvia."

Denis chuckled. Kester said to Eleanor, "Forgive us. But we have a great many cousins, and some of them are nuisances."

"Aren't everybody's?" Denis asked with amusement. "Or what do you think, Miss Upjohn?"

"I'm afraid I can't answer. I haven't any."

"No cousins?" Kester exclaimed.

"Neither of my parents had any brothers or sisters."

"I'm tempted to call you lucky," Kester said.

"I think it's fun to have a lot of family," said Eleanor. "I've never had to bother about it, because I have five brothers and sisters of my own, but my mother says it's pretty lonesome to grow up without anybody who belongs to you."

"I should think it would be," Lysiane nodded. "Your mother is quite right. Where did she grow up?—with a remote uncle, or something like that?"

"No, ma'am, in an orphan asylum in New Orleans."

"Indeed!" Lysiane exclaimed with such sympathy that Eleanor hastened to add,

"Oh, it wasn't as bad as that, Mrs. Larne! Mamma says they were very good to the children."

"Those times were so difficult," Denis said gently. "Everyone was in straits."

"Everyone?"

18

"Why yes," said Lysiane. "The carpetbagger days. When I was a little girl, a new dress was such an event!"

Eleanor thought of the buried coffee service. "It must have been a fantastic period. Kester was saying a little while ago he didn't believe there was ever any such thing as the good old days."

"No," said Kester, "I'm glad I live now. Aren't you, Miss Eleanor?"

"I've never thought much about it. But I'm glad I don't have to wear their clothes. Imagine having to go about in hoops, or a bustle."

"I can't. But neither can I imagine wearing a hobble-skirt."

"At least," she retorted, "I can sit down in a hobble-skirt, and I've never understood how anybody ever sat down in a bustle." Eleanor put her glass on the tray. "Mrs. Larne, it's very pleasant being here, but I simply must go."

Lysiane graciously asked her to stay for supper, but Eleanor shook her head. They made their farewells, and Eleanor and Kester went back to his car. As they drove toward the camp they did not talk much, but at length Kester said, "May I come back to see you tomorrow?"

"That's very soon."

"Not too soon," said Kester. "I've been waiting years to meet a girl who could spend a whole afternoon without tucking her hand under her belt to see if her shirtwaist and skirt were coming apart. Tomorrow?"

She laughed. "All right. About three. I'll be working until then."

He stopped the car by the levee and walked with her to the main tent. "Gee, I like you!" he exclaimed, and strode back across the levee, whistling the *Horseshoe Rag* like a young man well pleased with the world.

Chapter Two

1

AFTER THAT Eleanor and Kester saw each other nearly every day. Conscientiously, Eleanor forbade him to call until afternoon, but for the first time since she had been her father's

19

secretary she found herself watching the clock. Until now she had liked her work and had gone out in the afternoon merely for rest and exercise, but suddenly the morning was only a dreary prelude to the golden hours when she would be with Kester, and even before he came her awareness of him was distracting.

She really tried to keep her thoughts away from Kester while she was at work. But as the days went by she found it increasingly hard to do so. In the midst of a statement to the Mississippi River Commission some gay remark of his would pop into her head and twenty minutes later she would discover her fingers still idle on the keys. She would jerk herself back, but her smooth typing turned into a chaos of wrong letters and dollar marks, and she could almost hear Kester laughing at her exasperation as she tore out the sheet and started over. Once she called Randa to bring her a cup of coffee, and Randa came in, her bediamonded teeth gleaming as she inquired, "You got a headache, Miss Elna?"

"No," said Eleanor, "but I think I'm losing my mind."

Randa gave her a flashing grin. "Yo' mind done gone kitin' over to dat plantation."

"Don't be an idiot," said Eleanor shortly.

Arms akimbo, Randa surveyed her. "Ah, go on, Miss Elna. You's just befo' fallin' in love wid dat gemman."

Eleanor sipped her coffee and did not answer.

"He's a mighty highclass gemman," Randa went on. "Give me fifty cents mighty near every time he come over. But you take care of yo'self, Miss Elna. He's the sparkin' kind."

"Will you press my dotted shirtwaist?" Eleanor asked. "I want to wear it this afternoon."

"Yassum." Randa went off, shaking her head and mumbling like an oracle. Eleanor looked after her. The sparking kind. Randa doubtless knew what she was talking about. Eleanor had observed before now that Negroes knew a great deal more about white people than white people knew about Negroes. Setting down her cup so hard it rattled in the saucer, she turned resolutely back to her desk. Kester was none of Randa's business.

Fred was good-natured when he and Kester met, but Fred's contempt for what he called the mildewed aristocracy of the plantations was too profound for him to have much approval of any specimen of that class, and Kester's blithe assumption that the world had been created only for pleasure would not in any case have won Fred's esteem. But except for occasional comments on her incomprehensible taste, Fred said very little to Eleanor about him, for he was too busy to pay much attention to anything but his levee. Eleanor was not troubled by her father's opinion of Kester—she was, in fact, hardly conscious of it. She was conscious of very little except her own sudden happiness.

She did not try to analyze it. She only knew that when she saw Kester the world turned radiant, and while she was with him she was aware of nothing but his charm and his genius for laughter. Kester laughed at everything. Bad weather, bumpy roads, the foibles of other people—Kester found them not irritating, but funny. Though she was by nature rather opinionated Eleanor found herself reflecting his tolerance. She thought she must have laughed more in the weeks she had known Kester than in all her lifetime before.

Except for some spontaneous gesture such as taking her hands and holding them while he told her how glad he was to see her again, Kester had never touched her, but his joy at being with her was evident. They took long drives through the plantation country, rattling over the roads in his little topless car or sometimes moving more sedately in a carriage. They crossed the river on a ferry and visited a suger plantation where the cane-cutting season was not yet over, and the Negroes peeled cane for them while they sucked out the juice, which trickled down their chins and stickied their clothes and made them nearly sick with an excess of sweetness. They found an old Negro who ground his own cane to make molasses for his family, in an ancient shed thatched with palm branches such as the earliest planters used when cane sugar was new; subject as everybody was to Kester's charm, he let them feed the stalks between the two big wooden wheels turned by mules, and they shouted with delight as the juice dripped into the kettle over the fire. Kester bought from him two big buckets of cuite, the thick dark molasses that is the last boiling of the syrup before it turns to sugar, and gave one of them to Eleanor to serve with hot biscuits for supper, warning her to serve it with a wooden spoon, for if you put a metal spoon into cuite it will granulate before morning.

Once they took a picnic lunch and drove toward the woods, stopping on a road built along the edge of a cypress swamp. They had hardly left the carriage when a mighty rain tumbled upon them, so they scrambled back inside and sat huddled

21

under the rug. Around them the swamp had a strange loveliness. The great cypresses were hung with moss in such thick draperies that there seemed hardly room for leaves to push through, though occasionally one of the trees was bare, holding up crooked white limbs to the rain. The leaves on the live oaks were dull, ready to drop when the new leaves would push them off in March. The only bright color in the swamp was the green of the tree-ferns growing along the branches. Under the oaks the sedges were brown, with a purplish tinge like a veil over them, and the lichens were gray on the cypress trunks growing out of the water, and over everything was the gray moss and the rain.

It was Kester who showed her the sullen magnificence of the swamp, while Eleanor looked, discovering the joy of becoming sensitive to the beauty of familiar scenes. When at last they drove back through the rain she felt as if she had been on a journey to a place of strange enchantment.

Often they went to Ardeith, and when she curled up on the rug by the fire and talked to him—on any subject, for sometimes she could hardly remember what they had talked about—Eleanor had a sense of rapture.

When she went to Ardeith, Kester's parents were sometimes, though not always, at home. While they were invariably gracious Eleanor could not help regarding them with a secret amusement. Denis and Lysiane, and their numberless cousins who drifted through the house, seemed to her so delicate, like relics that should be kept behind glass. It was the first time she had had a glimpse of the gentle, defeated civilization that in secluded spots like this went on still stunned from the blow of the Civil War. These people were strange to her, yet she could not deny that they had a curious emotional security because it had never occurred to them to doubt their own values. She was continually being surprised at their cool, devastating scorn of people who fell short of their standards; they dismissed everything such a person said and did as of no consequence, so that one felt strangely ill at ease and could not explain why it was so. And they could do this, she concluded with some astonishment, because they were so much more attractive than people could be after fighting the battles necessary for adjustment to a changing world.

Eleanor thought them pretty but absurd. She could not have made articulate how utterly she felt herself superior to their canons. She sounded Kester as to what he thought of all this, and discovered, not greatly to her surprise, that Kester had never thought about it at all. Kester liked his country; he liked seeing the cotton come up and put forth its white flowers, the flowers turning pink and dropping off to reveal hard little green bolls on the stalks, the bolls opening and the fields turning white with the ripe cotton hanging ready to be picked. He liked these blue February days, the fragrance of the earth turning under the plows, and the prospect of the summer ahead when the earth would go mad with blooming and men would work not to make the plants grow but to check their increase. He liked hunting and riding and dancing and swimming and gathering around the piano with his friends to sing songs.

"But you don't know whether or not you like to think," Eleanor said to him, "because you've never tried it."

They were driving back to the levee camp after a visit to Ardeith, and Eleanor's lap was piled with the last poinsettias of the season. It was still early, but two army engineers were coming in for supper and she had to be at home to supervise Randa's setting of the table. As she spoke Kester gave her a roguish look out of the corner of his eye. "What am I supposed to think about?" he inquired.

"Don't you like to find out how people happen to be the way they are?" she asked.

"No, I can't say that I do." He adroitly drove around a wagon lumbering along the middle of the road. "They are the way they are, so what can I do about it?"

"But don't you like to understand them?"

Again he glanced at her, with an eloquent flick of his eyebrow. "Eleanor, I understand more about people than you ever will."

"No you don't!"

"Yes I do," he returned serenely. "You see, I look at them as persons. To you they're like these mathematical equations you're always figuring out for the engineers."

Eleanor twisted a poinsettia leaf, considering. "You and I are very different, aren't we, Kester?"

He nodded. "Very. You're always surprising me."

"Which of us do you suppose is right?"

"Oh Eleanor, people aren't right or wrong. They're different. Like blue eyes and brown eyes." Kester turned off the highway into the cotton-road leading to the levee.

"Is that why you and I have so much fun together?—because we're so different?"

"That's probably one reason."

"Strange, isn't it? You and I—born in the same state, of the same race, the same generation, yet in so many ways we're unlike." She paused a moment, and added, "I believe I know what it is."

"What?" he asked, casually, as though it were not very important.

"You're a Southerner," Eleanor said, "and I'm an American."

Kester grinned. "You're bewitching," he told her, "and I'm appreciative. Well, you'll probably amount to something, and when I die they'll write on my tombstone 'Here lies a man who had a grand time.' "

She laughed. They had reached the levee, and Kester walked to the tent with her. At the door he said, "I'll be back tomorrow," and smiled at her admiringly. "You're very fetching above those red flowers. In fact, you're a splendid person."

"So are you," said Eleanor.

She watched him climb the levee. He was lithe as a dancer. At the crest he turned and waved. Smiling to herself, as he went on out of sight Eleanor separated one poinsettia from the rest and began counting off the petals.

"He loves me, he's the sparking kind, he loves me, he's the sparking kind—"

It came out even, on "He's the sparking kind." Eleanor threw down the stem, called herself a goose for trusting a flower, and went indoors.

2

Kester sang to himself as he drove back toward home. He was not given to thinking ahead of the moment in time he happened to be occupying, but he knew he enjoyed being with Eleanor more than with any other girl he had ever known and he wished she were not so scrupulous about her work so they could have more time together. Leaving his car by the front steps he ran into the house. His mother and father were in the parlor, evidently engaged in earnest conversation. Denis stood by the fire and Lysiane sat near him, looking up with troubled

24

attention. As Kester came in he heard Denis say, "It can't go any further."

Kester tossed his overcoat on the sofa and came to the fire. "Hello," he greeted them.

"Where have you been?" his father asked.

"Seeing Nellie home."

"I thought so," Lysiane murmured half under her breath.

Kester started to poke the fire.

His father made a gesture of exasperation toward Lysiane. Kester turned around, leaning his shoulders against the mantel and surveying his parents nonchalantly.

"You don't like Eleanor, do you?"

"We don't *dislike* her, Kester," Lysiane corrected him. "But—" she hesitated.

"But she shocks you, doesn't she?" he persisted. "You were displeased the first time you saw her when she made that remark about sitting down in a bustle, weren't you? You don't understand her father's letting her live in a levee camp, do you? You're missing the Carnival balls so you can stay here and keep an eye on her, aren't you?" He shook his head at them shrewdly. "I'm not impressed. She's the nicest girl I know."

"I have no doubt, Kester," said Denis, "that Eleanor Upjohn is a very deserving girl. But after all," he added tersely, "there is something called background, and your mother and I are not alone in believing it has value."

"You are alone, though," said Kester, "if you believe we're the only people who have it." He strolled over to the sofa and sat down, stretching his legs in front of him.

"Don't be absurd," said Lysiane. She turned her chair so that she was facing him, and spoke with a rare abruptness. "I've never been called a snob in my life, Kester, and I'm not risking any such description now when I say that Eleanor Upjohn is not one of us."

It was not easy to make Kester talk seriously about anything. He took a cigarette out of his pocket and held it lengthwise between his thumb and forefinger. He did not light it, because his mother disliked tobacco smoke, but he looked at it as though he found it more interesting than this conversation. "Why not?" he asked ingenuously.

Denis answered. "Eleanor Upjohn's mother came from heaven knows where and was brought up in an orphan asylum. Her father is the illegitimate son of a prostitute and a carpetbagger."

"How do you know that?" Kester demanded shortly.

"About her father? I've just remembered it. Ever since I met that girl I've been trying to think where I had heard the name Upjohn. Then I recalled a story I had heard from my mother."

"What was your mother doing," Kester inquired, "associating with prostitutes and carpetbaggers?"

"I'd prefer you to speak of my mother in more respectful terms, Kester. Not long before the war she gave work to a girl who came here one day asking for charity. Some time later the girl left, and nothing was heard of her till she reappeared during the Reconstruction period as the mistress of a tax-gatherer of the most vicious type. A child was born of that association."

"Fred Upjohn?"

"Yes."

Kester swung one leg across the other. His eye shifted from Denis to Lysiane and back to Denis. "So I'm expected to blame Eleanor for that, am I? Honestly, I'd thought better of you."

"Kester," Lysiane said reprovingly. She came to sit by him on the sofa. "We aren't trying to cast any aspersions on Eleanor Upjohn," she went on with gentle insistence. "But her people are *common*. It's inevitable that she should have absorbed some of their commonness." Kester did not answer and Lysiane went on, her voice low and pleading. "Don't you see, my dear boy, we are simply trying to save you for your own sake? You and she are too different to have any basis for permanent understanding!"

"Permanent—?" Kester got up from the sofa. He stared at them. "Holy smoke, do you think I want to marry her?"

They were silent.

"Hell and high water," said Kester slowly. "I do!"

He burst out laughing. "I do!" he repeated. Snatching up his overcoat he started to scramble into it.

"Kester!" exclaimed Lysiane. "Where are you going?"

"To the levee camp to ask Eleanor to marry me."

His father spoke sharply. "Kester, don't be a fool."

"I'm not. You two have been turning on a light in my head." He opened the door.

"Kester," said Lysiane.

He paused. Lysiane had not moved. She sat with her white hands holding each other in her lap. Her words came with quiet emphasis.

"You haven't seen what we saw when we were children, Kester, the pride and desolation—two sisters with but one presentable dress between them so they could never both come into the parlor at once, the anguish and the desperate smiling pretenses, all to save our civilization from the kind of people we have been talking about. Maybe it's because we know what it cost to give this to you that we shudder at seeing you try to throw it away."

Kester made a little annoyed movement of his head. "Mother, stop it."

Lysiane sprang up and came to him. "My dear child," she pled, "believe me. If I thought there was the faintest chance of you being happy with this girl—"

He was sorry for her, but at the same time he wanted to laugh. "This isn't the old days of the aristocracy and the trash!" he exclaimed. "It's 1912 and I've just found out I've been in love for six weeks."

He brushed a kiss on her forehead and went out. The sun had thinned to a golden sheen over the treetops. As he got into his car Kester began to whistle a ragtime tune. It seemed to him that Eleanor was like one of the Doric columns across the veranda, strong, clean-cut, austerely beautiful, and he marveled that his fondness for her had not long ago come to a climax. His little car panting at its utmost speed, he drove to the levee. As he burst into the main tent, Randa, who was puttering about the table, looked around and gave him her jeweled grin.

"Evenin', Mr. Kester."

"Evening, Randa. Can I speak to Miss Eleanor?"

"Sho, Mr. Kester." Randa lifted her voice. "Miss Elna! Gemman to see you!"

"All right," Eleanor called from the bedroom.

Kester stood impatiently by the desk. A moment later Eleanor came in, she had changed her dress for a white shirt waist and a close-fitting black satin skirt that glimmered with every movement of what Kester thought was the most regal figure of a woman he had ever seen. Eleanor gave an exclamation of surprise.

"Why Kester! What brought you back?"

"You're in the way, Randa," Kester said.

"Yassah." With a chuckle and a swish of skirts Randa left them alone. Kester came a step nearer to where Eleanor stood.

"Eleanor, will you marry me?"

For an instant Eleanor stood quite still. Then she put her hand to her forehead and pushed back her hair. Her dark blue eyes stared at him. In a low voice she answered,

"Say that again."

"Will you marry me?" asked Kester.

"Yes. Yes, of course I will." She spoke in a voice of unbelieving wonder.

He gripped her hands. "You mean it? You will?"

With a happy little laugh far down in her throat she answered, "I told you I would. I think I've been in love with you since the first day I saw you."

"I've loved you since then too. Only I'm such a fool I didn't know it till now. And think of it—I've never even kissed you."

"Then why don't you?" Eleanor asked smiling.

As he drew her to him Kester whispered, "I've been waiting for you all my life."

3

They fled the approach of the engineers and drove off together. Kester had remembered gratefully that his parents had an engagement for supper and auction bridge, and he knew them well enough to be sure no domestic crisis could make them overlook a social obligation. Having stopped on the way to verify this by a telephone call, he took Eleanor to Ardeith.

For a long time they sat together by the fire, in the silence of a miracle that seemed too vast and at the same time too simple to need words. At last Kester drew back and looked down at her.

"Eleanor, why didn't anybody in the whole stupid, inarticulate world ever tell me it was like this to be in love?"

She shook her head. "Maybe you can't tell it, Kester. Maybe it just happens. Like this."

They sat on the sofa between the front windows. The room was rosy in the firelight. After a moment Kester stood up. He bent and kissed her hair, and walked over to the hearth.

Eleanor watched him, thinking she had never known before how handsome he was.

Kester put a fresh log on the andirons and adjusted it with the tongs. The flames leaped up and glowed over him. Without looking around he said,

"Eleanor, I suppose you know I'm not nearly good enough for you?"

She leaned back, smiling at him slowly.

"Don't start that. You're everything in the world I want."

Kester set down the tongs and turned. Their eyes met.

"I love hearing you say that. But you make me sadly ashamed of myself."

Eleanor laughed lovingly. "You look like a little boy caught with his fist in the cooky-jar. Did you mean this to be the preface to a big confession scene?"

"If you think it should be," Kester said simply.

She shook her head. "No. It doesn't matter." After a pause she added, "Come here, Kester." He obeyed and sat by her again. Eleanor said, "Can I help it if other women have found you as irresistible as I do?"

"You darling," said Kester.

"I don't care at all," Eleanor repeated. "Or maybe I should. Tell me—"

"What, sweetheart?"

"Were any of those girls—well, important?"

"No."

"Just—regrettable incidents?"

He nodded. "Too much Bourbon or too much moonlight. Or possibly—"

"Yes?"

"Since I'm trying very hard to be honest, Eleanor, there was one girl who was temporarily rather important. But it didn't last long."

Eleanor smiled again. "Anyone I know?"

He shook his head, smiling too.

"And nobody I'm likely to meet?"

"Oh no. I haven't seen her for years."

"Then again, I don't care."

There was a pause, while they sat and looked at each other, rapt in the witchery that had come upon them. Eleanor slipped down to kneel in front of him. She crossed her arms on his knees and looked up into his face.

"Kester, I don't see how I can possibly be jealous of

29

anything that happened before you even knew I was alive. I'm so grateful to chance and destiny and God that I've got you now, I can't quarrel about any of the paths that brought you to me." She laughed a little. "Why Kester, if you hadn't been quite audacious about girls in general, you'd never have come dashing up to speak to a perfectly strange one just because you liked the way she looked standing above the river."

"That's right," he exclaimed in lovable relief. "I suppose I shouldn't have. Anyway, I feel as if I'm just beginning to live. The way all the poets say a man in love feels, and I thought they were so foolish."

"So did I." She rested her head on his knee.

For a long time they were silent. At last they realized it was midnight. Eleanor said he had to take her home. They drove in silence along the river road, through a still blue night thick with stars.

4

Fred had been sitting up late working on his monthly report to the state levee board. He was wondering where Eleanor could be. Eleanor was a sensible girl and could take care of herself, but Randa had said she had gone off with that Kester Larne and Fred was getting tired of her seeing him so often. Like a lot of fine intelligent girls who had never been bothered with puppy-love Eleanor was probably much more innocent about men than these little flirts who knew about men and nothing else, and while he didn't care how many dates Eleanor had, most normal amusement in the world for a young girl, Fred decided to warn her about that no-'count parlor ornament. Maybe he'd been selfish, Fred told himself; there weren't many men around a levee camp of a sort to entertain Eleanor. It was natural to her to be glad to see any presentable young fellow that came along. Great girl she was, and he shouldn't take too much advantage of her willingness to help him, though the Lord knew he'd have a hard time finding another secretary as good as she was. Well, anyway, he'd speak to her about Kester Larne in the morning. Don't want to be bossing you around, Eleanor, but he's really not worth your time.

For the love of Pete, it was past midnight and he had to be up and doing at five. He heard a car on the other side of the levee. So there they were. The canvas side of the tent next the levee was down, but Fred thought he'd better take a look out and be sure. He'd just glance sidewise around the edge of the canvas—he wouldn't want Eleanor to think he was sitting up to spy on her.

He saw Kester and Eleanor walking across the levee. As they neared the tent they started to say goodby and dropped into each other's arms.

Fred smothered an exclamation. He was angry. But well, girls kissed young men a lot more casually nowadays than they did when he was young. No reason for him to be startled. But Lord have mercy, that wasn't just a kiss. That was as passionate an embrace as he'd ever heard of in his life.

Fred knew Eleanor was not a girl to give herself lightly to that sort of lovemaking. He would have sworn Kester Larne was the only man who had ever held her like that. It meant Eleanor was in love: in love with that indolent hand-kissing scion of a wornout line.

Finally they broke apart, and Eleanor ran toward the tents as though afraid to trust herself to look back. She let herself into her own room softly, evidently thinking the whole camp was asleep. Kester looked after her. In the starlight his face was worshipful.

Fred turned around. His sense of decency forbade him to speak to Eleanor now. In the silence he could hear her sobbing, soft smothered sobs of thwarted ecstasy.

Fred went to his own room, but he could not sleep. He sat up and smoked till nearly morning. All the time he had known that no matter who it would be Eleanor married he would never think the guy good enough for her, but he had always figured that when she made up her mind he'd say, "Well, if he suits you he's all right with me," and let her go. But not with this faded rose of the old Southland. Kester Larne did nothing but amuse himself and keep a paternal eye on his debt-ridden plantation; and he'd never, Fred thought grimly, do anything else. Fred cursed the difficulty of this particular levee job, which had kept him too busy to see what was going on. Why, he asked himself now, couldn't he have taken time to pay some attention to his own daughter before she got herself bedazzled with this firefly?

In the morning Eleanor did not appear till after seven. Fred was having his own belated breakfast.

"I thought you'd be on the levee by now," she remarked as she sat down at the table.

"I had a lot of work last night," said Fred. "That report to the levee board."

"I suppose you want it typed? Show me where it is and I'll start after breakfast."

Eleanor had evidently not slept much herself. She was heavy-lidded, and sat playing with her bacon abstractedly and drinking a great deal of coffee. Fred was wondering how to speak to her. Whatever he said would be wrong. When a man had spent his life in levee camps he hadn't had time to learn diplomatic phrases. He was still wondering when Randa came in and gave Eleanor a box of red camellias.

She sprang up to receive it. As she read the card that lay among the flowers, a dreamy glow flickered over her face. She looked up. "Is the boy waiting, Randa?"

"Yassum." Randa grinned knowingly.

"Give him coffee in the kitchen while I write a note."

As Randa departed Eleanor went to the desk. Fred got up from his chair.

"Who're the flowers from?" he asked, though he knew already.

"Kester." She was writing.

"Wait a minute before you answer," said Fred.

Eleanor halted her scribbling pen. As though seeing his face for the first time that day, she started. "What's the matter, dad?"

He crossed the tent and stood before her. "Eleanor, you're in love with that man, aren't you?"

She nodded, smiling to herself. "How did you know?"

"I was still up when you came in last night," he said abruptly. "I saw you kiss him."

He had expected her to make an indignant retort. But at once he realized that he had underestimated her. Eleanor had never kept any secrets from him, nor did she now. She only said, her eyes on the camellias, "I'd have told you very soon. I'm going to marry him."

"No you're not," said Fred.

Eleanor stared at him. Her blue eyes stretched wide. In a thin, amazed voice she gasped, "Why—dad!"

Fred stood with his hands in his pants pockets. He did so hate to hurt her. Feeling very awkward, he fumbled with his matter-of-fact vocabulary.

"I don't reckon I'm very smart about some things, Nellie," he said gently. "If I was I could tell you better. But that fellow's not good enough for a girl like you."

"Yes he is." Smiling tolerantly, Eleanor stood up and put her hands on his shoulders. "Between you and me, dad, I think the same thing you do about his family. But they aren't Kester."

Fred sighed and started over. "Nellie, listen to me."

She was still smiling, as though he were trying to deny that the world was round. "Stop calling me Nellie. I'm not going to listen." She sat down again and was about to take up her pen.

"Yes you are," said Fred. He spoke with a tender vehemence. "Eleanor, I reckon this is about the hardest thing I ever tried to say. I guess you really are in love with him, and you're mighty happy about it right now, but if you marry Kester Larne you're not going to be happy long."

"Why not?" she asked as if hardly hearing him.

"He's just no good," said Fred.

Eleanor picked up a match and began breaking it into small pieces. "He told me he hadn't been an angel, if that's what you mean."

"Honey child," said Fred earnestly, "I'm not talking about anything he's done. I'm talking about the kind of person he is."

Eleanor was beginning to be angry. "So you think I'll have to wander around wearing a brave smile above a broken heart! But I won't."

"I want you to get more out of life," said Fred, "than just not having your heart broken." He repeated, "That fellow is just no good."

Eleanor's eyes had narrowed dangerously as he spoke. They looked like lines of blue fire. "You'd better be careful, dad," she said in a low voice.

"Why should I be careful? I'm saying what I know is true. And you're going to sit there and hear me." Fred caught his voice and went on as gently as he could. "Eleanor, honey, Kester don't know what it means to be a man grown up. He's a child in a man's body, and you deserve better than that."

As he paused, Eleanor stood up. Her hands were in the pockets of her skirt. Fred saw them swell the cloth as they doubled into fists. It was his own movement of determination.

33

"All right, dad," she said evenly. "I've listened. Now I'll tell you. I love Kester. That's all."

Fred thought he should have known that if Eleanor ever loved a man it would be like this. She was so intense. Feeling that he would have given anything he owned to pierce the armor of infatuation around her, he tried again.

"I know you think that's enough, Eleanor. But believe me, it's not."

Eleanor looked past him as though he were not there. "Maybe you've forgotten," she said slowly. "Maybe it never happened to you like this. I've heard a lot of people talk about love. But nobody seems to mean what I mean."

"No, Eleanor," he said wearily. "Everybody means what you mean."

But it was no use. Fred told her everything he believed was true, that Kester had never accepted the responsibility for his own life and was unfit to accept the responsibility for hers. As he persisted Eleanor grew furious. She flashed at him as she had never done, then she became penitent and pled for his comprehension, and at last she cried out despairingly, "It's no use, dad. I love him. Why can't you understand me? You always have before!"

She crumpled up by the desk and began to sob. It was the first time he had seen her shed tears since she was a little girl. He understood, with a pain that went very deep, that she was crying because all her life he had been her best friend. Eleanor was his first child and nearer to him than any of the others. She had run to him for comfort about her broken dolls and had accepted his rebukes for her childish sins, she had gone to him for counsel and he had talked over his own problems with her, and there had never been any anger between them. Fred stroked her shoulder clumsily. He was sure she was facing fierce disillusion, and the more he tried to tell her so the more he would succeed in making her hate him. But because he loved her he had not the faintest intention of being lenient. He wished they were back in the days when a man could lock up his daughter till she was willing to obey him.

5

Eleanor said nothing to Kester about her father's opposition. She went through her work as usual and continued to see Kester every afternoon. They generally went out in his car, for his parents still lingered at Ardeith and he seemed to think they would be in the way when he and Eleanor had so much to say to each other. Eleanor supposed he had told them about their engagement, but she did not ask. It was enough to get away from her father's hurt indignation into the wonder and peace that came to her when she and Kester were together.

But in less than two weeks the levee was finished and she was back in New Orleans, and now that she could not see Kester every day she found her battle with her father becoming a strain that increased as she grew tired of it.

Her mother was more tolerant. Mrs. Upjohn was a woman who took life as it came. Born Molly Thompson, she had lost her parents during her babyhood, grown up in a Methodist orphan asylum and gone from there to stand behind a counter in a department store, where she had met Fred Upjohn, who was then a sub-foreman on a levee job. When they were married she went up to camp and cooked for Fred and five other men, not accepting the help of a Negro woman until a month before Eleanor was born and then only because Fred insisted on it, Molly's opinion being that it was a shame to pay out wages when Fred needed the money to buy his engineering books. Molly had six children in eleven years, and with prosperity she had grown fat, comfortable and more than ever easy to live with. Having observed that the world did not always adjust itself to meet her convenience, she assumed that the Lord knew more than she did and good-naturedly let Him have His way. When Fred and Eleanor first came home Molly said of Kester only that she had not met the gentleman and therefore had no opinion, and her husband and daughter spoke of him with such contradictory violence that she could not form one. After he had been down to see Eleanor several times Molly said he was a mighty pleasing young man, but she'd hesitate before she'd marry a planter who left his cotton so often right in the middle of planting time just to see a girl

35

who wrote him every day anyway. Noticing that Eleanor had her mind made up, Molly was thereafter silent on the subject.

Eleanor blessed her mother's calmness, but she was so eager to escape Fred's troubled eyes that she would have been willing to be married in the courthouse at once. Kester, however, had assumed that their engagement would be properly announced in the New Orleans *Picayune* and that they would be married in her father's house by a minister. Eleanor finally had to tell him, one day when they were lunching at Antoine's, that Fred was so opposed to their marriage she did not believe he would consent to having it performed in his home. Kester was at first amazed, then he burst out laughing uncontrollably, and finally, when she insisted upon knowing what was so ridiculous about a situation that was racking her nerves beyond endurance, he told her his parents were also convinced the marriage would be disastrous, but for different reasons.

Eleanor was angry. "That pair of eggshells!" she blazed.

"That's why I won't run off to any justice of the peace," Kester ended. "I want you worse than I ever wanted anything, but I'm going to marry you like a man who's proud of what he's doing." He began to laugh again.

"I was never so mad in my life," Eleanor exclaimed, "and it's not funny."

Kester was shaking with mirth. "But it is, my darling, it is funny. Your father thinking the Larnes were blessing heaven for the infusion of some fresh red blood into their weary veins, my father thinking the Upjohns were gloating over the prospect of getting my precious name into their chronicles— and you and I not thinking of anything but how much we love each other and how we wish they'd leave us alone."

At that Eleanor laughed too. As Kester said it, the opposing viewpoints of their families did sound foolish. "What is it they say," she asked after awhile, wonderingly, " 'two shall be born the whole wide world apart'—"

"I think everybody must have gone mad but us," said Kester. Ignoring the uneaten half of his crêpes suzette, he asked the waiter for a check. "Come on," he said, "I'll attend to your father."

He did attend to Fred, with a gay serenity that Eleanor began to think it must have taken six generations to produce. They went into Fred's office, where Kester stood facing Fred across the desk and calmly stated that he was going to marry Eleanor.

"I'm sorry you don't like me," he went on, "but I'm going to marry her anyway. We're both of age and don't have to ask anybody's permission. But I happen to be a man who likes the pleasant traditions. I want to be married in her father's house and have him say 'I do' when the minister asks who gives her away."

Fred crossed his hands on the desk and his eyes met Kester's. "You're mighty confident of yourself, young man, aren't you?"

"Why, yes, sir," said Kester. "I am."

"Mhm. I am too." returned Fred. "I don't like her marrying you, and I don't like pretending in public that I do."

Kester grinned coolly. "You're a stubborn man, Mr. Upjohn," he remarked, "used to bossing everybody around you. But this time you might as well acknowledge that you've lost, and it's your own fault."

"My fault?"

"Certainly," said Kester. "I suppose it didn't occur to you when Eleanor was born that she could be just as stubborn as you are, because when you begot her you gave her your own weapons to fight you with. You might as well give in, Mr. Upjohn. It's the revenge of the chromosome."

There was a silence. Kester and Eleanor waited. At last Fred nodded slowly. "I know when I'm licked." He glanced at Eleanor. "You're going to marry him, whether or no?"

"Yes, dad."

"All right. Kester, I guess that's so, what you said. I'd never thought of it that way."

"Neither had I," said Kester, demurely, "till I walked in and saw Eleanor's face when she looked at you. Thanks, Mr. Upjohn."

After that Fred made no more opposition, and gave Eleanor a check to spend for clothes. But he could not hide his disappointment, and Eleanor was eager to be gone. She did not have much time to think, however, and but for the help of her sister Florence, who came home from school for the Easter holidays, she did not know how she would have done her shopping. When the engagement was officially announced in the *Picayune* (with a photograph of herself pled for by the society editor with an eagerness that made Eleanor recognize the Larne hand in the background, for she knew nothing about the society section), then she found herself breathlessly busy. Lysiane called the next day, and one would have thought this marriage was the consummation of her dreams— "I cannot tell you, Mrs. Upjohn, how happy we are that your lovely daughter is to be one of us"—and Kester's brother Sebastian called, and his sister Alice gave her a luncheon, and Alice's friends gave her luncheons, and wedding presents began to arrive with an abundance that made her understand that in marrying a man named Larne she was entering a tower of mighty significance. Her best friend, Lena Tonelli, whose family owned a tropical fruit company and had grown vastly rich from bananas, undertook the task of keeping the list of the letters Eleanor would have to write after she was married, and she sat competently among the gifts, collecting cards and scribbling on them with amazed exclamations. "Good heavens, Eleanor, these are all names out of the history books! I thought they were dead. What *are* you getting into?"

Eleanor sighed and then laughed. "Once I told Kester he was a Southerner and I was an American. I'm beginning to grasp what I meant."

"My dear," said Lena Tonelli, "you're marrying the Louisiana Purchase and the whole Confederate Army." She waved her hand in dismissal. "I wouldn't get mixed up with this outfit—"

"Neither would I, but for one reason."

Lena nodded soberly. "I never met him but once, the day I happened to be here when he walked in, but I do think he's enchanting. Eleanor, is he really worth all this?"

"Yes."

"I suppose you're right," said Lena.

Eleanor smiled to herself. There was a great deal about Kester's people Lena could not be expected to know, as she was only beginning to discover it herself. Their gallantry, for instance. The Larnes did not approve of this marriage. But once it had been decided on, they had accepted the fact with far more ease than Fred. No outsider could have guessed it was not all they had wished. They simply closed the door on their private lives. It was such a spirit, she thought, that had carried them through pestilence and war; for all their artificial graces they had their own invincibility.

But Fred too was gracious, in his own blunt fashion. The evening before Eleanor was married Fred sent for her. Eleanor went with some reluctance, for Fred's disapproval of what she was doing was still so keen that she had been avoiding him as much as she could. But Fred started the interview in a matter-of-fact way. He merely wanted her signature. He had made over to her a little of his stock in the Tonelli Fruit Lines, to give her an income of about a hundred dollars a month. Eleanor was astonished, and protested as she thanked him. No, no, Fred said, looking embarrassed, he could afford it. The Tonelli Lines owned a vast slice of Central America and were growing. What with his fruit stock and his levee work his income last year had been about twenty thousand dollars, and he didn't think she'd like to ask her husband's permission every time she wanted a dress. This was just income. He had tied up the principal so she couldn't do anything silly, because Tonelli stock was worth holding.

Eleanor kissed him impulsively. They were in the little study off his bedroom where Fred sometimes worked at night. She sat on his desk.

"Dad, you're rather splendid," she said sincerely. "I mean —I know you don't like my marriage any more than you did when I first told you." That was hard to say. They had not mentioned it since Kester's visit to the office. "Yet you're doing everything you can to give me a good start."

Fred crossed his arms on the desk and smiled at her. "I'm mighty fond of you, Eleanor."

"I know you are," she answered. "I'm mighty fond of you too."

Fred put his hand over hers. "Honey, you and me haven't been getting along very well lately. But I hope you're right about this and I'm wrong. And I'd like for us to be friends."

"I'd like it too, dad. I—well, I've missed you," she said with a little catch in her voice.

He patted her hand, and for awhile they said nothing else. It was like old times.

"That Miss Loring down at the office can't make up letters as good as yours," Fred remarked at length.

"I expect she'll learn. I didn't know much about it when I started."

"She hasn't got your education. I reckon I'll have to look around for a girl who's been to college."

Eleanor smiled lovingly. Fred's respect for college was always touching. "If you ever get into a really tight place,

39

dad, let me know. I'm sure Kester could spare me for a day or two."

"No, I guess I'll manage. I always have. But not many girls have your brains."

"Not many girls have fathers like mine to get them from."

He chuckled, then grew sober again. "What was it Kester said that day?—the revenge of the chromosome. I got the idea but I wasn't sure what chromosome meant. I had to look it up. And I had a devil of a time finding out how to spell it. But it reminded me of something I've been wanting to tell you."

"Yes, dad?" She pressed the hand that was still holding hers. "I'm not angry with you any more. I'll listen."

"Well, it's kind of complicated. But I mean, you're like me in so many ways I can see where you're liable to get mixed up, and I don't want you to. I don't want you to think what you do think, that you can get everything you want out of the whole world."

"I'm afraid," she said, "I don't quite understand."

"Well, it's like this," said Fred. "Nothing is as wonderful as you think this is going to be. There always do come times when things go to pieces on us. We've got to be ready for it." He looked into her eyes intently. "Honey, I know now, but I didn't always. The first time a levee of mine went down before the river it mighty near killed me. I'd built that levee myself from the ground up and I *knew* it was right. Then I had to learn that sometimes things go down. All you can do is the best you can. Do you believe me?"

"Why yes, of course," said Eleanor, in a happy voice that told him as well as herself that she did not.

Fred shook his head. "Anyway, try to. It makes things easier to stand. Eleanor, I don't care what you've got, some-how it always stops this side of glory. Now remember that. Not for me. For you."

"Yes, dad." She leaned forward and put her arms around his neck. "You're a very superior person, dad, and I love you very much. But don't have any sad premonitions about me. I'm going to be all right. I'm so happy—I'm going to be so happy with Kester—"

"Yes, honey, I hope you are," he said. "God bless you, Eleanor."

The next day Eleanor and Kester were married. It was the last week in May. They went down to the Gulf Coast, too happy to think of anything but that they were together.

40

Chapter Three

1

THE GULF was like a sheet of purple glass. Beyond the beach the palms waved their fans and feathers around the hotel, which in the sunlight glittered white as the sand. The days followed one another in dazzling succession. Eleanor and Kester swam and hiked, or lay on the beach in their tremendous space of sand and sun and purple water, looking at each other, saying little or sometimes for hours on end saying nothing at all. The miracle of their being together was endless. Eleanor wondered if all the years of her life would be time enough for her to get used to it.

It was her first acquaintance with tranquillity. She had been a busy, decisive person, wanting this and that and driving ahead to get it, bored with leisure, forever looking around for something to use up her tumultuous energy. But here she had drifted into quiet. Remembering the tension of the last months at home, she wondered now if its cessation were not less to her escape from Fred's disapproval than to her present physical release. She smiled sometimes as she recalled how little she had really known of that, though she had thought herself so wise. Kester was a magnificent lover. But she was too aware of happiness to care much about examining it.

There were the mornings when she would realize through her sleep that Kester had kissed her throat, and she would open her eyes and look at him in serene adoration. There were the long hot days when they went out and swam in the sea, and he brought her fruit punches while she lay on the wharf with her hair spread out to dry, the wide skirt of her bathing dress billowing in the wind and her legs in their long black stockings flashing as she swung them over the edge. "You're very beautiful like that," he would say to her as he sat down by her and they sipped their drinks quickly before the sun could melt the ice. There were the evenings when they danced in the lounge and she found that he was an excellent and tireless dancer who never seemed out of breath even in the fastest contortions of the turkey-trot. When she remarked that many people were horrified at these wild new dances Kester asked, "Didn't you ever read about the shudders they had a hundred years ago when the waltz was new?" She had not; it was always Kester who brought up such amusing scraps of imformation strewn in his memory by the library his ancestors had accumulated at Ardeith. Even if she had not loved him she would have found him the most enjoyable companion she had ever known, but she loved him with an intensity that increased by its own exhilaration, and at night when she went to sleep with Kester's arm under her and her head on Kester's shoulder she could feel herself asking with her last conscious thought, "Oh, dear God, is there anything, anything more wonderful than this?"

During this summer she grew familiar with his sunshiny virtues and his lovable if exasperating faults. Kester knew and loved everybody and everybody liked him. Waiters and bell-boys were devoted to him, and after the first day or two the other guests greeted him as if they were lifelong friends of his, while Eleanor, who could have gone from New Orleans to Shanghai without speaking to a soul, was amazed to find herself sharing the popularity Kester so effortlessly gathered. Everybody assumed that she must be like Kester, which she wasn't, but she enjoyed it; when people said to her, "Mrs. Larne, knowing you and your husband has made this the pleasantest holiday I've ever spent," she felt she was receiving a tribute that really belonged to him, but she glowed with pride at possessing such a husband. For with all his geniality Kester never said or did anything that was not impeccable. She had never encountered such habitual elegance of deport-ment as his. She was proud to be seen with him; she liked the admiring glances women gave him when he entered a restau-rant. Eleanor was not given to self-depreciation, but there were times she was filled with wonder that so captivating a man should have chosen *her*, and felt positively humble to be the recipient of such a favor.

But the ease with which everything came to him made Kester a stranger to the ideas of order and self-discipline she had been taught to consider important. He forgot to wind his watch, he could never remember where he had put anything, when he changed his clothes he threw things about wildly, and Eleanor often exclaimed that she spent her whole honey-moon picking up her husband's belongings. He bought quanti-ties of newspapers and scattered them about till the room

42

looked as if it might have been occupied by a political committe bent on informing itself of every phase of the Balkan War and the coming Presidential election, and if she threw away one of them he lamented that it contained a most important article he hadn't had time to read. "I believe you like disorder," Eleanor exclaimed to him. "You don't care whether Wilson or Taft or Roosevelt gets elected, you just like to have things lying around." Kester laughed at her attempts at tidiness and blithely went ahead as usual. When she protested at the way he wrote checks without making out stubs for them he answered, "Why, honeybug, the bank sends a statement. That's what they're for." Eleanor laughed at him rebukingly, and said, "You seem to think the angels are going to take care of you," to which Kester retorted, "Well, they always have. And now they've sent you to do it, haven't they?"

Whereupon he went to the bar and got a Manhattan cocktail, though it was mid-afternoon and the mercury was over ninety. Eleanor wondered that liquor on such a day did not make him miserable, but nothing seemed able to quench his buoyancy.

When their holiday was over they went to Ardeith. The servants and tenants were assembled in front of the house to cheer their homecoming, and Kester's mother, with twenty cousins and friends, stood on the gallery to welcome Eleanor among them. Eleanor and Kester went upstairs, to the room in which Kester and his father had been born, where tulips bloomed on the marble mantel and the great fourposter bed under its canopy of crimson silk looked like a couch placed there for the begetting of heirs to a great tradition. Opening from the bedroom was a little boudoir furnished in rosewood and damask for a lady of beloved fragility; and as she looked around it, and back at the bedroom, and at the oaks beyond the windows whispering as they had whispered to many generations, Eleanor felt the tradition enfolding her, as though she were no longer an individual but part of a unit, like a stone in a castle wall.

"It's so lovely," she murmured to Kester. "So—important."

Later, while her bath water was running, she stood before the old mahogany bureau and looked at herself, and thought of the other women whose reflections had come back to them from this mirror in years long past. The bureau drawer stuck slightly as she tried to open it to put in her clothes. Eleanor remembered her room at home, where the furniture was new and shining and practical. Nobody in the Upjohn family had time for drawers that stuck, or for idleness before ancient mirrors. She felt as if she had stepped into an enchanted world where nothing was quite real but everything had the vague loveliness of pleasant dreams.

2

"I am doing nothing in the most delightful fashion," Eleanor wrote her father. "Picture me if you can, waking up in this vast fourposter, reaching up to pull an embroidered bellcord (the bells work by a system of wires and pulleys of about 1840 construction and my bedroom cord jingles something far down in the back regions where I have as yet hardly penetrated), and then lying back to contemplate the canopy over my head until a black woman in a plaid tignon and gold earrings comes in with coffee. It is not always the same woman, for we have enough servants to run the White House, but Kester says that most of them were born on the plantation and he'd have to take care of them anyway. At length we get dressed and go downstairs to a breakfast room full of flowers and mahogany, to put away quantities of hominy grits, ham and hot waffles. Meanwhile another of these ubiquitous darkies has brought the horses around, and after breakfast Kester and I go riding to look at the cottonfields. I am learning a lot about cotton. At first Kester was startled that I should ride astride, but when I told him the nicest ladies were doing it nowadays and I couldn't learn to manage a sidesaddle anyway, he acquiesced. After awhile, leaving him in the cotton, I come indoors. On the assumption that I must be weary after my exertions another colored girl changes me into a diaphanous dressing gown trimmed with ostrich feathers, and I retire into my damask boudoir to sip lemonade and write letters of thanks for my wedding presents.

"As the adjustment to matronly responsibilities is assumed to be arduous enough to make assistance welcome, Kester's mother is here for a month to carry part of my new burden. While I am riding and writing letters she is doing the housekeeping—so far I am treated like a guest who must on no account trouble her pretty head about such matters. At two o'clock I get dressed for dinner, which we eat in a diningroom the size of a state banqueting hall. The food here is divine, it's like eating at Antoine's every day. Suspended from the ceiling over the table hangs the long fan (they call it a besom) that a little Negro boy used to swing during every meal to blow away flies. It has no purpose in these days of screened windows, but I am beginning to have a certain tenderness for these picturesque anachronisms.

"After dinner I get dressed again—this time very carefully, for I am about to be put on exhibit—and go down to the parlor with Mrs. Larne and sit nicely receiving calls. She occupies her hands embroidering an altar-cloth for St. Margaret's Protestant Episcopal Church. I occupy my hands with nothing, because if I sat holding stitchery everyone would think I was making tiny garments, and, though I am doing no such thing, any suggestion that such an event is possible would be indelicate. And the callers come. Apparently every lady in the parish thinks it necessary to interrupt her affairs during the first weeks so that my life can be enriched by her acquaintance. Most of the calls last exactly an hour. Mrs. Larne acts as my duenna. A bride being supposedly too young and innocent to choose her friends without guidance, Lysiane drops hints into my ears—Mrs. Thingumbob comes of one of the finest families in Louisiana and is to be cultivated; Mrs. Soandso was *talked about* before her marriage, no doubt unjustly but it's always wise to be careful. New people are generally those who have moved into the neighborhood since the Civil War. They all say 'since the war' as though it happened last Tuesday.

"Some of the ladies are charming, some irritating and some dull. Yesterday our butler, Cameo, announced the Durham girls. Three ancient ladies filed in, all in black, and sat weirdly in a row, surveying me so solemnly that I thanked heaven for Lysiane, who talked to them about their Sunday School classes. That evening I asked Kester why the three ladies were called girls, and with a wicked glint in his eye he answered, 'Their house caught fire one night when they were mites of fifty or so, and recounting the accident the next day their father said, "My wife and I were perfectly calm but the children got a little excited." '

"We have supper by lamplight. In the evening Kester's mother tactfully removes herself—either she goes to her room to read *The Winning of Barbara Worth* or to somebody's

45

house to play flinch—and Kester and I can giggle over the people I've seen.

"I can imagine you wrinkling your nose and saying, 'My daughter Eleanor, who can carry logarithms in her head!' Don't, dad. This marriage of mine is so ecstatic that there's nothing I can tell you about it except that it's *right*. I'm going to be one of the happy people who have no history."

Eleanor was surprised at the number of ladies who came to call. Obviously, if Lysiane's friends had whispered questions about Kester's unknown bride before his marriage, the fact of the marriage was an answer. She found the formalities droll, but since she expected to live at Ardeith the rest of her life she tried to sort out her callers, though it was not always easy. The ladies seemed much alike as they sat with bright smiles in the parlor. She did manage to distinguish a few of them—young Mrs. Neal Sheramy from Silverwood Plantation, who was pretty and frail, and coughed delicately, suggesting consumption; Kester's cousin Sylvia St. Clair, fortyish, with a scrawny neck and a face that looked like a whine, who hinted at her own unhappy marriage, gossiped about other people's, and asked Eleanor veiled but intimate questions about hers, which Eleanor parried with a wild desire to giggle, but so adroitly that she won Lysiane's commendation—"I must say you dealt with Sylvia better than most people do, my dear; even if she is my own second cousin I can't deny she is a fool;" and gathering that Sylvia was one of the people who would rather go to the gallows at once and have it over with than be condemned to a lifelong agony of minding their own business, Eleanor chuckled at Lysiane and received an amused smile in return; and she remembered Violet Purcell, a dark, vivid girl who wore a lavender dress and a black feather boa, and whose conversation, spiced with epigrams, had a bitter pleasantness like an olive. Eleanor did not mind the callers as long as she and Kester could laugh about them in the evenings. For Kester's sense of humor and his sense of people were alike so keen that he made comments far more penetrating than Lysiane's.

After Lysiane had gone home to New Orleans, their life settled down to the leisurely plantation routine. Kester and Eleanor gave parties and went to them, or spent long evenings alone, never done with what they had to say to each other. When cotton-picking was over Kester gave the Negroes a barbecue, at which he and Eleanor, with several of their friends, acted as hosts and guests of honor, enthroned in state on cotton-bales while the darkies brought them beer and pig-sandwiches; after which they were driven in a wagon to the big house to dance through the evening. The day they got news of Woodrow Wilson's election Kester appeared unexpectedly with a troop of guests to celebrate, and when Eleanor, not yet used to such impromptu parties, got him aside and asked how she was expected to feed so many people without notice Kester retorted merrily, "Vermont, Utah and Eleanor, all for Taft!"—and disappeared into the kitchen. Eleanor followed him, protesting that she was not for Taft, she was glad about Wilson, but supper for ten was something else; but Kester was chattering with Mamie, the cook who had been at Ardeith ever since he could remember and who understood these things, and he shooed Eleanor back into the parlor with orders not to worry.

The guests were already around the piano, singing while Violet Purcell played for them. Entering with a tray of drinks, Kester flung Eleanor a teasing glance. She whispered under cover of the music.

"Is it going to be all right?"

"Of course," Kester assured her, and shouted, "anybody want a drink?"

Nearly everybody did, and Neal Sheramy from Silverwood Plantation called, "Kester, may I dance with your beautiful wife?"

As they hopped off together in a bunny-hug Neal said to her, "It's fun coming to Ardeith, Eleanor!" She gathered that they must have been used to dropping in this way, and remembered what Lysiane had said about Kester's keeping the house always full of people. Violet had started playing *The Mississippi Dippy-Dip* and Eleanor danced with Neal until they were both out of breath, when they went over to sit by Neal's wispy little wife, who appeared too frail to indulge in these insane dances. Eleanor thanked heaven for her own rugged health and felt grateful that she could give parties. When the supper bell rang they went into the diningroom. The table held an omelet, a cheese soufflé, a dish of ham and various plates of hot biscuits and preserves; and seeing how easy it all was when everybody was used to it, Eleanor had a gay evening and later told Kester to have a party whenever he felt like it. Rather surprised, Kester answered, "Why, sugarplum, I do."

Now and then she gave a formal dinner, and sat in splendor among the silver and linen with her hair piled on top of her head and her bosom alight with antique jewelry Kester had brought up from the vault and given her to wear, but mostly the parties at Ardeith were hilarious affairs like this one, with everybody dancing while the phonograph played or Violet pounded out ragtime on the piano. Kester's friends were a gay, insouciant group, with beautiful voices and exquisite manners. They had been friends since childhood, and much of their badinage she could not share, but she always felt that they were doing their best to make her feel at ease among them because they were all devoted to Kester. Most of them were obviously going to be like Denis and Lysiane, decorative ladies and gentlemen of no earthly use but very pleasant to have around, and Eleanor began to understand that the reverse of her father's good qualities could be delightful. Of the lot she preferred Violet Purcell, whose cool terseness was refreshing.

She enjoyed the life she was leading and found it easy to forget that she had ever been used to any other. When Fred wrote her a description of the President's waterways conference in Washington she found his letter almost dull, and was astonished to remember how eager she would have been a year ago to be told about the advances in levee construction. But now Kester and Ardeith filled her thoughts so that anything else seemed a needless intrusion. Kester told her a dozen times a week that he had never been so happy. They had but one argument, when Eleanor insisted on being given a regular allowance for housekeeping. Characteristically, he said, "Buy what you need and send the bills to me," and it took her two hours to convince him that she could not spend money with any degree of wisdom unless she knew how much she had to spend. Kester asked then, "All right, how much do you want?" Eleanor sighed; she wanted whatever it took to run the house, and was aghast when he told her Cameo and Mamie had always done the ordering and he had simply paid the bills without keeping any record of their monthly totals.

At last she got out of him that Ardeith had produced about eight hundred bales of cotton last year, and that a good average price for cotton was ten cents a pound, which gave the plantation a gross income of forty thousand dollars. How much of this was clear she did not know, and it was impossible to make Kester be definite, so in despair she halved it, and though this did not seem a large income for a place like Ardeith she considered it adequate. The house was so lavishly equipped that it could be operated with no great expenditure. She asked Kester if he would give her six hundred dollars a month for housekeeping. Kester said "Certainly," but as she was sure he would forget to do it she drove to the bank with him the next morning to see to it that he made the first deposit. She was exasperated. But he came out of the bank as debonair as usual and gave her a book showing a deposit to her credit of eight thousand dollars. She gasped, but he said, "Now you won't pester me for a whole year, will you?"

"Are you angry with me?" Eleanor asked repentantly.

"My darling, no," said Kester, "but you know I'd never remember to make a deposit every month and I'm not going to waste a lot of time being called names because I am the way I am. You've got such—what's the new word they're using in factories?—efficiency."

Eleanor kept house with the exactness she liked, balancing her account books every week and doing the best she could to prevent Mamie from feeding her husband and children out of the Ardeith kitchen. Mamie was a trial, but she was a cook in a thousand and knew her power. They had eleven servants, which Eleanor considered about five too many, but she yielded to Kester's importunities and retained them, along with sundry black boys who kept turning up from the plantation ostensibly to ask if there wasn't something the young miss wanted done and actually to get some cold biscuits from Mamie's generous hands. Eleanor put these down under the heading of "Foolish but Unavoidable Expenses," and let it go at that. As long as Kester adored her as he did she was willing to compromise with everything else.

"You're an astonishing girl," Violet said to her. "Don't give me that innocent look out of your eyes, either, as if you didn't know you were married to the most comsummate heartbreaker in the United States. Remember what Washington Irving said?"

Eleanor shook her head.

"It's about a man, but reverse the sexes and it applies to you. 'He who wins a thousand common hearts is therefore entitled to some renown, but he who keeps undisputed sway over the heart of a coquette—' something about his being a real hero. My dear, how *do* you do it?"

Eleanor laughed and said she didn't know, but privately she was rapturous. That she should love Kester so passionately seemed to her to require no explanation; she did not know how any woman could help loving him. But that he should love her seemed a perpetually recurring miracle. She liked every evidence of it. Kester made frequent trips to New Orleans, sometimes with and sometimes without her, and brought back absurd and expensive presents—rhinestone combs for her hair, frilled camisoles, taffeta petticoats that made an enticing racket when she walked. At Christmas he gave her a watch to be worn on a long chain about her neck and tucked under her belt, with a card saying "I love you" in nine languages, the preparation of which had taken him a whole morning in the Tulane library.

After the opening of the new year Eleanor discovered that she was going to have a baby. She recognized it with some dismay, for though she had assumed that she would have children she had not intended to have any till she had been married a year or two and was tired of her carefree life, and besides, she was dubious about Kester's reaction to the responsibilities of fatherhood. Kester had said he liked children, but she suspected that he thought of babies as being like the curly angels on Christmas cards, and as the eldest of six Eleanor had been required to play nursemaid too often to have any such cherubic misconceptions.

But when she told Kester, he was thrilled. He immediately told everybody he knew, with the artless joy of a little boy promised a bicycle. He went up to the attic and brought down the carved rosewood cradle where the infant Larnes had kicked and squalled for a hundred years, and set it up in the old nursery six months before it would be needed. Eleanor's new acquaintances called with congratulations, bringing presents of silver thimbles and yards of muslin, which, as she couldn't sew, she put away in a drawer, and ordered a layette from New Orleans. Altogether, in spite of her amused and sometimes annoyed protests she found herself relegated to the place of a Brave Little Woman, and to her surprise she discovered it was not an unpleasant place to be. It was agreeable to be worshipped and waited on, and to receive Kester's delighted tributes. He brought her anything his eye fell upon with favor, without regard for whether or not she would have any use for it, and apparently believing that she was now too delicate to move he had an extension telephone

50

installed by her bed to save her going downstairs to answer rings. As if this were not enough, he asked her nearly every day if she wanted anything, so eagerly that Eleanor was at last emboldened to make a request that had been lying in the back of her mind ever since they came from their honeymoon trip.

Kester's untidiness irritated her and she had observed that her endless picking up irritated him. She was beginning to foresee that if they continued to occupy the same bedroom their mutual annoyance was going to result in a storm. "I don't want to quarrel with you about anything so unimportant," she pled, "but I can't, Kester, I can't live in a place that always looks as if the Chinese army had just marched through! If there was no help for it I'd try to be patient, but in a house with nine bedrooms I don't see why I have to. Would you mind very much if I had a room of my own?"

They were undressing. Kester's shirt was dangling from the chandelier and the floor was strewn with his undergarments. Eleanor stood in the middle of the room surveying its confusion with a look of despair. Kester began to laugh.

Of course she could have her own room, he exclaimed. He would be glad to be relieved of her eternal neatness. Only she mustn't move, he would. He'd take the room across the hall, which though less grand than this was every bit as comfortable. She thanked him joyfully.

That removed her last vexation. As the summer poured its hot richness upon Ardeith Eleanor passed her days in pleasant indolence. Young Dr. Bob Purcell, brother of Violet and son of the old doctor who had assisted Kester and Kester's father into the world, dropped in once or twice a week, but his visits were more social than professional. He and Kester sat drinking juleps and talking about the cotton crop, varieties of good whiskey and the doings of the neighborhood. Eleanor liked Dr. Purcell, who was both wise and humorous, and enjoyed his visits.

The three old Durham girls called to see her, with great interest in her preparations for the baby. Eleanor was not used to gentle old ladies with nothing to do, but she tried to be pleasant. One of them brought her an elaborately briar-stitched sacque and another a pair of crocheted bootees, while the third sister, Miss Agatha, explained bashfully that she had adhesions and couldn't stoop, but she brought an illustrated volume of fairy tales. Eleanor began to be aware that any one of the three sisters would have bartered her soul for a baby, and she was filled with sympathy and kissed them all. They told her they were happy that dear Kester had married such a sweet girl. It was the first time anybody had ever called her sweet.

Only once was she roused to look at herself, when Fred came to Ardeith at a time when his business brought him upriver for a few days. Beholding Eleanor, in a white satin dressing-gown, reclining on a sofa in her little boudoir, Fred was alarmed, embraced her tenderly, and asked why she had not let him know all was not well with her. When Eleanor exclaimed that she was perfectly well, and wanted to know what nonsense Kester had been telling him, Fred looked her up and down in astonishment. Then what, he demanded, did she mean by this ridiculous performance?

Suddenly, looking at his face, Eleanor saw herself as he saw her and burst into uncontrollable laughter. Fred continued to stare.

"Darling," she said at length, "you don't understand. I'm a flower of the Old South about to produce an heir."

"Do you really feel all right?" Fred repeated.

She nodded vehemently. "Yes, dad, I'm perfectly all right."

"When you weren't with Kester in the car at the train," said Fred, still unconvinced, "I began to be worried."

"At the train?" Eleanor gave him a look of mock horror. "My dear Mr. Upjohn, you don't think a lady in my condition would show her figure past her own front gate?"

"You mean they won't let you go out? But what do you do for exercise?"

"I cut flowers in the garden," she told him wickedly, "with one of the maids following me around to make sure a grasshopper doesn't frighten me."

Fred sat down on one of the dainty little chairs. "I declare to my soul," he said blankly. Then he added, "Before you were born your mother was cooking three meals a day for six men."

"My mother," said Eleanor, "was not married to Kester." She began to laugh again. "Dad, get that look off your face. I'm smothered in magnolias, and I love it."

Fred sat forward in the little chair, awkwardly, as though afraid it was going to crack under his weight. "This don't seem a bit like you," he said slowly.

Eleanor bit her finger, laughing at him.

"And you the smartest girl I ever did see," Fred added.

How sad it is, she thought, that we should be so inarticulate that we have to laugh at our profoundest joys. She could not explain to Fred the happinesss that was hers when her eyes met Kester's across the room and they exchanged a fleeting smile. She and Kester teased each other, laughed at each other's eccentricities, pretended to scold each other's faults, with an unspoken understanding; she could not tell Fred about the moments when she had lain in Kester's arms sobbing with the ecstasy of loving him. But Fred should have comprehended it. That he appeared not to comprehend puzzled and hurt her. I'm the first person who ever proved him wrong, she thought, and he can't be sporting about it. She was relieved when he left, and it made her feel guilty.

3

The baby was born in October. Kester, of course, behaved as anybody might have foretold he would behave: he paced the hall, refused to eat, got sick from the fumes of chloroform, kept coming in at inconvenient moments to make sure Eleanor was not dying, and in general made a nuisance of himself; and about six o'clock in the afternoon when the nurse came to inform him that the baby was a girl he groaned "Thank God she'll never have to go through this," rushed into the bedroom and had to be forcibly restrained by the doctor from smothering Eleanor with his kisses. And when Eleanor murmured, "Please go away and let me rest," he was persuaded that she did not love him any more and without having laid eyes on his daughter he went downstairs in anguish to call up his cousin and chum Neal Sheramy, and the two of them went out and got drunk and at sunrise had to be assisted to bed by Cameo.

But he was delighted with his fatherhood, sent telegrams to everybody he could think of and for a week kept open house, serving wine and eggnog in the parlor to a stream of congratulating visitors as though it had been New Year's. Dennis and Lysiane came up to see the baby—"Well, well, now where did you get this?"—and Fred, who could not get away until the following Sunday, came up at Kester's urgent invitation, bringing Molly and Eleanor's sister Florence, and they spent a merry day admiring the squirming pink object that was still called "the baby," for though Kester and Eleanor had discussed dozens of possible names none of them seemed quite right. Eleanor lay in the great fourposter under its crimson canopy, vastly enjoying her homage. She was glad to see her parents; they were so frank, so strong, laughing at the elegance of her surroundings and reminding her that she had been born in a tent. Here in the legended quiet of Ardeith they seemed to Eleanor refreshing, like a wind in summer, and she thought how proud she was that she could pass on to her child such an unconquerable heritage as hers. They took the night train back to town. Though she was tired, she told the nurse she wanted to speak to Kester before she went to sleep.

The nurse brought him and left them alone together. As Kester sat down by the bed Eleanor told him she knew what she wanted to name the baby. "I'd like to name her for a very courageous woman," she said. "My father's mother. Unless you mind."

Kester was sitting on the bedstep. He laid his head on the pillow by hers. "My dearest girl, why did you think I'd mind?"

"Dad was illegitimate—had you forgotten that?—and you're so conservative about some things."

"Why no, darling, I hadn't forgotten it. Something about a carpetbagger during Reconstruction."

"I've never thought much about it until now," said Eleanor. "She was a poor creature who'd never had a pretty dress nor very many square meals until she took the only chance she'd ever had to get them. He deserted her before dad was born. When dad was a child she used to take in washing, and somehow she brought him up and made him go to school. She couldn't read, she didn't know any of the sort of things we know, but I think she must have been splendid. She died when I was a little girl, as triumphantly as any soldier who had won a battle, for she knew dad was a great man and she had made him one. She had the courage that makes the mothers of heroes. I'd like to name my daughter for her."

Kester smiled. "I suspect you're very much like her. What was her name?"

"Corrie May Upjohn."

He took a long breath. "Eleanor, forgive me, but I think that's atrocious."

"So do I, but can't we arrange it somehow?"

Isn't Corrie sometimes short for Cornelia?" he suggested after a moment's consideration.

"Cornelia. I like that. Let's name her Cornelia."

"All right."

Eleanor moved to rest her cheek against his hand as it lay on the pillow. They went on talking about the baby. Kester began to outline her future. He wanted Cornelia to have a hobby-horse with a real hair mane and tail. Eleanor began to picture her as she would come down the spiral staircase in bridal white.

"And maybe taking her wedding trip in a flying-machine," Kester suggested.

Eleanor shivered. "And scare me to death. Do you suppose they'll be practical by then?"

"Why not? Automobiles weren't practical twenty years ago. Why, Eleanor, she may live to see anything—even rockets going to the moon."

Eleanor could not help laughing at his romantic imagination.

"Well, she might," he persisted. "The world's getting to be an amazing place. Did you read the list of inventions they made speeches about at the German Kaiser's silver jubilee?"

"I don't think so."

"It was a gorgeous celebration—a sort of handshaking-and-eternal-friendship party for all the kings and queens and writers and scientists in Europe. The Kaiser combined the anniversary celebration with the marriage of his daughter, and the bridesmaids were English, Rumanian, Russian and Italian princesses—to symbolize the unity of Europe, you know—and visiting kings made speeches and called the Kaiser Europe's man of peace. You needn't laugh at what I said about rockets, either. The Kaiser conferred the title 'Greatest German of the Twentieth Century' on Count von Zeppelin."

"Who's he?"

"He invented the dirigible balloon. And they can go anywhere."

"Not to the moon, stupid. When was all this?"

"Last summer. Stop being so practical. Don't you like the idea of your daughter's growing up in a world that's turning into a sort of wonderland?"

"I don't know. It's rather frightening. But I do think I'd like to go up in a balloon."

"So would I," Kester agreed. In the ancient cradle near the

bedside Cornelia began to kick. Eleanor kissed Kester's hand as it lay against her face. She was very tired, and drowsy, and very happy indeed.

Chapter Four

1

ELEANOR LOVED the baby very much, but she was not by nature passionately maternal, and she had never dreamed of such abject adoration as Kester poured out on his small daughter. He lavished toys and clothes upon her, listening to her every gurgle as a sign of intelligent notice. and he not only thought Cornelia the most remarkable child in the world but told everybody so in terms that made Eleanor protest.

"Kester you've got to stop it!" she exclaimed one evening when they came home after having taken supper with the Purcells. "When Cornelia was born she was not pink and white and dimpled, she was red as a bricklayer's neck. All babies are."

"Cornelia wasn't," he insisted. He was on his knees building up the parlor fire.

"All babies are born ugly," Eleanor returned, "and practically all parents say *their* baby was the one exception in history. and I've always laughed at them and declared that if I ever had a child I wasn't going to talk about it like that—"

"You've got such a factual mind " said Kester. He got up and brushed off his hands. The fire crackled.

Kester took a chair on the opposite side of the hearth from Eleanor, leaning back in it lazily his hands clasped behind his head. He was such a dear, she thought. nobody could ever succeed in convincing him that the earth was the dull and monotonous place most people found it Kester had made her life so rich; it was January, almost two years to the day since they had first seen each other and it seemed to Eleanor that nothing that happened to her before then was of any importance except as one of the steps by which she had moved toward him. She smiled reproachfully as she noticed his day's mail still on the side table unopened.

56

"Is that the way you used to treat my letters?" she asked, glancing at the pile.

"I used to haunt the box waiting for them," said Kester, "and carry them around to peek at while I was riding the cotton." He reached for the mail and began to look it over. "Here's one from my sister Alice. She has no literary talents, but she feels it a matter of family duty to write me once a month. What's this one that's been opened?"

"That's addressed to Mr. and Mrs.," said Eleanor. "It's from Mrs. Neal Sheramy reminding us we're having dinner with them at Silverwood tomorrow."

"Oh yes. I'm going with Neal after dinner to help him buy a car. These others are bills, and something from the bank in New Orleans. See what Alice has to say while I look at them."

He tossed the letter into her lap and Eleanor opened it. Alice's news, as he had foretold, was not interesting. Alice was well, her husband was well, it had been a rainy week in New Orleans, and as Alice said "Mother had a large party Wednesday to play bridge," Eleanor assumed that Kester's parents were also well. She had started to replace the letter in its envelope when Kester sprang to his feet with an exclamation.

She looked up at him, and the pages slipped out of her hand.

Kester was holding the letter from his bank in New Orleans. His eyes seemed all of a sudden hollow, and he stared at the sheet as though it told him he had been unwittingly eating poison. She gasped, "Kester, what is it?"

For a moment Kester did not answer. Then, in a strange, unbelieving voice, he said, "The bank is threatening to take Ardeith."

Eleanor heard a sound come out of her throat. It was not a word. It was merely a noise, like the croak of a frog in a swamp. She felt dizzy. It was as though a blow had distorted her senses, and she had just enough wit left to remind herself not to speak or move now because in a moment everything would come back to its place and she would be glad she had not done anything foolish. She could see Ardeith all at once, the oaks and the palms and the house, the rows of cotton, the cabins and the Negroes. She saw Kester, and her baby who was going to come down the spiral staircase in a wedding veil. And strangely, she saw the print of the horseshoe on the step of the stairs, and the dent in the silver coffee-pot, and Kester's little knife with his name engraved on the handle because he was always losing things.

At last—she did not know how long she had been staring at him—Kester bent and kissed her forehead. She heard him say,

"I'm sorry, darling. I shouldn't have worried you. I'll go down to New Orleans and get an extension."

Eleanor put up her hand to her forehead with a curious feeling of resentment as though a stranger had touched her with his lips. Things were not coming back to their places. She said vaguely, "An extension? How do you know you can get it?"

He shrugged. By a great effort she focused her attention upon him, and saw that he looked normal again, the untroubled and delightful young man who had never failed to have what he wanted fall into his hands. "I always do, sweetheart," he assured her. "This is just a form letter. I shouldn't have let it scare me." He continued with soothing cheerfulness. "My dearest, don't glare at me like that! I'm sorry I frightened you. Didn't you know I'm always hopelessly in debt? That I'm the bad child coddled by the Southeastern Exchange Bank? That my one talent is being able to borrow money from anybody?" As though bewildered by her hurt amazement, he added wonderingly, "Didn't you know me, darling, when you married me?"

In a voice so cold and hard that her word dropped like a lump of ice on his self-confidence, Eleanor said,

"No."

Kester did not answer. He took a step backward. It seemed to Eleanor that this moment was like a blade that cut through her life, dividing all that lay ahead of it from all that lay behind. She stared at Kester through the minute of transition, seeing him with the clarity with which one sometimes sees through pain. She saw him as though for the first time, Kester who had been given everything and so had never been faced with the necessity of deserving anything. Blessed with an honored name, a great inheritance, compelling personal gifts, Kester had never thought of guarding what he received so easily. And money was one thing—perhaps the only important thing in his life—that was not subject to his charm. So Kester had refused to look at it. He preferred to make believe that its demands were not relentless. But that, in the code to which Eleanor had been bred, was unforgivable.

She remembered the tent in the levee camp, and her father's implacable voice. "I'm not talking about anything he's done. I'm talking about the kind of person he is."

She got to her feet slowly, feeling stiff as though she had been sitting still for hours. Kester was still regarding her with a hurt surprise.

"I don't understand," said Eleanor. "What have we been spending?"

He shrugged. "I've wondered myself."

"How much money do you owe?"

"I haven't," said Kester, "the faintest idea."

"Don't talk to me like that!" she exclaimed. "I'm not a child. Where did you get it?"

He made a wide gesture, his hand taking in the room. "Ardeith. Funny how it piles up on you."

"You mean you've mortgaged it piece by piece?"

"Something like that. The place was mortgaged a little when I took it over. My grandmother had kept it clear of debt, but father never had much more sense about money than I have. Since he's retired he's lived on the income of some sugar land across the river. It's rented."

"But how did you do it?"

"How does anybody do it?" he answered patiently. "I haven't paid much attention. You borrow on the cotton when it's planted. You think the crop will pay it off but you need the money for something else, so you give a piece of land as security. Then all of a sudden something happens to make you realize every teaspoon in the house is carrying all it can stand. Eleanor," he exclaimed, "don't look at me as if I'd killed somebody! I tell you it's all right. There's some pine land across the road, not worth a picayune, but I can make Mr. Robichaux think it is."

She looked him up and down, standing opposite him with her anger like a cold lump in her breast. "Tell me, Kester." Her voice was hard. *"How much do you owe on this plantation?"*

"I told you," he retorted, "I didn't know."

He stood by the fireplace, his elbow on the mantel. She took a step nearer. "Kester," she asked, "were you in debt when we married?"

He tilted his shoulder. "I'm always in debt. It's my normal state."

His casual answer flung her into a fury. "You were in debt

when you took the best suite in the hotel for our honeymoon?" she cried. "When you were tipping the bellboys a dollar for bringing you a paper? When you served sixteen-year-old Bourbon to your guests? When you brought Cornelia handmade dresses and imported—"

"Shut up," said Kester quietly. "And stop screaming."

"I didn't mean to scream. But suppose I do? You can't keep this a secret forever. That we've been living on money that didn't belong to you. On your smile and your dishonesty. Funny," she added. "My father told me all this before I married you."

"Then why didn't you listen to him?" asked Kester. He walked over to the liquor cabinet at the side of the room and began pouring himself a drink. His hand was steady, and even when he asked his last question his voice had not changed.

"I didn't listen to him," said Eleanor, "because I loved you. I loved you so much I thought nothing else mattered. But he knew me better than I knew myself. He knew I'd rather scrub floors than spend money that wasn't mine to spend."

Kester did not answer. He was quietly sipping whiskey from a little glass. She wondered if the whiskey had been paid for.

Eleanor twisted her hands together, feeling crushed under the burden of her disenchantment. "Some day," she said, "you may know what it has done to me to find this out about you."

He gave her an oddly intent look across his glass, and smiled, a bitter little smile. "I always thought," he said slowly, "you were the one person in the world who'd never let me down."

"What have I done except tell you the truth about yourself?"

"Will you have the kindness to go upstairs?" Kester asked.

His voice was so icy polite that Eleanor turned without answering and went out. She climbed the spiral staircase and went into her own room. Through the front windows she could see the draperies of moss swinging from the trees and the little feathers of fog blowing in the dark around them. She sat down by the fire, wishing she was given to tears, and wishing it was daylight so she could go out and walk for miles and miles. Any physical reaction would have been easier than merely bearing this silence and this smothering weight of disappointment.

After a long time she heard Kester climb the stairs and go

60

into his room across the hall. The sound of his door closing gave her a devastating sense of loneliness. There had never been a night before when they had parted in anger. At first she would not believe that he intended to go to bed without speaking to her again. But she heard nothing else. She wished she had never asked that they sleep in separate rooms. If he had had to go to bed in here they would have talked to each other, and they could not have helped saying they were sorry. She stood up, almost ready to go to him and ask his forgiveness. But she stayed where she was; it was not her fault the plantation was mortgaged or that they had lived in luxury on money they had no right to spend. Eleanor resolutely began taking off her clothes. She opened the windows and got into bed.

She could not go to sleep. She tumbled about, unable to get warm and then unable to find a comfortable place to lie, while her mind was blurred with what for a long time was merely an unthinking confusion. The little clock on the bedside table ticked loudly. The clock had to be there so she would know when to go to Cornelia, but its ticking worried her nerves. Slowly, her unhappiness began to turn to self-analysis. She told herself that she had merely hurt Kester without suggesting any solution of the problem, and in the fierce inner light of sleeplessness she knew that she could not endure to hurt him because she loved him with a passion that had in no way diminished. She wanted him and she would want him as long as she lived. Whatever price she had to pay for her life with him, she would not relinquish any chance to recapture what they had had together. The next step ahead of her was plain: she was going down to New Orleans and make the bankers tell her exactly the plight of Ardeith. If there was any salvation to be had she would wrest it from them with every shred of strength she possessed, because if she recognized Kester's faults it was only with a violent desire to save him from their consequences.

There was a faint little cry from the nursery. Eleanor sat up. It must be after four o'clock. Usually she set the alarm, but tonight she had forgotten it. Hurriedly putting on a bathrobe she went down the hall to the nursery, where Cornelia lay in her crib protesting the world's neglect. As she felt Cornelia cuddle against her in warm helpless trust Eleanor thought how much she loved her. She was not demonstrative like Kester, but she gave her child the simple, quiet love that

61

meant protection. Remembering the unconquerable grand-mother for whom Cornelia was named she smiled to herself. Kester had the grace born of many self-assured generations, but she had somethng else, the pitiless strength of a race that had fought its way through the dirt and cruelty of the poor, and she liked to think Cornelia was drawing in something of this harsh vigor with her mother's milk.

Eleanor put the baby back into the cradle and covered her up. Out in the hall again, she hesitated, then went to Kester's room, opening the door softly. His clothes were tossed about on the chairs and floor as usual, and he was fast asleep. Wondering resentfully if any crisis could disturb the healthy rhythm of his life, Eleanor nevertheless bent down and kissed him. He stirred slightly, but did not wake up. She left him, and went back to her room.

But the compulsion to immediate activity still would not let her rest, so she took a coat from her armoire and drawing it around her she crept down the chilly dark stairway to the little room Kester called his study, where there was a big roller-top desk piled with ledgers. The desk drawers were so stuffed with papers that it was hard to open them. Eleanor pulled out a drawer and began to go through its contents—circulars, restaurant menus, old letters, racing forms, ticket stubs, theater programs, bills, bills, bills. With hands that were stiff with cold she went to work sorting the bills.

Her exasperation rose in her again. Kester had evidently paid for nothing until he had to. The presents he had given her, the dresses he had bought Cornelia, were all unpaid for; and she shivered with anger when she found Bob Purcell's bill for his attendance upon her at her delivery three months ago. Eleanor thrust that into her coat pocket. Thank heaven she had some money, her income from the Tonelli Fruit Lines. Nine hundred dollars of that lay in the bank. She had been putting it up to buy a car of her own, but that was out of the question now. She would pay this bill herself tomorrow—no, today. It was nearly dawn.

To think that Kester had neglected such an obligation made her sick with shame. But she promised herself fiercely that nothing at Ardeith would be neglected again. Whatever her talents might or might not be, she had a good head for business. She had not majored in mathematics at Barnard for nothing.

With grim resolution she pulled open another drawer and

rummaged for more bills. As she found one, and then others, Eleanor felt her wrath turning to fear. With all these to be paid besides the accumulated mortgages on Ardeith, the possible total of Kester's indebtedness began to assume terrifying proportions. Tucked in the back of the drawer was a white cardboard box. Eleanor lifted the lid, and started at the sight of envelopes addressed to Kester in her own handwriting. They were the letters she had written him before their marriage, kept here together with a handkerchief and a silk vanity case she must have dropped one evening, and several other trifles nobody but a fond lover would have thought precious, the only objects in the desk he had thought to store carefully away. A wave of affection swept over her, smothering her anger, and she dropped her head, pushing her cold fingers back through her hair; she loved him, she could not help it, and it was easy to understand why everybody else who knew him loved him too. He was the most lovable person she had ever known, although, by all the standards of righteousness, he was not worth a picayune.

Eleanor put the box back in its place. She took the unpaid bills upstairs with her and filed them in a pigeonhole in her desk. Though her fingers were so cold she could hardly hold the pen she wrote a check for Bob Purcell and put it with his statement into an envelope and addressed and stamped it. When she stood up and turned out her desk-lamp it was six o'clock in the morning, and she was trembling with fatigue.

Then at last she went to bed and fell asleep, waking only when Dilcy, the baby's nurse, brought Cornelia to her, and going to sleep again at once. It was nearly noon when she was roused by hearing Kester's voice in the hall outside. He was talking to Dilcy.

"It's gorgeous weather, Dilcy—cold, but the sun will do her good. Take her outdoors. Is Miss Eleanor still asleep?"

Eleanor could hear Dilcy protesting, with the conviction of mammies that cold air meant disaster to their darlings, and she heard Kester insisting again. Raising herself on her elbow, she called him.

He put his head in. "Hello! So you finally woke up. Such hours!"

Kester looked well, and he grinned upon her as though their last night's quarrel had never occurred. As he came in, Eleanor pulled the bellcord for coffee and lay down again, thinking how disheveled she must look beside Kester's fresh well-being. He came in and sat on the bedstep. "Did you go to bed late?" he asked her.

She nodded.

"Mad with me?" he inquired smiling.

She nodded again.

"I was mad with you too. But I'm not any more." He took her hand in his. "Not if you're sorry you yelled at me."

"I'm sorry," she murmured, and she turned her head and kissed his hand as it held hers. She smiled a little. "I can't be angry with you very long. You're a goose and I love you better than anything else on earth."

"I love you too," said Kester.

They did not say anything more until after Bessie from the kitchen had brought a tray with Eleanor's coffee. Eleanor sat up in bed, and as she drank it she began to feel better.

"Kester," she said, "I'm not in a fury now, or screaming. Let's talk about those debts."

"All right." He grinned. "I'm a worthless, trifling no-'count white man, and I know it, so let's start from there."

He was like a little boy confessing a fault with such endearing remorse that his mother had not the heart to punish him. But Eleanor sobered quickly. "We must go down to New Orleans right away," she went on. "Who is it we see at the bank?"

"Mr. Robichaux."

"—And find out just what we owe and what the terms are. Then we must somehow make him grant us a little time so we can start paying."

"You're right, of course," said Kester. "It's going to be tough. But Eleanor," he continued earnestly, "I don't think it's hopeless. There's no use saying it is until we know. I'll go to New Orleans—"

"I'm going with you."

"You can if you want to, but it's not necessary."

"I'd rather," said Eleanor. "I'm going to help you clear it up and I want to know just where we are."

"All right," he agreed.

Eleanor poured another cup of coffee and they went on planning. A new feeling of intimacy began to grow between them as they talked over the battle that lay ahead. Kester was no fool once his attention was roused, and now that the result of his carelessness had been brought home to him he was eager to fight. Eleanor started to push back the bedclothes. "I

64

shan't wait for a fire to be made in here. I'll get dressed and pack a grip. There's a train for New Orleans at three."

"But we can't go today!" exclaimed Kester.

"Why not?" she asked in astonishment.

Kester reminded her they had an appointment for dinner. Didn't she remember that there was a display of automobiles in town today?—and two weeks ago they had promised Neal Sheramy to have dinner with him at Silverwood and go with him later to try out the cars. To Eleanor's irritated protests Kester was unshakable. They had promised. Clara Sheramy was expecting them for dinner at two o'clock and had promised to have softshell crabs because Kester was so fond of them, and anyway he wanted to drive the new cars. Neal was considering getting an electric car for Clara, as she was so frail and driving out into the fresh air would be good for her. And Kester reminded Eleanor that he knew all about automobiles—he had been the first man in town to drive one, when they were considered horrid playthings meant to frighten horses—and besides, it was not necessary to dash off to New Orleans today. Tomorrow would be soon enough.

Eleanor sighed in annoyance. "Phone and tell Neal Sheramy we can't come. This is important, Kester!"

"But there's no harm in going to New Orleans tomorrow instead of today!" he persisted.

"Why can't Neal choose his own car? He's not halfwitted."

"Why do you have to be in such a hurry? I promised to have dinner at Silverwood and I'm going to."

"I'm not," said Eleanor flatly.

Kester obviously did not believe she meant it. To his mind an engagement for dinner was sacred; more sacred, Eleanor thought when he had left her and she sat up with her hands clasped around her knees, than an engagement to repay borrowed money. She got up and dressed and began to pack her clothes and Cornelia's. While she was on her knees fastening the grips Kester returned and stood in the doorway.

"So you're really going to New Orleans today?" he asked.

"Yes."

"What do you want me to tell the Sheramys?"

"Tell them I was called away on business."

"Do you want them to think you're a Hottentot?"

"Why should they?"

"If it's your father's affair he could be attending to it, if it's the plantation I could be."

"If you won't I've got to."

"I will. I told you I would. Tomorrow."

"I don't want to wait."

"You're taking Cornelia with you?"

"Certainly. I can't wean her in five minutes."

His hands in his coat pockets, Kester leaned against the side of the doorway and watched her fasten the buckle of the last strap. "Have you ever been spanked," he said, "and locked in a dark closet till you acknowledged you couldn't run the world?"

"Don't be silly," she said, getting up from the floor. "I'm doing this for you! It's your home!"

"I've been minding my business," he told her.

"Yes, and look where it got you," Eleanor snapped. She bit her lip. "I'm sorry."

"Where in heaven's name did you get that voice?" he asked, with the same ominous quietness he had used toward her last night.

"I didn't mean to shout. But I've got to go to New Orleans today; I ought to."

Kester lifted his eyebrows reproachfully. "Too much strength of character is a disagreeable trait, Eleanor," he remarked.

"*You* needn't worry."

"I don't. Not at all. Do exactly as you please." He started out, and turned around to say, "By the way, we've always stayed at the St. Charles."

He closed the door behind him. Eleanor stood still, hating herself. Hideous remarks were coming out of her unbidden, like the toads that dropped from the naughty girl's lips in the fairy tale; but how much more dreadful the girl's punishment would have been, she reflected bitterly, if the toads had fallen only in the presence of the one she loved best. Why *did* she talk to Kester so? Did she resent him because she was powerless to stop adoring him? She did not know, but she would go this minute and beg his forgiveness. She would even yield and go to Silverwood with him to prove how sorry she was.

But his room was empty, and as she started downstairs to look for him she heard the front door closing. Hurrying to the window overlooking the lawn from the front of the upper hall, Eleanor saw Kester driving down the avenue. He was driving much too fast for safety, and she felt a tremor of fright for him through her regret that it was too late for her to apologize. Taking from under her belt the little watch Kester had given her as a Christmas present she saw that it was half past twelve. Early to be starting for a two o'clock dinner at a plantation that could be reached by car in twenty minutes. She lowered her head, feeling hurt and conquered, and returned listlessly to her room to finish getting ready for the train. Perhaps it was better that now she had to go to New Orleans, but she wondered why it was that she could do anything to prove her love for Kester except be tactful enough to make him convinced of it.

At a quarter of two she shut the door of her room and rang up Silverwood from her bedside phone.

Clara Sheramy answered. Eleanor made her excuses for not coming to dinner. It was very important, she said, that she go to New Orleans at once. She was leaving at three. Clara was very regretful. Clara's voice was as delicate as her appearance. I can talk like that, Eleanor reminded herself while she listened, when I'm not mad; oh please God, help me to keep my temper! "May I speak to Kester, please?" she said into the phone.

"Why yes, of course," said Clara. "I'll call him. He's in the parlor having a cocktail with Neal."

A moment later Kester's voice came over the wire.

"Kester," said Eleanor, "I'm so sorry. I don't know why I talked to you like that. I won't again."

Kester replied without rancor. Either time or the cocktail had smoothed his disposition. "See that you don't."

"I really won't, darling. But I didn't sleep much last night, and I'm nervous as an alley cat."

"It's quite all right," he said as though he meant it.

"Kester, can anybody hear you talking?"

"No."

"Then tell me you love me."

"I love you enormously. Do you think I'd put up with you if I didn't?"

"I don't suppose you would."

Hurriedly, so as not to keep him too long, she told him she had tried to tell him all this before he left. "But you were on your way," she ended, "so I went on and got ready to go to New Orleans."

"Somebody has won a doubtful victory," Kester said dryly.

67

"But as soon as I start dissecting my feelings I stop enjoying them. Run along."

She took the afternoon train for New Orleans, Dilcy sitting opposite her with Cornelia. Dilcy was in a state of grim disapproval. She had worked for the ladies of Ardeith many years, and she had never before observed one of them leaving her husband to stay at a hotel unprotected.

2

In no mood to be a guest of either her family or Kester's, Eleanor registered at the St. Charles. She telephoned Mr. Robichaux, who gave her an appointment the next afternoon.

A night's sleep made her feel strong again, so in the morning she went to her father's office. Her brother Vance, a year younger than herself and a promising neophyte engineer, sprang up as she came in, to ask what she was doing in town. Eleanor said she wanted to see Fred. Dad was in his private office dictating, Vance said, and he detained her to give her the news. Lena Tonelli was engaged to be married, Florence was getting mighty pretty and kept the house in an uproar with her beaus coming and going, the Atchafalaya River was acting up worse than ever this year—that was a mean, nasty river if there ever was one. In spite of her low spirits Eleanor found herself listening with interest. Named for the foreman who had given Fred his first job, Vance had like herself drawn in knowledge of the Louisiana rivers from his birth. While he talked she remembered wistfully how she and Vance and Florence used to play coon-can and seven-up in the levee camps, and built little levees of their own by using tin cans for scoops. By the time he was nine and she ten they could build perfect miniature levees, complete with borrow-pit and berme and batture, the slopes graded by the aid of a tape measure from their mother's mending basket, and Florence, who was only seven then, was compelled to run their errands, her pigtails bobbing as she scampered about doing what she was told. Now Vance was an engineer and Florence a young lady, and she herself tired with her suddenly acquired knowledge that life provided nothing perfect. At length she said she had to see her father. Vance opened the door of Fred's private office and stuck his head in. "Dad, Eleanor's here."

Fred was sitting at his desk, scowling over a blue and pink diagram of a steam-grader. He sprang up when she came in.

"Why Eleanor! When did you get to town?"

She glanced at his secretary. "I'd like to see you alone, dad."

Fred made a movement of his thumb toward the door to the outer office. "Run along, Miss Loring." As the secretary and Vance went out he looked back at Eleanor. "Sit down, honey."

"I haven't much time to sit down," Eleanor said brusquely. "Dad, will you let me have my stock in the fruit lines?"

"Oh." Fred sat down again and folded his hands on the diagram of the steam-grader. He gave her a long look up and down. Their eyes met. Fred said, "No, I will not."

Eleanor felt a stab that was almost like physical pain. With no more words between them she knew he had given it to her because he did not trust Kester, and that was why he had tied it up so she could spend nothing but the income. She had between twelve and fifteen hundred dollars a year, which would be enough to keep her and her child from destitution.

"All right," said Eleanor. "If you won't you won't, and I know there's no use arguing. I'll go now."

"Not yet." Fred reached across the desk and took her hand in his. He gave her another intent look. "Honey," he said, "if you're having money trouble, why don't you tell me about it?"

"It's no use," Eleanor returned. "I can manage."

"How?" asked Fred.

"It's none of your business," she said shortly.

"Southeastern Exchange Bank?" Fred asked cannily. "Charlie Robichaux?"

"How did you know?"

He gave her a smile. "I'm not exactly stupid. That bank runs half those worn-out plantations up the river." Fred got up and came around the desk. "Why don't you tell me about it, Eleanor?"

"No," she said.

"All right, honey," said Fred. "I guess you're grown up." After a moment he asked, "Baby, do you want me to sign my name on something? Would that be a help?"

Eleanor shivered. Fred was not a rich man, but he had never owed a penny he had not paid. His integrity was beyond question. If he signed his name, that was enough for any bank in town. She had never thought before about how hard such a reputation was to win and how precious it was to keep.

She answered sharply to cover the fact that her voice might easily have trembled. "Dad, I wouldn't let you do that for a million dollars. If you don't understand there's nothing I can tell you."

"I understand, Eleanor," said Fred simply.

"Yes, dad, I'm your daughter," she said, and then she dropped into the chair he had drawn up for her and put her head down on the desk, resting it on her arm. She did not cry. But she had undertaken this interview first because she had known it was going to be the most difficult, and so it was; she felt naked and ashamed before her father's eyes. He put his arm around her shoulders, and Eleanor thought how much easier this would be to stand if he had been angry and had told her she could go ahead and take her punishment for not having listened to him. She wished she had not come to Fred; she might have known he would not yield to her request, but it had been her only chance to get her hands on some negotiable property at once and she had reached for it with a sense of desperation. When at last she lifted her head, making herself look into his eyes, Fred said only,

"The folks'll feel mighty sad if they don't get a chance to see you while you're here. Let me ring Molly and say you'll be up for dinner this evening?"

She wanted nothing less than to see any of them, but she did not know how to refuse. So she nodded. "And dad," she added, "nothing to the folks about why I'm in town."

"Oh, to be sure not," he said genially. "You're old enough to have business of your own. Like to come out now for a cup of coffee?"

"No, thanks, I have to get back to the baby, then I'm seeing Mr. Robichaux."

"All right. See you tonight, then."

Eleanor left him. She went back to the hotel and waited impatiently till it was time for her appointment at the bank.

In the afternoon she went to see Mr. Robichaux.

Mr. Robichaux had iron-gray hair and a pleasant face that became grim when she asked about the Ardeith mortgages. She told him she wanted the dates and the totals.

Mr. Robichaux cleared his throat. He said he had been compelled to write Kester a rather sharp letter. Kester's father had often borrowed money on the cotton crop, but he had

been more careful about keeping up with it, though of course
—he cleared his throat again and came to the present. Yes,
there had been of late, ah, some slight neglect about the
interest. Kester was becoming absent-minded. Besides, the
plantation had become—well, slightly run-down. It was not as
valuable security as it had been. Unless something was done
shortly, he was afraid—

"I understand," said Eleanor. "Now, how much do we owe
the bank and when do the notes fall due?"

Mr. Robichaux called in a clerk and got a pile of papers.

Inside of an hour Eleanor discovered that she and Kester
were living at Ardeith only by a lenient interpretation of
banking rules. Kester had apparently been willing to sign
anything that would relieve him of thinking about money as a
fact of life. She asked Mr. Robichaux for a sheet of stationery
and began to write down the figures. Mentally she began to
add these to the bills she had found in Kester's desk. Kester's
notes at the bank and his personal debts together totaled, as
closely as she could figure now, nearly one hundred thousand
dollars.

And the plain truth was, Mr. Robichaux reminded her, that
Kester had let half the plantation go to sharecroppers. The
land was being ruined with one-mule crops.

"Thank you," said Eleanor, "for giving me so much of your
time."

She left him and went out into the street. A January sun,
glittering without warmth, lit the pavements, Eleanor took her
watch from under her belt, wondering as she did so how long
it had taken Kester to pay for the watch and what it would
bring if she tried to sell it. She still had some leisure, and was
thankful.

She walked down through the wholesale district, and
among the factories, where the air was rich with the familiar
odors of coffee and molasses that she would always associate
with downtown New Orleans. When she reached the river-
front she stood on the wharf watching the creeping golden
river that had fathered Ardeith and the land on which the city
stood. Boats from Central America were unloading coffee,
and great refrigerator cars were lined up on railroads leading
to the wharf, ready to receive their cargo of bananas in the
morning. Far out in the river a dredge was working, keeping
the channel open. She could hear its puffing above the voices
of the men busy on the wharf around her. She saw a big sign,

"Tonelli Fruit Lines." Lena Tonelli's grandfather had come from Italy in the steerage, and picked up the overripe bananas thrown away on the wharf of New Orleans and peddled them in a pushcart at two cents a dozen. but at least he had had no debts when he started.

Turning her back on the fruit-ships, Eleanor walked down to Canal Street. She could see the west bank, a line of trees and houses made dim by distance, and the ferryboats going back and forth. The wind here was fresh; Eleanor thought of crossing the river on a ferry, but recollected that she could not afford to drop a nickel unnecessarily into the turnstile. So she stood still and looked at the river, remembering how she and Vance used to tease visitors to the levee camps by asking them if they knew which way the river flowed past New Orleans. Sometimes the strangers guessed east or west, but they almost never said north, which was right, and you had to draw a map and show them the bend whereby the Mississippi appeared to want to go back where it came from, before it turned around again and poured through seven golden mouths into the purple Gulf.

Eleanor caught herself. She was not often given to the yearning nostalgia that reaches for anything except the present. She turned around and walked swiftly back to the hotel, where she changed her dress and told Dilcy to stay with Cornelia while she went uptown to visit her mother.

Dinner at home was gay, friendly and noisy. After dinner the young Tonellis came in, with Guy Rickert, Lena's fiancé, and everybody talked at once. Lena asked Eleanor if she had learned to drive a car yet, and when Eleanor said Kester was teaching her, Lena said she had already learned and it was easy, she had an Overland coupé with an electric starter that had never yet failed to work, and these new slit skirts might be immodest but they did make it easy to reach the clutch and brake. Fred told about an exciting movie he had seen, in which Ford Sterling strapped Mabel Normand to a plank and started to cut her in half with a buzz-saw; he had forgotten how she was rescued, but it kept him on the edge of his seat and quite took his mind off the trouble the Atchafalaya River was making this winter. Florence said New Orleans had more than thirty moving picture theaters now, did Eleanor know that? Molly Upjohn reminded Florence that with a baby three months old, Eleanor probably didn't have time to be up-to-date on things like moving picture theaters. Florence began to play the piano and Guy Rickert asked Eleanor to dance. It was as though she had never been away. Eleanor had a sense of warm familiarity. These were her people, solid, sincere, utterly trustworthy. They took it for granted that you should take care of yourself. Guy and Lena drove her back to the hotel. Eleanor stood a moment looking after them regretfully, feeling that they were taking away with them the sturdy self-reliance to which she had been bred and leaving her nothing to put in its place.

When she opened the door of her room she saw Kester. He was reading an afternoon paper, and as she came in he sprang to his feet, letting the paper slip to the floor.

"Remember me?" he asked affably.

Eleanor went to him, and Kester put his arms around her. Eleanor dropped her head against him, wondering why it was that Kester's arms around her should give her such a sense of security even now. When she looked up she asked, "Are you angry with me for coming?"

"What good would it do if I were?" inquired Kester. "How does Cornelia like traveling?"

"She's fine."

"She seems to be; I played with her in the other room till she went to sleep." He helped her off with her coat, and Eleanor rescued her hat in time to prevent his tossing it upside down on the bed, for it was a velvet hat with a tall aigrette and she did not expect to buy another hat of such quality for a long time. "Now," said Kester as she put the hat into its box, "what have you been doing, Mrs. Manage-it-all?" He was regarding her with the reproachful amusement he might have given if she had interfered with his poker game by an excess of solicitude.

Fresh from the gay safety of home, Eleanor was in no mood for banter. Her reply was clear and terse.

"I've been adding up your bills. Altogether you owe nearly a hundred thousand dollars."

"A hundred th— Eleanor, don't be fantastic!"

"I'm not being fantastic. You told me you didn't know how much it was, so I've been finding out."

Kester gave a long whistle. Leaning back in his chair, he regarded the chandelier thoughtfully. Eleanor told him about her talk with Mr. Robichaux.

"You wait for me," Kester said abruptly. "I'm going downstairs and call him."

"This time of night?"

"It's not twelve o'clock yet. I'll ring him at home."

Soothed by his superb confidence that nothing could ever happen to *him*, Kester scampered out, and Eleanor went into the adjoining room to look at Cornelia. She bent over the crib. Cornelia had gone to sleep holding a rattle, which Eleanor slipped out of her fingers, lest she hurt herself with it in the night. Back in the light of her own room she noticed that the rattle was a new one, evidently brought by Kester when he came in this evening, and she flung it down with vehemence. With debts pointing accusing fingers at him from every corner, what right had he to waste even a quarter on a rattle for a child already amply supplied with unpaid-for luxuries? Kester came in, exuberant. He was going to see Mr. Robichaux at three o'clock tomorrow afternoon, he said, and he kissed her, assuring her that he'd take care of it and everything was going to be all right. Eleanor laid his hand against her cheek, with a wondering smile.

"Doesn't it distress you," she asked, "to know you're in debt?"

"Darling," said Kester, "I suppose it ought to, but I'm so used to it." He sat down and drew her to sit on his knee.

"Have you always been in debt?" Eleanor inquired.

"Always," he assured her solemnly. "I'll tell you about myself. When I was eight years old my father gave me a quarter and told me he was going to give me a quarter every week. I was to keep a cash book, recording what I spent for candy and such, and this was to teach me how to be a big business man."

"Yes, that's the way I was taught," she agreed.

Kester went on talking confidently. "But I didn't have any cash book, you see. So I went to the store and bought one. It was a funny little store kept by an old man named Mr. Parfax. The cash book cost thirty cents, and I only had a quarter. So the first entry I made in the book was, 'I owe Mr. Parfax five cents.'" He sighed. "And it seems I've never caught up."

Eleanor could not help laughing at him. Kester looked as ingenuous as his baby daughter. "Do you support your father?" she asked after a moment.

"No, darling, he has the rent from that sugar land across the river."

"What are you going to tell Mr. Robichaux tomorrow? He can foreclose if he wants to."

"Oh Lord, I don't know. I'll tell him something. Eleanor, I bothered about this for a long time the other night before I could go to sleep and all it did was give me a headache. I'm not going to tear my head to pieces again about it. It's late, and I'm sleepy, and if you don't get that serious look off your face you're going to have lines before you're thirty."

3

The next afternoon they went to the Southeastern Exchange bank to see Mr. Robichaux.

Mr. Robichaux greeted Kester cordially. Suspecting that this pleasantness was merely intended to soften what he would be compelled to tell Kester in about ten minutes, Eleanor was apprehensive as she sat down. Kester began to talk business.

That is, he began to talk what purported to be business, while Eleanor listened with increasing amazement. Her way of discussing anything was to slash through to its fundamentals. Kester's was to exchange opinions about the races, to ask Mr. Robichaux about his grandchildren (he knew all their names), to congratulate Mr. Robichaux on having won the chess tournament at his club (and how under heaven, she wondered, did Kester know he had won any chess tournament? Kester knew everything about everybody). Apparently Mr. Robichaux's chess was important to him. He grew more and more jovial. He told Kester about a tricky opening gambit he had used. Somehow the talk veered to politics. Mr. Robichaux thought the Americans who were having trouble with the Mexican bandits ought to come home and not expect the government to send soldiers to take care of them. That sort of thing would lead to war. And who wanted war with Mexico? Who indeed? Kester inquired agreeably. The United States got all of Mexico it could use during the old war with them, the one back in the eighteen-forties. But of course, said Mr. Robichaux, with that college professor in the White House you couldn't tell what might happen. Kester nodded. Mr. Wilson was a sort of experiment with a philosopher-king, as they said, didn't Mr. Robichaux think so?"

But what, Eleanor thought in wonder, had all this to do with the Ardeith mortgages?

75

From Mexico the talk drifted to Mr. Robichaux's trip to California last summer. Remarkable country out there, but with all that desert between, it was almost like crossing to another continent. Was Kester by any chance thinking of going to the exposition next year in San Francisco? They did say the Panama Canal would be open and ready for traffic, and they were planning to send boats directly from New Orleans to San Francisco, through the canal.

Kester smiled and shrugged. Mr. Robichaux must know he couldn't afford to go to any exposition. Why, he had to get busy and attend to his plantation. That was what he had come in for, you know, to talk over the mortgages Mr. Robichaux's bank had been so kind as to let him carry on Ardeith.

Yes, yes indeed, said Mr. Robichaux. By this time he and Kester had grown so sociable that Mr. Robichaux was speaking of the mortgages as a matter between friends, not at all in the grim fashion in which he had discussed them with Eleanor yesterday. Kester remarked that he had been planning to make a great many changes in his management of Ardeith, but what with his getting married and having a baby, he had sort of been putting it off. He leaned nearer his listener, across the desk. Now here was the idea.

Then, to Eleanor's astonishment, Kester coolly began to outline plans for completely revising the system under which Ardeith was conducted. He described the constitution of the soil and its possibilities for intensive cultivation. He talked about scientific improvements the Department of Agriculture had suggested for increasing the yield of cotton land, and improved sprinkling methods for fighting boll weevils. He used terms that were to Eleanor a foreign language, and possibly to Mr. Robichaux too, but it was obvious that the latter was beginning to be impressed. He asked questions. He nodded soberly. He listened.

Kester's deep, persuasive voice went on, laying fact after fact before Mr. Robichaux's attention. Cabbages could be grown on the cotton land in winter. The scrub pine land, so far considered valueless, could be planted in holly. Holly always had a profitable market at Christmas. You planted ten female trees to each male tree, and for maximum production you could graft female branches to each of the male trees. But holly and cabbages and such minor crops would just be lagniappe, something extra thrown in; Ardeith was a cotton plantation. It had averaged eight hundred bales a year recent-

76

ly, but there was no reason why it couldn't produce a thousand or even more. The government experts had been saying for a long time that a bale of cotton took twice as much land as it ought to, and there was no reason why it had to be grown so wastefully at Ardeith. That was what share-croppers did for a place. As soon as he got back to Ardeith he was going to start getting the sharecroppers off his land and have the cotton grown by paid laborers under his own supervision.

"Give me two years, Mr. Robichaux," said Kester. "This fall I'll pay you the interest entire on all these notes, and in the fall of 1915 I can start reducing the principal."

Mr. Robichaux thoughtfully adjusted the position of his ink-stand.

"You don't want a rundown plantation," said Kester. "What would the bank do with it? Let it be run at a loss by somebody who's hired and consequently doesn't care? Or cut it up into parcels and sell it for whatever you can get? Either way you'll lose money. Let me run it the way I've outlined and you won't lose a penny."

Mr. Robichaux was won. "I wish you had told me your plans before!" he exclaimed. "I had no idea you were counting on such improvements."

"Well, it takes time to work out details. I didn't want to come to you with anything that wasn't complete and clear."

"Of course," said Mr. Robichaux, "of course." But he explained that he could not, without consulation, renew the notes so as to postpone a payment on the principal until the fall of 1915, nearly two years ahead. However, Kester could come in tomorrow morning and outline his system of planta-tion management to a group of directors. Mr. Robichaux was confident they would agree to his proposal.

Kester lowered his eyes and was humbly grateful. "After the procrastinating idiot I've seemed to be, Mr. Robichaux, I surely appreciate it, sir."

"Not at all, Kester, my boy." Mr. Robichaux held out his hand. "Bankers aren't ogres. We live by lending money. Only, you understand, we've got to have certainty. Just had to check up on your plans, you see."

They shook hands. Eleanor wanted to gasp and laugh at once. By this time it was Mr. Robichaux who was on the verge of apologies and Kester who was bossing the interview. Mr. Robichaux shook hands wth Eleanor, and said if she was planning to come back to New Orleans for Mardi Gras she must certainly let Mrs. Robichaux know, maybe they could manage a luncheon one day.

Kester and Eleanor got outside, into the street. "Kester!" she began.

"Don't say anything. Come on. Hurry." He was nearly choking with smothered glee.

He made her almost race the short distance back to the hotel. When he had closed the door of their room behind them Kester dropped into a chair and began to laugh. He laughed till he was weak. Eleanor was still speechless.

"Now what was all your hurry?" he demanded at last. "I went to dinner, tried out the automobiles, had supper with the salesman, and settled everything here." He gave her a look of twinkling triumph. "You, young woman, are going to explode one of these days."

"But Kester," she exclaimed in awe, "with such marvelous ideas for rehabilitating Ardeith, why haven't you been doing any of it? And why didn't you tell me before I nearly lost my mind with worry?"

Kester gave her a blank look. "My dearest girl, you didn't assume I'd thought up all that before this afternoon?"

"But—you must have!" she gasped.

Kester pulled her down to sit on his knees. "My darling, my angel, the light of my eyes," he said to her, shaking with mirth, "I made it up as I went along."

She still did not understand. "But you seemed to know so much!"

"I do know a lot about cotton, sweetheart. I've known for fifteen years what ought to be done with that plantation." He squeezed her. "Honeybug, if some men are born with silver spoons in their mouths, I was born with a cotton boll in my hand."

For a moment she sat silent on his knees, while Kester still laughed at his own triumph. "You're very tactful," she said thoughtfully. "I'm not."

"No, you're not," he agreed with her.

Eleanor considered. "Tact is a form of fraud," she said. "Yes it is—to get what you want you've got to use either tact or force. By force you take what you want, leaving your victim hating you; by tact you take it too, but leaving him happy in the belief that he wanted to give it to you all the time."

"Bright girl," said Kester. He drew her head down and kissed her. "You have such soft little rings of hair on your temples. Eleanor, now that we've got the Southeastern Exchange Bank where we want it, let's have a drink and celebrate."

He had handled the situation so much better than she could have done that Eleanor consented, and let him mix her a highball.

But as the evening advanced, her reassurance began to change to apprehension. Kester's work that day had been inspired, but his joy now was as though the battle had been fought and won, and in his victorious merriment he was drinking more Bourbon than she thought could possibly be good for him, all the time outlining more and more grandiose schemes for Ardeith. While he celebrated his jubilance Eleanor began taking notes on what he was saying. If she was going to help him make his visions concrete now was a good time as any to begin understanding what they were.

In the morning when she woke him up Kester groaned that his head was like a balloon, there were corkscrews twirling in his stomach, his mind was paralyzed, and in short he had the grandfather of all hangovers.

Eleanor trembled with exasperation. Standing by the bedside, she told Kester exactly what she thought of him, and at the moment what she thought of him was not pleasant. Nothing stopped her but the clock pointing to a quarter of ten. She gathered up her notes, thanking heaven that last night she had had foreknowledge of her need for them, and went out.

She told Mr. Robichaux Kester had got hold of a bad oyster at dinner last evening and was suffering with indigestion. With a sympathetic cluck-cluck Mr. Robichaux led her into the room where a group of other men were waiting for her.

They looked businesslike and forbidding, and Eleanor's courage sank as her irritation rose. If I had the brains of a bat, she thought angrily, I'd give up and let him lose his plantation. Why on earth am I doing this anyway?—I don't care about Ardeith! But oh, heaven forgive me, she thought as she sat down before them, I do care about Kester.

Though she did her best to tell these men what Kester had told Mr. Robichaux yesterday, her exposition lacked not only the charm of his but its expertness, for she had not heard cotton talked about every day of her life till she could speak its language by instinct. The directors were not as impressed by the possibilities of Ardeith as Mr. Robichaux had been. But Mr. Robichaux, still under Kester's spell, insisted that Ardeith was capable of producing cotton enough to pay off all its mortgages. They listened to him, dubiously, and at last, when one of them asked, "Who's going to put all these plans into execution?"—Eleanor, feeling that she stood on the rock-bottom of what she knew about Kester, answered with bitter clairvoyance, "I am."

The doubtful director was as impressed by her cold determination as Mr. Robichaux had been by Kester's eagerness. He smiled, a little grimly.

"You sound as if you might be a good business woman, Mrs. Larne," he said to her.

Eleanor did not smile. "I don't know. I haven't had much chance to find out. But I have a habit," she said distinctly, "of finishing what I start."

The doubtful director nodded slowly. "Have you and I met before? You remind me of someone I know."

"You may know my father. He's Fred Upjohn."

"Upjohn? The levee contractor? To be sure!" The doubtful director's grim expression became cordial. He drummed his fingers on the desk. One or two of the others murmured recognition. Fred Upjohn had been doing business with the Southeastern Exchange Bank for twenty years. The doubtful director cleared his throat. It might be possible—ah—to obtain Mr. Upjohn's guarantee on these notes.

"*No*," Eleanor said vehemently.

There was a silence. Eleanor and the doubtful director looked straight into each other's eyes. His eyes were small, set deeply under heavy gray eyebrows, and his face was thin and hard like a tomahawk. Eleanor had a passion for privacy; she could not for the life of her have told these men that this matter of the Ardeith mortgages was an affair of her personal pride because her father had warned her against Kester and now that his warning had been proved she would rather die than have him pay the price of her marriage. She was ready to give them as much as they required of herself, and suddenly her deeper mind opened to her immediate consciousness and she realized that it was for her justification, and not because Kester loved Ardeith, that she was ready to throw herself down as a sacrifice to his thoughtlessness; and she wondered if it was merely her personal destiny or the fate of the whole human race to engage in battle with the people they loved. Aloud—the silence had lasted only a few seconds and might have appeared to have been caused only by her care in choosing words for her answer—she continued:

"My father would guarantee these notes without question if I asked him. If I should die or for any other reason fail to pay you, he would assume the obligation without any thought of asking for mercy, and it would bankrupt him." As the doubtful director did not shift his eyes from her, and the others waited as though expecting her to go on, she added, "I believe that as a parent he has given me all I have a right to ask for, a happy childhood, a good education, and—I hope— a sound character. The very fact that he is willing to give me more—he suggested this himself yesterday—makes it impossible for me to take it." She spoke clearly to the doubtful director. "Do I get that extension?"

He answered, "You get it, Mrs. Larne."

They gave her a series of papers for her signature and explained to her that under the community property laws of Louisiana Kester's signature must in every instance be coupled with hers. It was January, 1914; the interest was to be paid in full in November, 1914, and twenty thousand dollars of the principal in December, 1915. Eleanor put the papers into a big manila envelope and took them back to the hotel with her. As she walked she thought of the indentured servants of colonial days who had signed away the labor of half their lives for the chance to come to America, and she wondered if they had felt bound as she did.

Chapter Five

1

WHEN they were back at Ardeith Kester and Eleanor had the longest and frankest talk they had ever had.

He was ashamed of himself, Kester told her quietly. He had done more thinking than she knew since the morning when he had made her face the directors alone. He was ready to quit drinking and quit partying, and go to work. To keep their promises to the bank meant that he would have to work harder than he had ever dreamed of working, but it could be done.

"I'm going to do it too," said Eleanor. "There's no reason why I can't learn to be a cotton planter. You'll have to provide lots of capital in the way of information, but I can give you lots of labor."

Standing in his favorite attitude by the mantel, Kester turned to her a face puckered with an odd smile. "Willing," he said "and grateful, if—" he paused impressively—"you keep your temper."

"I promise, dear. I won't scream at you again."

"I'm not calling attention to your faults in order to minimize my own," he went on, "but frankly, I've never heard a self-respecting woman sound the way you do when you get angry. What you say is bad enough, but your voice gets up into your nose in a snarl that sounds—"

"Yes?" she prompted when he seemed to hesitate.

"Common," said Kester bluntly. He put his hand on her shoulder. "I love you so much, Eleanor, but when you yell like that I want to choke you."

There was a pause. Resting her chin on her hand, Eleanor looked into the fire. "I've been so busy throwing your deficiencies at you," she said, "I suppose it's about time I gave some attention to mine. I think—" she looked up at him, and smiled—"yours are the things you do, mine are the way I do things."

He smiled down at her. "Does that still mean you're American and I'm Southern?"

"I think so. Anyway, my virtues are so disagreeable and your faults are so attractive!" She took the hand that still lay on her shoulder, and held it in hers. "Kester, I'd like to talk about that now, to make it clear for both of us."

"Yes, dear, I'd like it too." He went back to his place by the mantel and stood waiting for her to go on.

Eleanor looked at him thoughtfully, noticing as she had on their first meeting Kester's casual, unconscious elegance, and contrasting it with the cast-iron vigor of Fred ordering the foremen about. "Tell me something, honestly," she said after a moment. "Kester, when you used to come to see me before we were married, didn't you find my parents crude?"

He smiled reluctantly. "Have I got to answer?"

"You have answered," she said.

"But, my dear girl," he exclaimed, "it doesn't matter! It never did."

"Now I'll tell you," said Eleanor. "When I used to come here I thought your parents were revoltingly useless. I felt superior to them because I had in me the hard streak that made my father climb out of the wretchedness where he was born."

Kester's forehead had crinkled ever so slightly between and above his eyebrows, giving him a look of surprise, like that of a schoolboy coming across some glint of philosophy that pleased his reason though it damaged his prejudice.

"But your people must have had a hardness in them once," Eleanor went on. "When they got here Louisiana was a trackless jungle. The American pioneers didn't hack their way across this continent by using romance and beautiful deportment. They did it because they were the most uncompromising realists the world has ever seen." She saw he was listening, and she continued. "But now you want to live only by the gracious trivialities they developed after they'd ceased having to fight for existence. And you can't," she said incisively. "It's nearly cost you Ardeith. If you want to get Ardeith back you've got to get it the way Philip Larne cut it out of the wilderness."

As she paused Kester answered slowly, as though the glint of philosophy was brightening, but its glow still so faint that he had to walk very carefully by the little light it gave him. "You're trying to tell me, aren't you, that I've got to learn hardness again, from your sort of people?"

"Yes. Because we're just now cutting our way out of the wilderness."

There was a pause, broken only by the snapping of the fire. "But what were the Upjohns doing all that time?" he asked at length.

"I don't know, except fighting to keep alive. Maybe we didn't have much strength to start with. Maybe only those of us who could fight survived at all."

Again there was a silence. Kester picked up the tongs and adjusted a log on the fire. He got a cigarette from the box on the table, lit it, and examined its tip with the concentrated look of a man who finds it easier to fix a thought in his mind while his outer attention is fixed on a meaningless object. "But don't you think," he asked finally, "that what you call the gracious trivialities are important?"

"Of course I do," said Eleanor. "I think they're beautiful. They're what I want to learn from you," she added earnestly, "gentleness and tact and how to make people love me. The civilization your people created is the most beautiful I've ever seen or heard of—the gallantry and high breeding and ideals, the moon over the cotton and the darkies thrumming banjos along the river. It's the South of legends and poetry, and it's true." She stood up and faced him. "Kester, that's what your people brought into being. Mine didn't do it. Yes, I know—you're too gracious to say it, but a generation ago we'd have been called poor white trash. But my sort of people are closer to facts than yours. And if you withdraw, if you try to live on gallantry and beauty alone—here we come. We're coming out of the tenements and the steerage. We're hard and brash and uncouth. We hurt your sensibilities. But we're Americans, more than you are, because we've got the qualities that made it possible for the American nation to be. We're the second pioneers."

Kester gave her right hand a grip that hurt it. "Anything I could say after that would be an anticlimax. But you mean that with what you have from your people and what I have from mine we can do more together than either of us could do alone. I understand. Let's see it through."

She nodded. "Yes. Let's see it through." His handclasp made her feel more closely married than she had ever felt before.

2

Under the double stimulus of Kester's ideas and Eleanor's energy, the plantation leaped into life.

Ardeith was deep and black and rich; it gobbled the cottonseed and thrust out plants that grew fast in the brooding sun. By a last desperate loan on the pine-lands they had obtained enough money to raise the crop this year, and they worked passionately. Up at six, they spent the morning on horseback supervising the labor in the fields, and came in for dinner at three. In the afternoon Eleanor attended to the bookkeeping while Kester either returned to the cotton or wrote business letters, and that done, they relaxed by reading the newspaper—which they rarely had time to look at earlier —and playing with the baby. After supper they worked again, though not for long, as by nine o'clock they were usually too sleepy to think.

It was backbreaking drudgery, tolerable in the velvet weather of February and March, but as the spring turned to a June of steam and fire there were days when Eleanor thought it beyond her endurance. She had never minded the summer, but she had never spent the six hottest hours of the day without shade. Yet she did not dare to wilt. Kester was working hard, the sun no lighter on his head than hers, but she knew her own driving resolution was the backbone of their labor. Though Kester could make a brilliant start he needed encouragement to persist in the doing of one thing over and over after it had ceased to be interesting. But they were both happy in their feeling of purposeful unity. They were hard and Indian-brown, and the responding fields, promising a thousand bales in the fall, gave them a sense of splendid achievement.

Eleanor was at first amazed at Kester's industry. But as the spring advanced and she saw how he looked around his acres, with the same look he gave her in their tenderest moments, she began to understand. Before Kester was old enough to make his knowledge articulate he had stood on his land and had known it belonged to him. He had loved all of it, the cotton rows dwindling toward the dip of the sky like spokes of a mighty wheel, the palms waving their fans above his head, the wild irises in the woods and hyacinths crowding the bayous. Before he could bound his own state or spell the name of the river on which he lived Kester could glance at a cottonfield and tell whether or not it needed rain; and by that time there had grown up within him a love for Ardeith so intense that he felt as much a part of his plantation as the cotton and palms, and he felt, without thinking it, that he would die as easily as they if he should be torn from his soil.

Without sharing this, she understood it, and promised both him and herself that she would give all she had to help him save Ardeith. They divided the work between them. Kester was not efficient, but he was creative, and his suggestions were so sound that Eleanor could readily put them into effect. It was Kester who had thought of holly on the pine-lands, but it was Eleanor who collected facts and figures, discovering that most of the holly sold in New Orleans at Christmas time came from Maryland, and Louisiana holly could undersell it because of lower transportation charges. Kester knew exactly why paid laborers were economically better than sharecroppers, but Eleanor undertook to reorganize the plan under which the plantation was run; by March she had reduced by half the land tilled under the sharecropper system and the other sharecroppers had been warned that they must either move or turn into wage-workers after they had raised this year's crop. Eleanor could make the laborers work well, but they did not like her, and she never understood how it was that by riding to the end of a row and spending ten minutes in conversation with a darky—conversation that included an exchange of gossip about Kester's baby and the darky's baby and the weather and the looks of the river this spring—Kester could guarantee her that the field would be plowed by sundown, and be right about it.

Eleanor was fair: she never balked at offering good wages or required overtime work without paying for it. Kester was not fair. He thought extra pay for extra work was silly, and when additional hoeing was needed after a sudden June rain he wandered casually into the field, took hold of a hoe himself and said something about a fish-fry one Sunday before long, and the field was hoed, and nobody mentioned money or apparently thought of it. Eleanor was surprised.

"How *do* you do it?" she asked that evening. "How do you make everybody like you?"

"Like 'em back," said Kester.

She sighed, her elbows on her account books and her chin cupped in her hands. "I still think they should have been paid for it."

Kester stretched out on the sofa to read the *Times-Picayune* from New Orleans. "My dear, if you ran the world all the sidewalks would be scrubbed and the trains would run on time and everybody would live to be ninety and nobody would have any fun. Now do your arithmetic and let me read about this murder."

"Save it for me if it's good," said Eleanor.

Already absorbed, Kester did not answer, and Eleanor went back to her accounts. Kester could not keep accounts. Any mathematics beyond what could be checked on his ten fingers was beyond him. Eleanor kept records of the household and the plantation separately but with equal precision. In a passion for economy she had stopped the handouts from the kitchen; she knew how many pounds of flour, how many tubes of toothpaste and how many bars of soap they used in a month and bought accordingly. She also knew how much fertilizer had gone into every section, how much had been spent for wages there and how much they could reasonably expect as profit when the cotton was picked this fall. Kester said she was wonderful. He was as incapable of carrying out the fine details of a scheme as she was of originating it in the first place, and their mutual awe made them congenial as well as complementary partners.

Cotton was high this year. It was quoted at between twelve and thirteen cents a pound, but this price was unusual, based on recent devastations of boll weevils, and with improved methods of sprinkling likely to increase the general yield Eleanor thought it unsafe to count on so much, so she was calculating on the average price of ten cents a pound. At ten cents on this year's crop they could pay for the improvements on the plantation (only a few matters of equipment that had been absolutely necessary, for they needed cash more than plows), send the interest to the bank and put by a sum against next year's payment on the principal. If the price this fall should be more than ten cents they could buy tractors and four-row cultivators to do away with so much hand labor. But that, she reminded herself firmly, would be lagniappe and she would not depend on it.

She smiled now as she visualized the prospect. Tractors, cultivators, motor-trucks to take the cotton to the gin instead of these rickety wagons pulled by mules. She had begun this job with no idea of liking it; it was simply something that had to be done. But now that she was doing it she was engrossed. She had no emotional fervor for the land or the crops as such, unlike Kester, who felt that in saving Ardeith for himself he was protecting a beloved spot from the sacrilege of alien feet, but she liked taking an enterprise in her hands and feeling it grow and move under her direction. Her own work at Ardeith gave her a sense not of creation but of conquest.

"This is exciting," said Kester.

She looked up, startled back into the present. "What? The murder? Read it to me and I'll finish this after supper. Is it somebody in New Orleans?"

"No, better than that. It's the crown prince of Austria-Hungary."

"Good heavens! Where was it? Vienna?"

"No, in—" Kester spelt the word painfully—"S-a-r-a-j-e-v-o."

"Where's that?"

"I don't know, somewhere in the Balkans. The fellow's name is G-a-v-r-i-l-o P-r-i-n-z-i-p. They caught him."

Over his shoulder she saw a three-column headline. "HEIR TO THRONE VICTIM OF ASSASSIN'S BULLET." Kester began reading aloud.

" 'Archduke Francis Ferdinand, heir to the Austro-Hungarian throne, and his morganatic wife, the Duchess of Hohenberg, were assassinated today while driving through the streets of Sara-whatever-you-call-it, the Bosnian capital. A youthful Servian student fired the shots, which added another to the long list of tragedies that has darkened the reign of Francis Joseph.' "

"Poor old fellow," murmured Eleanor. "He *has* had a hard life. Go on."

" 'On their return from the town hall, the archduke and the duchess were driving to the hospital when Gavrilo What's-his-name darted at the car and fired a volley at the occupants. His aim was true and the archduke and his wife were mortally wounded.' Now you may read the rest to yourself. It defies an American tongue."

He gave her the paper, his thumb pointing to the next paragraph. Eleanor chuckled as she read, "Prinzip and a fellow-conspirator, a compositor from Trebinje, named Gabrinovics, barely escaped lynching by the infuriated spectators. Both are natives of the annexed province of Herzegovina." She looked up. "I bet all the proofreaders wish the Balkans were sunk in the bottom of the sea. Look, Kester, here's an article under the archduke's picture saying that corn thrives well on reclaimed land, and celery should, too—do you know anything about growing celery?"

"I think we should stick to cotton awhile. Now that ours is beginning to bloom it's really showing itself, and I've never seen better cotton anywhere."

"But is truck-farming very profitable?"

"It can be. First you plant corn, and when you lay by the corn—"

"Lay by?"

"Hoe it for the last time, using a middle-splitter—when you lay by the corn you plant peas. When you cut the green corn you plant more corn. The second corn is used mostly for horses. Then you plant potatoes, and between the potatoes you plant shallots. When they're dug in the late winter you're ready to start the corn again. With five crops a year—two corn crops, potatoes, peas and onions—you make a lot of profit if you take care of the land."

"I should think you would!" she exclaimed.

"Give me back the paper and I'll look at that article you were talking about," Kester said, then his face lighted as the door opened. "Hello! Who let you in?"

Eleanor put down the newspaper and smiled as she saw Cornelia crawling across the rug toward them. Dilcy stood in the doorway remarking that she thought they'd like to tell the little miss good night.

Cornelia crawled about from daybreak till dark, never tired. Eleanor had had Dilcy make her overalls of blue denim to protect her legs, and Cornelia wore white spots on the knees with her ceaseless explorations. She came across the room and headed straight for her father.

Eleanor watched with a wistful envy. Kester had some instinct about winning a baby's love that she simply did not possess. She did everything that should be done for Cornelia with a smooth and loving competence, and Cornelia regarded her as she regarded the pieces of furniture in the nursery. Kester loved to perform offices for her and he did everything wrong, and Cornelia adored him with all her baby heart. Eleanor was ashamed that she could not help its hurting her. Kester did not think of it; he was only delighted that the baby had learned to recognize him. Eleanor looked on as he picked Cornelia up and swung her over his head and down again to his knees while she gurgled with joy.

"Dat's enough, Mr. Kester," Dilcy exclaimed at length. "You gon' get dat child so upset in her mind she won't get to sleep noways. Come here to me, little miss!"

"Let me have her," said Eleanor. She took the baby and kissed her. "Isn't she cute?" she said over Cornelia's head to Kester.

Cornelia wiggled and held out her arms to play again. Kester shook his head. "No, ma'am, you go to bed now," he said, and Eleanor gave her to Dilcy. Cornelia was carried off protesting.

Kester looked after her proudly. "I declare I believe she knows she's going to be put to bed and doesn't like it. She's a bright child."

Eleanor pretended to be examining her ledger. "Yes, I think she's going to be very clever."

89

"Pretty, too, with those big dark eyes. She looks a lot like me, don't you think?"

"She does, but I'm sorry to say I think she's going to have my chin."

"I hope she'll have your figure," said Kester.

Eleanor gave him a grateful smile. Kester had such a way of soothing her feelings even when he didn't know they had been hurt. She hoped heaven would help her never to let him suspect that she was so selfish as to resent the baby's preference for him. If I'm not a noble character, she thought as they went in to supper, at least I can try to behave like one.

After that she tried to fix her thoughts on the cotton and get pleasure enough from its thriving to make up for Cornelia's infant worship of her father. The cotton was beautiful; it was beginning to bloom, and the fields looked like a well-tended garden of white flowers. She read the papers, rejoiced that the price of cotton was still high and agreed with Kester that the new heir to the Austro-Hungarian throne, Charles Francis, was certainly a pleasanter looking citizen than Francis Ferdinand with his ferocious turned-up mustaches. Encouraged by the cotton market, Eleanor dared to go shopping. She bought a few necessary things for Cornelia, and after a moment's hesitation she thought of the cotton market again and yielded to temptation in the form of a black taffeta dress with the skirt slit to the knee and a cascade of white georgette falling down the bosom, and a black hat with three white feathers shooting up from the crown. When she wore it Kester gave her a long survey of admiration. "Magnificent," he exclaimed, "and—" he waved his hand toward the blooming fields—"you deserve it if anybody ever did. If cotton is over ten cents this fall I want you to get a car of your own, and a black coat with a big fox collar."

They smiled at each other in the pride of a job well done.

In mid-July the cotton blossoms began to turn pink. The weather was fiercely hot, hard on men and women but perfect for cotton, and there was not a boll weevil at Ardeith. In the most advanced acres the blossoms began to drop, leaving hard little green bolls on the stalks. Afire with impatience to see the open cotton blowing like flags of triumph, Eleanor could not understand when Kester began to relax his efforts. "What's the matter with you?" she cried as she saw him stretch out in the parlor with the newspaper and a glass early one afternoon. "Are you scared of the sun?"

Kester laughed at her. "Eleanor, you're just before working that cotton to death. Sit down."

She obeyed unwillingly. He lowered the paper.

"Honey child, if you keep stirring up the ground the plants won't grow. Between blossom time and picking time you only loosen the earth after a rain. Leave it alone."

She was incredulous. "It doesn't seem right just to sit, when I'm so impatient!"

"You'd have made an excellent helpmeet for one of the Pilgrim Fathers," Kester remarked, "but the Pilgrim Fathers didn't raise cotton."

Eleanor yielded. The room was cool, the curtains blowing in a welcome wind. The wind brought a whiff of mint. "Kester," she began.

"I told you I wasn't going to get drunk," said Kester. "I didn't promise not to drink juleps when I had nothing else to do. Behave yourself, Eleanor."

She began to laugh. "I'm a nuisance," she said. "Are they really very good?"

"Pull the bellcord. There are three more in the refrigerator getting frosted."

She sent for one and found after a tentative taste that she liked a julep very much. "What's that big headline across the top of the page?" she asked.

"Train robbery near New Orleans."

He had the paper folded so that she saw the top of the front page upside down. Eleanor idly began to spell the letters heading another story. "U-L-T-I-M—Ultimatum—to—Servia—"

"Quit mumbling," said Kester. "I'm reading about the train robbery."

"Gives—Scanty—Time," Eleanor finished. "I read that upside down. What are they doing in Servia?"

"I don't know. Isn't there anything you can read upside down besides my paper?"

Eleanor leaned back, enjoying the delicious coolness. If it wasn't necessary to pay such close attention to the cotton for awhile, there was plenty else to be done. Cornelia was outgrowing every garment she possessed. Eleanor decided to have a lot of rompers made for her, for she was beginning to toddle and her little legs would look so cute underneath bulges of starched pink gingham.

Cornelia continued to be the major delight of Kester's life, though she was breaking his heart because she refused to talk. Eleanor tried to tell him it must be several months yet before Cornelia could be expected to speak a word, but Kester would not be convinced. He was trying to make her say "Father." Kester did not like nicknames; he said a baby could learn to say father as easily as pop or dad or any other silly substitute. Between their cotton and their baby neither of them was much interested in anything else. Even when the paper flung at them a streamer headline, "Europe Trembles on Brink of War," they got no more than half an hour's conversation out of it, and returned to talking about the cotton. The next day, when they read "Austria Forces War upon Serbs," Kester began to laugh. "I must say," he exclaimed, "I think the Americans have a pretty right to be taking a holy attitude about Austria when you think what we forced on Spain not so long ago."

"That one was rather fun," Eleanor said, smiling at the recollection. "I was eight years old, and I wore a button to school with 'Remember the Maine' on it."

"I did too. I was mightily excited and was furious at being too young to join the army. San Juan Hill, and Hobson's Choice—remember?—and 'Don't cheer, boys, the poor devils are dying'?"

She nodded and glanced back at the paper. "I must say the Austrians have taken their own precious time about it. That archduke was killed a month ago."

"You think everybody should be in a hurry," said Kester.

The following afternoon they came in early from the fields, for the cotton was flowering magnificently and there was little to do but watch it. The sun was blazing and Kester announced that he was going to spend an hour in a cold bath. As Eleanor came out of her own bothroom, glowing from cold water and talcum powder, she called across the hall to him.

"Kester, are you still in the tub?"

"Yes, and I'm going to stay here till sundown."

"Do you want to read about all this rah-rah in Europe?"

"That's what I'm staying here for, to have a cool place to read it. Bring me the paper."

She took it to him and went into the nursery to pick up Cornelia, who had wakened from her nap and was clamoring for attention. As she plopped the baby into her own little bathtub she heard Kester calling her again. Eleanor shouted that she was busy.

She had Cornelia in her lap, and was shaking talcum over her and enjoying Cornelia's interest in her own toes, when Kester appeared in the doorway. He had pulled a bathrobe around him and was holding the newspaper. "Eleanor, did you see this?"

"See what?"

Kester crossed the room in what looked like one step, nearly running into Dilcy, who was bringing out the baby's clean clothes. He thrust the paper in front of Eleanor's eyes.

She looked up and began to read. " 'Grim War Cloud Overshadows Europe. Austria Sounds Appeal to Arms against Servia. Kaiser Stands Firmly behind His Ancient Ally—' Good Lord, Kester!" Catching Cornelia in one arm she sprang up and snatched the paper from him, for between a picture of Crown Prince Alexander of Servia and another of the French Madame Caillaux she saw a second series of headlines.

"World's Markets Demoralized ... European Bourses ... Wall Street . . . COTTON FUTURES SLUMP HEAVILY."

Dilcy ran to her. "My Lawsy, Miss Elna, is somebody dead?"

"Take the baby," Eleanor said mechanically without looking up. She was trying to read the article under the headlines. The only sentence she was seeing clearly was "Smart declines were recorded in cotton futures at New York and New Orleans."

She lowered the paper. Kester was still standing by her, his hands in the pockets of his bathrobe, as though waiting for her to explain what she understood no more than he did.

"Come into my room," said Eleanor.

They went in and shut the door behind them. Eleanor sat down, twisting the cord of her dressing gown. "What do you think?" Kester asked.

"I don't know what to think. What has this archduke business got to do with the price of cotton?"

He shrugged. "All I know is what I showed you in the paper."

Eleanor was tying the cord into a knot. Kester began to walk up and down, talking uneasily. This might be only a temporary slump, he said after awhile; international complications always made the markets stagger. Talking about it cleared the fog of the first shock for both of them, and they grew optimistic. "After all," said Eleanor, "this is only July.

93

We won't be ready for the market until September. It'll probably be straightened out by then."

"I tell you," Kester exclaimed, "I'll call up my brother Sebastian; he's a cotton broker and will know what's happening today—this is yesterday's news in the *Times-Picayune*."

She agreed eagerly. "Call him now. Do you mind if I listen from this phone here?"

"Of course not." Kester almost ran downstairs. She picked up the receiver from her bedside telephone and listened while he rang Sebastian's New Orleans office from the phone downstairs.

When Sebastian answered his voice had a tired sound, but his words were quick, as though he were speaking under a strain. He said cotton had begun to fall yesterday. It was still falling. In the world's three cotton exchanges—at New Orleans, New York and Liverpool—the situation was tense; several millionaire brokers were already dumping large sums of money into the market in an effort to bolster the price. Eleanor fancied that Sebastian's voice had a curiously familiar sound, as though she had heard it many times before, which was odd, for she barely knew him.

"But what on earth is the reason?" Kester demanded.

"Briefly, this," said Sebastian. "If there should be a general war in Europe and their markets should be closed, this country would have to absorb the whole cotton crop, and we can't do it. Normally two-thirds of it is sold in Europe. If that's all you wanted I've got to hang up—we're working like mad." Eleanor gave her head a little shake as she listened. She had heard voices like that before. With an irrelevance that was somehow frightening she was reminded of a levee camp. Kester's voice cut into her musing.

"But—"

"We're hoping it's only temporary," Sebastian interrupted. "They'll have to have clothes over there, war or no war. I've got to go, Kester."

The receivers clicked into place. For a moment Eleanor sat still by the bed. She could feel her heart thumping. This might not be important, yet she was trembling; and all of a sudden she knew where she had heard voices like Sebastian's voice today. He sounded like the men on the river saying. "I don't think it will break, do you?" when the river was creeping up inch by terrible inch and sweat was streaming into their eyes from their fight to hold a levee that was just about to go under, "Oh please, God, *please!*" Eleanor whispered involuntarily, and she sprang up and began to put on her clothes with the same swift desperation with which she had seen them drag sandbags to the levee crown.

As she dashed around the turn of the spiral staircase she called to Kester that she was not to be disturbed till suppertime, and she got out her ledgers. Though she had tried not to, secretly she knew she had been counting on selling the cotton for at least twelve cents a pound. But now she began to figure out how little they could possibly ask for it with safety. She and Kester had prepared for everything: they had cash ready to pay the cotton-pickers, they had provided for ginning and contracted for warehouse space to hold the cottonbales until it was time for shipment. Unlike some improvident planters (one of whom Kester had been this time last year, she was reminded as she worked) they had not waited until the last minute to attend to these details; every single thing human effort could arrange was in order at Ardeith, and this heaven-sent weather was taking care of the only item beyond their control.

She worked until she was called to supper. After supper, telling Cameo to bring her a pot of coffee, she went back to her ledgers.

At eleven o'clock she looked up at Kester, who had been pretending to read. Her shoulders and the back of her neck ached with weariness, and as she spoke she thought her voice had a tinny sound.

"Kester, if the worst comes we can get through this fall on seven and a quarter cents a pound."

He sprang to his feet, almost angrily. "Seven and a quarter cents? But my darling girl, we can't take that! It's giving it away."

"I know it. But we may have to take it. It will mean we can't do a thing but pay the interest and the outstanding bills. We can't put a cent into the plantation or buy so much as a pair of shoes this winter. And of course we can't put aside anything toward next year's payment on the principal."

"Seven and a quarter cents," he repeated, as though they were words unfit to use in decent conversation. "It's unthinkable."

"Well, you might as well start thinking about it," she retorted.

"I'd as soon plow it under," Kester exclaimed.

"Oh, good heavens, Kester!" she cried. "Do you suppose I'm having any fun telling you that people who are desperate have to take what they can get?"

"No, darling. Forgive me." He came around to the back of her chair and bent to kiss her forehead. "You've an astonishing mind for business. I couldn't even squeeze out the interest at such a price."

She leaned against him, aching with disappointment as much as with exhaustion. "I'm figuring on starvation wages to the pickers. Forty cents a hundred pounds—I hate to do it, but if cotton goes down that far they'll be desperate too. Oh—" she brushed her hand across her eyes. "I was planning on tractors and cultivators, and so many pretty things for Cornelia! She's been dressed like a pauper's child this summer."

Kester had his arm around her. "There's nothing I can tell you, sweetheart," he said in a low voice, "except that you've been splendid, and I feel worse than you do."

She held his hand, afraid to speak again lest she break down and sob, and crying made her feel like such a fool.

The next morning when they rode over the fields the cotton was still as lavish as though the bombardment of Belgrade had never started. With proud authority Kester told Eleanor that this was as excellent cotton as could be grown anywhere in the world. "But what good is that," she exclaimed, "if the price stays low?"

"How do you know it's going to be low?" he demanded. "We won't be selling for six or seven weeks."

She looked down, stroking her horse's mane. "I know. I'm ashamed of myself. But I feel so stricken."

"Oh, stop it," said Kester. He turned his horse abruptly and began hurrying back to the house. Eleanor followed, and found him at the telephone. "I'm ringing New Orleans again," he said. "The market may have turned up by now. Go upstairs and listen if you want to."

Eleanor climbed the stairs and sat by the bed, the receiver in her hand. She had a long time in which to resolve to be cheerful, for Kester had difficulty in getting Sebastian to the telephone. As Sebastian answered, Eleanor heard a confusion of voices behind him. To her strained attention they sounded like pandemonium. She heard Kester speak.

"Sebastian, what's happening to cotton?"

Sebastian took a sharp breath. "Still falling."

"But what's going on?"

"Can't you read? With Russia mobilizing, God knows who else will be in it by night."

Kester asked more questions. Sebastian answered shortly, as though in no mood to discuss anything with anybody. At length, with an evident attempt to be optimistic, he urged, "After all, cotton is still in the flower. The war may not last more than a few months."

"That's what they said about the Civil War," Kester returned, "and it lasted—"

At that Sebastian's own dismay got the better of him. "Oh for God's sake, Kester, do you think you're the only one who's in a panic today? The Cotton Exchange is a madhouse. There's never been anything like it. If it'll cheer you up I'll tell you what I've lost this week. Some of us—"

Eleanor put back her own receiver, feeling that she simply could not bear to listen any longer. She dropped her forehead on her hands, and found that in spite of the blistering heat her hands were cold.

Beyond her windows the cotton blossoms danced in the sun, their opulence mocking her despair. She remembered those hundreds of hours in the fields when the sun had pounded on her head and her back had ached till she could hardly sit her horse, and the nights when she had sat up over her accounts though her head was heavy with sleepiness; she had pretended she did not need rest or amusement, and had looked the other way when she passed shopwindows full of fluffy dresses for a baby girl. She had given all she had it in her to give, till a thousand bales of perfect cotton were flowering in the fields. And now a prince nobody cared about had been shot in a town nobody had ever heard of by a maniac whose name nobody could pronounce, and she might as well have let the plantation grow up in grass.

Too shaky to work and too restless to sit still, she and Kester walked up and down the gallery, trying to encourage each other. Maybe Germany wouldn't enter the war. And as for France and the British Empire, what concern could they possibly have with a dead Austrian archduke? It was beyond reason. Somebody in the Austrian royal family was always getting murdered, it seemed to be their destiny, and nobody had started a war over Prince Rudolph, or the Empress Elizabeth; the other kings had said they were sorry and had gone about their business as usual. But the fact that it was past understanding did not alter the fact that today the cotton

97

of Ardeith was worth only about half as much as it had been worth the day before yesterday.

"Let's have a party," said Kester suddenly.

Eleanor stopped short. "A party? Are you losing your mind?"

"No, but I will if we keep on like this. Let's call up everybody we know. Tell Mamie to whip up some sandwiches. I'll go down and get the best liquor in the house. Let's have a party!"

He had grabbed her hand and dragged her indoors. As he said the last word he pulled down the receiver of the telephone and shouted a number. Eleanor listened, aghast.

"Violet? This is Kester Larne. You and Bob come over at seven. We feel like dancing. Good! We'll be looking for you." He rattled the hook again. "Eleanor, tell Mamie about those sandwiches. Cameo!" he yelled over his shoulder. "Hello? Neal? This is Kester. We're having a party tonight. You and Clara—yes, I know, damn the cotton—we're expecting you." Cameo had appeared from the back and Kester began giving him orders. "Cameo, make a lot of Sazeracs, we're having some people in. Eleanor, go talk to Mamie!"

Giggling almost hysterically, Eleanor dropped a kiss on the tip of his ear. "You're wonderful," she whispered, and hurried back to the kitchen.

By eight o'clock the parlors were full and the phonograph was shrieking, "I want a girl, just like the girl, that married dear old dad!" Eleanor was dancing with Bob Purcell and Kester was mixing drinks for everybody. They talked a little about the drop in cotton, especially those who, like Neal Sheramy, were directly affected by it, but ragtime and Sazeracs were convincing most of them that things would be all right pretty soon. None of the guests knew how dangerous the state of Ardeith was, so nobody sympathized, and as the evening advanced Eleanor was more and more glad of it. She hardly sat down for hours. Though she had been up since six she kept going with a fierce inner stimulation that made her forget to think whether or not she was tired; she drank two Sazeracs before supper and two highballs afterward, more than she had ever drunk in an evening before, and for the first time in her life she smoked a cigarette. It gave her a welcome lightness in her head.

It was three o'clock before the guests left, clamoring that they had had a wonderful time and that Kester was really a bad influence, keeping people up till such hours on a Thursday night when tomorrow was a workday, but the all-of-a-sudden parties at Ardeith were such irresistible fun. As the door closed behind the last of them Eleanor stood still in the hall a moment, then all the strength went out of her and she sank down on the staircase, realizing that every joint of her body had a separate ache and her head was pounding.

Kester took her hands and helped her up. "Feel better?" he asked.

She nodded. He put his arm around her waist and they went upstairs. Kester was slightly drunk, but it did not seem important. She did not blame him.

But though she was so tired, she did not go to sleep at once. As she lay in bed, too tense to relax immediately and her thoughts clear with the cruel clarity of fatigue, she could not help remembering that if Kester had minded his plantation in normal times this drop would not have threatened disaster.

It was nearly eleven o'clock when she was wakened by Cornelia scrambling around in the hall outside. The room was hot but dim, and she noticed that somebody had tiptoed in early to draw the curtains so that the sun would not disturb her. Slipping out of bed, Eleanor put on her slippers and went to the door, where she saw Dilcy coming out of the nursery to rescue Cornelia. Pinned to the outside of her door was a torn scrap of paper on which Kester had scribbled, "Don't wake up Miss Eleanor."

Eleanor smiled. The darling. Taking care of her just as if he had not been up as late as she had. The door of his room across the hall was open and the bed was empty. She asked Dilcy where he was.

"He been downstairs quite awhile," Dilcy told her. "You want yo' coffee now, miss?"

"Yes, please." Eleanor went back into her room and began to get dressed. She drank coffee, but it was too hot for her to want breakfast. By force of custom she put on a riding-habit, though it was too late to see much of the cotton this morning.

Kester was downstairs, reading the paper and drinking iced tea. He sprang up as she came in. "Hello, darling. How do you feel?"

"Fine. Better than you do—how much sleep did you get?"

"Funny," he said. "I woke up at six, as usual."

"Thanks for drawing my curtains," said Eleanor. She kissed

99

him and rumpled up his hair. "Is there anything in the paper?"

He chuckled. "Panama Canal to be opened for world traffic August fifteenth, as if anybody cares, now that there's practically no traffic to go through it."

"I'd forgotten all about the canal. Remember how important it was a month ago?"

"Since you're all dressed for it," he suggested, "want to take a look at the cotton?"

She looked him over wonderingly. "Kester, I had a good sleep and feel very well, but if you were up at six—"

"Oh, I'm all right," he assured her.

They ordered the horses and went out. The sky was white with heat, but Kester said there was a feel of rain in the air. Last night's merriment had cleared away much of their despondency, and the sight of the cotton reminded them that markets went up as well as down. If there was any change at all, Kester said, it would have to be up. And no matter what cannibals the Europeans were turning out to be they hadn't given up the custom of wearing clothes. Unless, of course, the British went back to painting themselves blue like their ancestors. Laughing at his nonsense, Eleanor felt her spirits rising.

The cotton needed very little attention. They rode past the cabins, where most of the Negroes were idling in the sun, waiting for the bolls to open. A group of them were celebrating the slack period with a watermelon-cutting, and a pickaninny ran up with slices of watermelon for the master and mistress. They rode back to the house wiping the juice off their chins.

Cameo met them in the hall with a telegram.

"From Sebastian?" Eleanor exclaimed.

"It must be," Kester answered eagerly as he tore it open. "He promised to wire if anything happened."

Eleanor read it over his shoulder. As the words met her eyes she had a curious deathlike sensation. It was as though all the blood in her body had dropped, making her legs very heavy and the upper part of her feel as if it were not there at all.

NEW ORLEANS COTTON EXCHANGE CLOSED FIRST TIME IN HISTORY TEN TWENTY SIX THIS MORNING NEW YORK AND LIVERPOOL EX-

Chapter Six

1

THEN THEY HAD the experience of living in a country that was paralyzed.

From Virginia to Texas, the South had stood on a foundation of cotton. There were other crops of course, and other industries, but cotton was their staff of life Most of them had accepted their dependence on cotton like their dependence on the sun, never dreaming that either could be blotted from their reckoning. "The South clothes the world" was their proverb, and they were very nearly right silk and linen were luxuries and all but the most costly woollens were woven with a mixture of cotton. Cotton was the principal export of the United States.

Manufacturers abroad had contracted months in advance for cotton, and the merchant ships were embargoed in American ports: a city of ships clogged the river below New Orleans. There were vessels from all the warring nations, huddled so close together that the crews shouted to one another with an amiability that their kings overseas would hardly have sanctioned. In Europe the price of gingham was shooting beyond the reach of all but the wealthy. In the United States gingham was being sold for six cents a yard, because those who expected to profit by the havoc had ordered that cotton should not be moved.

Eleanor woke every morning with a sense of heaviness, looked around and remembered the cotton. She hated to get up. She hated the dragging days. She dreaded seeing Kester.

He said very little about their situation. apparently preferring to talk of any subject on earth but the fact that if their long overdue interest were not paid in November the bank would almost certainly foreclose. But sometimes when he was playing with Cornelia she would see him give the baby a look that made her remember that Cornelia was the seventh generation of the Larnes of Ardeith, and if they should take her away from it now she would not have even a memory of what her home had been.

It had never occurred to Eleanor to doubt that if she gave everything she had she could win this battle, and her courage to endure the labor of the past few months had been based on a joyous self-confidence. She had always believed things did not happen to you unless you let them happen. The defeated people were those too lazy or too stupid to make their way. Now she felt as if all her knowledge and religion were turning to mockery. She walked up and down her bedroom, trying to think of a way out till she was dizzy with thinking. The loss of Ardeith would mean a fearful blow to her faith in herself, and as she fought to keep from having to receive such a blow she was reminded at every turn that this was not her fault, but Kester's. All cotton planters were staggering under the shock, but those who had been provident were not facing utter ruin. And though she resolved to have patience with him, it was the first time she had ever had much need for such a quality and it was hard to acquire.

Fred wrote asking her if the collapse of the cotton market had put the plantation into really evil straits, and if so, was there anything he could do? Eleanor showed the letter to Kester. He read it soberly and went to his desk. Later in the day he brought her an answer he had written.

"Your kind letter to Eleanor would make me realize, if I never had before, what a fine and thoughtful man she has for a father. However, your anxiety is premature. We have no cotton to sell yet even if the times were normal, and there is every reason to expect the market to open by fall." There followed several paragraphs of news about Eleanor and the baby. "Shall I send it?" Kester asked.

"Of course," said Eleanor.

They read the papers, less to follow the war than to search for some indication that the warmakers were going to lift the embargo on cotton. The Germans were on their way to Paris and the Russians pushing through East Prussia toward Berlin. Eleanor wished savagely that one or the other army would get where it wanted to go; she didn't care which, if only that would end the war and open the seas again. Through September she and Kester worked doggedly getting the cotton in, and sent it to the warehouse to fill the space they had so exultantly contracted for three months ago. There were nine hundred and thirty-two bales of it, worth nearly fifty thousand dollars last July and today not worth two cents.

They went to New Orleans and talked to Mr. Robichaux. Mr. Robichaux was regretful, but he was firm. The banks simply could not carry the cotton planters. At first, Eleanor was indignant at such heartlessness then as the interview progressed she saw that Mr. Robichaux looked like a man straining under a burden too heavy for his shoulders, and his voice, as he talked to them, once or twice came perilously near to breaking. "How much power do you think we have?" he cried at last. "At least you can thank God you haven't had to listen to the stories I've heard this month while I've sat here feeling like a brute because I couldn't offer help. I've handed some of these people money from my own pocket, not people like you, but the little farmers with their one-mule crops, good decent men trying to get along, I've seen them break down and sob at having to take charity, and here you come telling me you're desperate."

"I am desperate," said Kester quietly.

"Yes, Kester, I know. Poverty is relative, of course—but all I can tell you is what I've already said. We're desperate too."

Kester began to push back his chair. "Thank you, sir, and forgive me."

They took the train back to Ardeith. On the seat by Kester, Eleanor was tense, her hands holding each other tight on her knee. It was the first time in her life she had ever sat facing defeat.

"You needn't look like that," Kester exclaimed at length under cover of the rattling wheels. "Even if the worst comes you won't have to take in washing!"

"I could stand taking in washing. I can't stand feeling beaten."

"For God's sake, Eleanor, it's not our fault we can't move the cotton!"

"It's not my fault we haven't any credit," she returned.

Kester said nothing. He fixed his eyes on the gray cypress woods through which the train was passing. After awhile Eleanor reached out and put her hand over his.

"I'm sorry, Kester," she said.

He turned her hand over, and looked at the darn on the tip of one of the glove-fingers. "I don't suppose you can help

103

saying that now and then, can you? You must be thinking it all the time."

"I try not to," she murmured. "Even if I don't sound like it, Kester, I love you very much."

Their hands closed on each other. Eleanor looked down, ashamed of herself, wondering why she could not hold her tongue.

As they went up the front steps of the Ardeith gallery Cornelia toddled to meet them. Kester picked her up and smiled for the first time that day.

Eleanor went upstairs and flung her hat on a table. The hat was two years old. Last summer when she was waiting for Cornelia's birth she had not needed hats, and except for that beauty with the three white feathers, quite unsuitable to wear on the train, she had not dared to buy any this year. The hat she had just pulled off belonged to her magical honeymoon on the Gulf Coast, a thousand years ago when she was young and confident, sure that going to sleep with Kester's arms around her meant that she would never have a problem in this world. Eleanor picked up the hat and tried to smooth the faded ribbon around the crown. She did so hate to be shabby; she had never been foolishly extravagant about her clothes, but she had always looked well-dressed. Always, she thought now, until she had married Kester the single act of her life that had been prompted by emotion instead of reason.

There was a knock on her door. When she called, Kester came in carrying her grip, dear Kester who had such delicacy that he never entered her bedroom unless he knocked first, and he came to her without speaking, and put his arms around her and held her close. Eleanor clung to him, because when Kester held her like this she could not be conscious of anything except of how much she loved him.

After a long time Kester said, "They've got supper nearly ready. Change your dress and come down."

"All right," she answered faintly.

"It's frightfully hot," he said. "I'll send you up a pitcher of ice water."

She kissed him lingeringly.

After supper Kester ensconced himself behind a magazine while Eleanor sat drawing curlycues on the page of a ledger, searching the wall in front of them for some crack for escape. They did not need a great deal of money. If Kester had not neglected the interest on his notes since long before they went to the bank last January they would have needed still less.

She went on drawing circles. Their payment on the principal would not be due until the following fall. Eight thousand dollars would take care of the interest this year, though it would not leave a penny to pay for the fertilizer they had bought, nor the equipment, nor any of their long-standing bills. Eight thousand dollars; it was no vast sum to mean the bridge between collapse and endurance, but she was reminded of what Benjamin Franklin had said: "If you would know the value of money, go and try to borrow some."

Alice's husband and Sebastian had both taken such heavy losses in the market crash that though they might have wanted to do so they could not offer help. Kester's father, living on his income from the sugar land, habitually spent the last penny he received. Her own father—the thought of asking his charity made her writhe. It might mean considerable hardship for Fred to dig up eight thousand dollars in cash on a week's notice.

Her own little income went for current living expenses as fast as she received it, for keeping a house such as this one in order, even with the strictest economy, cost a good deal. She felt herself smiling at the irony of being destitute amid such splendor.

The idea brought a flash of inspiration. Eleanor jabbed her pencil into the paper so hard that the point snapped. She sprang up.

"Where are you going?" Kester asked.

"To get my keys. I'll show you." By the time she had said it she was at the door. She dashed upstairs to get her keys and a flashlight and down again to the vault that had been built under the house for the safeguarding of valuables. With the aid of the flashlight she looked around.

Kester had said every teaspoon in the house was carrying all it could stand, which was an exaggeration. There were some things nobody had thought to mortgage: a few bottles of priceless liquor put here by a race that had understood the refinements of good living, and numerous bits of jewelry worn by dead ladies. Some of it she had worn herself on important occasions. Eleanor took the bottles down and pushed aside the cobwebs so she could see the labels. She knew very little about ancient liquors, but anything that could not be replaced was worth money. She knelt down, the dust blackening her skirt, and began unlocking the old safe, constructed long ago to be opened with a series of keys. Groping in the half-darkness, she found a silver cup given to some Larne baby of a past generation; Cornelia was cutting her teeth on a silver cup that had belonged to her great-grandfather, so evidently this had been offered to another child, and holding her flashlight close she read "Cynthia, June 6, 1849." Without pausing to wonder who Cynthia might have been Eleanor set the cup on the floor and went on rummaging. There were piles of documents—marriage certificates, wills, deeds to land and slaves—as these were of no monetary value she hardly looked at them. She found some earrings long and heavy for pierced ears, several brooches, a jeweled butterfly apparently made to hold up a lady's curls, a medallion with a lock of baby's hair on one side and on the other a space that looked as if it might have been meant for a picture. The space was set within a circle of diamonds

Holding these and other treasures jumbled together in a bag she made by gathering up her skirt, Eleanor relocked the safe. She left the jewelry in her room, and without pausing to wash her blackened hands she picked up the flashlight again and went to the attic. It was full of furniture, mahogany and rosewood that were merely odds and ends at Ardeith but that would be costly antiques in the shop windows along Royal Street in New Orleans.

As she came down she saw Kester in the upper hall looking for her.

"Eleanor, what *have* you been doing?" he demanded. He looked her up and down and burst out laughing. "Your hair is full of cobwebs and you're black from head to foot."

"Come in here." She opened the door of her bedroom. "Kester, do you know we've got enough salable stuff in this house to set an antique dealer mad? I'm going to bring one up from New Orleans."

Kester was amazed. He was, she guessed after a few minutes, shocked. It had never occurred to him that the treasures of Ardeith were separable from it any more than the columns that held up the roof. He looked at the silver and jewelry she had brought from the vault, and listened to her description of what else they could part with. Now and then he shook his head in wondering protest.

"The brandy I don't mind," he said after awhile. "Nor the things in the attic—I suppose the fact that they're there proves we don't need them. But these—" he indicated the jewels—"Eleanor, do we have to let them go? They mean something—I could tell you a story about every piece on that table—"

"Kester, we can't afford to be sentimental!"

He had picked up the diamond medallion. "My grand-mother—the girl in the blue hoopskirt downstairs—tried to sell this during Reconstruction when one of her children was very ill. It was midsummer and she was trying to buy ice. She couldn't sell it. The child died."

"Kester, my darling, it doesn't matter now. We can't let it matter!"

He slowly replaced the medallion on the table beside the other things. "The trouble with you," he said, "is that you're always so damn right."

They took the jewelry to New Orleans the next day and left it there for appraisal. After consideration. Eleanor told Kester they need not actually sell it, as the bank would probably accept it as security for the interest on their notes, and the reminder cheered Kester so that he submitted to her unsavory choice of a dealer in antiques to look at their discarded furniture.

The dealer smelt like lard. His hair was greasy, his face was greasy, even his voice had a well-oiled sound. In the lapel of his coat he wore a button bearing the legend "I love my wife but oh you kid!" There were many dealers of gentler appearance on Royal Street, but Eleanor had wanted one who would regard what she had to sell as merchandise and make a bargain accordingly. Cameo, who met them at the station with the carriage, gave their visitor a glance of distaste all the more eloquent because he abated not one jot of the silent respect with which he waited upon any guest to Ardeith. The dealer whistled as the carriage drove down the avenue and gave voice to some profane admiration. When they went indoors he looked around as though estimating the cost of everything within his vision.

"Swell layout you got here," he observed. "Now where's the stuff you want me to look at?"

Eleanor had had the servants move it all into a back room downstairs. She saw Dilcy and Bessie now. regarding the new arrival as Cameo had done. "Will yo' guest have some coffee, miss?" Bessie inquired with polite disdain.

"No time for coffee," said the guest briskly. "Where—"

107

"In this room," said Kester, opening a door, but the dealer had paused before the two companion portraits hung at the foot of the stairs. "Mhm," he said, nodding with approval. "Romantic. How much you want for those?"

"They are not for sale," said Kester. "Will you come in here, please?"

"Well, you needn't freeze on it. What'd you bring me up here for if you didn't want money?"

As this sort of trade was obviously not to Kester's liking, Eleanor took charge. "It's all in here," she said briskly, leading them into the back room. "This tip-table, as you can see, is solid rosewood. This nest of tables is made up of six, fitting one within the other—"

"Sure, I see." He bent down, tapping the wood and looking for wormholes. Eleanor nodded sagely. She had been right; this fellow wouldn't waste time talking. He knew his business.

Kester looked on, speaking only when he had to answer a question. But now that she was actually doing something, Eleanor was enjoying herself. Matching her wits with some-one else's for profit gave her a feeling of gay triumph, for she was good at it; they dickered and argued, and when they agreed on a price for anything she wrote it down in a notebook. Evidently having begun with the misconception that he was calling upon a lady who could be cheated because she wouldn't know any better, as the day advanced the dealer began giving her glances of unwilling respect. "You sure know what you're up to, don't you, Mrs. Larne?" he remarked at length.

"Certainly," said Eleanor.

"You ought to be in business."

"What do you think this is?" she retorted.

He continued to examine the seat of a chair he was holding upside down. "Funny. I don't mind telling you. Most folks who've got this stuff to sell out of old houses don't know a dollar from a biscuit," he confided.

She laughed. "Well, I do."

"So I observe. What you got total for this?"

"Two thousand one hundred and forty-two dollars."

"Make it two thousand for the lot and we'll call it quits."

"It totals two thousand one hundred—"

"Damn!" he said, and began to laugh too. "Ain't you a bit unladylike?"

"Not when it costs good money to be ladylike," said Eleanor.

"All right, all right, you win. Look, Mrs. Larne, any time you want a job selling let me know. I could use one like you." He went back into the hall and looked around again at the portraits. "Better think twice, you two. I'd like to handle some of these."

"I told you they were not for sale," Kester answered crisply.

"Your kinfolks?"

"Yes."

He surveyed the portraits wisely. "Sure, I knew it. You wouldn't have 'em if they weren't real. All your stuff is real. You can't fool me."

"Those are of no value to any family but my own," said Kester, evidently wishing his visitor would remove himself as soon as possible. "They aren't by great artists."

The dealer gave a low whistle of derision. "I can see you're new to this business, mister. Lots of them porky millionaires that come to New Orleans for Mardi Gras, they haven't got any portraits. Their folks were on the steerage when your folks were getting painted. So they buy 'em a couple of pictures and take 'em home. Don't you get it?—Aunt Minnie."

Kester gave a shrug. Eleanor began to laugh.

"I bet this little lady would sell 'em." The dealer made a gesture with his thumb toward Eleanor.

"You heard my husband say they were not for sale," she put in quickly. "Here's the list of prices you offered, so you can add them yourself if you like. And here's a pen."

"Yes ma'am," he said with exaggerated meekness. "Now what's the first name, please?"

"Kester," she told him.

"Oh, I make the check to him? All right, anything you say. There'll be a couple of boys around with a truck in the morning. And don't you get smart and slip a couple of pieces back in the garret, either."

"Good Lord," exclaimed Kester.

"Well, people have been known to. Don't get me wrong, mister, I ain't saying you're not honest, but we need to be careful when we got our living to make." He grinned at Eleanor. "If you change your mind about Aunt Minnie, say so."

When he had gone Kester shivered with relief and ordered a highball. Eleanor went jubilantly to him with the check. "Endorse this now," she exclaimed, "and I'll send it right to the bank. Kester, aren't you delighted?"

"I'm delighted he's gone," said Kester dryly. He wrote his name.

Eleanor picked up the check. For a moment she stood still, looking down at him, then she crossed to the desk, where she put the check into an envelope to be mailed to the bank for deposit. As she stamped the letter she turned around again and looked at him. Kester sat by the window sipping his highball.

"Aren't you even glad I got some money for us?" she asked.

"Of course I'm glad," he said without turning.

"Then what's the matter with you?"

"Do I have to pretend besides I enjoyed your haggling like a pawnbroker?"

"Somebody had to haggle," she exclaimed, "and it was evident you weren't going to."

"You were very good at it. That nest of tables you got eighty dollars for isn't worth more than fifty."

Eleanor walked across the room and stood in front of him.

"Then you might have said so. All you've done this afternoon is stand around with your lip curled. One would think trying to pay your debts was a matter beneath a gentleman's dignity."

She stopped, drew a breath and let it out audibly. She went to him and put her hand on his shoulder. As she was tingling with anger she waited a moment, then spoke slowly and carefully. "Kester, please don't make me mad! My nerves are in the same state as European culture, and if I lose my—"

He turned impulsively, put his arm around her and drew her down to sit on the arm of his chair. "I know, darling. Mine are too." He gave a sorry little shake of his head. "Odd, isn't it—we're just as bad as the Europeans. The minute people start fighting for civilization they start behaving as if they never heard of it."

For several minutes they were silent. At last Eleanor stood up restlessly. "I think I'll take a drive down the river road before supper. The air will be good for my disposition."

He smiled. "I'm sorry, darling," he said.

"So am I," Eleanor answered, and kissed his hair.

She piloted the automobile down the avenue and past the gates. The scenery along the river road was not a happy sight this fall. The oaks grew on either side, their branches lacing overhead so that the road was spotted with sunlight, but behind them in the fields unpicked cotton was lying, on the ground in dirty little curls, as numerous planters had not thought it worth while to go to the trouble of getting it in. Bales for which no warehouse space had been contracted beforehand were piled around the gins, for with none of the year's harvest moving, the warehouses had no more space to rent. Eleanor had come out because she wanted to relax and not talk about cotton, but she could not help thinking about it. With the cash she had acquired today and the jewels as security for the rest of the interest, they could doubtless pacify the bank into letting them stay at Ardeith through another year. But during that year—?

The future ahead of her was blank as a desert. They had no money for the laborers who would be needed to tend the plantation during the winter, they could buy no fertilizer till they paid for what they had bought already, and there were a hundred other needs from repairs and fodder to subscriptions to agricultural journals; and all that without considering the necessities of daily living, for which their credit was strained till Eleanor shrank from entering a shop. And suppose they somehow got through the winter, what in the name of reason were they going to plant next spring? The country had ten million bales of cotton on its hands. Planting more was folly, yet except for vegetables grown for their own table nothing but cotton had been planted at Ardeith since the Civil War. You could not revolutionize a plantation suddenly any more than a factory. Cotton, cotton, cotton—the word rattled in her head. Didn't those lunatics in Europe need clothes? Of all the harmless commodities to be swept off the seas!

It was getting late. Eleanor turned the car and drove back to Ardeith. As she stopped in front of the house, impulsively she rested her elbows on the steering wheel and put her head down on her arms. "Please, God," she whispered, "if you aren't going to let cotton move, let something, anything, happen to make me stop thinking about it!"

2

Something did happen, of a nature to make Eleanor remember that she had heard ministers warn their congregations to be careful what they prayed for lest their prayers be answered.

They left the jewels at the bank as security, and the money they received for the old brandy they put aside to be used for living expenses. It was impossible to say how long it would last, for due to the lack of manufactured articles from abroad the price of many commodities was rising, and a war-tax bill, to make up for diminishing customs receipts, sent the cost of living higher still. Though they had a breathing space Eleanor felt like a patient who was barely breathing. There was still no answer to the question of what they could plant next spring to give them the twenty thousand dollars they had promised to pay the bank in the fall.

In spite of her resolution, suspense made her temper uncertain and she was not always easy to live with. Kester urged her to go out. Their friends were entertaining again, saying you couldn't stay under a pall forever. It was true their gaiety had a hysterical quality suggesting that of the beleaguered cities overseas, but dancing was less destructive to the nerves than pacing the floor at home, so Eleanor yielded, and they had dinner with the Sheramys and went on a picnic with Violet Purcell. They also had a Sunday night supper with the three Durham girls, a rather lugubrious meal, as the old ladies habitually set a place at table for their sister Kate who had eloped forty years ago in defiance of parents and propriety, a matter that had grieved them so much they had felt it their duty ever since to ignore her departure.

Kester's Cousin Sylvia came around to sell them a pair of tickets to a dance being given at the Hunt Club in town for the benefit of the Buy-a-Bale movement, which had been begun with the hope that if everybody with any money to spare would buy a bale of cotton at the standard price of fifty dollars, the market would be eased. "Such a worthy cause," Sylvia urged, "and nobody is going to lose anything by it, because all the brokers say that as soon as the war is over the need for cotton in Europe will send the price to twelve cents a pound. So anybody who buys a bale now will make ten dollars by holding it."

"Really?" said Eleanor.

"Yes indeed." Cousin Sylvia was fluttering about the parlor. "Have you bought your bale yet?"

Eleanor gasped.

"We have all the cotton we need, Cousin Sylvia," answered Kester. He looked as if he wanted to giggle.

"But my dear boy, it's the *principle* of the thing!"

"We can't afford principles," Eleanor said curtly.

"Now Eleanor, you *mustn't* say things like that. President Wilson has bought a bale, and I'm sure he doesn't need it. And all sorts of people are buying bales and putting them on their front porches—"

"Doing their alms before men in the most delicate fashion," murmured Kester.

"And a great many of the leading merchants in New Orleans and everywhere are buying bales, and they put them on the sidewalks with a sign saying 'Bought by the Soandso Company, have you bought yours?' "

"A nice way to get free advertising by shoving the taxpayers off the sidewalk," said Eleanor. "I think it's silly. The cotton is all being held for sale again, so I don't see that it's easing the market."

"Now Eleanor, you don't understand." Sylvia opened her handbag and took out a rattling handful of buttons. "We are giving out these buttons to be worn on your dress, or your coat lapel, Kester. You see, they have 'I've bought a bale, have you?' printed on them."

Quivering with suppressed merriment, Kester took a button. "I see. Excellent. I tell you, Sylvia, I'll buy a bale from somebody if you'll buy a bale from me."

Sylvia gave a tolerant little laugh. "*Now*, Kester, you know I have *barely* enough to live on! My poor Conrad," she explained to Eleanor, "was not a practical business man for all his noble qualities. That's why I'm giving all I have, my strength and my time, to the cause. It's all I have to give." She proceeded to explain that, of course, she had known it all along, when people put their whole confidence into one staple commodity they were heading *straight* for disaster. As neither of them had ever heard her say so before, Kester continued to be amused and Eleanor irritated. Cousin Sylvia asked Kester if he would please look for her handkerchief, she must have dropped it when she got out of her buggy, and when he was gone she urged Eleanor in a confidential voice to be *very* cheerful these trying days. "And *don't* make such pessimistic remarks, my dear girl," she went on. "What every man wants of his wife is comfort and cheer. I know about these things."

Eleanor was tempted to slap her, but was saved from carrying out her impulse by Kester, who returned to say that he could not find the handkerchief, and remarkably Sylvia discovered that she still had it in her bag, how stupid of her to think she had dropped it. Now if they couldn't buy a bale today, would they at least take tickets for the dance? Such a worthy cause. Eleanor was moved to wrath when Kester bought the tickets.

"Did you have to do that?" she demanded when Cousin Sylvia had left.

Kester sank into a chair and began to laugh. "No, but I did it because I wanted to. Isn't she wonderful? The first time I ever got sent upstairs in disgrace it was for laughing at Sylvia out loud."

"I think she's odious," Eleanor exclaimed, though she was amused in spite of herself. "She sent you out so she could give me some advice on how to be happily married."

"I thought it must be for something of that sort. Sylvia was married twelve years to Cousin Conrad, who was a very affable fellow and endured her by a combination of Christian fortitude and good whiskey. I never saw a man so literally driven to drink."

"So now she tells everybody else—"

Kester was vastly tickled. "Certainly. Once he had gone to his reward she mourned him devotedly, had him cremated and set the ashes right up in her bedroom so she could worship them always."

"Revolting," said Eleanor.

"So be careful," Kester ended, "if you ever go to her house for supper and she takes you upstairs to primp. She keeps the ashes in a jar by the mirror and if you aren't careful you'll powder your face with Conrad."

Eleanor could not help laughing, though she still thought it was foolish to pay for any kind of dance when they had so little money. But she liked dancing, and agreed with Kester that she needed entertainment, so she was glad when the evening arrived and they dressed and went to the Hunt Club. It was there that she met Isabel Valcour.

For a week everybody had been talking about Isabel Valcour, and Eleanor had looked forward to making her acquaintance. Isabel had grown up in Dalroy, but she had married a German—an excessively rich German, they said— seven years ago, and since then she had lived abroad, apparently not remembering the United States at all until she had had to flee the war. The afternoon before the Buy-a-Bale dance was to be held, Violet dropped by Ardeith for a cup of coffee with Eleanor and reported that she had just been to call on Isabel, who had moved into her deceased father's old house on the river road. "Utterly incongruous, my dear," said Violet. "Cosmopolitan, better-looking than ever, dressed in clothes that are going to be in style sometime next year—how she's going to pass her time till the war's over I *don't* know."

"Where's her husband?" asked Eleanor. "In the army?"

"No, in heaven. It seems she's been a widow three years, following the seasons from Norway to Scotland to Monte Carlo to Paris—or wherever it is they go. I never thought I'd be trying to describe the odysseys of the international million- aires—and now to Dalroy, Louisiana. Imagine!"

Eleanor thought Isabel sounded interesting, and asked if she was going to attend the Buy-a-Bale dance. Violet didn't know; she had left Isabel's house because Clara Sheramy had come to call, and though Clara was a sweet little thing there were limits to what one could stand of her stupidity.

Her curiosity aroused, when they were driving to the Hunt Club that evening Eleanor asked Kester if he remembered Isabel. Certainly he did, Kester said, he had known her all her life.

"Is she as pretty as they say?" Eleanor asked.

"She used to be. I can't answer for her now."

"Shall we see her tonight?"

Kester had not inquired, but he supposed they would. Everybody else would be there, and it was a good chance for Isabel to meet her old friends.

A chill autumn fog had swooped down, and the club house was brilliant by contrast. The rooms were full of people, and when Kester and Eleanor arrived, the dancers were doing the fox-trot. Bob Purcell came to meet her, saying he had been waiting for her to dance with him; to Eleanor's protests that she had never tried the fox-trot he insisted that it was not difficult and quite an orderly pastime after the breathless hugs and hops of the past few seasons. She waved Kester a temporary goodby. In a few minutes she was having a very good time indeed, and she did not think of Isabel again until she saw her.

It was in the space after the first set of dances. She and Bob walked over to join the group around the punch-table, where a little lake of champagne sparkled in the hollow of a mold of pineapple ice. As they approached, Eleanor observed that in the center of the group was a slender blonde woman in sea-green satin, who stood with a glass in her hand answering questions with an air of amused detachment. Violet reached to take Eleanor's hand and draw her in among them, and the stranger paused, turning upon her a pair of enormous hazel eyes. Evidently this was Isabel Valcour. Eleanor hoped she was not staring.

Isabel was not only the most beautiful woman in the room but probably the most beautiful woman in the state of Louisiana. A product not only of good fortune but a carefully casual art, she looked like the archetype of a voluptuous and sophisticated group that had been used to moving among the capitals without seeing anything but the inside of its own circle. Though she was not tall, her figure was of the sort that seems to have been designed by heaven for the sole earthly purpose of wearing clothes, and her green dress, close-fitting except for a swirl at the hips, made an exquisite setting for her white shoulders and the perfect line of her throat. She had hair of a rare gold, brushed into shining ripples, and a face of such classic outlines that one could not help being surprised at the worldly cynicism of its smile. Without having been told beforehand, Eleanor thought she would have known that Isabel had returned to this town on the Mississippi River from a region as remote by philosophy as by distance; she was an alien, lost in her present situation unless she had—as she appeared so far to have—sufficient sense of humor to be amused by it. Surmising that the war must be the first event of many years that had found Isabel unprepared, Eleanor was suddenly sorry for her, and at the same time grateful for herself to be reminded that other lives than her own had been interrupted by the breaking apart of the world's order.

She must have been facing Isabel for only an instant, for she heard Violet say,

"We've been hearing about the horrors of war first hand— oh, I'm sorry, of course you two don't know each other. Mrs. Larne, Mrs.—Isabel, what *is* your name?"

116

Isabel answered with a slow smile. "Schimmelpfeng."

"There," said Violet to Eleanor. "You heard it."

Eleanor laughed. "Yes. But forgive me if I can't say it," she added to Isabel. "How do you do."

"Don't apologize. It took me a month to learn to say it myself." Isabel's voice was as lovely as her face. "Mrs. Kester Larne?"

"Yes."

"I remember Kester so well. Is he here tonight?"

"He's here, yes. Don't let me interrupt you. You were talking about the war?"

Isabel shrugged as though she would have been happy to stop talking about it, but Clara Sheramy chirped eagerly.

"She's been telling us about her adventures getting out of Europe. It's terribly exciting. Do go on, Isabel. It happened all of a sudden—" she paused expectantly.

Isabel yielded. "Yes, it was quite terrifying. Europe—well, galvanized, that's the only word I can think of. You woke up one morning to find every placid village turned into a center of mobilization. There were bright pink bulletins tacked up everywhere proclaiming the war and army orders."

Eleanor accepted a glass of punch from Bob Purcell. "Go on," Bob said to Isabel. "Where were you? In Germany?"

"No, in Italy, by the grace of God. If I'd been in Germany I'd probably still be there. Italy was technically neutral, though it was nearly as bad there as in the other countries. The streets were full of foreigners who had been called to the armies, saying tearful goodbys and promising to meet again as soon as it was over—"

"How lucky you were neutral!" Clara exclaimed.

Isabel gave a little astonished laugh. "But I wasn't neutral, dear child. Legally I'm a German, *hoch der Kaiser* and all that."

"Are you really?" breathed Clara.

"Of course she is," said Violet.

Isabel held out her glass. "Will somebody fill this for me? I haven't drunk champagne punch like this since the last time I went to a ball in Vicksburg."

Eleanor nearly chuckled at the vision of Isabel at a ball in Vicksburg. But of course, she reminded herself, Isabel in those days had not been the Isabel she was seeing now. Three gentlemen sprang to replenish her glass, and smiling gracious-

117

ly at them all, Isabel acceded to the requests around her that she continue.

"I went to Rome," she told them, "and began storming the American consulate like the rest. There must have been hundreds of us there every day, Americans who had suddenly discovered we were yearning for apple pie and Mount Vernon and willing to pay anything we possessed for a berth in any ship heading west. You know how those countries adore American visitors, bowing and holding out their itching palms to us—we'd been used to that, and here we found ourselves reduced to the status of public nuisances."

She talks well, Eleanor reflected. With that hair and figure I'll wager she didn't have much trouble.

Isabel's next line might have been an answer to her thoughts. "Then luckily, just as I thought I was going to have to stay in Rome or be shipped back to Germany for the length of the war, who should turn up at the consulate but a most delightful man, Louisiana born like myself, from Baton Rouge, of all places. I'd forgotten how Louisiana looked, but did I remember then! Crayfish bisque, river-boats, cotton, sugarcane, levees, cornbread—they began to trip off my tongue as though I'd never been a mile from the river."

Overcome by the image of Isabel's transformation into a honey child, Eleanor laughed out loud. Isabel's eyes met hers, at first surprised, then she laughed too. "You're quite right," she said to Eleanor, and went on speaking to the group at large. "We became very good friends. He had a steamship ticket he couldn't use, as he was there on business and his firm had cabled him to stay in Rome. So I got out, bringing such luggage as I had with me."

"Where are the rest of your things?" asked Clara.

"In Berlin, darling. Want to try and get them?"

Behind Isabel a voice called, "Hello, everybody!"

They saw Kester, approaching with a general grin at the company. Eleanor watched him, wondering how it was that no matter what his circumstances Kester always looked like a fortunate youth immune from the common plagues of life, and as always she was proud of him.

"Can a man get a drink here?" he was asking. "Bob, you left a treatise on leprosy at my house. Well, for heaven's sake —Isabel Valcour!"

They had moved to make way for him. Isabel turned her glass by its stem as she glanced up. "Hello, Kester."

"It's good to see you." He looked her up and down. "But that's not Berlin. It's Paris. Or am I wrong?"

"No, Paris." She smiled, watching him. "Don't tell me I haven't changed a bit."

"Of course you've changed," said Kester.

"Seven years?" Isabel asked.

"No," said Kester. "The world."

"You haven't changed," said Isabel.

Kester accepted his drink from the waiter. Instead of answering her last observation he asked, "How did you get out?"

"Isabel has been telling us," Clara contributed eagerly. "It was awful at first, then there was one man who thought she was wonderful."

"Why Isabel," asked Kester, "how did you happen to be in a place where there was only one man?"

"Act your age," said Isabel.

The orchestra began to play again. After promising several other men to dance with them later, Isabel went off with Neal Sheramy. Eleanor saw no more of her until they were summoned to supper, when she found herself again in a group around Isabel, who was holding her plate on her knees and still answering questions, though by now she was abrupt, as though bored with being a cynosure Eleanor did not blame her, for their queries about the war sounded silly.

"Isabel, why did the Germans march through Belgium?"

"To get to France."

"But why did they have to go through Belgium?"

"Because it's the way. Look at the map."

"But the French didn't try to go through."

"The Germans got there first."

"Why did they burn Louvain?"

"I don't know."

"But don't you think it was dreadful?"

"Yes, it must have been."

"Have you ever seen the Kaiser?"

"Yes, I've seen him."

"Where?"

"In parades."

"Has he really got a crippled arm?"

"I didn't notice."

"Is it true Belgium had a secret alliance with England?"

"I don't know."

119

"But the papers say Count Bernstorff claims—"

"Maybe they did, then."

"What do you think about the atrocity stories?"

"Flapdoodle."

"You mean the Germans wouldn't do such things?"

"Those I know wouldn't."

"But the papers say—why do you think not?"

"I don't know much about armies," Isabel returned shortly "but I should imagine that invaders with a campaign on their hands would be too busy to get drunk and drag naked women through the street."

"Mhm—maybe, but it all sounds so dreadful. You're pro-German, aren't you?"

Eleanor interrupted. "Why shouldn't she be pro-German? This is a neutral country."

Isabel gave her an astonished look. "Thank you, Mrs. Larne," she said after a moment. "This country is so neutral," she added tersely, "that I've noticed the restaurants are having their bills of fare printed in English throughout, because sympathizers won't order dishes with names in French or German or Russian."

They laughed, and with an evident attempt to relieve Isabel of more catechizing Kester asked, "Did you see that England has put another tax on tea?"

But Cousin Sylvia was there, and she persisted, "Isabel, do you think England was right in going into the war?"

Isabel drew a short breath. "Listen, all of you," she exclaimed. "I haven't seen a German newspaper since last summer, I didn't read a paper once a week while I lived there, I don't know anything about the war. I'm glad I'm off their blasted continent and I'm going to build a monument to Christopher Columbus in my front yard."

She was evidently on the verge of exasperation. Though an hour ago she had seemed to be enjoying her homage, she was behaving now like a cross child, and Eleanor wondered if it were merely boredom or if something had happened meanwhile to irritate her. With his usual tact Kester was intervening. "Let's sing songs. Violet, if you've finished supper, will you play?"

Violet complied with alacrity, obviously glad to give Isabel a chance for relief. Isabel followed them to the piano, and in a moment the room was full of merry noise: Violet was pounding out tunes, the waiters were bringing dishes and drinks, a group who did not want to sing were arguing about John Bunny's talents as a comedian, another group discussed the cotton trouble and a third disputed whether a mint julep was better with or without a rum float, while over it all those around the piano were blissfully warbling,

The neutral in the front of me was cheering for the Kaiser,
The neutral in the back of me was arguing for France ...

Leaning against the piano, Eleanor smiled at Kester, wondering how anybody ever gave a party without him. She heard Sylvia's voice under the music.

"... but I feel it my *duty* to warn you Isabel, that after Belgium most people in this country feel very *indignant* about the Germans—"

"Oh shut up, Sylvia, for heaven's sake."

"Isabel!" cried Sylvia. She turned her back, insulted, and walked off, and Isabel looked after her with a sigh of relief. Eleanor caught her eye and smiled.

"Don't mind her," she advised Isabel sympathetically. "She's a goose."

Isabel smiled, though a little grimly. "For that I came back to God's country!" She made a gesture as though to push away the lot of them. "How long have you and Kester been married?" she asked.

"Two years last May."

"Have you any children?"

"Yes, a little girl. She had her first birthday last week."

"How nice," said Isabel.

"Come to see us," said Eleanor. "We won't ask you about the Belgian atrocities, I promise."

"Why, thank you," said Isabel.

Violet pulled her down to the piano stool. "Isabel, play for us. You always did it much better than I could."

"Haven't they got any war-songs in Europe that we haven't heard over here?" Clara inquired.

Isabel gave her a bloodthirsty look, but Kester interposed with a sort of quiet authority, as though he were host and responsible for keeping the party in good spirits. "Play a war-song, Isabel."

Isabel shrugged slightly, but after an instant's hesitation she smiled obediently as though she had recovered her temper and sang a British recruiting song that began,

Where will you look, sonny, where will you look
  When your children yet to be
Clamor to learn of the part you took
  In the war that kept men free?

She went from that into dance tunes, told them about having
seen the Castles dance in Paris, and between talking and
playing the piano she kept them amused until they returned to
the ballroom. Eleanor did not see her again, but on the way
home she told Kester she thought she might like Isabel. "She
was having an annoying time of it tonight," she said.

"She certainly was," said Kester. "I was glad you came out
with what you did about its being all right for her to be
pro-German. It was a sensible remark, whether she is or not."

"I suppose she is. After all, her husband was a German."

She heard Kester give a chuckle. "Where your treasure is,
my dear girl, there will your heart be also."

"Was her husband's fortune so tremendous?"

"Colossal," said Kester dryly.

"Sylvia was being more of a pest than usual," Eleanor
remarked.

"For all Sylvia's spotless ancestry," Kester returned with
amusement, "she's a shining example of what I'd call poor
white trash."

Eleanor laughed. "You know, I'm never quite sure what
that phrase means."

"Why, I'd say—" he paused a moment to consider—
"people who have no fineness, no delicacy, no knowledge that
some things are Caesar's and some things are God's."

Eleanor watched the shadowy trees move past, thinking of
Sylvia's officious nonsense and Isabel's plight and then of her
own. A war in which they had no concern was doing a lot of
unpleasant things to a lot of people who were not being
directly touched by it. Dancing so a few patriots could buy a
few bales seemed such a feeble way of countering the havoc.

She went to sleep thinking of cotton, and woke up thinking
of it, and as usual she resolved with her coffee that she would
go through one more day without talking about it. She was
glad Kester did not seem to have any problem on his mind but
that of making Cornelia say "Father." He had set his heart on
her saying it for her birthday, and with that a week behind
and Cornelia still inarticulate he had redoubled his efforts, but

122

though Eleanor tried to co-operate Cornelia got the impression that all this attention was a new device for her enjoyment and laughed and kicked and tapped their cheeks with her porridge-spoon in high glee.

"Father," Kester repeated.

"Guggle," said Cornelia.

"Father!" said Eleanor.

"Blub," said Cornelia happily.

"Do you suppose she's not very bright?" Kester asked.

Eleanor looked at her watch. "I don't know, but she's out of castile soap and a lot of other nursery things, and I've got to go to town to get them. You teach her."

She went out, in good spirits in spite of the melancholy weather. A baby was such fun. Kester wanted another, though Eleanor had insisted she would not have any more children until they could be provided with assurance of a roof to sleep under. Before she got to town her mind was again on the eternal torment of cotton. By the time she reached the drug store it was raining. Clara and Violet were at the soda fountain having a drink and complaining about the weather.

"You can't even say it's good for the crop," said Violet. "The crop is in."

"I'm so tired hearing about cotton!" Clara mourned. "Neal is so bothered."

—but at least Silverwood isn't mortgaged to its death, Eleanor thought as she greeted them.

"—and I just decided I wasn't going to worry about it," Clara announced with a triumphant lift of her chin, as if by so deciding she had reopened the market.

Eleanor declined their invitation to have a soda. There were times when Clara's pretty ineffectiveness was too much to be borne. But as she drove back Eleanor was almost envying her. It must be very convenient to be able just to decide not to worry and so make somebody else do it.

She put up the car and ran through the rain to the back door, shutting it so hastily that it caught and snagged her skirt. Eleanor gave an irritated exclamation and hurried upstairs. Her room was chilly. She must order a fire downstairs this evening, she thought as she examined the skirt. The snag was a bad one, and a darn here would be obvious. "I'm beginning to look like an object of charity," she told herself. "Oh Lord, clothes, Ardeith, even the drug store clerk looked at me as though he knew our account was months overdue, cotton—the war—damn everything!"

The telephone rang.

She was in no mood to talk to anybody. If the servants were about their business one of them would answer downstairs. The phone rang again. She looked at the snag in her skirt and paid no attention. It rang again. Eleanor got up unwillingly and sat on the bedstep. You had to answer the phone. Silly, it wasn't a matter of life and death once in a thousand rings, but there it was, and she had never seen anybody with sufficient detachment to ignore it. She picked up the receiver, and as she did so she heard Kester answering the phone downstairs.

"Mr. Larne?" said a woman's voice over the wire.

"Yes," said Kester.

"Kester, this is Isabel."

"Yes," he said again, "I thought so."

Eleanor wondered what she could want with him. She made a movement to hang up the receiver, but Isabel's next words arrested her.

"Don't say anything obvious from that end. But is your wife—what's her name?"

"Eleanor."

"Is Eleanor around?"

"No, she's gone to town."

"Good, Kester, I want to talk to you."

"Go ahead."

"Kester, please. I mean I want to see you. Won't you come over?"

There was an instant's pause. Kester said, "Frankly, I'd rather not."

Eleanor listened. She sat on the bedstep, the receiver pressed to her ear. Her heart had started to pound.

"Oh Kester," Isabel exclaimed, "don't behave like a provincial puritan!"

He laughed. "I've been called a good many names in my lifetime, but that one's really new. But honestly, honeybug, I don't see the point of it."

"That's the first time anybody has called me honeybug since I left Louisiana. I believe I like it. But seriously, I do want to see you. Shall I explain?"

"You can if you like. There's nobody here."

He sounded casual, uninterested. Perhaps, Eleanor thought, deliberately so.

"Really, Kester," Isabel said with a little rebuking laugh, "I didn't come home for your sake. But since I'm here, tell me, does Eleanor know anything about—well, about us?"

"No," said Kester.

"Thanks. I thought not, from her attitude last night. I'm glad, for wives sometimes exaggerate such things."

"Aren't you exaggerating it too?"

"I had all but forgotten it," said Isabel. "Don't you know me?"

"I know you by heart," said Kester.

"And you're laughing at me."

"On the contrary, I'm sorry for you. Though I admit it's funny to think of your bursting into tears before the Statue of Liberty."

"Who told you I did?"

"Nobody, but I know your instinct for self-dramatization. Now you're doing it again."

"What?"

"Feeling looked at."

"Oh, *am* I!" she exclaimed fervently. "You know, Kester, you had drifted into the back of my mind, and had become, frankly, quite unimportant. It didn't occur to me to ask whether or not you were going to be at that party last night. I'd heard you were married—the girls have been running in, ostensibly to welcome me home and actually to see how I look among the ruins—and they've told me what's been going on. But then, all of a sudden when I saw you, I was self-conscious as a schoolgirl."

Kester laughed a little. "So I observed."

"You weren't."

"Seven years is a long time," said Kester.

"You're never awkward anyway. Well, after I got home I began to think of something I hadn't realized before. I'm going to be here all this winter, maybe till the war's over, because practically everything I possess is tied up in Germany and at least in Dalroy I have the old house. If you and I were perfectly wise I suppose we'd avoid each other entirely. But we can't. We know all the same people and will get invited to all the same places, and we'll see each other unless one of us becomes a hermit. And I should like to talk to you just once, quietly and privately, before I have to see you again in a room full of people."

"Do you think it's necessary? As I said before, I'd rather not."

"You'd rather not face facts, Kester. I know you too. But please try to face this one. There was a time when I was an absolute idiot about you—"

"Were you?"

"Kester, are you actually as capable as that sounds of shutting a door on your own memory?"

Kester's answer was low and clear, as though he had put his lips close to the mouthpiece and was speaking so that nobody in the hall could have overheard him. "Isabel, you were never in love with anybody but the girl in the looking-glass. And don't try to tell me anything different."

"You can be very cruel, can't you?"

"Am I the only person who ever told you the truth?"

"Yes. That's why I liked you. However, that isn't quite the truth. But never mind. Let's get back to the present. Suppose, for instance—"

"Yes?"

"Well, suppose Eleanor—I rather like her. What sort of woman is she?"

"She's a grand person. You wouldn't understand her."

"Who is she?"

"She lived in New Orleans. Her name was Upjohn."

"Funny, I never heard of anybody in New Orleans named Upjohn."

"In a city that size there must be some people even you never heard of. Isabel, what *do* you want of me?"

"I want you to tell me what I should do in the event of some likely complication such as Eleanor's inviting me to dinner. Last night she asked me to come to Ardeith, and she may do it again. Should I accept, or should I invent a polite excuse? And if I keep inventing polite excuses, won't she wonder why and start asking questions? After all, Eleanor must realize that you and I have known each other ever since we were born, and wouldn't it be perfectly natural for her to make friends with me as she has with Violet and Clara?"

"Now that you mention it, I suppose so. I hadn't thought of it at all."

"Kester, you have the most delicious quality of not think-ing. It will keep you young forever. But some kind soul—not to hint at Sylvia—is certain to mention that you and I were frequent dancing partners the year before I was married, and we'll both be happier this winter if Eleanor leaves it at that and doesn't realize there was anything more between us than a kiss. And don't you really believe it would be sensible for us to talk it over like a pair of civilized adults?"

"I reckon it would," said Kester. "Only remember," he added clearly, "we're both civilized and adult."

"Then you will come over?"

"Necessarily now?"

"Yes, Kester. You see, that isn't all I want to ask you about. I need some advice. I'm in a lot of trouble. Maybe you don't know what it means to have one's life cut in two. I fled like a fugitive from justice—"

"Like a fugitive from what?"

"Don't be cruel to me now!" she pled helplessly. "I really can't stand it, Kester. I'm so lost and tired. I've been dumped into a strange country—nobody but you would understand that."

"Yes, I understand."

"Of course you do. In this whole stupid place you're the only friend I have who can talk to me sanely. Won't you put up with my dismay for just one afternoon? Kester, I need you! Please!"

"You poor girl," he exclaimed, "I didn't know it was as bad as that."

"Yes, it's as bad as that. Can't I talk to you?"

"Why yes, of course you can."

"Then you will come over?"

"Yes. But listen—don't hang up yet—just this once. That's all."

"That's all I'm asking. Thank you, Kester, thank you."

Eleanor listened for the click of the other two receivers before replacing her own on its hook. When she did so she found that she had been holding it so tight her fingers were stiff.

"And I was *nice* to that woman," she said aloud.

She was trembling with anger. To have stumbled across one of Kester's juvenile sins was not particularly startling, but Eleanor was amazed and wrathful that Isabel should be reaching now into the enclosure of his marriage and that Kester should not have realized at once what she was doing. "Won't you put up with my dismay for just one afternoon?

127

Kester, I need you!" Anybody but a fool, she thought, could have translated that into "Now that I've seen you again, Kester, I want you!"

Hearing the clatter of a horse's hoofs in the avenue she went to the window and saw Kester riding toward the gates. The rain had stopped, and evidently thinking she was still in town he had not looked for the car. With characteristic belief in his ability to eat his cake and have it too, Kester was going over to hear Isabel pour out her melodious troubles. Eleanor twisted the cord that held back the curtain. She was remembering, as she had remembered while she listened to their conversation: the evening she had promised to marry Kester, herself asking, "Were any of those girls—well, important?" and his answering, "There was a girl who was temporarily rather important. But it didn't last long. . . . I haven't seen her for years." She had never referred to that again. Kester had given her no reason to doubt that he loved her.

And she had no reason, she assured herself, to doubt it now. Whatever had taken place between him and Isabel, it had been over, at least as far as Kester was concerned. Recalling his half of the telephone conversation she realized that it had been considerably less than half. There was nothing he had said to which she herself could take exception, nothing but his yielding to Isabel's importunities that he visit her. But Isabel—Eleanor doubled her fists savagely.

She was thinking, Isabel and I are very different. I couldn't possibly have talked to anybody as Isabel talked to him. I can go after what I want but I can't sneak up on it. I'm forthright. She's subtle. That's what the women of Kester's world have always been—clever, soft, sinuous, never asking for exactly what they want, asking for something easy and then working around for what they want so cunningly that men think they're giving it of their own accord. And here I was thinking of Isabel as a cosmopolite from the European capitals. Why, she's really one of these magnolias that bloom all over the old Southern tradition and hide their tough stems under frail white petals. She was brought up to that and seven years in Europe couldn't make her forget it.

All right, Isabel. Be as lovely and helpless as you please. But I'm Kester's wife, not one of his conquests. And you'd better leave him alone.

Suddenly she was ashamed of the violence of her reaction. Crossing the room she looked at herself in the mirror. Behave yourself, Eleanor, she mentally ordered her reflection. You're not one of these delicate females so unsure of themselves that they quiver with jealousy every time their husbands look at a pretty woman. You can take care of yourself. Kester didn't tell you anything about Isabel because he didn't think it was important, but now that she's trying to make it important he'll tell you. Only he probably won't if after spending an afternoon with that exquisite creature he sees you with your hair looking like a rat-nest and a snag in your skirt.

Eleanor took a bath and got dressed. She braided her hair carefully—Kester liked her best with a coronet braid around her head—and she put on a dress of navy blue serge with a starched white Medici collar that stood flatteringly across the back of her neck. It had been one of his favorite dresses, bought last year just before her discovery that she could not afford to buy clothes, and this was the first time she had worn it this fall. Looking herself over in the glass, she was well pleased. Crisp tailored clothes suited her.

The first fire of the season danced in the parlor, and as Eleanor sat down with a magazine Dilcy brought in the baby, adorable in her pink rompers, with dark brown curls fluffed all over her head. Cornelia was playing with two rag dolls. Eleanor smiled lovingly as she watched her.

She was looking at the war-map in the *Literary Digest,* trying to find Pforzheim and Przemysl, when she heard the horse approaching. A moment later Kester, who never walked when he could run, was bounding up the front steps. She heard him in the hall telling one of the boys to put up the horse, and then he opened the parlor door. Eleanor looked up from the map.

"Hello, darling," she greeted him.

Cornelia, playing with dolls on the floor, looked up, and very clearly she said,

"Fader."

Eleanor sprang up as Kester swooped to grab the baby from the floor. Together they exclaimed,

"Did you hear her? She can talk!"

Kester threw Cornelia up toward the ceiling and caught her, laughing with ineffable joy, while Cornelia shouted and crowed, every now and then repeating her triumph by exclaiming, "Fader, fader, fader," aware somehow from her elders' reaction that this achievement was quite the most notable event of her lifetime. Holding her on one arm Kester flung open the door.

"Dilcy!" he called. "Come hear the little miss! She can talk!"

Dilcy came running, and so did Cameo and Mamie and Bessie and every other Negro in the house, and Cornelia said her one word proudly, and while she was being given her supper everybody hovered around to listen on the chance that she might say something else. While Eleanor and Kester were having their own supper they talked of nothing but how pleased they were, with Kester exclaiming he had had no idea it was such fun to be a father and he'd like to have about five more children, and Eleanor saying all right, only that would take a lot of patience. It was not until Kester had finally told her good night that Eleanor, standing in front of the bureau to brush her hair, remembered that he had not mentioned his visit to Isabel.

But after all, she asked, how could he? Though he might have meant to tell her this evening, Cornelia's looking up like that to say "Father" would have swept everything else out of his mind. And to be sure, Cornelia's first word would be Father. It wouldn't by any chance have been Mother.

"For pity's sake," Eleanor exclaimed to her reflection, "what's happening to me? Am I getting jealous of my own child? Nearly all girls love their fathers best. I do. I wonder if my mother minds? I ought to be glad Kester adores Cornelia so, when before she was born I dreaded telling him because he's so light-headed I thought he'd regard a baby as a nuisance. And I certainly can't blame her for loving him. Everybody loves him. I don't even blame that Valcour-Schimmelpfeng woman for wanting him—wouldn't any woman want him? He'll tell me about her tomorrow."

But the next day Kester did not speak of Isabel. He spent most of the morning reading articles about the cotton situation and told Eleanor that the governors of the Southern states, in conference in Washington, had decided to urge all planters to substitute food crops on at least half their usual cotton acreage next spring, so as to give the country a chance to use the surplus already on hand. That afternoon Neal Sheramy called for him and they set out for the movies on their weekly expedition to watch Pearl White tumble off cliffs in the role of the imperiled but indestructible Pauline. After they had gone Eleanor sat by her desk, drumming her fingers

130

on a ledger and wondering if even Kester's happy-go-lucky mind could hold the idea that she had no right to know if he was renewing an acquaintance with a woman who used to be his mistress.

During the two weeks that followed Kester said nothing about Isabel, and for the first time in her life Eleanor kept silence on a subject that vitally concerned her. Her perplexity began to take precedence over everything else in her thoughts. She did not know if Kester had visited Isabel again, but whenever he left the house alone she wondered if that was where he had gone. Kester remarked on her abstraction, blaming it on the cotton crisis, and was glad when Bob and Violet invited them to a party. She needed diversion, he told her, to buoy her spirits.

Eleanor went to the party, but she did not enjoy it. Isabel was there, in a black dress of exquisite lines that made Eleanor more than ever conscious of her own tired wardrobe. The conversation drifted to old times—birthday parties, Sunday School. "Remember how Miss Agatha Durham made us memorize the names of all the books of the Bible?" Violet asked.

"Kester won the prize," said Bob.

"A silk bookmark with a motto embroidered on it," said Kester, and they all laughed.

"I can remember you now," Isabel said to him, "in your white linen suit and your hair very neatly parted, standing up piously to recite the Minor Prophets—" she folded her hands and cast her eyes toward the ceiling—"Hosea, Joel, Amos, Obadiah, Jonah, Micah, Nahum, Habakkuk, Zephaniah, Haggai, Zechariah, Malachi."

"How on earth do you remember them?" Kester asked.

"Miss Agatha's training," she returned. "Or maybe because you looked so cute."

They laughed again, and somebody mentioned the games they used to play on the levee behind the cottonfields. The talk had the gay, tender quality of talk among grownups investing their childhood memories with luster, and even if Isabel had not been there Eleanor would have felt out of it, because she had no childhood memories to share with them. Isabel sat at the piano. Turning to the keyboard she began to pick out a tune. "Remember this? 'Chickama, chickama, craney crow—' "

At length, when they told the others good night, Kester was

131

in high spirits. "Wasn't that a grand party?" he asked as they started home.

"I haven't anything to talk about to those people," said Eleanor.

"Silly. They all like you."

Watching the trees move past the car, Eleanor wondered if Kester's friends had accepted her because they liked her or because they liked Kester. She warned herself that she was getting too introspective for her own good. By the time they reached Ardeith she had decided that trustful bravery might have been all right for any other woman of Kester's circle but it was too remote from her own nature for her to keep it up any longer. "Are you sleepy?" she asked Kester as they went up the stairs.

"No, why?"

"Come in here," said Eleanor, opening the door of her room. "I want to ask you something."

Kester followed her in and sat down. "You look mighty grave, honeybug," he remarked as he lit a cigarette. "What's the trouble?"

The last time she had heard him call anybody honeybug was when he said it to Isabel on the phone. Eleanor sat down on the bedstep and looked up at him.

"Kester, I wish you'd tell me about Isabel Valcour."

He gave her a puzzled frown. After a moment's pause he asked, "What nonsense has somebody been talking to you?"

"Nobody has said anything. You don't think I discuss my private life with a whole lot of people!"

"No," he returned smiling, "I can't imagine your doing that. What do you want me to tell you?"

Eleanor looked down at her hands. They were like the rest of her, lean, hard-muscled, capable. She raised her eyes again to Kester.

"I'm rather ashamed of myself," she said frankly, "for not asking you about this before. But I thought you'd tell me of your own accord. And I'm rather ashamed of you for not doing it. You and Isabel had an affair before she was married, didn't you?—and the day after we met her at the Hunt Club dance she called you up and reminded you of it and asked you to come to see her. And you went."

Kester tossed his cigarette into the fireplace and rested his chin on his hand. He regarded her with a certain regretful surprise, but he did not look guilty.

132

"So that's what's been the matter with you lately," he said.

"Yes. Don't you think you should have told me?"

"I suppose so. But I'd like to know," he added coolly, "what sort of detective work you've been doing."

"I heard her talk to you that day. I was at this phone here."

He gave a low whistle. "And you," he said, "are the most honest person I've ever known."

"Good heavens above, Kester! I didn't intend to listen. But when I heard her say 'Is your wife around?' how in the name of human nature could I have helped it?"

"You couldn't have, evidently. But I wish you'd asked me about it then, instead of imagining awful debaucheries."

"I thought you'd tell me. When you didn't—anyway, tell me now. How many times have you seen her—I mean alone —and what have you talked about?"

He returned without hesitation, "I've had exactly three private conversations with Isabel since she came home. I've sat watching her pace the floor, listened while she told me she couldn't stand being prisoned in this place, and given her a shoulder to cry on. That's all."

"But what on earth is the matter with her?"

Kester answered as though trying to explain simple facts to an obtuse listener. "Eleanor, Isabel is in the status of an alien tourist in the house where she was born. She wants to get back her citizenship. She's having to learn how to live on an income that wouldn't have bought her slippers last year. She's trying to get adjusted to a life that has become strange to her, and she's discouraged and unhappy."

"Does she think she's the only person whose habits have been upset by the war?" Eleanor asked contemptuously.

He smiled a little. "Yes, Eleanor, she does. You don't know Isabel."

"It's evident you do. How can you waste time coddling such a fool?"

"All I've tried to be is a friend, honey. It seems to do her good to talk to me."

"I don't doubt it. If she needs advice, why doesn't she get a lawyer?"

"I've told her to get one. She's going to."

"I wonder," said Eleanor.

He looked at her keenly. "Just what do you mean by that?"

She answered with another query. "Kester, in those three visits you've made to her, have you ever kissed her?"

133

"Certainly I've kissed her," he answered. "That first afternoon, when she broke down and cried. As her uncle might have kissed her."

"Her uncle," said Eleanor. "That's what you think. That's what she wants you to think. You have a perfectly delightful time hearing her plead that she couldn't live without your counsel. That's all she'll say to you yet. But she wants you back where she had you."

Kester took another cigarette. "Eleanor, Isabel is no dolt. She knows I'm in love with you."

"That's why she's being artful," Eleanor insisted. "Tell me, Kester, how much did she ever mean to you?"

He shrugged. "For about three months I was infatuated. That was seven years ago. I didn't have any illusions about her, but she was the loveliest creature I had ever seen."

"I suppose she still is."

He did not contradict her.

"Can't you see she's trying to get you back as her lover?" Eleanor persisted. "You're so very attractive, probably more so now than when she saw you last. Oh Kester, when a woman lets go of a man it's usually with the feeling that she can pick him up again if she happens to want him. As long as that woman was running around Europe with everything she wanted and men tumbling down before her, she didn't think much about you, but now that she's stranded here she has a chance to see again how charming you are and she's sorry she didn't hold on to you. She won't start making love to you right away, she's too wise, but she's playing to get you back—oh, can't you see it?"

At that Kester laughed. He said, "My darling, you have more imagination than I thought."

"She asked you to come to see her just once," Eleanor said inexorably. "You've seen her three times."

"Eleanor, if you knew how unimportant all this is!" he exclaimed. "Listen. If you're really troubled—you've no reason to be, I'd have told you all this if I'd known you were worrying about it, and I suppose I should have told you anyway—but if you're troubled, I won't see Isabel again. Is that what you want?"

She nodded.

"All right." He came over and kissed her. "I won't see her except when we happen to be thrown together at other people's houses, like tonight."

"Thank you." Eleanor took his hand. "That's all I wanted." She drew him down to sit on the bedstep by her. "Kester, does anybody know about what happened between you two a long time ago?"

"No."

"I'm glad of that. It makes things simpler for me. I'd like to hear what did happen."

"I can't tell you without being very unchivalrous, I'm afraid. However—"

"Go on," said Eleanor.

She had such a sense of relief that she felt light-hearted. Kester was reckless, he never thought ahead of the present, but he loved her and would do anything to make her happy; and Eleanor wondered why she had not had sense enough to talk this over with him earlier instead of submitting herself to the most uncomfortable fortnight of her marriage.

Chapter Seven

THE VALCOURS were Louisiana French, descendants of a marriage made in the year 1794 between the Widow Gervaise Purcell, née Durand, native of New Orleans, and Louis Valcour, bachelor from the same town. Nearly a hundred years later one of their posterity, Mr. Pierre Valcour, became captivated late in life by a golden beauty from Memphis, who survived their marriage long enough to bequeath him a small income based on a cotton comeback after the Civil War, and a daughter whom the cross-breeding between the Latin and Anglo-Saxon strains had endowed with provocative charm. Mr. Valcour was not dubious about how to dispose of either legacy. You enjoyed money and you sent beautiful daughters to schools distinguished for their success in turning out well-bred young ladies.

At the age of eighteen Isabel graduated. She was gentle, gracile and soft-voiced, with a lovely face, golden hair a yard long and large, innocent eyes.

But under its abundance of waves and velvet fillets Isabel's head contained a brain that was clever, calculating and

135

productive of ambition. Convinced that a girl's life was determined by the kind of marriage she made, Isabel had channeled all her talents toward making a very superior marriage indeed. Her upbringing had been exactly what she needed. She could dance beautifully, listen ardently, tinkle tunes on the piano, and dress in such a fashion as to make everybody look in admiration when she entered a room. Her teachers had taught her French and English, so that she read both with equal ease; that they had failed to convince her of the desirability of reading anything in either language was the fault not of her teachers but of Isabel, who privately disdained them, for if they had known as much as she intended to know they would not have had to teach school for a living. They were obviously not as wise as she, and they were downright simpletons compared to what she intended to become.

Isabel graduated in a fluffy white dress with a blue sash and everybody said she looked quite like an angel. This remark gave Isabel some amusement, for did not the Bible say that among the angels there was neither marriage nor giving in marriage? But she went docilely home with her gray-haired father, made her debut and attended the parties, assiduously studying her chosen vocation. For while she had no intention of spending her life as a giver of teas and fondler of babies in a river town, the young gentlemen she met in Dalroy were typical specimens of manhood and what she learned from them now could doubtless be applied advantageously as the horizon of her opportunities widened.

She learned that while her face and figure were invaluable assets, looks were not sufficient working capital; for the best results one must also use one's mind. Recalling that somewhere in her schoolbooks she had seen a line about speech being given to man to conceal his thoughts, she reflected very soon that cleverness was given to woman to conceal her intellect: simply, that if a girl wished to captivate young gentlemen the best use she could make of her intelligence would be to employ it in devising means to prevent their suspecting that she had any. For Isabel to pose as less gifted than some of the young beaus she met that winter required mental agility of a very high order. But she did it, walking through the first weeks of the social season in a flutter of helpless loveliness.

Then, gradually, she became wiser. She discovered that the

more brilliant of her male acquaintances did not admire such an utterly brainless beauty as she was pretending to be. She observed then that the cleverer a man was, the more he liked a clever woman, his only requirement being that she be just a trifle less clever than himself; he wanted her to look up to him, but the higher the pinnacle on which she could convince him she must stand in order to be just beneath him, the more he would be flattered by her adoration. And while she had not yet come across a young gentleman whom she sincerely considered wiser than herself, none of them suspected it.

Before Christmas Isabel was rewarded by becoming the most popular girl in town. Her date-book had no blank pages. When a cotillion was given her card was full weeks in advance, with many of the dances split to make room for all her admirers. Her room was piled with trophies consisting of flowers, chocolates, and handsomely bound copies of the *Rubáiyát of Omar Khayyám*. She had declined three proposals of marriage.

All these she looked upon as a candidate for the Legion of Honor might have regarded preliminary medals. Very gratifying, they proved she was on the right path, but this was still far short of her goal, and she moved carefully toward the extremely desirable man somewhere ahead of her. Popular as she was, she kept her reputation immaculate. Granting kisses, permitting too close an embrace in a waltz, staying out late without a chaperone—from these one gained nothing. Anything that commands a high price, she knew, does so because it is hard to get.

In fact, she had long since made up her mind to be so hard to get that nobody in her present surroundings could get her. Some relatives of her mother's lived in New York, and they had invited Isabel to spend the next winter with them. They were very well-to-do, and Isabel expected them to show her a whiter harvest. She was not impatient; she was young, and she had already learned enough to convince her that there must be a great deal more to be learned.

Then Kester Larne, having graduated from Tulane, came home.

In her plans, Isabel had not given Kester Larne five minutes' thought. She and Kester and his brother and sister had played together as children, but school had divided their paths and she had hardly seen Kester for several years. Ardeith was a run-down plantation, riddled with debt and sharecroppers by Kester's extravagant father, and Kester himself was a thoughtless young man who had narrowly missed being expelled from college for his escapades. He certainly had no place on the map of her destiny.

But here was Kester, of course invited to all the parties, here was Kester calling to ask for dances at the cotillions—to which she casually said yes, for he was a handsome young fellow of good family and she had set out to bewitch him as a matter of course—and then, suddenly, here was Kester, who though he might be an idle youth was the most fascinating idler she had ever beheld, not only good to look at and a winged-heeled dancer, but the only man she had ever seen who gave her the impression of knowing more about women than she knew about men.

As they began to waltz one evening, Isabel in a cloud of pale blue tulle, Kester asked abruptly, "You're too young to wear black, aren't you?"

"Why?" asked Isabel.

"You're marvelous as you are, Miss Isabel," he answered demurely, "but if you wore black satin your technique would be irresistible."

Isabel felt herself floundering, not sure whether or not he meant to be as horrid as he sounded. He was smiling very slightly, a smile that was caressing and almost tender, but his eyes were on her in a fashion that made her feel like an arithmetic problem being reduced to its simplest terms. "I don't know what you're talking about," she said.

"Oh yes you do," Kester retorted. "However, I'm already fascinated, so you can relax now."

She stopped dancing. "I'll thank you to take me back to my chaperone," she exclaimed.

As though he had not heard her, Kester exclaimed in a voice of inspiration, "I have it—black won't do yet, but have you ever tried a really violent blue? I shouldn't put many blondes into bright colors, but in a regal blue you'd be gorgeous, like a heathen idol."

Isabel was so much interested that she forgot she was angry and let him lead her to the side of the room and sit down by her while the others went on dancing. He was still talking.

"Those pale colors you wear make you too remote. You look like Elaine, and you ought to look like Francesca."

"Who was Francesca?" she asked.

"A lady who went to hell for love," said Kester. "You'd

138

never do that, would you?—but you ought to look as if you were willing to."

"Really!" she exclaimed, and she felt uncomfortable.

"Yes, really. You've mistaken your type, Miss Isabel. You're lovely, as I suppose you've been told a thousand times, but don't go too far with being the daughter of a hundred earls—"

"Why not?"

"Oh, Miss Isabel, don't tell me you've already forgotten your Tennyson, and you not a year removed from a young ladies' academy."

"But I have," she admitted easily, this time on more familiar ground. "I'm not a bit clever with books."

Kester's eyes, brown and frosty as a mint julep, looked upon her keenly, and his mouth quivered at the corners. "You're too charming to need that approach, Miss Isabel."

Isabel stood up. Now she really was angry. "Thank you. I know exactly what you mean. The line is, 'The daughter of a hundred earls, you are not one to be desired.' Now will you please take me back to my Aunt Agnes?"

Kester, who had risen when she did, laughed approvingly. "That's much better. Now I like you. Please, ma'am, won't you finish this dance with me?"

Later Isabel thought that if she had been strong-minded enough to say no, her whole life might have been different. But she laughed too, and consented. She and Kester were together that evening as much as her other engagements would permit, and as he was finally delivering her to her Aunt Agnes to be taken home he said in a low voice, "Thank you for a delightful time. And will you try a startling blue gown?"

Isabel smiled frankly. "Yes. But I really don't know who Francesca was."

"I'll send you a book about her tomorrow morning," Kester promised. He bent his head nearer lest the chaperones hear him. "By the way, did I tell you you're the most devastatingly beautiful woman I ever saw?"

The next day, instead of the pale sweetheart roses he should correctly have sent, there arrived a magnificent copy of the *Inferno* of Dante, with a length of royal blue ribbon marking the place where she read about the lovers whose ardor Dante had thought should be chilled for all eternity by the blowing mists of the pit. The book also contained a note from Kester saying he would be calling that afternoon to take

139

her for a drive. He didn't ask if it would be convenient, and she decided that since he was so sure of himself it would be good for him if when he called she sent a servant to say she was out because of a previous engagement, but when he arrived she was ready and waiting.

None of her other admirers would have sent her a story about a lady who indulged in unhallowed love, but somehow it seemed all right for Kester to do so. For in the weeks that followed Kester coolly refused to deal with her according to the accepted system of formalities that prevented a young gentleman and a young lady from getting to know anything about each other. He treated her like a reasonable individual, which for Isabel was a new and fascinating experience. From seeing each other frequently they soon reached the place where they were seeing each other every day.

Isabel knew she was being reckless. If she kept this up everybody would be taking it for granted that she and Kester were engaged. They were not engaged; he had not mentioned it, and she had no intention of accepting him if he should. Kester had nothing of what she intended to have in a husband, but he was so delightful, so interesting to talk to, so pleasant to be with—and soon, Isabel, who was not given to praying, began to plead in the solitary hours of the night, "Oh Lord, please don't let me fall in love with Kester Larne."

She could feel it happening. She could feel that Kester, without any effort on his part, was knocking down the castles of her dreams. Much more of this and she would not be able to leave him in search of that brilliant marriage on which she had set her ambition. Over and over she resolved to be out the next time he called, and over and over her resolution went down at the sound of his footsteps on the porch. And finally, when one evening in her own parlor she let him kiss her, it first lifted her to ecstasy and then thrust her into a farsighted terror. She rushed away from him, and upstairs in her own room she stood trembling, and thought, "Those foolish women, those women I've laughed at, who have given up their lives for a short bright passion—this is what conquers them. This is love. Oh, Lord God in heaven, don't let me give in to it! To spend my life on an old plantation, wearing stockings silk halfway up and embroidering a new shirtwaist to freshen up last year's suit and pouring coffee for the ladies' guild of the church—me, Isabel Valcour, with real golden hair a yard long and the whole world in front of me! I can't. To be that

140

kind of a fool because Kester Larne kissed me. But isn't it strange, I never knew it before, this is what conquers them."

She was so apprehensive that an unexpected invitation from her New York relatives to spend a few weeks at their summer place in Westchester was like a miraculous answer to prayer. She fled from Kester. He wrote her a jolly letter, saying he hoped she was having a fine vacation and he was lonesome without her, but not including a single ardent line. This increased Isabel's determination to be done with him, for though she could not rid her thoughts of Kester neither could she rid herself of the conviction that she cared a good deal more for him than he did for her. She did not answer his letter.

Isabel's aunt and uncle were delighted with her. Not having seen her since she was a little girl, they were unprepared for the beautiful young woman she had become. At their Westchester house Isabel met numerous young men, and was an immediate success. Here, away from Kester, she began to look around with her customary shrewdness. Among the guests was a young German named Schimmelpfeng who was touring America and had been invited to her uncle's country house because her uncle's export firm sold raw cotton to the textile company owned by the German's father.

Aside from his baffling name young Schimmelpfeng was not unacceptable, but neither was he exciting. He was a negative sort of person, the sort of whom one says, "Haven't I met that fellow somewhere?" and then discovers one has conversed with him a dozen times. But he evidently admired Isabel, and was so assiduous in his attentions that she began to ask questions about him. Why, didn't she, her uncle asked, know who the Schimmelpfengs were? No, she didn't. But Schimmelpfeng dyes, Schimmelpfeng textiles, in short, Schimmelpfeng millions? No, said Isabel, she hadn't known. What else? Why, not only a fine old family, but a most desirable business connection for her uncle. They were happy that she had been so beautifully courteous to him.

Were they really, said Isabel. That evening there was dancing, and though Herr Schimmelpfeng was a trifle heavy-footed, Isabel's beautiful courtesy became as warm as was congruous with what she believed a Continental millionaire's ideas of young ladyhood to be. By midnight it was evident that Herr Schimmelpfeng was enchanted with the beautiful American. In his thick English he regretted that she was returning to the South so soon, and was delighted when she told him she planned to come to New York in November and spend the winter with her aunt. Did she indeed? Herr Schimmelpfeng had planned to cross the great West this fall and have a look at the magical California, but if Miss Valcour was certain she was coming to New York in November—?

Miss Valcour lowered her sweet hazel eyes demurely.

Again in her own room she sat down to think. Herr Schimmelpfeng was not so very young. He was in his thirties and looked older, a serious business man whose property, you might be sure, would at his death be worth double what it had been at his birth. Not like Kester, who would spend everything he owned and run up as many debts as he could persuade the tradesmen to allow him. Not like Kester, oh no, not like Kester with his sparkling conversation, his eternal good humor, his beautiful sunburnt body, his air of timeless and indestructible youth. Again Isabel remembered Kester's arms around her, and the morning was turning red when she finally dropped off to sleep after a night of balancing Kester's charm against Schimmelpfeng's millions.

Shortly afterward, it was time to go home. She said goodby to Schimmelpfeng, who every morning for a week had sent her a gardenia and now sent another for her to wear when she took the train. But as the train pulled into Dalroy, there with his carriage was Kester, like a light in the dusty little depot. Kester was glad to have her back. The town had been dull without her, and he had pestered her father to find out when she was coming home. "Now tell me about Westchester," he urged. "And your conquests."

"Conquests?" she echoed. Then, slyly, "You won't be jealous?"

"Certainly not. I like knowing my best girl has been a success. I don't want something nobody else wants."

Isabel prattled, telling him about everything but Herr Schimmelpfeng. They sat down in her parlor with coffee and biscuits and were talking merrily when there was a noise outside and up rumbled a mule-drawn truck. A boy came to the door asking for Miss Valcour. He bore a telegram from Herr Schimmelpfeng, and behind him, there by the front steps, stood the truck piled to overflowing with gardenias.

Having sent her a gardenia every morning in Westchester, Herr Schimmelpfeng had thought that upon her return to Louisiana he would demonstrate his regard by increasing the gesture, so he had sent the Dalroy florist twenty dollars with orders to deliver gardenias to Miss Valcour upon her arrival. And thinking he was some wag who meant it as a joke, the florist had taken him at his word. As this was midsummer and gardenias were scenting the air of the country lanes throughout Louisiana, the florist simply sent several little darkies out to gather them, piled the result into a truck, and gave orders that they were to be dumped on Isabel's front porch.

By the time Kester and Isabel reached the doorway the flowers were all over the floor of the porch and two Negro boys, agrin with glee, were dropping armfuls more on top of them. The consequence was rather horrible. For while the odor of one gardenia is pleasant the odor of a wagon load of gardenias is enough to make one quite sick.

Kester gave the Negroes a stare of amazement and then looked at Isabel. She had turned scarlet. He exclaimed, "May I see?" and without waiting for permission glanced over her shoulder at what he thought was going to be a teasing telegram. He read, "A very small tribute to convey a very great admiration. Hermann Schimmelpfeng."

Looking again from Isabel's red face to the gardenias, Kester gave a war-whoop. He laughed and laughed, he shouted, he all but rolled among the flowers. She was ordering, "You boys take those things away at once! Do you hear me?" and meanwhile Kester leaned against the wall, weak with laughter. And still came the gardenias.

Old Mr. Valcour appeared, shouting that he had smelt a nauseating smell upstairs in his room and what on earth did this mean? Isabel tried to explain, stammered, and Mr. Valcour demanded of Kester, "Please tell me, sir, are you responsible for this insulting performance? There's no excuse for this but a funeral over a stale nigger corpse!"

Between explosions of mirth Kester replied, "One of Miss Isabel's Northern admirers, sir. Gardenias don't grow in ditches up there."

Mr. Valcour gave the florist's boys five dollars apiece to remove the gardenias, ordered that the porch be scrubbed with strong soap, and retired upstairs still thundering his wrath. Kester had drawn Isabel back into the parlor, where the odor followed them through the open windows, persistent as the smell of moth balls. He was demanding to know who on earth was named Hermann Schimmelpfeng.

"He's a German," said Isabel. "And I think you're horrid."

143

"Oh, Herr Schimmelpfeng," Kester apostrophized, "the fragrance of your memory will be in the curtains for days. Isabel, my dear Isabel, isn't it enough for you to conquer every American you see without starting on Germany? Who is this fellow?"

"He is a very nice young man," said Isabel, "and he has millions of dollars."

She felt like a fool. Kester betrayed no jealousy. He merely thought Herr Schimmelpfeng ridiculous. And so, against her will, did Isabel. At last Kester asked if she would play tennis tomorrow afternoon. She did not like athletics, but glad to promise anything that would keep the conversation away from gardenias Isabel said yes.

For the rest of the summer, the contrast between Kester and Hermann Schimmelpfeng became clearer every day. Kester was merry, adorable, alluring. Kester was almost irresistible. Isabel felt that she was no longer falling in love, she had fallen in love beyond argument. Calling herself several kinds of a goose she was nevertheless unable to say no whenever Kester asked for a date.

She was frightened. Her life was dropping to pieces and she felt unable to resist. September that year was sultry, and the doctor advised Mr. Valcour to go to the Virginia Springs until cooler weather. Isabel, who had never felt or manifested much filial attachment, suddenly became a model daughter. Let her father go to a watering-place alone? Certainly not. She would go with him. She would read to him and bring him drinks of the healing waters. Though old Mr. Valcour, who was a gay soul and perfectly capable of taking care of himself, intimated that she would be a useless impediment to his holiday, Isabel turned deaf and accompanied him. Never dreaming that Isabel was fleeing to the springs as a drunkard desirous of reform would flee to a spot where liquor was unobtainable, Mr. Valcour was puzzled and somewhat annoyed by this excess of devotion. But Isabel adamantly established herself in the hotel among the invalids and elderly vacationers, thanking heaven that there were now five states between herself and Kester Larne.

She forgot that the trains were public conveyances. They had not been at the springs a week before Kester appeared, remarking that he thought the waters might be good for him too. Mr. Valcour mildly observed how nice it was for Isabel to have a youthful companion, and turned in for his nap.

Isabel was half joyful and half angry. It was flattering to be pursued for such a distance by the most attractive man she knew, but it was dreadful to think that he was destroying her future. But there was Kester, who beckoned her by merely being alive. Kester asked her to marry him.

Isabel twisted her hands together and said, "I don't know. Please give me time to think, Kester!"

Instead of persisting with telling her how lovely she was and how he couldn't live without her Kester stood up and looked down at her a moment, and then said coolly,

"Americans don't marry foreigners for their money, Isabel. It's the other way around."

She sprang up furiously. "What do you—"

Kester said, "It's bad form, honey, it might start international complications."

Then, before she could bring out an angry retort Kester had his arms around her and his mouth on hers, and Isabel felt that in spite of herself the battle was over. After a long time she heard him whisper, "How many millions would you take for this, Isabel?"

At last she made herself let him go. But she hardly slept that night, for though her emotions were convinced her mind was not.

But the next day and the next evening Kester was still there.

The product of a generation that set a mystical value on virginity, Isabel knew it would wreck her fortunes if her reputation became smirched. But she was surrounded by a community of elderly hypochondriacs interested in nothing but their own ailments. Her father was paying her not the slightest attention. She and Kester might almost have been on an island. By evening she had decided that if she could not have a life-time's happiness she would at least have what she could. Her conscience, being virtually non-existent, gave her no qualms; the only question that disturbed her was whether or not she would be caught up with, and Kester was discreet.

For several weeks she was divinely happy. Then she and Kester began to quarrel.

He was courtly and full of poetic gallantries, but Isabel was sure that secretly he despised her. Whatever his faults, Kester was not mercenary. He regarded life as a blessed gift to be enjoyed, but he would not have enjoyed selling his personal integrity. He knew Isabel loved him; her tumbling into his

145

arms because she loved him Kester regarded as the most natural and delightful occurrence in the world, but he regarded her intention of marrying a millionaire for no reason except that he was a millionaire as calculated prostitution. She suspected that he felt an amused sense of triumph when he thought of Schimmelpfeng, and chuckled privately at the knowledge that the excellent German would not be getting all he was paying for.

Isabel could stand anything but being laughed at. There came to her the ego-crashing suspicion that instead of considering her with awe like other men Kester had been laughing at her since the first evening they had danced together. In this frame of mind she could hardly be sweet-tempered. She and Kester quarreled about every subject except the one she was constantly thinking of. Finally, in exasperation, Kester packed his grips and went back to Dalroy.

Isabel came home a week later, staying just long enough to get her clothes in order before going to New York. She saw Kester only once. He was riding horseback through town, and seeing her come out of a shop he dismounted and went over to speak to her. He only said, "I didn't know you were home. I just wanted to tell you I'm frightfully sorry for losing my temper when you criticized my tennis stroke."

She had forgotten that had been the start of their last quarrel. Wondering if he were merely being polite, Isabel answered, "I was pretty bad-mannered myself. I'm sorry too."

He smiled. "When are you leaving for New York?"

"Tomorrow."

"I hope you have a pleasant trip," said Kester.

"Thank you," said Isabel.

He mounted again, and as she watched him ride off Isabel saw him glance back at her regretfully, and she thought, "I believe he doesn't want me to go. If I told him I'd given up the Schimmelpfeng idea I believe he'd marry me still."

But she threw the idea out of her mind and went to New York. The next time her friends at home heard of her was when her picture appeared in the society section of the New Orleans *Picayune*, with the caption, "Miss Isabel Valcour, daughter of Mr. Pierre Valcour of Dalroy, whose engagement to Mr. Hermann Schimmelpfeng of Berlin, Germany, is announced today by her father. The wedding is expected to take place in the early spring."

Isabel came home to get ready, and in Dalroy there was

tremendous flurry about her brilliant marriage. Several of her girl friends observed, "We were so surprised, you know we'd always had an idea you were going to marry Kester Larne." At such remarks Isabel laughed a little and answered, "Why for pity's sake, I never thought of such a thing! And I'm sure Kester never did." The girls gave her showers, the older ladies gave parties in her honor, everybody began sending her berry spoons and salad bowls that would cost more than they were worth to transport to Berlin, and the girls and their mammas were alike envious, wondering why heaven should equip some people with angelic faces and golden hair and the chance to meet millionaires from foreign parts. Herr Schimmelpfeng and his brother and his mother were all coming to Dalroy for the wedding, and Violet Purcell asked if Herr Schimmelpfeng traveled with a Man. "Because you can all entertain Mr. What's-his-name if you want to, but as for me, I'm going to entertain the Man. I've seen a millionaire," she said, "but I've never seen a Man."

Kester's sister Alice insisted on giving Isabel a boudoir shower. Unable to escape it, Isabel had to go play the guest of honor at Ardeith, where the parlor was strewn with bits of lingerie the girls had embroidered for her trousseau. Gentlemen had been invited to come in for the evening, and after the maidenly flutter of putting away the garments so they would not immodestly greet the gaze of the masculine guests, there was dancing. Of course Kester was there.

As brother of the hostess Kester could hardly avoid asking the guest of honor to dance, and as guest of honor Isabel could hardly refuse. They waltzed. Kester was impeccably courteous. But as she felt his arm around her waist Isabel thought that even now she might weaken if he gave her a chance to do so. She thought how cruel fate had been in giving her two chances to dispose of her future and so arranging circumstances that no matter which of the two she took she would spend her life wishing she had chosen the other. They had been dancing several minutes in silence when Kester said, "That ribbon around your hair is just the right color. Remember the time I told you to wear that shade of violent blue?"

"Yes," said Isabel.

She bit her lip, afraid she was going to cry out, "Oh Kester, don't let me go!" She thought of all she would have with her German marriage: a gorgeous house in Berlin, holidays on the

Riviera, wealth, splendor, pleasure; for she knew Schimmel-pfeng well enough to know he considered possession of her such a miracle he would give her anything his money could buy. She looked up at Kester, and down again, and in spite of herself she asked,

"Kester—tell me—if I should break my engagement now—would you ask me again to marry you?"

He answered, "I honestly don't know, Isabel. So maybe you'd better not risk it."

"You needn't worry," she retorted. "I shan't."

They did not speak again till the dance was over and the couples were breaking up, when in the hearing of half a dozen others Kester said gallantly, "Thank you for a delightful waltz, Miss Isabel. May I take this opportunity of wishing you happiness?"

"Thank you," said Isabel.

Those were the last words they were destined to exchange until she came home from Germany at the outbreak of the war.

Chapter Eight

1

ELEANOR'S OPINION of Isabel was scornful and briefly expressed.

"And you asked her to marry you! You're a very fortunate man, Kester Larne. All right, since you've promised to ignore her I'll do the same."

"Good," said Kester. "Then it's quits all around?"

"Quits," said Eleanor.

Kester gave her a humorously grateful smile.

Eleanor pushed Isabel into a back pigeonhole of her mind, telling herself that now she could be calm, but she still found no peace. For without the problem of Isabel to occupy them her thoughts leaped back to the torment of cotton. The exchanges reopened on the sixteenth of November, and cotton was salable at five cents a pound.

At such a price Kester and Eleanor could not have repaid what it had cost to grow the cotton, to say nothing of financing the plantation for another crop. They held the cotton desperately. The newspapers were trying to bolster the courage of the planters by reminding them that Europe needed cotton duck for tents and cotton cloth for uniforms, and that the rising cost of living in the United States would force the people to buy more cotton clothes instead of silk and wool, so that the crop would eventually be disposed of at a reasonable price. But they urged that very little cotton be planted in the spring, and the Secretary of Agriculture in Washington publicly demanded that bankers and merchants refuse to extend credit to any planter who did not first promise a sharp reduction in his cotton acreage.

Kester and Eleanor spent the winter studying the possibilities of food crops. Before the Civil War part of Ardeith had been planted in sugarcane, and another part in oranges, but today most cane was grown west of the river and the land nearer the Gulf had been found more suitable for orange trees. "Rice?" Eleanor suggested hopefully. Kester told her they would have to build siphons to bring the water across the levee to flood the fields, and import laborers who knew how to grow rice. "Nobody up here knows rice any more," he said. "It's grown in southwest Louisiana. We might try corn, but the country had a bumper corn crop last year and half the cotton planters are already planning to put in corn next spring."

One day in January Sylvia came in to ask for a subscription to the Belgian Relief Fund. Eleanor told her curtly it was all she could do this winter to feed her own child, let alone feeding the Belgians. If she wouldn't help the Belgians, Sylvia persisted, would she at least promise that when she served gelatine desserts she would insist on getting Hooper's gelatine? "You see, dear, they have a yellow label on one side of the box," she explained, showing a sample package, "and if you cut off the label and send it to the Housewives' League they'll send it to the company and the company will redeem the labels for one cent each and give it to the Red Cross—"

"Why don't they give the Red Cross all the postage that will take?" Eleanor inquired.

"Now, Eleanor, you don't understand."

"I understand perfectly. The gelatine company wants to play on public sympathy to sell more gelatine."

"Eleanor," said Sylvia, "I'm disappointed in you. Some of us are working so hard!"

When she had finally gone to call on her next prospect Eleanor went upstairs. She found Kester reading a letter from Sebastian, who said cotton was now six cents a pound, and did they want to sell?

"The cotton is all we've got," said Eleanor. "If we let it go it means utter bankruptcy."

He agreed. She sat down and took his hands in hers. "Let's hold it awhile longer, Kester. A lot of people are saying the war will be over this year."

"A lot of people," he said moodily, "are saying it won't be."

"If I'm wrong, if the bottom drops out of the market again, I can stand it. I've learned a lot recently."

"You're a great girl, Eleanor."

She smiled. "I can stand anything, darling, except Sylvia cackling as if she'd laid an egg."

"What did she want?"

Eleanor told him about Sylvia's peddling gelatin for the Belgians. He chuckled, but he said,

"You could have told her I gave five dollars to a Belgian fund yesterday."

"Kester! How could you? When we need it so!"

"I couldn't stand it. Those children. I kept thinking of Cornelia."

"If you'd thought of Cornelia you might have remembered that five dollars would buy her two pairs of shoes, and she certainly needs them."

"Oh, be quiet," said Kester, and she bit her lip remorsefully. But he was evidently glad to accept when Neal Sheramy called him up a few minutes later inviting him to the movies.

Eleanor was doing her best to be cheerful. She went out, and now and then she had their friends in for supper. When she saw Isabel, she said "Hello" politely and then paid her as little attention as possible. Like their acquaintances, she and Kester sang *Tipperary* and tried to pronounce Ypres and Prysansyz; they laughed ironically at the news that Gavrilo Prinzip had received a sentence of twenty years for starting the holocaust; they argued about the newly announced difference between Kultur and Culture; they learned the new war-game, played on a map of Europe, with armies and navies of Germany, Austria, Belgium, France, Great Britain and Russia carrying on strategic warfare. And meanwhile their creditors were becoming so insistent that they dreaded

150

driving through town. They could buy nothing else at the druggist's or the grocer's or the dry goods store. They could not buy nails to mend a loose board on the front gallery. The car was in such need of repair that it was unsafe to drive it. For two months they had been brushing their teeth with salt instead of toothpaste.

In February cotton was eight cents a pound. On the first of March Sebastian wrote urging them to sell. Cotton was being shipped overseas in small quantities now, he said, but the German submarines were getting continually more successful in their attempts to halt Allied commerce and nobody could tell what day the risks of international shipping would send the price down again.

For several successive evenings they sat up late talking it over. At eight cents a pound the crop would cover their immediate bills, but it would not leave a penny over toward the twenty thousand dollars they would be required to pay the bank if they were to keep Ardeith longer than the first of December. There was no chance that the plantation in its first year as an experimental truck-farm could be made to show a profit of twenty thousand dollars. In their extremity they at last confessed to each other that they might have been willing to turn to Fred for aid, but Eleanor knew her father's business well enough to know that twenty thousand dollars in cash represented an impossible demand. In the present plight of the cotton-stricken banks Fred could have raised such a sum only by mortgaging the machinery that built his levees and the home in which his family lived, a step that would reduce him to a state comparable to the one in which she and Kester found themselves today. After Fred's long struggle, which nobody understood better than she did, Eleanor felt that she would rather accept any defeat for herself than ask for that.

"I doubt if he'd do it anyway," she said. "There are the younger ones still in school. He has no right to jeopardize their security for my sake."

"You mean for my sake," retorted Kester. "Of course he hasn't. Your father is not going to risk losing everything he's worked for just because you took it into your head to marry me."

After a moment Eleanor asked, "How much money have you got?"

"I have—" Kester reached into his pocket, took out his cash and counted—"eleven dollars and thirty-four cents."

151

"I have about six dollars in my purse," said Eleanor, "and thirty-two dollars in my bank account."

"And that's all," said Kester.

He sat with one leg swung across the other. She could see the sole of his shoe, with a hole worn through the first layer of the leather. They had held their cotton with a frantic hope. It was their last negotiable possession. But now what they faced was no longer the possibility of saving Ardeith, it was a lack of the simple necessities with which to go on living. The bills at the local shops would absorb Eleanor's little income for months ahead. Their eyes met in despair.

"We've got to let the cotton go," said Kester.

"Yes," said Eleanor.

They sat looking at each other, bleakly.

In the morning Eleanor sat down at her typewriter and wrote Sebastian a letter telling him to sell the cotton. Kester, who could not typewrite, sat watching her. Eleanor began the letter four times. It was to be very simple, only a few lines long, but she kept making mistakes as though her hands refused to take the orders her mind was so reluctantly giving them. She tore out the fourth false beginning, wadded the sheet into a ball and flung it into the wastebasket. Without speaking, Kester came over to her and put his arms around her, and for a moment they stayed like that, saying nothing. At last Eleanor asked,

"What shall we do after December?"

"We may be able to rescue fifty or a hundred acres," said Kester. "I can be a one-mule farmer."

"And if we can't have even that much?"

"Oh, I don't know," said Kester.

Eleanor put her hands into his. Kester pressed them, then suddenly let them go. He walked over to the window and stood looking out at the swaying moss on the oaks and the azaleas thick with their bright, fragile blooms.

"Ardeith," he said. "Philip Larne built a log cabin here. He raised indigo."

"Kester, please stop."

Without giving him a chance to go on she turned back to the typewriter and began the letter again. Its crisp phrases did not sound like a death-warrant. "This will give you authority to sell the cotton represented by the enclosed warehouse receipts. . . ."

"Here it is, Kester," she said at length.

152

He leaned over the desk, read the letter and wrote his name at the end. "I'd better take it to town right away and mail it," he said. "The price may drop any time."

Bessie came in to announce dinner. They went into the dining-room and tried without much success to swallow what was in front of them- -chicken and vegetables raised on the place, for they had not been able to buy groceries for weeks. "We're living like sharecroppers already," Eleanor thought, but she did not say it. During dinner neither of them said anything, except for Kester's remarking that the peach orchard was beginning to bloom and looked mighty pretty.

As soon as their pretense at dinner was over Kester ordered his horse saddled and rode to town to mail the letter.

Eleanor walked around the house, feeling that she was saying goodby to the place she had grown to love. At last she got out the rickety little car and went for a drive, hesitating at first at the waste of gasoline and then remembering that it no longer mattered. She drove along the river road, wondering how much they were going to be able to rescue from the ruins when they had to move.

The fields were full of fragrances and chirps and colors, and the peach orchard was glowing with bloom. As she drove Eleanor thought she had never known how sensitive to the countryside she had become, until now when she was about to lose it. Then she put her foot on the brake so suddenly that the car jerked and sputtered. In the peach orchard, sitting on the grass under the trees, she saw Kester and Isabel. They were engaged in such close conversation that they did not notice her as she passed.

Eleanor stepped on the gas-feed and the car jumped ahead. Around the curve she saw Kester's horse tethered to a tree, and near it the smart little roadster Isabel had been driving since she came home. for though her income might be minute compared to what she was used to, it seemed enough to keep her supplied with all she needed.

Turning her car Eleanor drove past the orchard again. They had not moved. Isabel held her hat in her lap and the afternoon sun glinted on her hair. She sat with her ankles crossed in front of her looking up at Kester as though his words were the most interesting she had ever listened to; it was the flatteringly seductive attitude of a woman wise in the ways of men, pleasing by letting herself be pleased. As Eleanor passed the orchard for the second time Kester said

153

something that caused Isabel to throw back her head and laugh.

Eleanor was shaking with rage. She drove home, smothering her first impulse to interrupt them with the thought that she would not give Isabel the pleasure of seeing that Kester's wife knew how successful she was. Leaving the car in the avenue, she went indoors and began to walk up and down the parlor. She was still pacing when Dilcy came in with Cornelia.

"Take her outdoors," Eleanor said shortly.

"Fader?" asked Cornelia. Her eyes searched the room for him. "Fader?"

"Miss Elna," said Dilcy reproachfully, "it's gettin' cold out dere."

"Did you hear me tell you to take her out?"

"Yassum." Dilcy retired in dudgeon.

Eleanor went on pacing. "He promised me!" she said to herself, over and over. "This time I won't be quiet."

Since last November when Kester had promised he would not see her alone again, she had not mentioned Isabel to him. This was the first week in March. Kester had given the promise of his own accord, and it had not occurred to her to doubt that he meant to keep his word. She remembered how readily he had said it, as readily as he would have offered a child a stick of candy to keep her quiet. She had a disgusting sense of having been cheated and secretly laughed at. It set her on fire. Today they had let go the cotton, unless a miracle happened they would lose Ardeith, yet she had not said a word blaming Kester for their tragedy. And this was his gratitude. It was too much.

The sun was going down when he returned. She heard the horse's hoofs in the avenue, and Kester running up the front steps.

"Hello," he said as he came into the parlor. "Eleanor, don't you think it's chilly for Cornelia to be out? Dilcy said you told her—"

Eleanor wheeled around. "You promised me not to go to Isabel Valcour's house again," she exclaimed to him. "I suppose you decided that didn't mean you weren't to meet her in the peach orchard?"

Kester had stopped short as she spoke. He banged the door behind him. "You're the biggest fool I ever saw in my life," he said.

Eleanor's chest rose and fell with a short indignant breath.

"Am I a fool to want to know why you said you'd let her alone if you didn't mean it?"

"Good Lord, Eleanor, can I help passing anybody on the public highway?"

"I didn't notice that you passed her."

Kester stood with his back to the door, facing her. His answer had the deadly clearness that anger always produced in his speech. "Isabel was driving along the road. She stopped and called to ask if she could have some blossoms. I went in to help her cut them."

"You weren't cutting blossoms when I saw you."

"Is it a crime," he demanded, "to engage in civil conversation?"

"What did you find to talk about, I wonder?"

"The lurid subject." he returned evenly, "happened to be Sylvia. Isabel started by telling me Sylvia was asking everybody to dress dolls to be sent to the Belgian children. I had told her once how Sylvia had wanted you to buy gelatine."

"Gelatine? Sylvia didn't mention gelatine to me till after Christmas. Have you been meeting Isabel all winter?"

By this time Kester was furious. When he was furious he did not, like Eleanor. let his words tumble out in a flood. He answered in a low voice more cutting than any display of temper could have been. Certainly, he said, he had seen Isabel several times this winter. Isabel's house was on the river road not far from the southern border of Ardeith and they couldn't help running into each other now and then. When she asked his counsel it seemed the simplest friendly response to give what he could. Isabel needed a friend. Her father had died while she was in Germany, she had nobody to talk to, and besides it was his own business. He had not mentioned it to Eleanor because he preferred to avoid the kind of jealous tirade she had started now and that he had known she would start if she got the chance to do it.

Eleanor's wrath had risen as he talked. She was so angry that her voice quivered when she spoke. "Are you going to keep on seeing her?"

"I'm going to do as I please," said Kester. "I wasn't bought on a slave-block."

Eleanor felt as if her head were about to explode. Her months of labor her worry about Ardeith, her despair at having to sell the cotton her whole piled-up burden of fatigue and frustration crashed as though glad to find a concrete

155

object on which to fling itself. She began to talk. Her words came out of her without any conscious arrangement behind them. Every line she spoke was prompted by another detail of the past year's tedium but they were all thrown at Kester and Isabel. At the moment she was aware only of her anger that Kester had not kept his promise, so her words were aimed at nothing else, but they carried the weight of her anger at everything else and piled it on his shoulders.

Kester was amazed. He did not realize what she was doing, any more than she did; he knew only that she was accusing him of sins he had not committed and had not meant to commit. Once or twice he tried to stop her, but he might as well have put out his hand to stop the river rushing through a break in a long-strained levee. At last he cried,

"Will you in God's name shut up?"

"Why should I? Are you going to let that woman alone?"

"Why should I?" he exclaimed in return. "For the joy of watching you as you look now?"

"She's lovely, isn't she?"

"You look like a witch," said Kester. "And you sound like one."

"I can't work fourteen hours a day and look like a siren. If you'd wanted a woman who was helpless and adoring and sweet why didn't you marry one?"

"I wish I had," said Kester. He said it slowly, his hands behind him holding the doorknob.

"One who would spend her life telling you how wonderful you were, no matter what you did?"

"Yes!" said Kester. He opened the door.

"It's too bad," she said scornfully, "that my manners have not been polished by centuries of ladyism."

"You're mighty right they haven't," Kester replied. The parlor door banged, the front door banged, and a moment later she heard the car rattling down the avenue.

Eleanor dropped into a chair. She put her hands to her throbbing temples. For the moment she was not thinking at all. Her rage had exhausted her mind, so that it felt pumped dry of words and ideas alike, and she sat where she was, holding her head, her elbows on her knees.

She never knew how long it was that she stayed there, blankly watching the shadows as they drew in, but slowly her numb consciousness began to waken. As it did so she found that she was trembling, not with cold—for though the fire had burned down to a pile of glowing ashes its warmth was still in the room—but with an unfamiliar sensation of terror. As she moved her hands down from her temples and sat up, she knew why it was; she was afraid of a situation that she had not had to face in her marriage before, but that was there now, and she was afraid less because it was there than because she had put it there herself. No matter what she had said to Kester in those dreadful minutes when she had been half insane, she had never really believed he had been unfaithful to her. She had simply believed Isabel wanted him to be, that since Kester had been infatuated with her once he might be tempted again if he continued to put himself in her way. But now—Eleanor stood up. She walked toward the fireplace, drawn by the little glow of the ashes, for the room was quite dark. Mechanically, she picked up a stick of wood and dropped it across the andirons, then sat down on the rug, watching the wood catch fire while she realized more and more clearly that she had pushed Kester toward Isabel with a force none the less powerful because she had not while she was talking been rational enough to know she was using it.

It came back to her with a rush, what she had said to him and how she must have looked and sounded as she said it. She could not remember the words she had used but she was understanding now that the storm she had let fall upon him this afternoon had been gathering ever since the war had broken her hopes; she had said Isabel, but she had meant weariness, disillusion, defeat. And Kester had heard her with an understanding that was also weary, disillusioned, defeated. As she sat on the floor by her weak little fire she had her first experience of blaming herself and not something else for a disaster that had overtaken her.

Bessie called her to supper. Eleanor roused herself long enough to tell her to go away.

At last she got to her feet and went upstairs. She waited for him, watching the darkness from her bedroom window, where above the trees was a moon like a withered onion. She watched the morning break, and as the light came among the oaks she felt utterly spent, but she had learned that nothing that anyone or anything could do to her could be as terrible as what she could do to herself.

There was a knock at the door. Eleanor sprang up, shaking with hope. She ran to open it, stumbling across a chair in her haste and nearly falling, and flung the door wide open. When she saw Bessie the sight of her was like a blow in the face.

"Why miss!" Bessie marveled. "You done up and dressed already?"

Eleanor had forgotten that she had not undressed. She hoped Bessie was not looking past her to see that her bed had not been occupied.

"Yes," she said, "what is it?"

Bessie gave her a special delivery letter from New Orleans. The address was typewritten. Eleanor sat down, twirling the letter in her fingers, and feeling too much disappointed to read it, though it was important enough to bear a special delivery stamp. At last she tore open the envelope. A sheet of paper and two printed slips fell into her lap. The letter was from her father. He thought she should be interested in these, he sent love.

Eleanor was not interested. But she picked up the smaller clipping and began to read it. Fred had penciled on the side, "New York *Times*, March 2."

It was a brief report, stating without comment that the British dreadnaught *Queen Elizabeth*, now at the Dardanelles, used a bale of cotton every time she fired one of her fifteen-inch guns.

2

Cloudy with weariness, Eleanor's eyes tried to focus on the other piece of print her father had sent her. This was not a clipping, but a page torn out of a chemical encyclopedia, containing part of an article headed "Explosives." The words were long and unfamiliar: "guncotton ... nitrocellulose ... cordite."

Eleanor stood up, moving her arms and shoulders to relieve their tenseness. Slowly, past the turmoil of Kester, Isabel and her own remorse, a discovery was making its way into her mind. She went into the bathroom and threw cold water over her eyes, and came back to pick up her bedside telephone.

Sebastian would not be at his office yet, so she rang him at home. When he answered she made herself speak with terse resolution.

"Sebastian, you'll get a letter today from Kester telling you to sell the cotton. I've called to tell you he's changed his mind. He wants to hold it."

"Why Eleanor, what's happened?"

"Kester will tell you later. But do you understand me?—hold the cotton."

"Eleanor, I can't advise you too strongly to sell now. Germany and England—"

"Did you ever hear of guncotton, Sebastian? Nitrocellulose? Cordite?"

"What are you talking about?"

"It doesn't matter. Hold that cotton."

She hung up the receiver. The spurt of determination had drained out of her all the strength she had. As the telephone clicked Eleanor let herself relax on the bed, and without taking off her shoes or loosening her belt she went to sleep.

When she awoke the sun was high. For an instant she was surprised that she had slept so late, and surprised to find herself still dressed as she had been yesterday, then she remembered and sprang up. Kester had not come home. The servants looked as if they would have liked to know why, but Eleanor paid no attention. She gave her household orders, saw Cornelia safely in her high-chair for dinner, and made herself eat strawberries and drink coffee. When she had changed her dress she sat on the gallery steps, leaning back against one of the columns, and waited for Kester.

It was nearly four o'clock when he turned the car in between the gates. Eleanor sprang up. Kester stopped the car. As he got out she ran to meet him, and they reached for each other's hands, while they both exclaimed, "Are you ever going to forgive me?"

After that she did not know exactly what they said. She was trying to tell him everything at once, and he was trying to tell her. They went into the parlor by the fire, and she sat on the sofa while he knelt in front of her with his head in her lap.

She was trying to make him understand that he had had her forgiveness long before he came home, and all she wanted was to know that she had his, but he wanted to talk. He had not meant to go to Isabel when he left her, at least, he did not think he had, though he had been so angry it was hard to say what he had meant to do. But before it was very late he was very drunk, at least he thought he must have been, though he could remember everything that had happened, especially the bartender at Joe's Place begging him not to drive and himself insisting that he could drive any car anywhere at any time; he remembered that out in the air he had felt better, and had taken the car with elaborate carefulness around the corner where the Colston Dry Goods Store projected dangerously into the street, but all that the clarifying of his head had done was recall her cruel speeches and make him angrier with her than ever, so that he had told himself he didn't care if he never saw her again, and hoped he wouldn't have to; then he had driven aimlessly along the river road, not going anywhere, just driving there by force of habit—at least he hadn't consciously meant to be going anywhere, though it was hard for anybody to say just what his intentions had been when he was as drunk as that—but pretty soon he had discovered that he couldn't keep the car at the right side of the road, or the left side, or the middle of it, and he hadn't been so completely addled as not to know he wasn't likely to get anywhere alive if he didn't stop driving, and about the time he realized this, there in front of him was Isabel's home, all dark except for a light from one upstairs window. And if Eleanor could know, if she could possibly by any wild reach of fantasy imagine, the rat and the brute and the worm he had felt like when he woke up this morning, she would understand how it was that he had spent most of the day driving through the woods, throwing sticks into the bayous and trying to make up his mind to come home and face her.

Eleanor told him she did know. She understood, because she had spent a sleepless night realizing that the puritans and clergymen who had dictated the laws hadn't known more than half what they were talking about when they had assumed that there was only one sin that broke the marriage vows. She had broken them as well as he. They had both been disloyal, and all they could do was swear to each other that they would not be disloyal again.

There was a long silence. With his arms around her waist and his head in her lap and her hands stroking his tousled hair, Eleanor wondered why it was that this had made her more intensely than ever conscious of how closely she was bound to Kester, and no matter what he might do, of how completely she belonged to him.

At last he lifted his head. "What I need now is some self-respect," he said.

Eleanor bent and kissed him. "What you need now, darling,

is a bath and a clean shirt. Nobody can have any self-respect who looks the way you do."

"What a woman" said Kester, and she smiled with a poignant sense of happiness.

But in the middle of the night Eleanor woke up. She stirred restlessly, and turned over. It was foolish and she forbade herself to think about it, but all the same she could not rid herself of the feeling that her marriage was like a mended garment, which though it may be mended so dexterously that only a sharp eye can see that it was ever torn, will always have a weak place where it might tear again.

Chapter Nine

1

IN THE MORNING the papers Fred had sent her were still lying on Eleanor's bureau, and she snatched them up and began telling Kester what was about to happen to cotton. She talked briskly, fastening her attention to cotton for relief as much as for its own importance, because she had heard last night all she cared to hear about Isabel Valcour and felt that she could not endure the sound of that woman's name again, even coupled with Kester's protests of penitence.

He listened with amazement. At first monosyllabic exclamations were all he could answer, then his mind grabbed the idea and tossed it about in delight. "Guncotton—cordite— why Eleanor, it's wonderful! If the war lasts till fall the price for the new crop may be high enough for us to make that payment!"

But at length Eleanor reminded him that at present they had no money with which to raise another crop. As she spoke she realized that she must have been unconsciously thinking of this all night, for a plan began to tumble ready-made from her lips.

"I'm going down to New Orleans and talk to Mr. Tonelli, dad's friend who owns the banana lines," she told Kester. "We'll offer to mortgage to him the cotton we have now in the warehouse."

"Can you convince him the war will last two years more?"

"He'll be taking a chance, of course, but what investor doesn't? And Mr. Tonelli has made millions by taking chances like this."

"Wait a minute." Kester had sobered abruptly. "We wrote Sebastian to sell our cotton."

Eleanor looked down, rolling up the edge of one of the clippings between her thumb and forefinger. "I telephoned him to hold it."

"You did? When?"

"Yesterday morning early," she said in a faint voice.

Kester did not say anything. He came over and drew her head to his shoulder. There was a silence, but when Eleanor spoke again it was with crisp alacrity, for she still did not feel equal to talking about anything but cotton.

"I'll go to New Orleans this afternoon," she said. "You'd better manage the planting while I attack the financial end of it—we always work better that way."

"I'll start today." Kester spoke in the same fashion. He grinned down at her. "How was I ever lucky enough to marry a woman who had majored in mathematics?"

He gave her a squeeze. Eleanor laughed, and hurried to begin packing her bag. Later that day she drew the last dollar out of her bank account to pay for the trip to New Orleans.

When she got there she spent two days in the library reading about explosives and studying the international laws that governed neutral shipments to belligerents. Then, equipped with enough information to talk for hours if need be, she called on Marco Tonelli. Would he, she asked, lend her money on the cotton, taking the chance that the war would last long enough for her to pay it back?

Mr. Tonelli tapped his pencil on his thumb, considering. He was a fat little man with shrewd black eyes and creases in his cheeks left as the tracks of many triumphant smiles. His father had picked up overripe bananas on the wharfs of New Orleans and peddled them in a pushcart. He himself had once financed a Central American revolution for the sake of getting a government that would make more liberal terms with his banana plantations. Mr. Tonelli drove a twelve-thousand-dollar car and gave liberally to charity, but he had never knowingly wasted a quarter in his life.

"Now what's all this you've found out about ammunition, Miss Eleanor?" he inquired.

She was ready. "The details of the processes are trade

162

secrets, but the general principle is this: the raw cotton is treated with ether and alcohol to break up the fiber. As the ether and alcohol evaporate they leave a sort of jelly, and this is treated with nitrate. When the process of this treatment is fired, it forms an expanding gas—it explodes and there's absolutely nothing left."

He nodded and she went on.

"They have plenty of nitrate in Europe, but no cotton except what they can import. At the outbreak of the war they had reserves of ammunition, but it's giving out and they are working madly to produce more. I knew that, but I didn't know gunpowder was made of cotton. Evidently most of the general public doesn't know it either. They'll find out soon, now that it's getting into the papers, but by that time it will be too late to plant and the 1915 cotton crop is going to be a small one, so the price will be good. Meanwhile, the American munitions factories are going day and night making ammunition to be sold in Europe."

"How're they going to make sure it gets there?" Mr. Tonelli asked sharply.

"It's already getting there. Haven't you read those arguments in the papers about whether or not there should be a law prohibiting Americans from selling munitions to the countries at war?"

"Mhm, I believe I have. Suppose they should pass such a law?"

"Mr. Tonelli, you're not soft-hearted or soft-headed enough to think Congress can stop the American people's selling anything they can get paid for!"

He began to laugh. "You aren't either, ma'am, that's evident."

But Eleanor was not laughing. She went on, concisely and impressively, giving him facts. "The only question is how much longer the war will go on," she concluded. "The best estimates I can find give it three years, and so far it's lasted only seven months."

Chin in hand, Mr. Tonelli drummed his fingers on his little fat cheeks. "How much cotton have you got, Miss Eleanor?"

"Nine hundred and thirty-two bales."

"Unencumbered?"

"Yes, except that we are three hundred dollars behind on storage payments."

"How much do you want to borrow?"

163

"Thirty thousand dollars."

Mr. Tonelli whistled. "You've got nerve, young woman, haven't you?"

"If it isn't worth sixty by October," said Eleanor, "you may eat my head."

"I don't want to eat your head. I want that thirty thousand dollars back plus eight per cent."

"Eight per cent! You've got nerve too, haven't you?"

"Sure I have. The Germans got too close to Paris last fall for me to be counting on the duration of this war. Take it or not?"

"Take it," said Eleanor.

He promised to have the papers ready in a few days. Eleanor left his office decorously, but once on the street she almost scampered along. This was what she enjoyed, a challenge and a fight with the chance for victory. She wired Kester to come to New Orleans and sign the papers mortgaging their cotton to Mr. Tonelli. Kester arrived the next day, won the stern heart of Mr. Tonelli by his exuberance, thanked Fred with blithe gratitude for having noticed the mention of the British dreadnaught, and characteristically signed the agreement without reading it, though as Eleanor had already examined every word it did not matter. He and Eleanor went back to Ardeith ready to work as they had worked last summer, only, if possible, harder.

2

By April cotton was quoted at ten cents a pound, and the spring exports had exceeded any previous record for the corresponding period of the year. Eleanor discovered that she was going to have another child.

She was glad of it. Though it meant that she would be carrying a double burden, she welcomed a living reminder that the event that might have broken her marriage had ended by reestablishing its unity. Kester, when she told him, was delighted, and quite unconcerned over the fact that some of the energy she had planned to give the plantation would have to be used this year for other purposes.

But Eleanor was a healthy woman and nobody had ever called her indolent. During the first months of her pregnancy she worked eagerly to make up as much as possible for the time when she would not be able to work at all. She and Kester were hopeful again, and happy. Without verbally agreeing not to, they understood that neither of them wanted to mention Isabel. She had gone away—to Washington, Clara Sheramy said, where she was attending to her citizenship status and trying to get some of her property out of Germany —and though Eleanor assured herself that she was no longer troubled about her, she could not help thinking how convenient it would be if Isabel should bewitch a diplomat and get married.

But she had little energy to waste on thinking of Isabel. Between keeping accounts and checking orders, she gave frequent parties, for Kester was not capable of working long without amusement. In mid-summer, after creeping up fraction by fraction, cotton reached eleven cents a pound.

The war showed no sign of drawing to a close. Experts were saying that the Russian drive in eastern Europe and the British-French offensive in France had both failed for lack of ammunition, but the armies expected to have all they needed for next winter's campaign. As for the Germans and Austrians, they seemed to have ammunition in plenty. The Allies were doing all they could to keep cotton out of Germany, but even British diplomacy had a hard time stopping American shipments to other neutral countries, and the neutral countries of northern Europe had suddenly found they stood in need of astonishing amounts of cotton. During the past few months Sweden had imported twenty-five times as much cotton as in the similar period the year before the war, and Holland fourteen times as much; Eleanor chuckled as she read, wondering what they got for the cotton when they resold it in Germany.

She turned the pages of the newspaper, while on the steps Cornelia prattled to her dolls and Dilcy sat nearby mending rompers. Kester was indoors making mint juleps and setting them on ice to frost, for they were having guests to supper. Ardeith would not have a thousand bales this year, not with Kester's alternate spurts of diligence and gaiety, but the crop was going to be a good one, and next year when she was free again, she was confident that she could make the plantation produce a thousand or more. Eleanor wished that either the King of England or the Russian Czar would shave, as their pictures looked confusingly alike. She dropped her eyes to read a description of a weapon called Skoda Forty-two, the great Austrian gun that threw a shell weighing twenty-eight hundred pounds. The shell penetrated soft ground twenty feet before exploding. It killed every living thing within a hundred and fifty yards; the pressure of its gas would break roofs and partitions. As for men, the gas got into their body cavities and exploded there, blowing them into fragments so tiny that soldiers who disappeared in these explosions were reported missing, as there was no proof of their death.

Eleanor shivered and swallowed, uneasily broke off in the middle of the story and shifted her eyes to the adjoining column. A paragraph was joyfully informing the cotton planters, "It is estimated on good authority that the German and Austrian armies alone are shooting into space a thousand tons of cotton a day besides what is being used by the Allied armies. Every machine-gun keeps by it a reserve of ammunition averaging half a bale of cotton per gun. . . ." She let the paper slide off her knees to the floor, and looked across Cornelia's head to the gardenia and hibiscus bushes and the cottonfields beyond. It was hard, in this dreaming landscape, to be conscious that every stalk in the fields was putting forth a fruit of death She did not recall that she had ever really thought about it before.

Eleanor got up and went indoors. Kester came down the hall, a julep in his hand.

"Eleanor! Oh, there you are—I was about to look for you on the gallery. Taste this. Seems to me I've made these first ones too sweet."

She complied. "I think you have, only don't be too sure of my opinion. I'm not very expert." She set down the julep. "Kester, tell me something."

"Yes, honey. What is it? You look mighty serious."

Eleanor sat down on the sofa between the two front parlor windows. "I've just been reading a description of one of the big guns. It did something rather awful to me. Have you thought about it? I mean, thought about what we're doing, feeding those guns?"

With an odd little smile, Kester made a mark with his finger in the mist on the side of the julep-cup. "Why yes, I've thought about it."

"You haven't said anything."

"I'm still old-fashioned enough," said Kester, "not to want to point out some of those horrors to a woman who's about to have a baby."

"What I read made me quite sick for a minute," said Eleanor. "It's shocking to see myself as a maker of instruments of murder."

"We aren't responsible for the war," said Kester. He spoke quietly, and added, "What did they expect when they began it? People who don't like spiders in their tea shouldn't go on picnics."

"Oh I know," she agreed, "we can't do anything to stop it, but wouldn't you feel less responsible if we were growing something harmless—food crops, for instance?"

He shook his head.

"Why?"

Kester crossed the room to adjust a curtain that was letting in the glare of the sun. He turned around and stood leaning with his arms crossed on the back of a chair, searching for words that would make his rationalization articulate. She was somewhat surprised at him, for Kester had such facility of ideas that he could not often be induced to press one of them to its conclusion. Presently he spoke.

"Here's the fact. Eleanor. We have a plantation. We've got to raise something in order to make a living. Anything we grow this year will be used in some fashion to further the war. Food, clothes, ammunition—there's no difference. The armies can't fight without all of them."

She nodded.

"We sell to both sides," Kester continued. "Certainly. Why not? The right side and the wrong side—there isn't any. I've read their arguments till I'm sick of them. They both say they're fighting for civilization, for culture, for home and mother and flag. They both talk about 'the spiritual nature of the war' but they neglect to say what they hope to get by victory except the joy of having licked the pants off their enemies."

Eleanor laughed shortly. "Yes, I've noticed that."

"And as far as ammunition is concerned," Kester went on, "there was plenty of war before gunpowder was invented. There isn't any decent method of murder. If you're going to kill a man it doesn't make any difference whether you shoot him or knock him down with a club or lock him up to starve to death. We were horrified at the German's dropping bombs on defenseless towns, but the British are killing as many babies with their blockade as the Germans are with their bombs." He lifted his shoulder expressively.

167

Eleanor scowled thoughtfully at the corner of the room. "And if we didn't grow cotton, we'd lose Ardeith."

"We certainly would, to somebody who isn't too idealistic to grow it. I'm not the stuff martyrs are made of, Eleanor, and you aren't either. We'd better just grow as much cotton as we possibly can and be thankful the price is rising."

She gave him an ironic little smile. "Be thankful? To whom?"

"Honey child," said Kester, "everybody else has God on his side. Why shouldn't we?"

3

The plantation produced eight hundred and sixty-four bales that fall. The price in October was twelve cents a pound. With two crops in the warehouse, Kester and Eleanor found themselves possessed of more than one hundred thousand dollars' worth of cotton. and after a long siege with her books Eleanor announced that they could hold part of it.

"We can pay Mr. Tonelli and also that twenty thousand dollars to the bank " she said, "and if we are very careful we can cling to a little of this and wait for 1916 prices. Please let's do that. The war is not over, Kester."

He agreed with her, but added, "Now I'm going to see my tailor."

"Do," said Eleanor, "and as soon as I get my figure back I'm going to get some clothes too. An allover embroidery dress with a parasol to match. and patent-leather shoes with white kid tops and black silk lacings, and a suit of that new battleship gray, and a hat with a Paradise feather—stop me, Kester! I'm getting silly."

"Go on and be silly. How long since you had a new dress?"

"Don't you remember? That black one with the slit skirt, just after the archduke was killed."

Kester pulled her to him impulsively and kissed her.

Their son was born in January. Kester romantically insisted upon naming him Philip Larne, in memory of the periwigged founder of Ardeith whose portrait hung in the hall. He brought Cornelia in to see her brother and Cornelia regarded him with grave interest. "A yive doll," she commented, for she had difficulty with the letter L.

Kester smiled and put his finger through one of her curls.

168

Watching them from the bed, Eleanor said, "I observe that somebody's nose is not out of joint."

He laughed and said he should hope not. When he had gone out, Cornelia toddling after him in abject devotion, Eleanor turned her head on the pillow to look at the cradle, where she could just see one of baby Philip's hands on the coverlet. It was a very tiny, very pink hand, and she loved it very much.

She went to sleep, and when she woke it was because Kester had put his head in to tell her that though submarine attacks on merchant ships were scaring the market, cotton was twelve and a half cents a pound.

Eleanor opened her eyes. "Have the Allies got through the Dardanelles?"

"No."

"Are the Germans any nearer Paris?"

"No."

"Cotton will be fifteen cents by fall," said Eleanor.

4

By the time the 1916 crop was in flower, cotton was fourteen cents a pound. That autumn they harvested a crop of one thousand and thirty-two bales, and in October, the month when the Ardeith cotton was usually sold, the price was sixteen cents.

They sold what they had to, to pay the bank. About the rest, Eleanor hesitated with a sensation of mentally catching her breath. "Let's hold it till after the Presidential election," she pled.

The truth was, she needed a respite. Kester simply did not work with the fierce consistency that was needed if the plantation was to be made to produce to its utmost, and her knowledge of this had made her return to the battle sooner than she should have done after the birth of her second child. She had nursed little Philip for six months, driven by a sense of duty that would not let her admit that this, coupled with the efforts that had raised the plantation's yield by nearly two hundred bales, was costing more than she could safely give. Her experience of illness was small—except at the births of her children she had not been confined to bed for as long as a fortnight since she had had measles at the age of thirteen—

and she had taken it for granted that her bodily endurance was limitless. She dreaded being compelled to own that it was not.

Kester was different. When Kester was tired he went to sleep. When work grew dull he called up some people and had a party. The inexorable, persistent fact that Ardeith was still groaning with debt and that the madness of Europe was a temporary boon that could be used only while it lasted, seemed to trouble him not at all. He enjoyed their present prosperity, bought a new car and restocked the liquor-closets, and as usual let the future take care of itself. In her leisure after the cotton was in Eleanor was compelled to acknowledge what she had not been willing to admit during the summer, that he was increasingly restless. Kester was tired of being a hard-working planter. He wanted something to happen. In the summer when they were working from daybreak till dark, Kester had talked yearningly of going to one of the new preparedness camps; when she had exclaimed in horror that he could not leave her with the plantation and a newborn baby both to be cared for, he had given up the idea, but she had seen him looking at the pictures of the camps wistfully, like a little boy denied a holiday. Eleanor sighed as she recalled it. She had learned Kester's nature and knew there was no changing it; he was brilliant, generous, charming, but he reminded her of the rich young ruler to whom the Lord had said, "One thing thou lackest." He had no talent for drudgery.

But she had, and she was forced to conclude that hers must be enough for them both. When she compared other women's husbands with hers she felt blessed. Whatever Kester's shortcomings he had two virtues she prized above all else: he was never dull, and he never gave her a chance to doubt that he adored her. He told her so often, never more fervently than when Isabel came back to town. They were out riding in Kester's new car and saw her with Violet, standing on the street in the shadow of a billboard flaunting a huge picture of President Wilson and the proclamation "He Kept Us Out of War."

"I didn't know she was here again," said Eleanor.

"She's been here several weeks," said Kester, "but this is the first time I've seen her."

Violet waved, but if Isabel saw them pass she gave no

evidence of it. Eleanor looked down at her shoe-lacing. "Kester?"

"Yes, honey?"

"Have you talked to her at all since—" she stopped.

"Once."

"When?"

"Not long after that. I told her I was ashamed of myself and didn't intend to let any such thing happen again. That's all. It was a very short interview. You aren't concerned about her, are you?"

She shook her head. "No. Of course not."

"You shouldn't be. You see. Eleanor. I love you. I love you more than I've ever been able to tell you. You couldn't get rid of me unless you threw me out and locked the doors.

She put her hand over the one that lay near her on the steering-wheel, and pressed it.

"You don't wear darned gloves any more," Kester remarked.

The market hesitated until Mr. Wilson was safely re-elected, then cotton leaped to eighteen cents a pound. It was a magnificent price; though they had had to raise the wages of their laborers their profits were higher than they had dared to expect. Kester suggested that they give a dinner-party to celebrate, and Eleanor joyfully acceded. buying for the occasion the most beautiful dress she had ever owned. They had a glorious Christmas tree for the children and though golden-haired bisque dolls with lashed eyelids could no longer be obtained from Germany Cornelia did not miss them and baby Philip was so delighted with the bright tree that he kicked and gurgled without paying any attention at all to his toys.

By the time the excitement of Christmas was over they became aware of a feeling of expectancy. It did not come suddenly; it had been growing. as when a sound of rain becomes noticeable and one realizes that one has been hearing it, without noticing for a long time. The United States was going into the war. Nobody knew just when, but there it was, unmistakably about to happen. The feeling of expectancy was hard to analyze: it was not caused by such disasters as the *Lusitania* attack—one was used to them by now, and said shrugging that Americans who didn't want to be bombed should stay home; it was not the horror-stories—one was used to those too, so used to them that readers skimmed nightmarish accounts with bored eyes; it was not even the vast American loans to the Allies; it was an odd, resentful feeling that something tremendous was going on and Americans were missing it. Eleanor observed that everybody she knew seemed to share Kester's feeling of restlessness. The preparedness camps, the army expedition to chase Villa along the Mexican border, the defense appropriations, seemed like rehearsals for a show too long delayed. When she took the children out to play one afternoon and found Kester with half a dozen of his friends practising shots at a target set up in a meadow, she began to be frightened. Cornelia clapped her hands, shouting, "Father's a sojer! Aren't you a sojer, father?"

"Not yet," Kester said merrily, "but watch! Hold them, Eleanor."

Eleanor kept the children back while Kester put a shot neatly into the middle of the target. Baby Philip, alarmed at the noise, began to cry, and that gave her an excuse to take him and Cornelia indoors, but when Kester came in she demanded, "Kester, if we should get into this imbroglio—"

"It does look as if we're about to get into it."

"You haven't any wild notion of going, have you?"

"I don't know. Why not?"

"If you aren't scared of being shot—and I suppose you aren't—don't you know you have a job to do here? Who'd raise the cotton if you went?"

"I haven't gone yet," said Kester easily. "And if Mr. Wilson dilly-dallies much longer it may be over before anybody goes from here."

But his efforts were more spasmodic than ever that spring, and getting the fields planted required incessant labor from her. She was not surprised when the United States entered the war, but she was increasingly irritated that with cotton now at twenty cents a pound Kester seemed to think the plantation could run itself while he watched parades and read and talked about the war.

"Listen, Eleanor. Whatever they say about Wilson, they can't deny he's got a tremendous talent for words. 'We are glad to fight thus for the ultimate peace of the world and for the liberation of its people. . . . The world must be made safe for democracy—' "

"Kester, did you order fertilizer for the south field?"

"I forgot about it. I'll phone in the morning. This is really good, Eleanor, did you read it? 'To such a task we can dedicate our lives and our fortunes, everything that we are and everything that we have, with the pride of those who know that the day has come when America is privileged to spend her blood and her might for the principles that gave her birth and happiness and the peace which she has treasured—' "

"You promised to order that fertilizer yesterday. How do you expect to raise cotton if you won't pay any attention to it?"

"Oh Eleanor, be quiet! I said I'd order it tomorrow. Do you want to hear any more?"

"Good heavens, no! I haven't got time for democracy. What's that phone number? I'll call."

She went to the phone in the hall and ordered the fertilizer. When she came back Kester was still buried in the President's message to Congress, apparently having quite forgotten his earlier cynical attitude toward the war. Eleanor felt a pang of apprehension. The plantation had become a tedious job, nobody knew it better than she did. while the war was new and exciting. It beckoned a man of Kester's temperament with an imperative thrill. She thought of the work that still lay ahead if they were to save Ardeith, and shivered at the possibility of facing such a battle alone.

She could see it happening, though she tried not to see it and argued to herself that Kester simply could not go now and leave Ardeith to her. Kester did not have to go, for he was thirty-two years old and only men from eighteen to thirty were being required to register for the draft. But she knew he was going, and when he went she was not surprised, but despairing.

Kester came in happily, singing at the top of his voice, and burst into the room where she was working on her records and at the same time trying to keep an eye on Cornelia and Philip, who were playing on the floor. He picked up Cornelia and swung her around and as he put her down he turned to Eleanor. "How do you think you'll like me in a uniform?"

She dropped her pen, making a blot on the figures. "Kester! You haven't!"

He grinned and nodded. "Yes I have."

"You've signed up?" she asked in a voice that came out of a throat tight with dismay.

"I've promised to. I'm signing up finally this afternoon."

Eleanor got up slowly. She walked to the wall where the

bellcord hung and pulled it. When Dilcy appeared she told her to take the children out. As the door closed behind them she turned back to Kester, who was watching her with puzzled astonishment.

"Eleanor, what's the matter? Don't you want me to go?"

She held the back of a chair tight with both hands. "Kester," she exclaimed sternly, "you can't do this to me. If you've only promised somebody you'll enlist, you don't have to do it. You can't leave Ardeith now."

"My dear darling," he exclaimed, "don't start being one of those wives!"

"I'm not being one of those wives. I'm talking as your business partner. What will happen to Ardeith if you go away?"

Kester's face went blank. "Why, Eleanor, you know all about it now!"

"Knowing about it is one thing. Doing it is something else." She tried to plead with him. "Kester, this plantation is a full-time job. Running this house and taking care of two children is too much to add to it. You have responsibilities at home!"

He took a step toward her. "But this is war! Don't you understand?"

"Certainly I understand," she retorted. "The terrible Huns. Hang the Kaiser. Berlin or bust. I understand. You're running away."

"Running away?" He was hurt and astonished.

"Yes," said Eleanor.

Kester was angrily patriotic. Didn't she know the country needed men? That every billboard, every newspaper, was urging women to keep the home fires burning while their husbands went out and saved democracy? Didn't she want the children to be proud of him when they grew up?

"They might be more thankful to have a home to live in," said Eleanor. "This place is only half paid for."

"But you'll take care of Ardeith," Kester exclaimed.

Suddenly she felt very calm and cold. "Yes, Kester, I'll take care of Ardeith. But don't tell me I won't understand why I'm having to do it. You want drums and flags and glory and an excuse to make somebody else carry the responsibility for your life. If I were a helpless featherbrain you'd be more concerned about Ardeith than about saving the world. But you know when I've started a job I don't quit in the middle of

174

it, so you can run off to a new adventure." She ended with a scornful shrug.

"My patience is of the durable variety," said Kester, "but I wish to God you'd shut up."

"All right, I'll shut up. Go on and get your laurels."

Kester gave her a sardonic little grin. "You have a positive genius for taking the color out of anything I want to do. It must be a gift." He went to the door and opened it. "Have a good time being virtuous," he said over his shoulder, "because I'm going to town to enlist."

He went out. Eleanor sat down and rested her head on her hands, feeling as if the burden of the months ahead was already weighing on her shoulders.

But after a few minutes she began to regret what she had said. It was no use arguing with him. Kester was incapable of accepting the tiresome challenges of everyday living, and scolding him for it simply made him indignant without changing him in the slightest. With a sigh Eleanor turned over the blotted sheet of her ledger and started again on a fresh page. She might as well, she was thinking, accept the rôle destiny had assigned her, and spend her life wearily finishing what Kester had enthusiastically started. Since he was going into the army and there was no stopping him, she would be wise to hold her tongue as became the wife of a hero.

When he came in Eleanor told him she was sorry for her outburst. Kester, who was so delighted with himself that he had already forgotten it, replied that it didn't matter in the least, every man expected his wife to make a scene when he joined the army. He thereupon sat down and began giving her innumerable instructions about operating the plantation in his absence, talking to her as if she were a dear, noble creature but not very bright.

But he was in such hilarious spirits that they really had a very good time together during those last few days, and Eleanor drove to the station to see him off to the training camp with every intention of making a proud and tender farewell as properly as possible.

And then, suddenly, as he kissed her goodby, she felt a lump like a potato in her throat. Tears began to gush out of her eyes and she found herself clinging to him in an agony of terror. Somehow it had not actually come into her consciousness until this moment that Kester was going to a war where men were being killed; she heard the phrase "Twenty thousand casualties a day" going around and around in her mind, and when at last he tore himself away from her as other men all around them were tearing themselves from other weeping women, Eleanor stood quite still, feeling lost and dizzy, and not troubling to hide the tears that were dripping off her cheeks.

As the train pulled out she stumbled back into the car and put her head down and sobbed like any other frightened wife who adored her husband and could not keep him out of the war. It was a long time before she could quiet herself sufficiently to drive the car home.

She shut herself up in her room and sat down, still trembling. Guncotton, nitrocellulose, cordite—the words began to repeat themselves as they had done on the morning when she had first read them, only then they had brought her hope and triumph, and now they howled at her till she was stiff with fear. Guncotton, nitrocellulose, cordite. Twenty-cent cotton meant twenty thousand casualties a day.

Eleanor looked blankly at the wall.

"Twenty-cent cotton," she said aloud. "Strange—this very minute there must be twenty million women in the world who are feeling just as I do."

Chapter Ten

1

SHE HAD NEVER realized how large and empty the house could be without Kester.

During the five years of their marriage they had never been apart more than a few days at a time. There was always the knowledge that tomorrow or the next day they would be together again, so she had not missed him, but now the fact that he was not here and would not return for months or maybe years gave her a feeling of being lost in big rooms full of echoes. Kester had gone to an officers' training camp in Tennessee—to be on the safe side he had dropped four years off his age, a patriotic fib for which sworn corroboration was easy to get—and though he wrote often, his letters were far too small to fill up the vacancy he had left. Eleanor had thought she had been working all day long, and now she was astonished to find how much time she had spent in simply talking to Kester. It was hard to remember what they could have talked about that occupied so much time. But evidently they had said a great deal to each other, for when she followed her regular schedule there were so many blank spaces in the days.

She hung out a service flag, took snapshots of the children looking up at it and enclosed them in a letter. As she addressed the envelope the click of her typewriter was loud in the strangely quiet house.

"I've got to stop this," Eleanor told herself grimly. "I can't spend the whole war behaving like a child left in a dark room." She got up and rang the bell. "Bring me a pot of coffee," she said when Bessie answered, "and the *Times-Picayune.*"

The front page of the paper was full of battles. Remembering that she had been neglecting the market page, Eleanor turned to see what the battles were doing to cotton, and as she did so she stared and nearly spilt her coffee. Since Kester's departure the price of cotton had risen to twenty-five cents a pound.

Eleanor felt her spine stiffen as though her body felt her resolution before her mind. At twenty-five cents a pound a thousand bales of cotton would be worth one hundred and twenty-five thousand dollars. Even with mounting production costs, profits this year could be enormous.

She stood up slowly. Her indignation at Kester's going, and then her fear, had made her forget the simple truth that as long as she could not stop the war she could use it. With such a price as this she could provide the machinery she had begun dreaming of three years ago, and increase production at Ardeith beyond Kester's idea of possibility. The more cotton she fed the guns the sooner they could shoot a path clear for him to come home, and when he came back—she could not let herself consider any other possibility, because if she continued to do so she would go mad and not be able to raise any cotton at all—when he came back she would give him Ardeith of his ancestors not only clear of debt but a model of efficient abundance. What a welcome!

Eleanor looked down at the newspaper, smiling at an odd, guilty little realization that had begun to creep into the back of her head. With Kester away there would be no more

177

dawdling. She would not expect him to do things and then discover the work was awry because he had not done them. She missed him, she would have been willing to put up with his ways forever if only he could come home, but since she had to endure the lack of his adorable presence she might as well be frank with herself and acknowledge that the work would go faster under her sole authority. By the time he came home she could have Ardeith so expertly organized that its operation would require no more than he was in the habit of giving it.

Pulling the bellcord again, she told Bessie that hereafter she wanted to be called at five o'clock every morning.

She went to work now with the feeling that she was digging in for a siege. Her first step was to engage a competent overseer who could relieve her of details. He was hard to find. She knew what she wanted, but she had already observed that there was something about growing cotton that made too many people pleasantly vague, caught—if they were the old-line aristocrats—in a confusion of moonlight and mint juleps, or if they were dirt-farmers, in a fatalistic dependence on variables from the weather to the market. Those who knew how to raise cotton profitably were likely to be busy on their own fields and not looking for the chance to tend the fields belonging to somebody else. But after writing to the state university and the state department of agriculture, inserting advertisements in rural journals and interviewing two dozen applicants, she secured a man named Wyatt, a lean, saturnine individual who evidently knew the cotton business and had both sense and energy to give it. Wyatt had been working at the cotton station maintained by the government several miles up the river, where the men experimented with fertilizers, varieties of seed and methods of combating pests. He asked for four hundred dollars a month, a house with water and electricity free, and an automobile.

Eleanor agreed. They signed a contract.

"Now I want the utmost production this place can give without hurting the land," she said to him. "I'm not stingy and I don't expect to run a sweatshop. I'll pay the best wages in the parish but I won't have any banjo-thrummings or watermelon-cuttings when there's work to be done."

Wyatt did not smile. It was evident that he rarely did. "I get it."

"Look the place over and tell me what I need."

"Tractors," said Wyatt.

"Yes, I'm going to have those. With the right machines we ought to get twelve hundred bales this year. By the way, how old are you?"

"Forty-two," said Wyatt.

"Get this straight before we start," said Eleanor. "I'm twenty-seven. I'm not so dimwitted that I think I know everything. Give me any suggestions you can. You'll have a telephone and can ring me at any time. But this is my plantation and I'm running it. You understand?"

"Yes ma'am," said Wyatt. The corners of his somber mouth quivered slightly. "You didn't have to tell me that, Mrs. Larne."

"Good," said Eleanor. They shook hands.

With joyful audacity she set about fulfilling her dream of the plantation's renaissance. She installed tractors, cultivators, sprinklers, motortrucks; she paid good wages to the Negroes, repaired their cabins, scrupulously avoided asking or giving favors. Delighted with the new speed of the field work she turned her attention to the house, where except for a few routine additions such as plumbing and electric lights everything went along much as it had before the Civil War. Eleanor had the old bathrooms torn out and new pipes and fixtures installed. She added an electric stove, vacuum cleaners and an electric washing machine, and put in an inter-room telephone system. Never having heard of such goings-on the servants protested and several of them left, but as she no longer needed them it did not matter. There were not so many laborers in the fields either, as the machinery had enabled her to reduce human labor to a minimum, a change that was invaluable this year when factories and the army draft were making agricultural workers increasingly scarce in spite of the highest wages in history.

Around her the country blazed and shouted with the war. Aeroplanes sputtered, soldiers marched, billboards yelled "Give Till It Hurts!" Eleanor hardly heard the commotion. When she was asked to do war work she answered, "My husband is in the army. I'm taking his place. I can't do any more." It was obvious, even to the embattled ladies of the Red Cross, that she could not. She was plunged into a maelstrom of work that sent her to bed every night fairly drunk with weariness. The weather was very hot, and war-prices shot her costs to such heights that her bookkeeping grew more trying

179

every week. She began to lose weight, her head and back and legs so often throbbed with fatigue that she almost forgot how it had ever felt to be really rested, at night columns of figures reeled in her dreams till she sometimes woke feeling as if she had hardly slept at all But she felt rewarded whenever she looked at the teeming fields. From the romantic wastefulness of cotton tradition she was guiding Ardeith toward a crisp and impersonal efficiency. Wyatt received her orders with admiration, the laborers were getting used to regular hours, even Mamie and Dilcy were beginning to like the household contrivances that relieved them of so many backaches. When Eleanor watched the tractors at work she felt a surge of strength within herself like a response to their noisy power.

The cotton grew and flowered, dropped its flowers and opened its bolls to the sun With Wyatt's help Eleanor went out to comb the country for pickers. This was the only operation where her tractors could not relieve the cotton of its dependence on hand-laborers with their picturesque, wasteful sitting around. Mechanical cotton-pickers simply did not work. Eleanor offered first a dollar a hundred pounds for picking, then a dollar and a half and finally two dollars. She took her car and toured the countryside, stopping to urge a job upon every able-bodied man or woman she saw, and sent her trucks to bring them to the plantation from miles around. Some of her cotton fell to the ground for lack of hands to pick it, but when she was finally done she had gathered a crop of eleven hundred and sixteen bales and she was content. She sold the cotton for twenty-seven cents a pound. In spite of unprecedented costs of production her profit for the year was slightly more than seventy thousand dollars.

2

That winter she tried to relax. She went out, and even gave a party herself, but there was so much to do!

The war was complicating the simplest routines of daily life. Eleanor enjoyed buying clothes for herself and the children, for she felt prosperous enough to afford war-prices, but much of what they needed she could not buy at all. Sugar was nearly unobtainable: meat went to the army; coal was needed to run troop trains and civilians were forced to buy it by the bucketfull. As fat was used in the manufacture of explosives, butter cost eighty cents a pound. Wheat flour was scarce and expensive, so that bread was full of substitutes and had a dirty look as though somebody had wiped up the floor with it. Eleanor had the Negroes cut wood, but labor was so precious that she could not spare enough of them to cut all she needed, so though the children always had a fire in the nursery she herself often had to do without. She raised hens and winter vegetables, had her own butter made on the place, and thanked heaven for Mamie's skill at corn muffins and spoonbread. By using all her resourcefulness she managed to keep the war from encroaching on the children's comfort, but she got very little rest.

Kester's letters were exuberant. Emerging from the training camp as a first lieutenant, he had been sent to Camp Jackson at Columbia, South Carolina, where he was drilling, marching, stabbing straw Germans and enjoying everything he did. Sometimes as she read his letters Eleanor could not help a half humorous, half resentful feeling that it was just like Kester to have managed to get himself into the one situation where the inconveniences of this wild winter could not touch him.

"This is the most amazing adventure of my life," Kester wrote her. "The town looks like San Francisco of the forty-niners, it's jammed and frantic and everybody in it seems to have a case of wandering head.

"But no wonder. Before the war Columbia was a pleasant little city of about thirty thousand population. It had two skyscrapers, the Palmetto Building (sixteen stories) and the National Loan and Exchange Building (twelve stories); a fine new high school, shady streets with white houses, and a noble state capitol on which could still be discerned some cherished smoke-smudges left from the time when General Sherman set fire to the town in 1865. Since Sherman's time Columbia had thrived peacefully until the United States went to war with Germany.

"But now, at the edge of town the government has set up Camp Jackson. Aeroplanes are zooming overhead and down the streets come endless parades of infantry, cavalry and war machines camouflaged with stripes of pink and purple. Almost literally overnight the population was swelled by the addition of a hundred and fifty thousand soldiers, and then by a swarm of wives, families, nurses, friends and the usual accompaniment of harlots. Lodgings are in such demand that any household with a spare bedroom can rent it for thirty dollars a week. Many of the officers' wives are rich, and to supply them with the kind of goods they are used to buying merchants have flung up unpainted shacks where only half protected from the weather they display fur coats and hand-made shoes and gowns from the best designers in the country. There simply isn't enough food to go around. In front of the grocery stores are lines of customers, waiting; when they get in they sign their names in a book for the privilege of buying a pound of sugar (only one pound apiece) for forty cents.

"Money is tumbling about. Office boys who used to make three dollars a week are getting twenty. Elevators and cabs are being operated by girls who quit high school to earn salaries higher than those their fathers used to get before the war. Coal is a dollar a bucket and Negro women are hawking bundles of wood in the street, for Nature has gleefully added to the jambalaya by giving South Carolina the coldest winter it has had in fifty years. It is snowing about once a week. The Northern soldiers in camp are making ungracious remarks about the Sunny South (I don't blame them, for the icicles are three feet long), but we haven't any right to complain, for in spite of the coal shortage the cantonment is kept beautifully warm. We have all the coal. Civilians simply can't get it. They've closed the churches and schools to save coal for us, and so, as though the streets were not jammed already, the shivering citizenry pours out in the morning and doesn't go home till bedtime, for in the street there's at least excitement to keep them warm.

"Since there's no school, children are out all day. They go to the movies. The theaters aren't heated, but the pictures are lurid enough to make the audiences forget it. The movies have fearful names—*The Kaiser the Beast of Berlin, Auction of Souls, To Hell with the Kaiser*—and with our breath raising white clouds between ourselves and the screen we of the khaki brigade sit alongside the boys and girls deprived of algebra and watch Turks crucifying Armenian girls, babies being stabbed and German soldiers tearing lustfully through convents. The children believe all of it and cheer eagerly; I frankly don't know how much of this stuff I believe, about half of it, I suppose. Anyway, Europe's in a mess and I'm glad we're going to clean it up before Cornelia and Philip are grown.

"Eleanor, why don't you come to see me? You really won't

know anything about the war until you've had a look at a cantonment town. I can find you a room somewhere and I think I can get a couple days' furlough, and I miss you terribly."

Eleanor lowered the letter and smiled at her empty fireplace. It was midwinter and the room was like an igloo, but as she read Kester's letter it had been as though filled with his warm, laughing presence and the pain of her loneliness was as sharp as during the first days after he went away. She wired Kester to let her know when he could get a furlough.

Kester managed to get two days. Eleanor scrambled on a train that was crowded, smoky and full of cinders. She spent the night with her head on a pillow wedged against the red plush back of the seat and her feet resting against the knees of a bearded stranger who looked like a Bolshevik. In Columbia she and Kester stayed in a ramshackle hotel on a side street, in a back room for which Kester was paying fifteen dollars a day. The room had no heat, it contained a bed with sheets that were not long enough to tuck under both ends of the mattress at once and such inadequate blankets that they had to sleep under their coats; a bureau with a gray-spotted mirror that made them look like victims of some strange disease; a carpet with holes that caught their heels whenever they crossed the room; two shaky chairs, and a washstand with a bowl and pitcher for which they had to draw their own water from a pump at the end of the hall.

None of it made any difference. They were together for forty-eight hours. Eleanor thought she would have been glad to live in such quarters for the rest of her life if only Kester would swear never to leave her again.

Though when she got home Louisiana was bright after the Carolina snows and the camellias were flowering on the lawn, Ardeith looked grim and cold without Kester. She was glad it was time to get ready for the spring plowing. Kester had noticed how thin she was, and she had not had time to tell him how she was working, but it did not matter very much; she was sure she could hold out, for every glance at the market news gave her an infusion of courage. Cotton was climbing toward thirty cents a pound.

3

In April there came a break in Kester's letters, an unexplained silence that she knew by now did not need to be explained. The men were never told when they were to be sent overseas until just before they left, and when they made ready to go they were not allowed to notify their families, for the transport ships sailed in secret. Eleanor waited and waited, trying to ease her nerves by plunging into work with such intensity that she had no time to think, and wondering if the risk of German spies could possibly be great enough to justify this cruelty of not letting her know. During that period of uncertainty she was finally forced to seek counsel from Bob Purcell. Bob put two fingers on the leaping pulse in her wrist and shook his head at her with a reproachful smile, like a schoolmaster.

"If I thought there was the slightest chance of your listening to me," he said, "I'd tell you to go to bed for a month."

"Don't be silly," said Eleanor. "I can't desert my plantation."

He drew down her lower eyelid and looked at its lining. "Did you ever hear." he inquired, "of the Irishman who said he'd rather be a coward for ten minutes than be dead the rest of his life?"

"You know there's no chance of my dying."

"I know you're dangerously anemic," Bob said shortly.

He gave her a great deal of iron and advice. Eleanor took the iron, but as the advice consisted of impossibilities such as nine hours' sleep and a rest in the afternoon, she ignored it. When at last she received a letter from Kester she immediately felt so much better that she concluded that her ailment had been not anemia. but nerves. Kester was in France, he could not tell her where. but it was a lovely country, shell-scarred but trembling with spring, and full of birds chirruping above the noise of the guns.

"I am driving a car," wrote Kester. "I convey colonels, messages and supplies. Although the rule of the army seems to be that a guy's having been a cobbler for twenty years is good reason for making him a cook, some genius has appreciated my talent. Driving here is quite a job. No lights before or behind. No roads half the time, and if you strike one it is so full of ruts and shell-holes it is an invitation to suicide, or if not shell-holes it's mud. My Lord, the mud of France! I was under the impression that Louisiana was a muddy place. Don't ever let me say so again. The only thing in Louisiana that resembles French mud is New Orleans molasses. Thank God I know how to take a car apart and put it together again, so I always get through. But it's rather fun. If there are no lights on my car neither are there traffic lights to stop me, nor speed limits, nor white lines that I mustn't cross, nor smart-tongued ladies to say 'So Kester is driving you home. Have you said your prayers?'

"I wish I could tell you more. But it isn't allowed. Send me a new picture of yourself, and new ones of Cornelia and Philip. Those I'm carrying in my pocket are nearly worn out. How tall is Cornelia now? Does she remember me? Good night, my darling, and don't worry about me. I'm having a grand time."

Eleanor kissed his signature, tingling with thankfulness that Kester was at least somewhat safer than he would have been among the barbwire barricades of the trenches. She need not worry, she told herself. Kester bore a charmed life if man ever did and was probably destined to outdrink his great-grandchildren. The children were racketing on the gallery. Carrying a picture of Kester, taken at Camp Jackson, Eleanor went to the door and watched them. They were playing soldier. In cocked hats made of newspapers—evidently supervised by Dilcy, who had some idea that all soldiers should look like the Spirit of '76—they were marching up and down with hearth-brooms over their shoulders, singing what they believed to be a ferocious melody for the vanquishing of Germans,

> *There ain't no cooties on me,*
> *There ain't no cooties on me,*
>   *There may be cooties on some of you beauties,*
> *But there ain't no cooties on me!*

Eleanor laughed at them and held out Kester's photograph.

"Cornelia," she said.

Cornelia looked around in some annoyance. "Ma'am?"

"Come here, Cornelia."

"Comp'ny *attention!*" ordered Cornelia, and while Philip painfully held the hearthbroom—which was taller than he was

185

—she advanced to her mother. "I'm cap'n," she objected. "What do you want?"

Eleanor showed her the picture. Instead of facing the camera with the well-what-do-you-want-now look of most men having their pictures taken, Kester had regarded it like a chum. Cornelia's face broke into a smile as she looked at the picture, and her eyes softened. She had beautiful dark eyes.

"It's father," she exclaimed. Smiling at the picture, she said, "Ain't he pretty?"

Whenever she showed her photographs of Kester, Eleanor envied him for the way Cornelia loved him. Cornelia could not be supposed to know that the house she lived in and the pleasant luxury that surrounded her were the gifts not of her father's charm but her mother's strength. She took it for granted that her mother was a strained and tired person too busy to play with her, and adored her recollection of Kester. Looking up at Eleanor, she asked,

"When is he coming home?"

"When the war's over, dear."

"He's shootin' Boches!" said Cornelia.

Eleanor called Philip to see the picture too. Philip surveyed it solemnly and said "Sojer boy." He was two years old, and had no remembrance of Kester. "Father, Philip!" Cornelia corrected him severely.

"I'm a sojer," said Philip.

"Yes, Philip," said Eleanor, "you're a soldier, and your father's a soldier too."

They began to march and sing again. As she had several errands to do in town Eleanor went upstairs to get dressed. She went into Kester's room and paused a moment by his bureau, yearning for him. His clothes were in the drawers, too orderly in their piles to suggest his presence. Among his handkerchiefs was the little silver knife with his name on the handle. Eleanor picked it up and kissed it, remembering it was the first possession of his she had ever held in her hands.

From the window she could look out toward the fields. Again this year they were promising returns that made her feel triumphantly rich. Eleanor smiled proudly at what she was achieving.

When she went into her own room, even the simple process of changing her clothes reminded her of how well she was accomplishing the task she had set out to do. She liked the silky feel of warm water in her beautiful bathtub, the convenience of the electric irons that curled up the hairs straying on her neck, the ease of dressing before a mirror with sidelights. Eleanor looked herself up and down in the glass. She was no ravishing beauty, but she was a good-looking woman, tall and slender, with a figure excellently proportioned, and she carried herself well. It was good to feel herself in luxurious clothes again, a dress of crisp brown taffeta with a hat to match, boots and gloves of champagne-colored kid that looked as if they had never been worn before. It was good to drive into town in a smart little car, to be successful and to know she looked it.

Tradespeople hurried to serve her, deferentially. That was pleasant too, when she remembered that three years ago they had been closing her accounts because she could not pay. The town looked prosperous. The shops were full of customers and the streets full of cars. In the park girls strolled under parasols that matched their dresses, gay and fluttery in the sunshine. Everybody seemed to be in good spirits. The soft rustle of the palms in the park seemed to whisper, "Thirty-cent cotton!" Thirty-two cents, Eleanor corrected her musings as she drew up in front of the drug store and honked for the services of the soda-jerker, thirty-two cents and still rising, while everybody, from herself to the druggist rejoicing in the increased ability to buy merchandise, was profiting by it.

When the soda-jerker appeared she told him to bring her a box of face-powder and a glass of lemonade. The weather was already summery, and the lemonade looked cool in its tinkling glass. As she put her lips to the straw Eleanor noticed Isabel Valcour with a blue linen parasol on her shoulder, wandering along the sidewalk. Eleanor had not seen her for a long time. Probably she was consumed by ennui, Eleanor reflected as she watched Isabel approaching the drug store as though in search of some other idler who could help her get rid of an empty afternoon.

Two dirty little urchins wandered along the pavement from the other direction. They caught sight of Eleanor sipping lemonade. With quick shrewdness their eyes took in Eleanor herself, her sparkling car and the parcels piled on the seat. Looking elaborately away from her the taller of the two thrust his hands into his pants pockets and began to sing as he strolled ahead.

She's the army contractor's only daughter
Spending it now,
Spending it now. . . .

Isabel glanced up, started, and burst out laughing. She turned around instantly, lowering her parasol to cover her mirth, but her shoulders were quivering as the singer, sensing a kindred spirit, sidled up to her with a practised

"Lady gimmya nickel to go t'a show?"

"Surely, I'll give you a nickel to go to a show," said Isabel. Eleanor could hear the suppressed amusement in her voice. Opening her bag Isabel bestowed nickels on both of them. As they scampered off down the street Isabel disappeared into the drug store. Eleanor pressed the horn.

She was ashamed of her irritation. It was silly to let a street-gamin's taunt and Isabel's laughter annoy her. "Thanks, Mrs. Larne, come back to see us," the soda-jerker said genially as she returned the glass, and Eleanor managed to smile at him. But as she drove toward the plantation she was calling Isabel names, and it was not until she was out of town and driving once more along the oak-lined river road, her fields stretching on either side of her, that she could calm her temper. But the sight of her cotton plants could always soothe her. She compared her own achievement with Isabel's bored and useless life and smiled as she went indoors.

Wyatt was waiting for her. Eleanor was surprised to see him, for he rarely came to the house.

He greeted her more grimly than usual. "Mrs. Larne, I don't want to scare you or anything, but you'd better start getting pickers together early. Some of the hands are getting sick."

"Sick? What's the matter?"

He examined his dusty shoe. "Well ma'am, I don't rightly know what it is. They're calling it the Spanish influenza."

"Spanish influenza? I never heard of that. Thanks for telling me. I'll have the doctor come over. But I don't think you need to worry, for we won't be picking for a good while yet."

"No'm, but there seems to be a lot of it around. I thought you'd better know."

She thanked him again, and Wyatt took his lugubrious departure. Eleanor went to the telephone and rang Bob Purcell.

188

"Could you drop around sometime tomorrow, Bob?"

"Surely. What's the matter with you now?"

"Nothing, but some of my darkies are getting a new form of the misery."

"Not flu?" said Bob.

"What?"

"Spanish flu. Is that what they have?"

"Yes, influenza, Wyatt called it. Why?"

"There's a lot of it all of a sudden."

"Is it serious? What is it?"

"I don't know, to both questions," said Bob frankly. "But I'll come over."

In the morning he visited the quarters, and then came to her in the house. He was wearing a mask consisting of several squares of gauze tied over his mouth and chin. His eyes looked grave.

He told her to wear a mask too, since she was with the Negroes so much. and to keep the children inside the boundary of the lawns. Nobody knew whether or not this ailment was dangerous, but there was no good in taking chances. Eleanor promised to be careful, and ordered the children's dishes washed with antiseptic soap before their meals.

The next day Neal Sheramy telephoned to cancel an invitation to a Sunday night supper Clara had been planning. Clara was ill "—this strange thing everybody's getting," said Neal. "The flu."

Eleanor was not concerned, as Clara spent half her life catching something or other and apparently enjoying it, but when she got a letter from Fred telling her that her sister Florence was stricken she began to be worried, for like the rest of the Upjohns Florence was almost never ill. Eleanor wrote home that she would like to come to see her, but her mother answered with a special delivery letter telling her no. "Don't you dare run any risk of taking flu back to your youngsters," Molly wrote. "New Orleans is full of it, and it's a bad thing."

Eleanor telephoned Wyatt's house. "I'm doing my best," said Wyatt in answer to her queries. "But I don't know what we're going to use for hands if this keeps up."

Eleanor went out and rode through the fields. The cotton plants were covered with little green bolls. In a short time they would be open, and cotton did not wait to be picked. But who in the name of reason was going to pick it? Pickers had been hard enough to get last year when the general health had been normal. She was ready to cry out in dismay. Her laborers were well fed and housed, they did the most healthful outdoor work, yet Wyatt said they were collapsing like old men, and those who were left standing whispered sepulchrally to each other, "He's got it," and were too scared to work.

During the next few weeks Eleanor had Bob Purcell come to Ardeith frequently. He could not get there as often as she wanted him, for he was working from daybreak till dark. His face was thin with fatigue. "What started this thing?" she demanded of him one morning.

"I don't know," said Bob.

"Have you heard what some people are saying, that it was German spies in this country?"

He shrugged. "That might be credible if it hadn't appeared almost at the same time in China and Sweden and the Fiji Islands, and Germany too."

"What can we do to keep well?"

Bob took a long tired breath. "Eleanor, I don't know what it is nor how to prevent it nor how to cure it. Nobody knows. If you get it go to bed and stay there till you get well."

Her hands held each other tight. "And it's nearly time to pick cotton! What can I do?"

"Good Lord, Eleanor, this isn't a problem of cotton. It's life and death. In some towns the supply of coffins has already run out."

He left her. Eleanor paced the floor of her room till late that night, too restless to sleep. She had read about plagues—the Black Death in Europe, the yellow fever horrors that used to sweep American ports before anybody knew that mosquitoes were more than a harmless nuisance—but it had never occurred to her that she would be called upon to fight one. After a lifetime of taking it for granted that she lived in a world where white-coated men and women in laboratories manipulated test tubes for the public health, she felt stunned before this onslaught. One thought things like this belonged in the times when people prayed to spirits instead of being vaccinated. One did not expect to stand up in the most civilized nation of the twentieth century and see it helpless before a pestilence. One thought that on a plantation equipped with every wheel and engine modern ingenuity could provide, the most scientific planter in the parish could get her cotton in!

The next day Dilcy collapsed with flu. The children missed her, and Eleanor found that she had not known until now how much she had counted on her. While she herself was in the fields she left them with Bessie, but Bessie did not know much about caring for children and Eleanor was frightened lest they catch the infection. When she came in a day or two later to find that Mamie also was ill, she went into the kitchen and cooked their supper herself, clumsily, for she knew very little about cooking and was already trembling with weariness. The children were cross and she herself so nervous she had a hard time being gentle with them.

The cotton bolls opened on nearly empty fields. Eleanor put up signs facing the road and inserted advertisements in the newspapers offering work to anybody who would take it. She advertised two dollars a hundred pounds for picking, but got only scanty results. Billboards and patriotic speakers were proclaiming that America must feed Europe, clothe Europe, fill Europe's guns, but with thousands of workers in the army, thousands at new jobs created by the war, and half the civilian population jamming the hospitals, there were simply not enough laborers to be had at any price.

Eleanor felt sick as she watched the meager lines of pickers. Cotton was now thirty-seven cents a pound, and with the labor shortage lessening the yield the price might go higher. With this crop in the warehouse she could lay Ardeith in Kester's lap, the best equipped plantation in the state, not only free of debt but well on the road to making him rich. But unless she performed a miracle half her cotton would never reach the warehouse.

She sent for Wyatt. "You've got to do something!" she exclaimed, not because she thought he could do anything but because talking relieved her tension.

He shook his head gloomily watching her as she paced the floor. "I'm doing my best, Mrs. Larne."

"Your best? Suppose it should rain and soak those open bolls? We've got to get that cotton in!"

Wyatt sighed. "Honest, Mrs. Larne, I'm no slacker. But I can't make people sprout out of the ground."

Eleanor sat down, twisting her hands together on her knees, and stood up again. "Wyatt, go back and change those signs to read two-fifty a hundred."

"Two-fifty a hundred? My Lord, those pickers will go

nigger-rich with pink silk shirts and yellow shoes and all like that."

"If they get the cotton in I don't care how nigger-rich they get. Go on and do what I told you."

He sighed and retreated. Eleanor walked out into the hall, racking her head for some other means of getting cotton-pickers. On the gallery the children were quarreling. She wearily pacified them and went into the kitchen to make broth for their supper. The household was in a state as muddled as her own nerves. Dilcy and Mamie were still unable to work and two of the other maids had been sent home with influenza. The servants who were left simply could not do all the work. Dust was thick, papers and toys lay scrambled on the floor because nobody had time to pick them up. Always irritated by disorder, now with dust and fretful children added to her plantation worries Eleanor felt driven to the limit of her endurance.

She gave the children supper—used to Mamie's delectable concoctions they grumbled till she felt like giving way to hysterics—and when at last she got them to bed Eleanor went back to the kitchen to find something for herself. She was standing by the table eating a bowl of cornflakes when Bob came to see how the servants were. He was accompanied by Violet, who was driving his car so he could rest on the road.

While Bob was upstairs Eleanor and Violet sat looking at each other in the disordered parlor, both of them too tired to talk much. Violet had been driving Bob from house to house since early morning.

"My idea of heaven," she remarked, "is a place where one can eat white bread and buy a whole ton of coal at once and read every morning in the paper 'The War Is Over.' "

Eleanor laughed grimly. It was the only speech made by either of them until Bob came in.

Bob gave Eleanor a fresh pile of flu-masks, and reminded her to keep up her daily ration of iron.

She tried to smile. "I've already taken enough iron to make a railroad."

"You don't look it," he returned.

Eleanor walked to the door with them. Violet put her hand comfortingly on Eleanor's shoulder. "Don't let yourself get so distracted," she urged. "You'll come through this mess. You're the sort that comes through anything."

Eleanor did not reply. She closed the door behind them and

went up to her room, where she lay down across the bed with her hands pressed to her throbbing temples. Wasn't there anybody in the world, she wondered, who realized that the valiant people to whom nobody ever thought of giving sympathy because they always pulled through, sometimes reached a place where they would give anything they owned to be weak and babyish and have a strong loving bosom to receive their heads?

The next morning when she looked at her haggard face in the mirror she decided to get away from the house and think quietly. Ordering Bessie to stop washing the breakfast dishes and stay with the children, she got out the car and began to drive slowly toward town, for she had learned before now that the motions of driving required just enough attention to free the under part of her mind for thinking through a problem.

The streets were bright with billboards. Pictured soldiers grinned at her, while pictured mothers regarded them with noble eyes; Eleanor wondered why the mother of every eighteen-year-old doughboy should be painted as looking about eighty. But this did not tell her where she could find cotton-pickers. Lovely women in Greek robes waved flags on the posters urging the public to buy Liberty Bonds or join the Red Cross. There were portraits of President Wilson and Herbert Hoover. "Food will win the war! Don't waste it!" "Every home in which cornmeal is used becomes thereby a bulwark of democracy!" "Save sugar! An American girl of 1918 should be as offended at the offer of a box of candy as a girl of 1776 would have been at the offer of a cup of tea." "Food will win the war—every boy and girl who works in a vegetable patch is a Soldier of Freedom!"

Eleanor jammed on the brakes. She had an idea.

Turning the car to the curb she stayed there a moment, gazing up at the picture of an urchin in overalls striding along with a rake over his shoulder. After looking at him awhile she chuckled, wondering if she could make a speech. The papers were full of addresses by Four-Minute Men the country over and it should not be hard to find resounding phrases. Alternate feelings of boldness and guilt scrambled for precedence as she considered. She looked ahead at the road. "I didn't start it," she told herself. "I can't stop it. I might as well use it." She started the motor and drove to the high school.

The principal was in his office. Eleanor told him her plan.

"The boys and girls want to help win the war. But they feel there's so little they can do. They buy thrift stamps, but most of them have such small allowances that they can't buy many. Have you had a hard time filling your quota?"

Yes, the principal admitted, he had.

"I'm paying two dollars and a half a hundred pounds for picking cotton." said Eleanor. "Here's a battle they can fight. They'll be the army behind the lines. If you'll urge them to buy thrift stamps with their wages the Dalroy school will go over the top with it quota before the end of the month."

He was listening with interest. Yes, it was a good idea. She could make a speech in the auditorium tomorrow morning.

"I'll be glad to," said Eleanor. "By the way, who's the leader of the high school band?"

He told her and as soon as school was out Eleanor went to see the band leader.

She had the band on the platform in the auditorium when she spoke the next morning. The students were assembled before her.

"It takes a bale of cotton to fire a fifteen-inch gun," she exclaimed to them. "The winning of the war depends on the American South, the cottonfield of the world! The armies fighting for peace and freedom are counting on us. Come to Ardeith and fight there for salvation of the world's democracy!"

They began to applaud.

"Thank you!" she cried. "You boys who are too young to go to France, you girls who are sorry you can't be soldiers, mobilize to give the soldiers means to fight. Every bale of cotton we get this year brings nearer the day of universal peace. Be soldiers in the Harvest Army and win the war!"

The band forewarned struck up *The Star-Spangled Banner*. This brought them to their feet. They started to cheer.

"Thank you!" Eleanor shouted again above the din. "There'll be trucks at the schoolhouse at three o'clock."

That afternoon the trucks were there, draped with flags, and the band played patriotic music in the first one while the volunteers rode to the plantation. The fields of Ardeith were blazing with posters.

THIS COTTON IS GOING TO AMERICAN GUNS!
COTTON-PICKERS WILL WIN THE WAR

She had placarded the weighing-house:

194

BRING IN THE COTTON FOR AMERICA
AND BUY THRIFT STAMPS
WITH YOUR WAGES

By the first of the next week she had billboards on the streets all over town

COTTON WILL WIN THE WAR!
A SCHOOLBOY ON A PLANTATION
FIGHTS THE KAISER AS WELL
AS A SOLDIER IN THE TRENCHES.
FIGHT WITH US AT ARDEITH!

Five afternoons a week and all day on Saturday, Eleanor sent the boys and girls into the fields. Every Saturday morning they began with a ceremony. The band playing at their head, they marched to a platform outdoors where a flagpole stood, and as the flag was raised Eleanor led them in their pledge of allegiance. Then the band struck up *Dixie,* or *The Stars and Stripes Forever,* and they marched two and two into the fields to pick cotton for democracy.

To each one she gave a card marked in squares, each square meaning twenty pounds of cotton picked, so Wyatt could keep up with payments. "Pay them in single dollar bills, Wyatt," she instructed him. "It looks like more. And be sure the bills are crisp."

He gave her a long look and sighed. "I declare to my soul, Mrs. Larne," he announced somberly, "I never did see a lady like you."

Eleanor laughed. "What did I tell you?"

She even got them public notice. She told the New Orleans papers about her Harvest Army, bringing in the crop for the sake of the men overseas, and they sent photographers to Ardeith. Pictures of the boys and girls in the cottonfields appeared a few days later, and between publicity and patriotism Eleanor found herself one of the few employers of the year who had an abundance of labor. Some of the children caught flu that fall, others got tired and dropped out, and still others broke down cotton plants in their clumsiness, but the scheme worked. She got the cotton in.

The crop totaled twelve hundred and ten bales. She sold the cotton for thirty-eight cents a pound. The gross value of the 1918 crop was a little over two hundred thousand dollars.

195

4

There was one more morsel of a task, and then she would be done. She had to write the last checks that would clear her of owing a penny to anybody in the world.

She was sick with fatigue and at the same time thrilled with victory. It was ten o'clock at night when she realized that a few minutes of check-writing was all that was left for her to do. Her deposit slips had been returned from the bank that afternoon, and she had turned them over in her hands, too tired to grasp at once that the goal for which she had been striving so passionately was lying within reach. How much of this year's return was clear profit she could not tell until she had balanced her books, but her thoughts wandered happily among the possible figures. She was so tired now she could hardly see to write checks, but she concluded that a night's sleep would refresh her and she could attend to her ledgers in the morning.

But though she was exquisitely happy, she did not sleep well that night. Her head ached persistently, and the ticking clock made her so jumpy that she got up at last and put it in the bathroom. When at last she fell asleep she had muddled dreams in which she was alternately working among rows of cotton the pages of figures that seemed to stretch through all eternity. She woke aching in every joint, and writing the checks loomed ahead of her as a task too onerous to be performed.

Disgusted at her weakness, Eleanor dragged herself downstairs and boiled an egg she did not want and made herself eat it, along with a pot of coffee in the hope that it would ease her throbbing head. It did no good, but she gave orders that she was not to be interrupted and went into her study.

The joints of her fingers hurt so that she found it hard to open the desk, and she fumbled with the fountain pen like a child, finding it hard to unscrew the cap. She opened her checkbook. "In ten minutes," she reminded herself, "I'll be done. Ten minutes."

She could see everything at once—her realization that the plantation was mortgaged, the collapse of the cotton market, her discovery of guncotton, her tractors, her years of work. Now, after ten minutes of pushing a pen, it would be over.

She had her victory, and strangely, she felt so wretched that she did not care. She began to make out the first check.

It was hard for her to write. Her fingers moved slowly, and what she wrote was not clear before her eyes. The curious creeping aches would not leave her.

A paralyzing fear struck her, and she pushed it violently out of her mind. She was not sick, she never was, she had no time for it. She had to write these checks and the letters to go with them. She could not have influenza.

But there was no fighting back her sensation. Influenza crept into her hips and knees, wrenching at them till she felt as if the joints were coming apart; into her feet, till she was conscious of ten separate toes, each one with a drag of its own; into her shoulders till she could hardly raise her hand to push the hair back from her pounding head; into her fingers, till she could not support her head at all and let it fall down on her chest. There was an empty feeling behind her forehead. Her skin was blazing with fever and inside her was a chill as though a great icicle had been thrust down beside her spine.

Eleanor sat there, aware that the room was misshapen and moving around. Then for a moment her eyes cleared. She had one more check to write. Moving her hand slowly she grasped the pen; she took a deep breath, steadied the checkbook, and wrote it, moving the pen slowly and heavily, and signing her name like a child just learning how to write. The pen fell out of her hand again. It slipped down to her lap, leaving a blot on her dress, and rolled on the floor. Eleanor looked at it, blinking. The pen moved around. Everything in the room was wavering like shadows in the firelight. She did not care. Through the fever and the thousand aches a small clear spot in her mind knew that she had finished.

She felt herself slip down to the floor, and she caught at the chair she had been occupying. She was not unconscious. She knew she was on the floor, her head on the seat of the chair, and her hands holding it because it felt solid in the tottering room. A hundred ideas tumbled about in her head. Somebody had to get the children's dinner, Bob Purcell had warned her she would go to pieces, she couldn't help it, but it did not matter very much now because she had finished everything. Somebody would mail those checks and Ardeith was safe, and she had enough money to live on a long time even if she did not plant any cotton at all. When Cameo found her an hour later she was still on the floor, mumbling that she had finished.

Cameo called the yard-boy, and between them they carried her upstairs. By this time she was quite delirious.

5

Eleanor was aware of fever and of an acute discomfort that reached from her head to her feet, making her surprised that there should be so much of her to ache at once. It was dark, with spots of light piercing the black now and then and hurting her eyes, and she kept remembering figures and saying them out loud, seventeen cents, twenty cents, twenty-seven cents, thirty-eight cents. She said them over and over.

After a long time she realized that she was lying in bed and that it seemed dark because her eyes were closed. Somebody was drawing the covers over her arms. She opened her eyes. She was in her own bed, under the crimson tester, and bending over her was a strange woman in white with a white mask over the lower part of her face. Eleanor said "Thirty-eight cents," and the woman paid no attention. She moved away and Eleanor saw, sitting at the foot of the bed, a curiously familiar man whose mouth and nose were hidden by a square of gauze. She looked at the man and he looked at her. He was big and thick, and his eyes were blue and what she could see of his face was ruddy. Eleanor moved uncomfortably. He reached to pat her, awkwardly, with a big hand that had square nails, and when she saw his hand she knew him. She stopped saying figures. A strange peace came over her aching body. She lay quiet for a moment, and then said, "Dad."

He sprang up and came to the head of the bed. It seemed quite impossible for her to say anything else. He sat down on the bedstep. Eleanor managed to draw her hand out from under the cover, and he took it in his. From behind his mask he said, "It's all right, baby." She held his hand and let her eyes close again. He was here, he was always around somehow when she needed him, and he would take care of her because he knew she could not do any more. She could give herself up to being just as sick as she pleased.

In the weeks after that Eleanor was aware of very little except her own suffering. There came what seemed like years

198

and years of torment when she could not breathe or speak and her only wish was that they would quit worrying her so she could die and get it over with. Without recalling that anybody had told her, she gathered that her attack of war-flu had turned into the particularly frightful type of pneumonia that sometimes followed it in a constitution too depleted to fight back.

But she came up out of it, white and weak and tired, and slowly she began to take an interest in things and ask questions. Her father was frequently there—he made quick trips between Ardeith and his levee camps—and in his absence her mother was with her, or one of her sisters. The children were in New Orleans with her family. Mamie and Dilcy were well. The horror was passing.

The nurse put her into the wheel-chair one bright morning and let her sit by the window in a shaft of pale winter sunshine.

"You have several letters from your husband," she said. "Your father has them."

"Please!" said Eleanor.

The nurse smiled and went to call Fred, who was downstairs having a mid-morning cup of coffee. Fred came in accompanied by Bob Purcell. Eleanor gave Bob her hand.

"Don't say 'I told you so,' " she begged.

Bob smiled at her. "I won't. You've been punished enough."

"You'll be all right now," said Fred. He sat down near her.

"Have you got those letters from Kester?" Eleanor asked.

"Sure, right here." Fred took them out of his breast pocket. "I hope you'll forgive me for opening and answering them. I hated to, but I thought I should since you couldn't."

She held out her hand and received them. "What does he say?"

Fred chuckled. "A lot of stuff I won't embarrass you by repeating but I guess you're sentimental enough to appreciate it. He ought to be coming home soon."

Eleanor sprang forward in her chair with such force that Bob put restraining hands on her shoulders. "Home?" she cried, "Is he hurt?"

"Quiet," said Bob. He asked gently, "Eleanor, haven't any of us had the grace to tell you the war's over?"

"The war's over? Oh, my God." Eleanor covered her face with her hands and turned her head on the pillow behind her to hide the tears she was too weak to stop. When she could

199

turn around Bob and Fred were looking guiltily at each other, shaking their heads.

"That anybody could have missed the racket of Armistice Day," said Fred. He got up and leaned over Eleanor's chair. "Go on and cry, sugar," he added. "Don't be ashamed. Everybody but you got rid of those tears a week ago."

She managed to sob out, "Dad, the plantation is all clear. Cotton will drop now, won't it?—but it doesn't matter. I've done everything."

"Yes, baby," said Fred.

Chapter Eleven

1

ELEANOR spent the rest of the winter waiting for Kester to come home. As by the first of the year she was quite recovered, she occupied her impatience by preparing Ardeith for his welcome. The house was polished and painted till only by its design and furniture could anybody have guessed it was nearly a hundred years old. Eleanor had the oak trees pruned and trimmed, and the gardens landscaped. Bringing electricians from New Orleans she had Kester's bedroom equipped with a telephone connecting with the servants' phones downstairs, a heater for chilly mornings and a concealed fan that in response to a push-button would send forth gusts of air on hot afternoons. She had his bathroom doubled in size, its walls and floor tiled in two shades of blue, and provided it with sybaritic devices—a gigantic blue bathtub, glassed-in shower, shaving mirror with indirect lights, a long dressing mirror in the door, a wilderness of faucets for sprays and steam, brushes, mats, and colored towels with his monogram. Remembering how he hated figures she installed an adding machine in his study. She bought him an automobile, long and gleaming, and had a new garage built for the protection of this and her own smart little roadster.

Looking around at what she had accomplished Eleanor was aglow with pride. Everything from the nursery to the boundary line of the plantation was a pattern of smooth mechanical order. In the house there was little to do that could not be done by the pressing of a button or the turning of a switch. Outdoors, except for cotton-picking, human hands were needed only for the guiding of machines.

She lived on her anticipation of Kester's joy when he first saw the plantation, and tried to imagine his words. At first he would be speechless. Then he would turn to her. "Eleanor, I never dreamed it could be so beautiful! You did all this for me!" His delight would repay her for everything. She would not mind those weary days in the fields nor the influenza terror nor having worked herself nearly to death. They would have Ardeith, a model of prosperous efficiency, and would live here the rest of their lives together.

It was spring when Kester came. The gardens were shining with camellias and roses, magnolia flowers were starring the trees and in the fields the lines of young cotton were green from the road to the river. Eleanor met him in New Orleans. She stood in a shoving mob of people, not seeing any of them, and watched hundreds of soldiers, all of whom looked alike until she saw Kester. She caught sight of him before he saw her, Kester taking in the throng with his hello-everybody grin while his eyes searched for her, then when he saw her his grin became like a light of victory. Before she could struggle through the crowd to him he had somehow reached her, coming through the press of people as though he had leaped across it, and he had her in his arms. They were so starved for each other they might have been a thousand miles from any human company; Eleanor was conscious of nothing but his arms around her and his kisses on her mouth and eyes, and she never remembered what they said or if they said anything at all. She was simply aware that he was at home and that they would never be separated again.

After awhile—she never knew how long it was—she became conscious that bands were playing and people were cheering and a confusion of orders was being given around her. From somewhere she heard a group of shrill young voices triumphantly singing,

> *And it's oh, boy,*
> *It took the doughboy*
> *To hang the wash on the Hindenburg Line!*

She and Kester moved apart. They stood looking at each other, and began to laugh. He must parade and be cheered, he

201

told her, no, he couldn't help it, everybody seemed to have peace these days except the soldiers who had won the war. Eleanor had to relinquish him to the army, to his parents and his brother and sister, to what looked like thousands of friends. It seemed to her that half the population of New Orleans must have been waiting almost as eagerly as herself for Kester to come home. Though she had always enjoyed his popularity she wished now that nobody in town wanted to see him but herself.

But at last they came home to Ardeith.

Cameo met him at the train with the glittering car. Kester sprang forward and shook hands with Cameo, while Cameo beamed and stammered and looked him over and told him proudly, "Dey sho didn't need to tell me, Mr. Kester, it was gonta take you to win dat war!"

"How's Dilcy?" Kester inquired. "And Mamie?"

"Fine as pie, Mr. Kester. Just spoilin' for a look at you."

Kester took a look inside the car. "But didn't you bring the children, Cameo?"

"Dey's on de gallery waitin', Mr. Kester. Miss Cornelia, she jes' jumpin' up and down, 'bout to bust."

Kester gave Eleanor a wistful smile. "I suppose Philip won't know me at all, will he?"

"He has a mental picture of you—I think something about eight feet high, clanking swords. Kester, do you like the car?"

Kester looked at it. "Holy jumping Joshua." he gasped. He got in slowly, adjusted the mirrors, turned on the yellow fog lights and got out to examine the effect before turning them off again, and stared at her. "How much will she do?"

"Seventy or eighty. I'm not sure."

"Like driving her?"

"I don't know. This is yours."

"Mine?"

She nodded happily. "I have another. A roadster."

He looked around again, not yet used to it. "I thought I'd get a roadster. A little snappy one. I never dreamed of having anything like this."

"You're going to have lots you never dreamed of." Eleanor squeezed his hand. "Don't you want to drive it home? Cameo can sit in back with the bags."

"No, let him do it. I'd rather talk to you." They got into the back seat. Kester played with the inside light and the speaking-tube, raised and lowered the windows. "Why Eleanor, it's a circus on wheels."

Eleanor settled back. "Beautiful, isn't it?"

"Why yes, beautiful," said Kester. He looked eagerly as they started to drive through Dalroy. "Why, Colston's Dry Goods Store is all painted up. So's the drug store. And all those new flower-beds in the park! Gee, the place looks prosperous."

Eleanor chuckled. "Thirty-eight-cent cotton, darling."

"Thirty—eight—cents!" he gasped. "Did it really go that high?"

"Didn't I write you? Or maybe I didn't. That was about the time I got sick."

"Are you all right now?" he asked anxiously.

"Oh yes, I never felt better in my life."

"Lord, it's good to be home!" Kester looked out, his eyes greedy for the sight of familiar things. The car turned into the river road, purring softly under his exclamations. "Eleanor, I can't tell you how I've dreamed about this place. The wide shady streets and the palms with rosa montana climbing over them, the mules and Negroes in town on Saturday afternoons, the drug store with everybody getting cokes and lemonade, the darkies hoeing the cotton, watermelons and cornbread and crab gumbo—there's Ardeith, beyond the pomegranate trees!" His hand closed on hers. "How I've missed it," he said in a low voice.

Eleanor was breathless in her desire to watch him as he saw Ardeith's new beauty. Kester exclaimed,

"What gorgeous cotton! I never saw it so high this time of year."

He watched the fields, his back to her. She tingled.

"Oughtn't there to be some hoeing, about now?" asked Kester. "I haven't seen any darkies yet."

"I don't use so many laborers now. We don't need them."

"But why not?" Before she could answer, he asked, "What's that thing like an engine with claws, kicking up all that dust?"

"A cultivator. That's why we don't need so many Negroes."

He turned back to her with an astonished little smile. "I reckon I'll have to get used to them. That looks odd, somehow."

"I wrote you."

"But I don't think I exactly imagined them here. Funny, isn't it?"

"They do wonderful work."

"Evidently they do. That's fine cotton if I ever saw any." His attention was back on the fields. "What are those little white houses with green trimmings, over near the river?"

"That's where the Negroes live."

"Holy smoke, you mean that's the quarters?"

She nodded. "No more rickety cabins. They have screens and everything."

"Amazing," said Kester. He grinned. "I bet they've every one of them cut a hole in the screen door to let the cat in."

"They tried that sort of thing at first. I put a stop to it."

"Oh, I wouldn't."

"Why not?"

"If they're happier with mosquitoes, why not let 'em have mosquitoes? It's none of our business, you know, as long as they tend to the cotton."

She laughed at him. The car turned into the avenue. "Ardeith," said Kester. He said it reverently, looking around. "Eleanor, what's happened to the oaks? They seem smaller than I remember."

"They've been pruned down. I had a couple of tree-surgeons attend to them."

"Oh. The lawns are kind of—formal, aren't they?"

"The flowers were running wild. I brought a landscaper here to do them over."

The car stopped in front of the house. Kester sprang out. There was a shout from the gallery. Cornelia had said "Father?" tentatively, then as he ran toward her she screamed "Father!" and sprang to him in an ecstasy of delight. Philip, though he did not know him, was excited too, for Eleanor had told him so much about the wonderful man who was coming, and Kester stood up holding them both, each on an arm. They were all talking at once.

"Look at my new dress," said Cornelia. "It's got pink spots and a sash."

"Baby, how you've grown!" Kester was exclaiming. "Philip, do you know who I am?"

"Sojer," said Philip, "and father."

He carried them into the house. Eleanor followed. She found Kester down on his knees in the parlor, an open suitcase on the floor beside him, from which he was taking such an assortment of dolls and toys that the children were shouting with glee. Eleanor smiled as she watched. The

204

children were so pretty and so healthy, any man would be proud of them. And Kester certainly was. At last, when they had scampered away to show their treasures to Dilcy, he got to his feet.

"It's such fun to see them be persons," he said, "not babies any more. Eleanor, isn't Cornelia the loveliest child you ever saw?"

"She knows it, too," Eleanor returned. "If we aren't careful she's going to spend her life in front of a looking-glass. How do you like Philip?"

"I like him enormously. But I've got to get acquainted all over again with both of them."

She slipped her hand through the bend of his arm. "Come with me, Kester. I've got so much to show you, I hardly know where to start."

He looked around hungrily. "Ardeith," he said. "I want to see every room, every chair of it. Let's tell Cameo to take the bags upstairs." He took a step toward the wall and turned back to her with puzzled eyes. "Why Eleanor, where's the bellcord?"

"In the attic." Dropping his arm she went to the black button-studded rectangle in the corner and took down the telephone receiver. "Bessie? Tell Cameo to take Mr. Kester's things to his room. And have Mamie make a pot of fresh coffee and send it up. We'll be there in a few minutes."

Kester was staring. "What—in the name—of conscience—is that thing?"

"A house-telephone. They save an endless lot of running about. Come along."

She guided him through the house, showing him the convenience of buttons and switches, and the calculating machines in his office. Kester looked at everything with amazement.

"I don't suppose you're so much interested in the kitchen," she said, "or the laundry, but would you like to take a peek?"

"Why—yes," said Kester.

Eleanor opened the kitchen door. Kester stared at the expanse of white tiles, the curtained windows, Mamie presiding over the electric stove.

"It looks like a restaurant," he said in a low voice.

"Mighty fine doin's we got," Mamie announced to him.

"I'll say you have. But Mamie, can you cook on that thing —I mean, cook the way you used to?"

"Well sah, it was kind of funny at first. But it's mighty nice and clean, Mr. Kester. Right highclass, after you gets used to it."

"I suppose it must be," said Kester.

He and Eleanor went back into the main hall. "Don't you like it!" Eleanor exclaimed.

"Why yes, yes, of course. Only it's all so new. It's like coming to a different place. I'll have to get used to it, as Mamie said."

They went up the spiral staircase and into Kester's bedroom. Eleanor proudly pushed the button that controlled the hidden fan.

"I can't say anything yet," he murmured. "I'm too astonished. I feel like a horse and buggy."

She laughed. Kester crossed the room and opened the bathroom door.

"For the love of the Lord," he breathed. "Eleanor, this isn't mine!"

"Yes it is. Watch." She pressed a button. A brush came out of the wall, spinning, and she showed him how to hold his foot under it so as to get his shoe brushed without stooping. She displayed the faucets and mirrors and lights. Kester stood in the middle of it like a child before a baffling toy.

"All this," he marveled, "just to take a bath. Have you got one like it?"

She nodded. "You can see mine later."

There was a knock, and Cameo entered with the coffee-tray and the old silver service. "I could stand a cup of coffee," said Kester. "My head's positively addled."

They sat down by the bedside table and Eleanor began to pour the coffee. "Kester, tell me what you think of it!"

"Why—everything must be very convenient," he returned slowly. "I mean once you learn how to work all these things."

"Oh yes, it is. Living here is so easy now. Everybody has so much more time."

Kester stroked the handle of the silver coffee-pot. "It's good to see all this again, and drink Mamie's coffee. She makes the best coffee on earth. Why Eleanor!" he broke off.

"What's the trouble, darling?"

"Where's the dent?"

"Oh, that! You had me scared for a minute. I had it straightened."

"Oh, I see. You had it straightened." Kester set down his

206

cup and stood up. "Eleanor, run along, will you? I'd like to get washed up before dinner."

"Why—all right." She stood up too. "Don't you want me to help unpack your things?"

"No, I'll do it."

She moved away from him. He was looking out at the landscaped gardens. "Kester, what's the matter?" she asked.

"Not a thing. But I'm all cindery from the train, and famished. What have we got for dinner, by the way?"

She smiled at that. "River-shrimp and stuffed crabs, and rice—"

"Ah!" He grinned. "Wonderful. And we haven't—just by the merest possible chance—we *haven't* got pecan pie for dessert?"

She nodded vehemently. "Yes, we have."

Kester looked around. "Imagine, pecan pie in the same house with that bathroom. Eleanor, you—" He broke off again and began to laugh.

"What's so funny about pecan pie?" she exclaimed.

"Nothing, Eleanor. I'm just so glad to get it. Tell Mamie to hurry up, and I'll be down in a couple of minutes."

Eleanor went out and shut the door. She walked across to the middle of the hall and stood with her hand on the balustrade of the staircase, looking back at the door of Kester's room. She could hear him moving around. From downstairs she could hear the voices of the children.

Within her was a feeling of emptiness. It was very strange. Kester's homecoming was flat. He had not said or done anything to justify her having such an impression, but there it was. She slowly went downstairs.

"Nothing is as wonderful as you think it's going to be," she advised herself as she stood at the foot of the staircase. "He's so full of things to say he can't say any of them yet. That's all. I'm just overworking my imagination."

Kester called her, leaning over the balustrade above the turn. "Eleanor, have you invited any people over for this evening?"

"Why no," she answered, looking up. "I haven't." She felt a pang of disappointment; she had thought he would want to be alone with her.

"Oh, call them up—Neal and Bob and Violet—you know, everybody. I want to see them."

"All right," said Eleanor.

He went back to his room, whistling. Eleanor shook her head. She could not get rid of a feeling of having been delicately, perhaps unintentionally, snubbed.

2

She did not get rid of it as the weeks passed. Kester rode with her through the fields, praising the cotton and admiring her rejuvenation of the land, but he never showed the joy she had expected. He had an abstraction she had never observed in him before. In the midst of her explanation of how the tractors worked she saw that his eyes had wandered over to the river; when she demonstrated the new fertilizing machine he answered in phrases that would have looked all right had they been written down, but in a manner that was in some indefinable way not quite as enthusiastic as it might have been. It was not like Kester to be absent-minded. One of his most enjoyable characteristics was his quality of being absorbed in the affair of the moment as if nothing else existed. Knowing how he loved every clod and corner of Ardeith, she had expected that he would want to examine everything and visit every field to see how it was growing. But he did not. He followed her deferentially, giving generous praises, but only rarely did she hear a spontaneous expression of pleasure.

Eleanor was beginning to hear about the war's effect on some men, who had come back from France shivering neurotics unfit to resume normal life, but she was sure that was not what was wrong with Kester. He had seen very little of the war's worst aspects. He talked about it freely, though with his usual tact he was quick to sense the increasing reaction of "Oh let's not talk about the war, everybody's so tired of that," and change the subject. Their friends said, "Isn't Kester delightful? How did we ever do without him!"—and she smiled to hide an increasing pain. Kester was delightful. But what she could confess to nobody was that Kester was just as delightful in their hours of privacy as he was in a roomful of people, and hardly less superficial.

Kester was not pleased with her; he did not say so, but she could feel it. His conversation was copious, born of a prodigal mind too long deprived of its most eager listener. But being with Kester was like attending a banquet where the food was choice, the wine exquisite, and her partner quick to anticipate and please her every desire, but where intimacy died in its trappings of gaiety. There had been a swift physical intoxication at their being together after their long separation, but that could not last forever and they seemed to have very little else. They had not recaptured their old sense of being one person with a single aim and a single desire; they were separate, with an empty space between them that kept them apart. They played with the children, and it was obvious that Kester was very fond of them both. They went to parties or gave parties at Ardeith, and he was as merry as ever. But they rarely spent an evening alone. They did not have their long hours of alternate silence and chatter, tossing back and forth between them the tiny unimportant threads that in the course of years became an unbreakable web of union. Kester was knightly and adoring, but that was not what she wanted.

He treats me, she thought despairingly, like a mistress, a mistress he has to woo and please and charm because he doesn't dare admit her behind the barriers of his personal pride—what have I done?

Again and again she tried to bridge the gap by pretending it did not exist. She gossiped about what their friends had been doing in his absence, and he was pleasantly attentive. She talked about the plantation, and he was interested, but when she asked his advice she rarely received more than a polite, "But Eleanor, I hardly know. Everything is so different here, I'm afraid my ideas are antiquated."

"You know more about cotton than I ever will!" she protested.

"Don't pretend to flatter me, sugar. You've done it all so magnificently, you don't need anything I can tell you."

Eleanor fought the emptiness with a passionate yearning. She could not get through.

"Do you love me, Kester?"

"Sweetheart, how can you ask me? When your picture wasn't out of my pocket five minutes during the whole war except when I was showing it around?"

"Do you still love me as much as that?"

"I've always loved you, I love you now, I always will. Don't you know it?"

"Yes, but I like to hear you say it." That was all she could think of to answer.

He did love her, she could not doubt it. When Kester invited an army friend of his to spend a week at Ardeith, the guest walked directly to her with an eager smile, exclaiming, "And you are Eleanor? Forgive me if I can't think of you except by your first name but it's all I heard from Kester for six months at Camp Jackson." Eleanor laughed, more grateful than she would have liked for him to guess, and told him to go on calling her that He told her about Kester's popularity at camp—"Everybody liked him, but I suppose you're used to hearing that?"—and later, when Kester had gone to select a special Bourbon for a nightcap, he added, "I never saw a man so proud of his wife. His voice positively lowered with reverence when he spoke of you."

They gave a party the next evening, Kester playing his rôle of superb host and evidently enjoying it. Eleanor watched him, baffled. With other people he seemed not to have changed. It was only toward herself that he seemed to feel a curious shyness. His attitude was, she was sure, unintentional on his part and he did not know she sensed it, but she felt he wanted something of her that she was not giving him and that he thought it useless to ask for.

When their guest had gone Eleanor tried again. She asked Kester what he thought of the postwar conferences. They exchanged opinions. How did he regard Mr. Wilson's idea of a League of Nations? Not very highly, Kester said, he admired Mr. Wilson but he thought the United States had had enough of Europe and should mind its own business for a change. It was no use. He was as affectionately polite as he would have been to one of her sisters.

By the end of the summer Eleanor was nearly desperate with pleasant pretenses. She had thought the ripe fields, heavy with such a harvest as he had never seen before at Ardeith, would rouse him, but Kester's admiration, though she could find no fault with a word of it, seemed to be merely admiration; he did not, as she used to see him, take an open boll in his hand and stroke the cotton as tenderly as if it had been the hair of a beloved woman. He was not enthusiastic about anything that she could see, except parties—and he was drinking too much, though she so dreaded widening the breach between them that she never said so—and the only event that seemed to rouse his unalloyed interest was Cornelia's beginning to go to school. He got a great deal of pleasure from his children. Eleanor wearily returned her attention to the work of getting the cotton in.

She had no trouble finding pickers this year, for the influx of returning soldiers was beginning to cause a labor surplus and Wyatt had more applicants than he could use. The price of cotton was still high, as most of the product of recent years had been nitrated and shot away, and the world was in dire need of clothes; and Eleanor felt a resurgence of hope as she calculated what the profits would be. Unable to believe that Kester would remain indifferent to the plantation, Eleanor welcomed the realization that there was a problem now on which she needed his advice. With the war over, less cotton would be wanted and it would be wise to substitute other crops on part of the Ardeith acres. She asked Kester about it one afternoon after dinner.

"Do you mean you want to try truck-farming?" he asked.

"I thought we might. What vegetables grow best here?"

"Strawberries?" he suggested.

"We can try them. Do you think it would be a good idea to try a number of crops in different places, and see what we can do? Of course that would mean taking a good-sized loss at first, but we can afford it."

He smiled a little. "Can't we afford to stay with cotton?"

"Oh, we can, of course, but there's no reason to. Cotton prices are going to drop. I'm certain we'll do better with food crops on part of the land. Don't you think it would be fun to experiment, anyway?"

"But you've got the whole place organized for cotton. And we can live, and live well, Eleanor, on the production we have now, even if the price goes back to ten cents a pound."

"But there's no sense in living on that if we don't have to!" she exclaimed.

"I think there's pretty good sense to it," said Kester. "We can be mighty comfortable."

"But there's so much else to do, Kester! So much we *can* do. It's so exciting to work at a challenge like this. To organize it and feel it grow, and be rewarded when you've done it right."

"But you don't get time to do anything else," said Kester. He stood up. "Try reorganization if you want to. Put in strawberries very early to catch the February market. And don't risk anything on figs. They're so hard to ship they aren't worth it. Try—oh, lettuce, cabbage, celery, corn, shallots, turnips—they'll all grow well."

She shook her head at him, wondering. "When you know

so much about it," she said, "it's strange that you aren't interested in doing it. Why Kester, we can be rich!"

Kester smiled. "You like being rich, don't you?"

"Of course I do. Who wouldn't?"

He came over to where she sat. Bending over her, he pushed her hair back from her temple and kissed her. "You're an odd person. You're not like anybody else I've ever known." He added, "It's frightfully hot. I think I'll have Cameo make a Tom Collins."

"I'll order it." Eleanor gave the order at the telephone, tempted at the same time to scold Kester for drinking and make him mad. At the moment it seemed to her that any honest expression from him, even anger, would be easier to bear than his courteous apathy. "I'm going to town," she said abruptly. "I've some errands to do."

She got out the car and drove hurriedly down the avenue. Once on the river road she went more slowly. She had no errands. She simply drove, welcoming the cool wind in her hair, asking herself over and over, What have I done? What *is* the matter with him? Why doesn't he like me?

She had no answer.

3

When the cotton was baled Wyatt came to her triumphantly. Eleanor went out on the gallery to meet him, and found him looking almost jaunty, his hat on the back of his head.

"Here you are, Mrs. Larne," he said. He handed her his statement and stood back, waiting for his laurels.

Eleanor glanced down, and gasped. The crop totaled thirteen hundred and twenty-six bales.

"Wonderful!" she exclaimed.

"Yes, ma'am," said Wyatt.

"Great work, Wyatt." She shook his hand warmly.

The cheeks on either side of his lantern jaw began to crease with one of his rare proud grins, "Well ma'am, I wouldn't say it was bad, myself."

"I think this calls for a bonus," said Eleanor.

"You mean it, Mrs. Larne?"

"Certainly I mean it. Shall we say a dollar a bale?"

"Well now, ma'am, that's nice of you. You're mighty fair."

"Wait a minute. I want to tell my husband." She ran to the door and called. "Kester! Come here."

"What's all the excitement?" Kester asked, coming out to the gallery. "Oh hello, Wyatt."

"Good morning, Mr. Larne. Nice day."

"Kester," Eleanor was exclaiming, "do you know what we've done this year? Thirteen hundred and twenty-six bales!"

"Holy smoke," said Kester. He gave Wyatt a smile of congratulation. "I'm beginning to think you must be as smart as my wife says you are."

Mellowed by his bonus, Wyatt was in a mood to be generous. "Well sir, I wouldn't take all the credit. Not more than a third of it, I'd say. I never did see a lady could get things done like this lady here."

"Yes, she's great, isn't she?"

"Yes sir. You're mghty right she is. Thirteen hundred and twenty-six bales." Wyatt gave a glance around as though taking in all of Ardeith. "Not bad for a plantation that six years ago was barely topping eight hundred, is it?"

"Not bad at all," said Kester dryly.

"Don't go yet, Wyatt," Eleanor said to him. "I'll write that check for you." She hurried in, and when she came out with the check in her hand she saw Kester leaning against one of the gallery columns in affable conversation with the overseer. Wyatt was evidently finding him pleasant to talk to.

"—at Louisiana State," Wyatt was saying. "Doing mighty well up there. Got a scholarship for this year, pretty good, don't you think?—competitive examination in a big university like that?"

"Who's that you're talking about?" Eleanor inquired.

Wyatt glanced down as though embarrassed. "Why—er, my daughter, Mrs. Larne."

"Oh." She recalled having seen a young girl around his house, but they had never discussed his family. "here's the check, Wyatt, and thank you."

"Thank *you*, ma'am."

She sat down on the step and began giving him instructions about having the tractors overhauled before the winter's work. While she was talking Kester wandered off.

He gets intimate with everybody but me, she thought while she and Wyatt were discussing the tractors. Thirteen hundred bales of cotton and all he does is smile politely, he looked more interested in hearing that Wyatt's daughter had won a

213

scholarship. If Wyatt's so proud of her it's odd he never told me about it. What *have* I done to Kester? What except work till I collapsed making this the finest cotton plantation in Louisiana?

"Yes, that's all," she said briskly to Wyatt. "If I think of anything else that needs doing I'll call you in the morning."

She went into the house. Kester was in the library reading. Eleanor went across the hall to the parlor and sat down, a magazine on her knee so she could pretend to be reading if he came in. She was hurt more deeply than he had ever hurt her. For nearly six years, since she had first learned Ardeith was in danger, she had given herself to Kester's plantation without stint, sustained by her passionate anticipation of the day when she could give him her dream of Ardeith complete. And now, apparently, he did not want it. She thought she could have borne anything more easily than this pleasant indifference.

At supper Kester was talkative and amusing, as always, and when they went up to tell the children good night he recounted a bedtime story that sent them into happy chuckles. At least with Cornelia and Philip he had no reticences.

"Have you asked anybody to come in this evening?" she inquired as they left the nursery.

"No, I don't believe so."

"Then come into my room. We can talk."

"All right. I did want to talk to you."

She was glad of it. A fire was burning in her room—mainly for decorative purposes, as there was little need for it yet— and Eleanor listened eagerly as she sat down by the hearth. Kester was taking a travel folder out of his pocket.

"This came in the mail today. It's about a Central American cruise, lasting six weeks. Wouldn't you like a holiday?"

"I'd love it!" she exclaimed fervently. If they could get away now, in the idleness of the Gulf they might talk to each other frankly and recapture what they had lost. "In fact," she added, "I'd like it so much I can start getting ready tomorrow."

"Good," said Kester. "This sounds like the best cruise of the sort I've read about in a long time, a beautiful ship, stopping at all the interesting ports."

"Let me see." He handed her the folder. The pictures and descriptions were inviting. But the boat was not scheduled to leave New Orleans until the first of February, and when Eleanor saw the date she looked up dubiously. "But Kester, they're always having Central American cruises. Couldn't we take one this fall?"

"Why? This one sounds perfect." He chuckled. "You always want to be in such a hurry. Most women would be glad of two or three months to buy clothes."

"Silly. I can do all the shopping I'd need in a week. I was just thinking, if we took this trip we wouldn't get back till sometime in March, and that's just the wrong time to be away from the plantation."

"Oh, Eleanor," he objected, "what have we got an overseer for?"

"Wyatt's a cotton man," she reminded him. "If we're going to try any experimental crops—don't you remember we talked about that the other day?—we ought to be here."

"I'd forgotten that." He picked up the folder, which lay in her lap, and returned it to his pocket.

"I'll write New Orleans tomorrow," Eleanor went on, "asking about boats leaving in the next few weeks. That won't interfere with our work here." She smiled at the fire. "Experimental crops are costly at best, and there's no reason to deplete our profits any more than we can help."

Kester sat down. He looked at the fire. Suddenly he stood up again. "Eleanor," he exclaimed, "don't you ever think about anything but money?"

"Why, Kester!" She sat forward. "What do you mean?"

"I mean, don't you ever stop gloating over the money you've made? Don't you want to do anything besides go on making more?"

"I—don't—understand," she said slowly. "Aren't you glad we're prosperous at last?"

"Of course I'm glad. But you aren't just comfortably prosperous. You run money through your fingers like a miser. What's happened to you?" He spoke vehemently.

Eleanor pushed her hand over her forehead. "So that's it," she said. "That's why you don't like me." She was hurt, and she was still bewildered.

"I love you very much," Kester said earnestly. "But I don't like this streak that's come out in you, this passion for making money as though a bank account were the only important thing in the world. Eleanor, I don't care whether we take a trip now or next spring, or whether or not we take one at all, but I do care about your thinking of everything on the face of the earth in terms of what it costs! Ardeith is organized now to

215

run with only a reasonable amount of supervision—can't you let it alone? You're so imbedded in the idea of profits!"

"Wait a minute," said Eleanor. She spoke slowly, trying to be reasonable. "Kester, you don't understand. For so long I've not had the chance to think of anything else. When you left, Ardeith wasn't half paid for. I had to battle the highest prices and the worst labor shortage in history. I had to think about money every hour I was awake."

"But you don't have to now. We don't owe a cent to anybody on earth. We're making a splendid income, much more than enough for everything we need."

"But now that we've got such a victory," she pled, "we can't let it go! We can't slip back to being indolent dreamers!"

"Nobody's asking you to. But you don't have to work incessantly to get rich, as you did during the war."

Eleanor shook her head at him. She was still hurt, but she felt a sense of relief at the clearing of the mist. "But shouldn't we run the place carefully? Efficiently? I can't believe we should sit back and take it easily now! I like the sense of doing a job well. I want the results of all I worked for, Kester! You don't know what it was like. You weren't here."

"You're damn right I wasn't here," Kester said in a low voice.

She stood up. "If you had been—"

"If I had been here the place wouldn't be like this."

"Aren't you pleased with what I did?" she cried in astonishment. "Don't you like to have Ardeith free and rich and all your own again? Think what it is now, compared to what it used to be!"

"I've thought of nothing else all summer," said Kester.

"Aren't you glad the mortgages are paid?"

"Yes, yes, of course."

"Then what? Please tell me! Aren't you proud? Don't you love it?"

"Love it? In the name of God, Eleanor, how can anybody love living in a place that looks like the Ford factory?"

He turned around and walked to the door, while she stood still, breathless with amazement. His hand on the doorknob, he went on.

"There. I've said it. I've tried not to say it every day since I've been at home. I hate what you've done to Ardeith. I hate every button and every engine. I hate that God-damned bathroom and your telephones and your adding machines.

216

This place was beautiful when I had it. It was lazy and wasteful and nobody did very much and everybody had a grand time. Now it's a mill for the manufacture of cotton-bales. It's hideous."

He opened the door.

"Wait a minute " said Eleanor.

She stood feeling as though he had lashed her across the face with a whip Trembling with her effort to keep a tight hold on her temper she said,

"You don't quite know what you're talking about. Kester. Your picturesque way of running the plantation had it bankrupt."

"It was bankrupt the year before the war, but after that we were paying the mortgage. And we weren't doing it this way."

"At the rate we were going," she answered tensely, "it would have taken years and years. This way, we've nearly doubled our rate of profit."

"Yes, I know, and that's all that matters to you. This way, you've cleared out everything that made Ardeith warm and lovely, a place to be born in and live in and die in. You've swept away every track of the people who built it and loved it. You straightened the dent in my great-grandmother's coffee-pot."

Her chest rose and fell with a breath that had to be drawn with an effort because her lungs seemed paralyzed with anger.

"I think—you're—a fool," she said.

"Yes, by your standards I'm a fool. A sentimental fool. And by my standards you're a fool. Eleanor, man does *not* live by bread alone!"

Her chest was full of pain. "I thought you were going to like it. I thought you'd be glad to be rich."

"I don't like to be nigger-rich," Kester said deliberately.

"Nigger-rich?" She was so angry that her breath was coming with difficulty and she could hardly speak.

"Yes. You've seen darkies in prosperous times. Pink silk shirts and hanging-lamps and phonographs, anything bright or noisy—yes. I'm saying it now and you can stand up there and listen. Before I came home I'd seen cartoons of the war profiteers, complacent and porky, but it didn't occur to me I was going to have to live with one."

"Complacent. Porky." Eleanor was too shocked to do more than echo. Her hands were holding each other so tight that the knuckles were prominent and the skin was stretched across their backs.

"Just because you haven't gone in for diamond sunbursts on your bosom," said Kester, "do you think there's any difference? Your machines and your push-buttons and all your ostentatious efficiency!"

"That's—what—you—think of me," she said, slowly because she did not have breath enough to speak fast. "That's what I get for the work I've done."

"I know how hard you've worked. I've tried not to say it."

"I worked every minute I could stay awake," said Eleanor. "It didn't matter how tired I was or that I nearly died of pneumonia. I was doing it for you."

"For me?" He smiled wisely. "I'll listen to a lot of nonsense from you, Eleanor, but don't try to tell me that. You were doing it for your own self-esteem, to prove to yourself that you could do an almost superhuman job without anybody's help. If you'd been remaking this plantation for me you'd have done it with some regard for what I wanted. You knew me well enough to have realized I wouldn't like this shiny exhibition. I'm not saying you haven't as much right to your ways as I have to mine, but try to make me believe you were doing this for anybody's pleasure but your own."

"I thought," she managed to say, "you were going to be delighted."

"You thought I was going to be a rapturous audience. All you wanted from me was accolades. God knows I tried to give them to you."

She looked him up and down. Kester stood just in front of the half-open door, hands in his coat pockets, talking to her with the smile of passionless cruelty she had seen on his face once or twice before, and that she dreaded more than any other expression he could assume.

"You're having a good time telling me all this, aren't you?" Eleanor asked.

"Yes, I think I am. I've held it back so long."

"Why didn't you tell me earlier? When I was nearly distracted wondering what was wrong?"

"I didn't know you were wondering. I thought I was applauding very well."

"But why didn't you tell me?"

"I couldn't. I suppose in the back of my mind I knew I

218

couldn't go on forever without saying this, but I kept putting it off. I was so sorry for you."

"Sorry for me?"

"Why yes. You were so pleased with yourself. You thought it was all so pretty."

"I did think so," said Eleanor. "I still think so. I like convenience and efficiency and order. And whether you like them or not I'm going to keep them."

"Not like this," Kester retorted. "I want to enjoy life and I can't enjoy this kind. I'm going to have that horrible bathroom ripped out and a plain white one put in. I'm going to take that gadget-ridden automobile down and turn it in for one that doesn't look as if it had been made to show off a pawnbroker's opulence. I'm going to plant a few watermelons in these exquisite fields and let a few pickaninnies eat them on the levee. And as long as we make a living I don't care if I cut your precious profits in two. I'm going to get Ardeith back to something like what it used to be."

She crossed the room and faced him. "Oh no you're not."

"Why not?"

"I'll tell you why not. It's your turn to listen." She stood in front of him, speaking clearly. "I've paid the price of your irresponsibility and now that I've done it I'll be damned if I'll take your contempt. Has it entered your head that by every shading of right and justice this plantation belongs to me?"

Kester did not answer. He simply stared at her. She went on, speaking so that every word was separate from every other.

"Certainly it does. When I came here Ardeith wasn't yours. It belonged to the Southeastern Exchange Bank and they were letting you live here. When they threatened to make you move out I went to work. In the beginning you had to tell me what to do but even in that first summer I worked more than you did. When the market collapsed I sold the furniture and got Mr. Robichaux to take the jewelry as security for our interest. When dad sent me that clipping about guncotton I telephoned Sebastian and told him to hold our cotton because you were spending the night with Isabel Valcour. I got the loan from Mr. Tonelli that let us raise the crop that year. When you thought the war would be more exciting than paying your debts you merely said to me, 'You'll do it.' And I did. If I had run around to patriotic tea-parties after you went to camp you wouldn't have come home to Ardeith. You're living here because I bought this place and paid for it. If you don't like the way I operate my plantation, I'm sorry."

Kester had not moved as he listened to her. Now as she paused he stirred slightly, moved his head and shoulders, and slowly took one hand from his pocket to reach for the doorknob behind him.

"You are perfectly right," he said in a low voice. "Forgive me for being a very ungracious guest."

He went out.

As he started across the hall Eleanor leaned against the side of the doorway, watching him in bitter triumph. Kester opened the door of his own bedroom, went inside and closed it.

Eleanor could hear him moving around, opening doors and pulling out drawers. Suddenly her heart gave several quick little jumps and she caught her hands over it. She had not meant to be quite so cruel. Her words came back to her with their simple and unmistakable implication, which no man of Kester's nature could have failed to hear. The walls began to totter as she realized that he was acting upon it.

She ran across the hall and flung open the door of his room.

Two suitcases were on the floor, half full of a jumble of shirts and shoes and pajamas. The drawers of his bureau stood open, and he was going back and forth between the bureau and the suitcase, bringing garments and dumping them on the piles. As she came in he glanced up, but he did not pause or speak to her.

"Kester," she gasped, "where are you going?"

"I really don't know," said Kester. He was on his knees putting his toothbrushes into a case.

"I didn't mean that!" she exclaimed. "I never thought of it!"

"I should have thought of it myself," Kester returned quietly. "Stupid of me not to have realized that six months is a long time to ask for free lodging."

Eleanor laced her hands together, moving them till she could hear the little swishing sound of her palms against each other.

"Won't you forgive me, Kester?" she pled. "I was so angry —I hardly knew what I was talking about. I didn't mean to say what you thought I did."

"Would you mind moving so I can get that coat?" asked Kester.

She took a step to one side, mechanically observing that it was just like Kester to have slung his coat over a projecting light-bracket on the wall. He took it down and began folding it.

Eleanor stood where she was, silenced by her utter helplessness against what was happening. Kester went on packing his bags, muddling clothes and shaving-brushes in the most disorderly fashion and putting in shoes where the polish would be sure to smudge his handkerchiefs. She had an impulse to say, "Let me do that, you'll never find anything when you open those bags," but she did not say that or anything else; she simply stood there, watching him throw his things together and then close the suitcases. He had stuffed them so hastily that the lids and bottoms would not meet until he had put his knee on the top of each one in turn and strained at the straps. Then he stood up, carrying a suitcase in each hand, and went past her, through the doorway and into the hall.

She came after him. He was about to start down the staircase.

"Kester," she said, "Kester, I told you I was sorry. My darling—why are you going away?"

He set down the bags. Turning around, he looked at her. He looked her up and down, his face expressionless but for a flicker at the corner of his mouth.

"If you weren't poor white trash," he answered slowly and distinctly, "you wouldn't have to ask."

He picked up the bags and went down the stairs. Standing with her hands on her throat, which was closing and choking her so that she could not move or speak and could hardly breathe, Eleanor heard the front door closing and then the sound of the gadget-ridden car in the avenue.

Later that night a Negro man brought the car back. Cameo, who answered the doorbell, brought Eleanor a note.

"Sorry I had to borrow your car, but I had the tank filled. Kester."

Chapter Twelve

1

FOR A WEEK Eleanor heard nothing more from Kester, then she received a note four lines long telling her he was working at the government cotton station up the river. He did not write her again. She could not tell if his silence was a weapon he was deliberately using to hurt her or if he merely had nothing to say.

Eleanor had never been more uncertain or more wretched, for never had she had such a blow to her self-respect. Whether Kester's hand or her own had been heaviest in dealing it she could not decide. All she knew was that Kester had walked out of Ardeith and she had no way to tell if he had any intention of returning.

At first she could not think. It was like the winter before when she had been so ill that physical discomfort had been like a shell separating everything else from her consciousness, only what enclosed her now was pain of the spirit. She walked around the house, or drove into the country for such distances that she was half hypnotized with the motions of driving. Usually so clear and sure of its purposes, her mind now was muddy with confusion. Kester despised her. He had called her poor white trash. She lay awake at night remembering it, trembling with rage and shame. Long ago Kester had given her his own definition of the term: "No fineness, no delicacy, no knowledge that some things are Caesar's and some things are God's."

She recalled their last dialogue. Her concluding speech to Kester had been intolerable. She had driven a hateful truth into him like a knife, with a power to hurt him that she would not have had if he had not, by loving her, given it to her. But he had plagued her past endurance, she told herself savagely; nobody could remain patient before his habit of substituting charm for a sense of moral obligation.

Over and over she retraced her analysis this far, and stopped. She could go no further because she loved Kester, she loved him for the very levity and glitter that had driven her to exasperation, and she wanted nothing in the world but to have him back.

She wrote him a letter beginning, "The children ask for you a dozen times a day," and then tore it up. It was true, the children did ask for him, but that was a bludgeon she would scorn herself for using and he would scorn her for attempting it. She pacified Cornelia and Philip by telling them their father would be back soon. To other inquiries she said Kester was at the cotton station upriver, and said it so crisply that before long she was receiving no more questions. With a fierce desire for privacy, she went about as usual, willing to discuss any subject on earth but her personal life.

Then, vaguely and tormentingly, she began to be aware that her affairs were not private. At first the rumor was like a cobweb that one brushes away on a dark street, not sure whether one has encountered a cobweb or a trick of the shadows. But though she tried to believe it was a figment of her strained imagination she began to feel like a schoolgirl suspecting that everybody but herself was sharing a secret.

She went into the drug store and saw Clara and Cousin Sylvia talking in undertones to each other over glasses of Coca-Cola. As she approached the table they stopped abruptly, and said, "Why hello, Eleanor!" with exaggerated cordiality. Clara added. "Won't you sit down?"

Eleanor said no, she was in a hurry. While she was buying a jar of cold cream and a brush for Philip's hair—he had goldenish curls that were shamefully wasted on a boy—she heard Sylvia make a carefully indifferent remark about the weather. Eleanor glanced around, wondering why Sylvia should wear ruffles around her scrawny neck, trying to look young when she so obviously wasn't, and Sylvia moved her eyes away a fraction of a second too late to conceal from Eleanor that they had been on her.

When she reached home she went to the kitchen to give an order about the children's supper. Dilcy and Bessie were talking, and through the half-open door Eleanor heard Dilcy exclaim, "Why, it ain't *so!*" and Bessie retorted, "Well, dat's what dey's sayin'." As Eleanor entered they both turned sharply, saying "Yes *ma'am?*" with an excess of deference, and looking as if they might have blushed had they been white.

Eleanor had promised to go to a tea at Silverwood the following Sunday afternoon, in honor of Clara's sister, Mrs.

Meynard, who was coming down from Baton Rouge on a visit. The tea was placidly uninteresting until during a lull in the conversation Mrs. Meynard asked innocently, "What's Isabel Valcour doing these days? Is she still in town?" Clara answered hastily, "Oh yes, she's still in town," and as she said it her face pinkened and she began urging Violet to play he piano. Two or three others joined, fluttering as though to cover the embarrassment of a guest who had upset the gravy on the tablecloth. Violet complied with a coolness that was in itself a rebuke to them, while Eleanor sat nibbling wafers and feeling as conspicuous as a flagpole. But she blessed Violet's self-possession. Violet was a practical woman who took no pleasure in minding other people's business.

These occurrences were too frequent for her to overlook them; all she could do for the sake of her own dignity was pretend not to notice them. The chatter was all around her, in kitchen and parlor alike. She heard it and she did not hear it. Nobody told her anything, yet from everybody she learned something. Isabel was never invited anywhere Eleanor went and except for that slip at Clara's Eleanor never heard a mention of her name. Several of Eleanor's acquaintances began to be officiously kind. It drove her to fury. The whole business made her feel that an indecent advantage was being taken of her, as she might have felt had she seen the neighbors examining her clothesline in an attempt to discover how often she changed her underwear.

The fact that she was helpless drove her to bravado. She continued to go out, greeting her friends on the street and accepting invitations with offhand pleasantness. She gave a party for the children, she invited people to dinner, she went to entertainments and was very gay when she got there, and bought more clothes than ever before in a single season. When she was alone she paced the floor of her room till she thought she must have trodden miles across the rug, blaming herself, blaming Kester, hating Isabel; but her one aim in life had become that of not giving anybody a chance to guess what she was bearing. She walked through the halls and looked up at the pictured faces of her predecessors at Ardeith. Her eyes searching these women who had married men named Larne—women in Colonial powder, Napoleonic high waistline, balloon sleeves of the eighteen-thirties, Civil War hoopskirt—she wondered what they had in common and what lay behind their painted dignity. Happiness, disappointment, secure joy or desperate grief—they could not all have experienced the same destiny, but one thing she was sure they had shared, the power of endurance. They would have turned nothing but serenity to the artists who painted them, holding their conviction that a lady wore an enigmatic smile above her personal life. They were part of a great tradition. Eleanor had never thought much about that until now, but now she thought of it and understood it. They bore pain bravely because they could bear pain more easily than pity, knowing that pity was very close to contempt.

2

Late one morning during the first week of December Cousin Sylvia made Eleanor a visit. Eleanor was surprised when Cameo summoned her to the parlor, for the day was raw and gloomy with mist, hardly a time to be chosen for a round of ceremonious calls. Her knowledge of Sylvia suggested that it was more likely to have been chosen as a day when one could be sure of finding the object of one's efforts alone by her own fire, and as she descended the stairs Eleanor was buckling on an armor of unconcern against the pricks of Sylvia's lance. She entered the parlor smiling brightly.

"Why Cousin Sylvia, how good of you to drop in! And in this doleful weather, too."

"I've been *so* wanting to see you, Eleanor dear." Sylvia clasped Eleanor's hand ardently.

Wondering why anybody of Sylvia's age and disposition should think an over-use of rouge would cover the querulous lines in her cheeks, Eleanor exclaimed, "Your hands are cold. I'm sure you'd like a hot cup of coffee, wouldn't you?"

"How nice of you," said Sylvia.

Eleanor continued to be nice. She took Sylvia's coat, talking pleasantly while she made uncomplimentary mental remarks upon her visitor's girlish frock and floriated hat— Eleanor would have considered them both too juvenile for herself, though she was about twenty years younger than Sylvia—and settled Sylvia comfortably in an armchair by the hearth. Cameo brought coffee. "Now we can have a good long chat," Eleanor said as she filled the cups.

Sylvia smiled gently. "Yes, a good long chat. Bad weather makes a fireside so comforting, doesn't it?"

225

"Yes, doesn't it?" Eleanor agreed.

"Your poinsettias are especially pretty this year. I noticed them as I drove up."

"Thank you so much," said Eleanor.

For a few minutes they sipped coffee and discussed poinsettias. After awhile Sylvia remarked that everyone's garden would be full of weeds after this wet spell. "But you don't work your own flowers, do you?" she asked.

"No, I have a man for that."

"Gardening is such healthful exercise," Sylvia reminded her. "You should really take it up. The air and the beautiful sunshine, they make one's troubles seem small," she said invitingly, but as she got no response she edged her chair an inch nearer to ask, "How have you been amusing yourself lately?"

"Why, I've had a great deal to do, getting the children's winter clothes in order and making my Christmas list, and I've taken advantage of the dull weather to catch up on my correspondence."

"You write a great many letters?" Sylvia inquired.

"I have five brothers and sisters, you know," Eleanor returned blandly, "and there are my parents, besides all my old friends." And if you're trying to find out whether or not I've been writing to Kester, she added in her mind, you're going to be disappointed.

But Sylvia was not so easily disappointed. "You don't find it lonesome out here on the plantation?" she asked innocently.

"Lonesome? Why no. With two small children and a household as large as this, one doesn't get much chance for solitude."

"But that's hardly companionship," suggested Sylvia.

"Why Cousin Sylvia, I get the most delightful companionship in the world from my children."

As that remark was blameless Sylvia rested a moment, while Eleanor, watching her across the coffee-pot, wondered how long it was going to take her to come to the direct questions Sylvia was evidently yearning to have answered. "My dear," murmured Sylvia, "I have been thinking of you a great deal recently."

"How kind of you," said Eleanor.

Sylvia drank the last coffee in her cup. "Yes, my dear, I have. You aren't looking well. Are you feeling quite yourself, Eleanor?"

"I'm perfectly well, thank you."

"There are aches of the heart," Sylvia said darkly.

"Let me give you some coffee," said Eleanor. She refilled Sylvia's cup and her own.

Sylvia looked around the room and then at Eleanor again. "I have wanted to come to see you before, dear child," she continued. "But I have put it off. Sometimes one's duty is not clear. It is difficult to bring up unpleasant problems, even from the loftiest of motives. And yet, I am convinced I should speak to you. For your own good, Eleanor."

Eleanor silently observed that Sylvia would have loved to be a dentist and say gloatingly, "Now this *may* hurt a little."

Sylvia was talking on in her gentle whiny monotone. She toyed with her subject, drew it around and around. Eleanor listened, pretending a sweet impassivity while inwardly she burned with resentment.

"We were so happy when you and Kester were married," Sylvia informed her at length. "And yet—I am sure you never suspected this and I would be the last to tell you except that the time has come when it seems right to speak frankly— there was some surprise."

"Was there?"

"Indeed yes, my dear. Of course you are startled. You are a lovely, well-educated girl, and your people are most *deserving*, your father merits a great deal of credit for his honorable career, with so few opportunities as he has had, we are proud to know our country gives a chance to men like that, that's what America is for, isn't it?"

"Do you think so?" Eleanor asked fatuously.

"Yes, it is good to know we have no classes in this happy land. But there was astonishment, I shan't deny, when Kester stepped outside his own circle—not that I mean to imply he hadn't a perfect right to do so, but you and he had not been brought up alike, you must admit."

"I've never thought of not admitting it," said Eleanor.

"Certainly, my dear, everyone thought it so courageous of you to have no false pride. And I think I should tell you, lest you misunderstand my making this plain, that I championed you from the very *beginning*."

"Did you?"

"I certainly did, Eleanor. When Miss Agatha Durham said to me—such fine girls the Durhams are, devoted to good works, but a bit conservative—when Miss Agatha said to me,

'But what is this girl's *background?*'—I said right out to her, 'Now Miss Agatha, I am sure Kester Larne would not have married anyone whose antecedents were not unquestionable, and just because we don't know so much about the Upjohns as we do about some other families does not indicate that they aren't very *worthy* people, and anyway,' I said, 'this is a *Christian* country,' and I was happy to observe that the Durham girls called the next day, the very next day."

"How obliging of you," said Eleanor.

"My dear, with all my faults nobody can say I have not always tried to do my duty. And I'm sure your forebears were quite flawless, were they not Eleanor?"

Eleanor smiled upon her with all politeness. "In my home, Cousin Sylvia, we gave very little attention to the dead except to see that they were properly buried."

"Ah," murmured Sylvia. But though baffled, she was not silenced. She pursued her subject. "I have told you all this, Eleanor dear, not to hurt you—I should be very sad if I thought I had hurt you—but to make you understand that there has been certain, ah, unkind gossip of late." She waited for Eleanor's reaction, but as Eleanor showed none Sylvia went on. "Oh my dear, if you knew how it pains me to tell you!—for there have been those malicious enough to say that a man cannot be condemned for returning to his own people. How *can* anyone be so cruel? How can anyone have such foolish, hurtful interest in the concerns of others, talking, tattling, injuring—" She paused dramatically.

"I don't understand it myself," Eleanor responded. "Maybe you can explain it."

"Oh, I cannot! I shall never understand it. My dear, if you could know how my heart has bled for you! But of course you don't know what I'm talking about?"

"How should I?"

"Indeed, how should you? How could you? I have dreaded this, I have prayed over it, till I have finally concluded it is my duty to tell you. it was somebody's duty to do so and it was evident nobody else was going to. Oh, how I have shrunk from undertaking such a task! I'm related to Kester, his dear mother is my cousin, you know, and while I hesitate to speak evil of my own flesh and blood I must say Kester was always a wild boy, broke our hearts almost, and we did think, oh, we hoped, marriage might be the making of him—"

With a blank smile on her face, Eleanor was thinking, I

won't give her the satisfaction of seeing me writhe, not if it kills me. She listened stolidly.

"But *don't* you understand what I mean?" Sylvia was pleading.

Eleanor continued to smile, and shook her head. "I'm quite in the dark, Cousin Sylvia. Won't you have another cup of coffee?"

Sylvia declined. She talked ahead in her expressionless voice, probing, hinting, watching. Eleanor remained obtuse. "The wife is always the last to hear these things," Sylvia lamented after awhile. "And that is shameful. People mean to be kind about not speaking, but somebody *ought* to speak, and someone in the family is better than an outsider, don't you agree with me, someone related to Kester?"

"I thought nearly everybody in town was related to Kester."

"Yes, the family had many branches. But someone who has been intimate with the household all her life is certainly better than a more remote relative, don't you think, when something has to be spoken of?"

"But what has to be spoken of?" Eleanor civilly inquired.

"My poor, innocent girl, can it be possible that you still don't understand?"

"Understand what, Cousin Sylvia?"

"Why my dear, you cannot believe everyone doesn't know Kester is working at the government cotton station, has been there for two months?"

"Why of course, I thought everybody knew that. Why shouldn't they?"

"But Eleanor, have you heard no whisper of anything further?"

"No whisper? What sort of whisper?"

"Oh you poor woman, about Isabel Valcour." Now that she had said it Sylvia's glance sneaked over Eleanor's face. Eleanor smiled and waited until Sylvia resumed her babbling. "Poor Isabel. Such a charming girl, and from such a lovely family, it's all so sad. So very sad. Her brilliant marriage, and then her being left a widow like that, so young. Until now we thought she had no interest in anyone hereabouts, we thought her heart was in another hemisphere." Sylvia said it with a slow shake of the head, as though the world contained dozens of hemispheres and she would not betray confidence by revealing in which one of them poor Isabel had left her heart.

"But being alone, and then returning here for the duration of the war, it must have made the poor girl so unhappy, and she had no parents. no children. A woman should not be alone, she should have children and a home, and yet it does seem as if we good women who try to do our duty get least appreciation of all. doesn't it?"

"If you mean me, I've been quite well appreciated, Cousin Sylvia." Eleanor spoke rigidly; by this time she was so angry at Sylvia's meddling that she could have choked her with pleasure.

"Oh my dear, can it be that your affection for Kester blinds you so? That you really cannot see what is happening? Kester, Isabel!—"

She paused expectantly. Eleanor had planned no answer, but she was suddenly possessed by a cool disdain. She looked straight at Sylvia and began to laugh. "Really, Cousin Sylvia!" she exclaimed.

Cousin Sylvia stared incredulously.

Eleanor continued to laugh at her. "Why Cousin Sylvia, have you come all the way over here in this fog to tell me Kester has been having an affair with Isabel Valcour? Did you, could you possibly think I didn't know it?"

Cousin Sylvia gasped. She was amazed, and resentful that her own hope of triumph had been wasted. "So somebody has told you before?" she managed to ask.

Eleanor poured herself a third cup of coffee and lifted her eyes to look at Sylvia's ridiculous fluffy clothes, her rouged effort to look young, and she felt no pity. "I'm afraid you're still living in the nineteenth century," she said. "Kester and I understand each other perfectly."

"Glub," said Cousin Sylvia.

Eleanor gathered up her own weapons. "To be sure, a woman of your age couldn't be expected to understand the younger generation. I suppose you cling to the quaint old notion that once people are married they should treat members of the other sex like lepers. Dear dear, how boresome such a life must have been! But people were expected to be stodgy in your day, weren't they?"

Sylvia managed to say, "Then you know about Isabel—and you don't mind?"

"Oh Cousin Sylvia, even at your age one must realize the modern world has changed. We've become so much more broadminded since you were young. The new freedom, you know. Kester and I wouldn't dream of keeping each other in that old-fashioned bondage."

"Each other?" Sylvia echoed. She was leaning forward, her hands fidgeting on the arms of her chair.

Eleanor reached over and patted Sylvia's hand kindly. "Now don't be troubled. I know you meant to be very helpful when you came over to tell me what you thought I didn't know. It was just your goodness of heart that prompted you, and I appreciate it. But try to understand that modern people regard these things differently."

Cousin Sylvia blinked, while Eleanor regarded her with a little smile of pitying amusement. After a moment Cousin Sylvia stood up. She lifted herself to her full height, which was not very high.

"To laugh at such things!" she exclaimed in horror. "Eleanor Larne, you have no moral sense whatever. I am ashamed to have tried to do you a kindness."

"I think you should be." Eleanor stood up too, offering Sylvia her coat and handbag. "It makes you quite ridiculous, you know, busying yourself with things you don't understand."

"I understand morality and decency!" Sylvia retorted. She snatched her coat and scrambled into it. "I do not understand people who have no power of righteous indignation. When you talk like that it wouldn't surprise me at all to see you breaking your marriage vows too, not at all! Stop laughing at me!"

Eleanor did not obey her. "Kester used to tell me you were funny," she said. "You certainly are." She opened the door. "Thank you for a very diverting morning."

Sylvia stepped grandly into the hall. "We might have known. When a man of fine breeding marries a woman who's common as pig-tracks—we might have *known.*"

"You might have known," Eleanor said gently as she followed Sylvia out, "that if I had needed your advice I should have asked for it. Of course I understand your interest—it must be very dull to have nothing to do but stagnate among the tombs of your ancestors." She opened the front door. "Thank you so much for calling, Cousin Sylvia."

"I'm not *your* cousin," Sylvia snorted in farewell.

Eleanor watched her marching across the gallery and down the front steps. She went back up to her own room, her lips curling with rage as she climbed the stairs.

231

Then, regarding the matter of marital infidelity exactly as she would have regarded it had she lived in the administration of President Millard Fillmore Eleanor dropped down on the bed and put her head on the pillow miserably and cried. She cried until she had to give her red eyes a long treatment with hot water and ice before she was willing to face the children at dinner.

3

Cornelia came in from school lamenting the cloudy weather, which had prevented her playing outdoors at recess and promised to keep her in all the afternoon, while Philip, who had not objected to staying indoors during the morning, immediately joined her. Eleanor cheered them by promising that as tomorrow was a Saturday and Cornelia would not have to go to school, if the weather cleared she would take them both to town to buy new clothes for a Christmas party to which they had been invited. This put them into better humor, and to keep them amused for the afternoon Eleanor got out a set of cardboard cutouts she had meant as a Christmas present and gave it to Cornelia and Philip to play with. The set consisted of heads. legs and bodies of animals printed on sheets of thin cardboard, ready to be cut out and put together. As they both liked to make things, when they were provided with blunt-pointed scissors and a pot of paste they settled down by the nursery fire, happily prepared to create disorder. They were so lovable as they sat on the floor chattering with each other, and their exuberance so remindful of Kester's, that Eleanor felt a thrust of pain as she talked to them.

Leaving the children in Dilcy's care she went to her own room and sat down in front of the fire. She wondered what Kester was doing what he was thinking, if he was missing the children. Whatever he thought of her, she could not believe it possible that he would continue to neglect Cornelia and Philip. She had never seen a man who appeared to enjoy his children more than Kester did. But she did not. she told herself for the hundredth time, want him to come back to her merely for their sake; that would be a blow neither her love nor her pride could endure. She wanted Kester to come back because he loved her. He had loved her very deeply, and no matter how much she had hurt and angered him on their last evening together one did not with a single stroke tear down a structure that had been so many years in the building. If it were true about Isabel, she still was convinced that Kester loved her; she believed he had turned to Isabel as some men turned to gambling or alcohol in periods when they could not face themselves. But there were men, she remembered, who eventually found their means of evasion a necessary curtain between themselves and impossible reality.

Or was this, she asked merely her pride speaking in its own defense, unable to acknowledge that she had failed in the one thing she had tried hardest to do?

She did not know. "Eleanor, stop it!" she begged herself. "*Do* something!"

But she had no idea what should be done. Maybe fresh air and exercise would be a help. It was cloudy but not raining, with occasional flecks of sunshine breaking through the gloom. If she took a long walk it might clear her mind. She changed into a pair of flat-heeled shoes, put on a coat and started walking along the river road.

After a few minutes she was glad she had come out. The wind was damp, and blew refreshingly through her hair, for she had come without a hat. The countryside had a look of peace. On either side of the road were the oaks, their draperies of moss blowing and behind the oaks the fields were resting for their spring rebirth. In the trees the wind was like a serious and simple melody. Hands in her coat pockets, Eleanor walked fast, following the turns of the road and paying no attention to the occasional car or wagon that passed her. In times of turbulence the outdoors could always quiet her spirits.

She walked and walked, finally dulling even such slight thought as she had with the rhythm of movement. The wind was increasing. Eleanor paused a moment to place several hairpins more firmly, and went on. Veils of mist began to blow in from the river.

She became conscious that she was getting tired. Looking around, she thought she must have walked four or five miles, though she did not seem to have come very far. Her idea of distance on the river road had been fashioned by automobiles; in premachine days the plantations must have been remote. Eleanor remembered having heard that it used to be a four days' journey from Ardeith to New Orleans. River steamboats had reduced that to less than a day, and now trains did it in less than two hours. Aeroplanes—

Suddenly she realized that it was quite dark.

She had known it was late, but had paid little attention to the day's declining. Eleanor stopped where she was, unsure how long it had taken her to walk this far and calling herself stupid for not considering before that she was going to have to walk home along this lonesome country road. A wisp of hair blew across her face as she turned around and started back the way she had come.

The wind was screaming in the trees. Eleanor shivered and turned up her coat collar. Though the coat was not a heavy one, walking had kept her warm, but now the wind had begun to cut down the back of her neck and come through the fabric across her shoulders. As she fastened the collar around her throat a splash of rain struck her eyes.

The rain came violently. There was nothing invigorating about it; it tumbled down in a drowning torrent, lashing her like whips. In a few minutes she was soaked to the skin. Rain was pouring across her eyes and down her back, and the road had turned to a strip of mud. The wind blew her from side to side like a stalk. She could not see at all. More than once she stumbled into a tree, and as she put her feet blindly into puddles the mud caught and held her shoes till it was hard to take another step.

She was less frightened than irritated at her own lack of foresight. Any idiot could have noticed the weather, especially an idiot who had been born in Louisiana and experienced scores of these winter rains. It was going to rain for hours, drenching the earth and not pausing to give any peace to those who might be struggling through the downpour. Above her the oaks were creaking as the wind lashed through them. Her hair full of water and her shoes heavy with mud, her skirt flapping wetly aginst her legs, Eleanor fought her way along. Several times she nearly fell down, for her feet were so cold as to be almost without sensation. Through her battle with the rain came recollections of her last year's pneumonia.

The headlights of a car cut a blurry shaft through the rain. Eleanor stopped short, ready to cry out with thankfulness. The car was going slowly and carefully, and she stepped in front of the lights, too miserable to think beyond the bliss of dryness. The car drew up alongside her and a Negro chauffeur leaned out.

"Evenin', miss. Can we give you a lift?"

"You certainly can," Eleanor exclaimed above the beat of the rain. The rear door of the car opened and a woman's voice called,

"Get in."

Eleanor scrambled inside. "Thank you! You're very good." As the door closed she sank back on the seat, still shivering so that it was hard to say anything else. The chauffeur turned to ask,

"I'll take you on home, Miss Isabel?"

Eleanor turned her head. Beside her was only the shadowy outline of Isabel's figure, though she supposed she herself must have been clearly visible in the glare of the headlights.

Isabel said, "Why yes," and addressing Eleanor she added, "You won't mind? We're almost at the gate."

Her voice was cool, courteous. Eleanor was startled, though she remembered that either by chance or by some unrecognized impulsion she had been walking directly toward the old Valcour house. "Not at all," she returned with as much dignity as she could muster in her sodden state.

"I'm sorry I can't offer to send you home," Isabel continued, "but the chauffeur has a cold already and I don't like to keep him out on a night like this."

"I'll telephone for a car," said Eleanor, feeling that she was receiving the same consideration that would have been given a wet puppy. She felt so much like a wet puppy that she added, "I hope my dripping clothes won't ruin the upholstery."

"I'm sure not. The seat is leather," Isabel assured her politely, and asked, "How did you happen to be caught in such a downpour?"

"I was taking a walk." Eleanor spoke through chattering teeth. "The rain overtook me."

"A walk? Four miles? No wonder you have such a fine figure. I never was much of a hiker."

Eleanor fancied that Isabel was carrying off their meeting better than she was. But she was so cold, so wet and so wretched that she could not summon such urbanity. In the dark of the car her nostrils caught a warm whiff of perfume and her wrist brushed the end of a fur. She sneezed.

"Good heavens, you're catching a chill," said Isabel. The car stopped by her front steps, and she exclaimed, "Come in and get dry."

Eleanor helplessly obeyed her. They ran up the front steps,

and the driver touched his cap and drove off toward the garage. Isabel opened the front door. While she spoke to a servant, Eleanor stood just inside the doorway, her skirt dripping little puddles to the floor and water running into her eyes from the soaked braids of her hair. She sneezed again, and felt in her pocket for her handkerchief, though it was nothing but a useless ball of wet cloth. With impersonal grace Isabel turned to her. "We'll go upstairs. There's a fire in my room."

She looked suave and smart in a dark green suit edged with squirrel fur. Eleanor was conscious that she must look not only forlorn but hideous, and more ridiculous than either. Her hair was plastered across her cheeks, her skirt spattered with mud, and her shoes so crusted one could hardly tell what their color had been. She had left muddy footprints on the floor. "I can wait here," she returned. "I'll ruin your furniture if I try to sit down."

"You'll have a fever if you don't get warm," Isabel said reasonably. "Come on by the fire, and Ophelia will bring us some hot lemonade."

Suddenly through her shivers and chatters Eleanor felt herself pushed forward by an imperative curiosity. It occurred to her that Isabel had a reason for wanting her to stay or she would not have dismissed the car. To accept hospitality from her was the last thing Eleanor would ever have thought she wanted to do, but it would be only for the few minutes required for another car to come from Ardeith, and she rationalized her impulse by remembering that Isabel was right in saying that if she didn't get warm she would almost certainly be sick. She followed Isabel up the stairs.

Isabel opened the door of her bedroom. A fire was leaping behind the andirons, and it seemed to Eleanor that never had she felt a more delicious sensation than the warmth that came over her as she stood dripping by the hearth. Isabel took off her own hat and gloves, making an occasional remark about the joyless weather.

Downstairs Eleanor had been too uncomfortable to notice her surroundings, but now as she held out her numb hands to the fire she began to look around her. The room contained a mingling of furniture in the style of about seventy years before and the accessories of a modern woman who spent half her waking hours taking care of her person. There was a great fourposter bed, a marble-topped bureau, an armoire with mirrors in the doors, several tip-tables and rosewood chairs with seats made of horsehair. The old bureau was incongruously scattered with powder-boxes, atomizers, bottles of astringent, facial packs; a bathrobe of quilted blue satin lay across the bed and a pair of furred blue mules stood by the bedstep. As Isabel put her hat on the shelf of the armoire Eleanor sneezed again.

"Won't you get out of those clothes?" Isabel exclaimed, so urgently that Eleanor wondered if Isabel were afraid she was going to collapse and be stranded here for a week. Without waiting for an answer Isabel had opened the side door leading to the bathroom and started the water running. "Come in here," she called. "The plumbing looks early American and is, but there's plenty of hot water."

Realizing that nerves and discomfort together were making her foolish, Eleanor gathered what was left of her self-possession and crossed to the bathroom door. "Thank you. But first, where's your telephone?"

"I'll tell Ophelia to call." Isabel brought the blue robe and slippers. "Put these on, and I'll have her iron your things dry. Here she is now."

The Negro girl came in with a thermos bottle and two glasses on a tray, and a moment later Eleanor was handing over her own clothes to be pressed. She stepped into the tub. As the warm water crept over her, soothing her goose-pimples, Eleanor began to feel her assurance rising. She wondered what she and Isabel were going to say to each other. She was regarding the minutes ahead with simple curiosity, as though she were a tourist about to enter an unfamiliar place of interest. Isabel's bathroom was, as she had said, inconveniently out of date; the tub stood high on four claw feet, and the pipes groaned at the effort demanded of them. Evidently she preferred to spend her inadequate income on clothes and cold creams rather than on modernizing the quarters in which unmerciful destiny required her to live.

Eleanor dried herself on Isabel's towels, shook Isabel's talcum powder over herself, put on Isabel's bathrobe and slippers, and combed her wet hair with a silver-topped comb on which were the initials "I.S." in German script. When she came out of the bathroom rubbing her hair with a dry towel, Isabel began to pour the hot lemonade.

"This will be good for both of us," she said, offering a glass. "I do hope you're going to be all right."

"I'm sure of it," said Eleanor. "I'm very hard to kill."

Taking the drink she sat down by the fire. She felt quite well. Somehow her being here made Isabel seem curiously vulnerable. They had never talked to each other except on that first evening at the Buy-a-Bale dance; that was five years ago and seemed a thousand, and Eleanor was realizing that in her own mind Isabel had begun to lose the proportions of an ordinary person and become an idea frightening by its unfamiliarity. Tonight she was observing that Isabel was merely a beautiful, vain and idle woman whom she disliked exceedingly.

Now that excuses for being active were over, Isabel seemed uncertain of how to proceed. She sat down before the fire opposite Eleanor, by the little table where the maid had put the tray, and tasted her own drink tentatively. Eleanor began the conversation herself.

"It was kind of you to pick me up," she said.

Isabel smiled slightly. "I couldn't let you drown in that rain."

"Did you recognize me?"

"Why yes."

There was a pause. They looked each other over with an appraising interest that was fast dropping its mask of politeness. Observing that Isabel was extremely good to look at, Eleanor acknowledged her possession of a quality that in principle commanded her admiration, that of guarding one's assets. Beauty, she knew, was a gift of the gods at twenty but was more than that at thirty, and not one detail of Isabel's appearance—her face, her figure, her exquisite hands, the flawless line under her chin—had a suggestion of the slackness that would have betrayed its having been left to chance. Eleanor had never had reason to be distressed by her own lineaments; she was handsome in a cool, functional way, but between Isabel and herself the difference was that of a flower and a diamond drill. Isabel looked, as she almost certainly was, appealing and entirely useless. Eleanor despised her, not because Isabel knew what she wanted and the best means of getting it, but because what Isabel wanted was evidently the chance to be a soft and lovely parasite. She had no intention of living on her own strength if she could help it. Eleanor wondered how Kester, or any other man, could possibly be fond of such a creature.

With a scornful resolution that she would make Isabel be downright for once, Eleanor asked clearly,

"Isabel, why don't you say whatever it is you brought me here to listen to?"

"Why do you think I brought you here for anything?" Isabel's voice was even.

"You could very easily have told the chauffeur to take me home. It wouldn't have delayed him long enough to matter."

Isabel considered. After a moment she returned slowly, "Why—yes. You're right, I did want to talk to you." She tasted the lemonade again, watching Eleanor over the rim of the glass.

"What do you want to know about me?"

With a slight smile, Isabel answered, "Nothing more. I've had a good deal of time to observe you."

"Is that what you do with your time?"

Isabel gave an ironic little laugh. "Really, Eleanor, have you imagined me like that? Solitary female in an old house, fussing over a bird and a pussy cat, crocheting centerpieces and eying the neighbors? What a picture!"

"I haven't formed any image so silly, or even so detailed," Eleanor retorted. "I've been very much occupied lately."

"So have I. Most of my relatives and friends are in New York, you know. I've been there frequently. Only now and then I have to come home for the obvious unhappy reason."

"Obvious?"

"Poverty," Isabel replied with a cool frankness. "Oh, I know you don't understand that. In my place you'd have tripled your income and done without a car and chauffeur till you could really afford them. But I'm no financial wizard. I can't increase my income. It's all I can do," she added as though the fact were amusing, "to live on it."

Eleanor looked down at a slice of lemon in her glass and back at Isabel, thinking again how different the two of them were. It was not her way to admit that she had any inadequacies. Isabel, on the contrary, made capital of hers. Eleanor said,

"I've never thought about how you manage your property, but I suspect you're not as helpless as you sound."

Isabel regarded her gravely. After another slight pause she said, "How straightforward you are. You're direct in thinking and speaking and acting. You don't like to be told things gently, do you?"

239

"No, I don't."

"Then—" Isabel set her glass on the table. She linked her hands on her knees and looked straight across at Eleanor. "Will you give Kester a divorce?" she asked.

Eleanor felt herself stiffening. Remembering what her temper had cost her in the past she vehemently ordered herself to hold it tight. She said, in a voice as level as Isabel's, "He hasn't asked for one."

"That's not an answer," said Isabel.

"It's as much of an answer as I feel required to give."

"Don't you know Kester wants one?" Isabel asked steadily.

"I know if he did," Eleanor returned, "he wouldn't send you to tell me so."

Isabel shrugged. "He'd wait a long time before he told you so himself, too, because he has such respect for the forms of tradition. But what makes you think he doesn't?"

"If Kester ever mentions this subject to me," Eleanor said, "I'll discuss it with him."

Isabel was giving her a shrewd scrutiny. "You can't take it, can you? You asked me what I wanted, but you don't like my having answered. I knew you wouldn't. I told you I knew all about you I needed to know. Would you like to hear what else I think of you?"

Eleanor leaned down to put her glass on the hearth. Her pulse was quickening, and her skin was getting the unpleasant hot tingle of anger. Speaking carefully to keep her voice under control, she said, "No, I wouldn't. I'm really not interested in your opinions."

"Then maybe you'll be interested in this. I love Kester. He's the only man I've ever loved in my life."

"I don't believe you," Eleanor said shortly. "You're not capable of loving anybody very much."

Isabel gave her a sardonic little smile. "Then why should I want him?—and I do want him, Eleanor."

"I'll tell you why you want him." Eleanor spoke with deliberate certainty. "You've been bored to desperation. The war made you a pitiful and rather laughable object. If you could get Kester away from all he loves best in the world—from me, from Ardeith, from his children—it would re-establish your conviction that you're irresistible."

Isabel sat forward, holding the arms of her chair. "Do you mean my self-respect requires that I persuade somebody to marry me? Don't be childish, Eleanor. I can get married next week if I please." Her eyes fixed on Eleanor she added distinctly, "And he's worth about six million dollars. Does that answer you?"

"If it's true it surprises me."

"Does it indeed!"

"Not to hear that you can make a rich man fall in love with you. But that you should hesitate at taking him."

"Do you think I'm utterly mercenary? Yes, you do—and I said that to prove I love Kester more than you think. Now do you believe me?"

"No."

"Why not?"

"I told you. You do love luxury, but you love your own ego more than that. Kester will do more for your precious self-esteem than anybody else. That's what you're proving."

"You are stubborn, aren't you?" Isabel took out a handkerchief and began rolling it between her fingers. "But you might as well be pliable now, Eleanor. You've had your chance with Kester. And look what you did with it," she exclaimed. "What right have you to want him now?"

"Forgive my slowness," said Eleanor, "but as I don't know what has been said to you about me, I don't follow you."

"What has been said to me?" Isabel echoed with scorn. "Do you think I need to be told anything? Do you think I can't see what happened to him? Oh, you're a fool, Eleanor!"

"Am I? It seems to me you are. I don't know what visions you're cherishing, but it's evident you like believing them."

Isabel challenged her swiftly. "Why don't you stop that, Eleanor, and acknowledge you've lost? Can't you confess just once in your life that there's something you can't do? Why don't you get an office on top of a skyscraper and run a chain of factories? Why don't you let Kester alone? He's a human being!"

"Then why don't you stop talking about him as if he were a library book?" Eleanor demanded. "He can't be handed around."

"He might as well be a library book from the way you've treated him. Why don't you let him go while there's still time for me to repair the damage you've done?"

"Damage? For you to repair?" Eleanor was holding herself so tensely that her back hurt. "You? A piece of mistletoe looking for something to cling to—"

"That's what you'd call it," exclaimed Isabel. "You're so

invincible! Don't you know Kester wants to be needed? 'After all I've done for him,' you say, and you won't understand that a man like Kester wants to believe he's doing things for you. You thought you were giving him so much—oh, I've watched you, I've laughed at you—but you never gave him anything he wanted. The little triumphs, the little applauding whispers —Eleanor, Kester is coming to me because I can give him back his faith in himself and you needn't try to hold on because it's no use. You've wrought destruction enough."

Eleanor was hardly listening. She was so angry that Isabel's taunts meant no more than a jingling of syllables. She realized that she was standing up and Isabel was standing too. When they had risen to their feet she did not remember, but Isabel was going on, hardly having paused for breath.

"Kester comes from a long line of heroes—no matter what the Larne men were like the women who loved them made them feel like heroes. What men call the charm of Southern girls—I mean Southern girls who come from families like ours—is simply that quality of giving a man faith in himself. We do it by instinct, all the time, even when we aren't trying to, but give one of us a man she really loves and she can make him anything she pleases, and do you know how we do it? Of course you don't, you imbecile—we do it by praising him for the qualities we want him to have." She began to laugh. "Remember that next time, Eleanor. This time you've lost, and I mean it. Kester is so sick of you he hates remembering you're alive. You'd better yield with whatever grace you possess."

She turned and started for the door. Eleanor was holding her hands in the bathrobe pockets, clenched into hard fists. Her fury shook her like a storm. She was thinking, over and over, "If I say anything it will be something dreadful, God help me to keep still."

At the door Isabel said over her shoulder, "That's all I've got to say to you. I'll send your clothes up, and see about your car."

She closed the door behind her. For a moment Eleanor did not move. She could feel her heart pounding. When she finally took her hands out of her pockets and opened them the fingers were so stiff it hurt her to unbend the joints. All her muscles ached with tenseness, but she was glad she had not moved or spoken, for whatever she would have done would have been not a response but an unreasoned expression of rage. There was a knock at the door and she turned sharply, but it was only the Negro maid with her clothes.

The girl explained that she had pressed the dress and underwear with a hot iron and thought they were dry enough to be worn, but the coat was still wet and so were the shoes. Here was a pair of shoes that belonged to Miss Isabel. Eleanor gave brief thanks, and after the girl was gone she got dressed quickly. She put on her own shoes, however, preferring the risk of a cold to wearing Isabel's. Gathering up her hairpins she went to the bureau.

Her hair was nearly dry. Eleanor braided it hurriedly, and glanced down to be sure she had left none of her hairpins on Isabel's bureau. A sparkle from something lying near the mirror caught her eye.

She looked at it, and looked again, and her heart resumed its pounding as she reached to pick it up.

It was Kester's little silver-handled knife. Eleanor turned it over and read his name in tiny letters on the handle. The sight of it made her hot all over, and then cold; it was so like Kester to have left it lying around. Eleanor closed her hand around it, and then opened her fingers and looked at it lying on her palm, and the thought came into her head, "It is very sharp, I could slash her pretty face with it," and she started, for she had never known before what it felt like to be tempted to physical violence. There was another knock at the door. Eleanor closed her hand again quickly and wheeled around, saying "Yes?" in a voice louder than necessary. The Negro girl entered to say the car had come from Ardeith.

Eleanor held Kester's knife in her fist. The maid held out the damp coat and Eleanor threw it over her arm. She walked past the girl and went downstairs.

Isabel stood by the open front door, telling Cameo that Mrs. Larne would be down in a minute. As Eleanor reached her Isabel said, "Good night."

"Good night," Eleanor answered, and she went out and got into the car, holding her coat on her knees over the fist that held the knife.

The rain was still pouring down. Cameo drove slowly and carefully, and in the back seat Eleanor sat shivering both with cold and with the reaction from her gust of fury. She was weak from her efforts at self-restraint. It was the first time she had ever been savagely angry without giving herself any

release whatever, and she had not realized before how ex
hausting such a struggle could be.

Dilcy and Bessie met her in the hall, full of queries. Dilcy
took the wet coat, gave her a pair of slippers she had warmed
by the fire, and insisted on bringing supper. Eleanor said she
did not want any, but Dilcy urged that she drink a cup of hot
milk, and Eleanor consented more to get rid of their solicita-
tions than because she felt capable of drinking it.

Sitting down by the parlor fire she looked at the little silver
knife in her hand. She had not used it, but she was horrified
that she should even have thought of doing so. "Except that
this is a silver knife instead of a razor," she was thinking, "I
might as well be a darky in a honky-tonk tent on the levee." It
was appalling to discover how close primitive impulses lay
under the surface of civilization. She stared at the knife until
she heard Dilcy's footsteps in the hall, when she started
guiltily and thrust it under a magazine lying on the table. As
Dilcy bustled in with the milk and a plate of biscuits, the sight
of her broad, homely smile gave Eleanor a sense of rescue.
Dilcy must know from the telephone call that she had taken
refuge from the rain at Isabel's, but Dilcy could not know
what she had been thinking of, and ashamed of her tremors
Eleanor smiled back at her, realizing that she was herself
foolish with weariness. The day had been a hard one. She
wanted a long night's sleep.

"Now you jes' drink dis, Miss Elna, and eat a biscuit,"
Dilcy was urging, "den you go right up to bed. It sho is a bad
night to get caught in."

"Yes, it is," Eleanor said. "How are the children?"

"Dey got dere supper and dey's gone to bed. Don't you
worry 'bout 'em."

"I don't." Eleanor made herself smile again. "You take
very good care of them, Dilcy. I don't know what I'd do
without you."

"Yes ma'am, I tries to do right by my chirren. Now you
drink dis milk befo' it gets cold."

Eleanor obeyed her, and ate a biscuit too, since it was
easier to do so than to protest. Dilcy shepherded her upstairs
and helped her undress for Eleanor was so tired she was
hardly capable of getting out of her clothes unaided. Dilcy
put a hot water bag at her feet and told her nobody would
come near her till she woke up in the morning.

"And maybe you better stay in bed tomorrow," she went on.

"No, I'll be all right," Eleanor murmured. "Thank you, Dilcy."

"You weccome. Might as well coddle yo'sef, Miss Elna. You don't do it much." Dilcy gave her a comforting pat. Eleanor stretched out under the bedclothes. Before Dilcy had put out the light she was asleep.

Chapter Thirteen

1

IN THE MORNING it was no longer raining, but the ground was so wet that Dilcy would not let Cornelia and Philip go outdoors. She sent them downstairs to play lest they wake their mother. Cornelia and Philip were cross. The weather was gray, the animal cutouts were difficult, and Dilcy could not give help because she was cleaning the nursery. Cornelia stared out of the parlor window disconsolately. Her mother had promised to take her to town today to buy a dress, but with the weather like this it would be just like grown folks to say she could not go.

"Cut out the effalunt," said Philip, approaching her.

Cornelia thrust out her lip, wishing she had somebody her own age to play with. She was six, and Philip was only a baby not quite four. She was always having to help him to do things he was too little to do himself.

She took the card from him and struggled with the elephant while he watched her anxiously. The elephant's tusks were complicated and the blunt-pointed scissors not sharp enough to do the job neatly. Unwilling to admit that there was anything a big girl of six could not accomplish, Cornelia went over to the table and turned on the reading-lamp as though in need of more light, while Philip followed her to look on. But the scissors would not do; she needed something with a point. As she paused in perplexity her elbow shoved aside a magazine lying there, and she saw a man's pocket-knife. Cornelia put down the scissors and picked it up.

"I reckon this would cut the tusks," she suggested.

245

"What you got?" Philip inquired.

"Why, it's father's knife the one he's always using. He must have left it when he went away. I bet he misses it. Mother ought to send it to him." Philip watched her as she turned the knife in her hands. Cornelia smiled proudly. "I bet you can't read what this is on the handle."

Philip shook his head He could not read anything.

"I can read it," said Cornelia. "K, e, s, t, e, r. That's Kester. Kester Larne. When father comes home he won't know what to make of it, me reading so good. I can cut out the elephant's tusks with his."

"Let me do it!" begged Philip.

"No, don't you try to open this knife. You're too little. I'll cut the elephant right." Cornelia carefully got her finger-nail into the depression at the edge of the blade and drew it out.

"Dat's got a good point." Philip said. "I can do it."

"No, let me! You're too little. You'll cut the elephant all up."

"I want it!" cried Philip. He tried to take it from her.

Cornelia pulled her hand back, but Philip grabbed the knife. She tried to get it from him, loudly demanding respect for her age and superior wisdom. They scuffled, and Cornelia's foot slipped on the rug. As she fell down she gave a scream that frightened the servants in the kitchen and reached Dilcy in the nursery and pierced the ceiling to wake Eleanor in her room overhead.

2

Eleanor stirred unwillingly, annoyed that the house should not have been kept quiet enough for her to go on sleeping till she felt like waking up. There was such a lot of racket—the children yelling, the servants running about, a door banging down the hall. She might as well have tried to sleep through a football game. One of the children—it sounded like Cornelia —was screaming disgracefully; she ought to be stood in the corner for such behavior. unless she had been really hurt— and Eleanor sat up in bed. her mind suddenly clear enough to realize that what she was hearing was not the yells of a temper fit, but screams of pain. Something dreadful had happened.

She sprang out of bed. The windows were open and the

damp air blew sharply through her nightgown. Thrusting her feet into slippers and snatching up her bathrobe Eleanor ran to the stairs. The cries were coming from below.

Dilcy was rushing down ahead of her, and another servant was running up, her dustcloth still in her hand. She nearly collided with Eleanor at the turn.

"It's Miss Cornelia," the girl gasped breathlessly. "She fell down."

Eleanor hurried past her. The parlor was already full of servants who had come running when they heard the screams. Philip was sobbing, evidently scared by all the commotion, and after a glance to make sure he was unhurt Eleanor dropped on her knees by Dilcy, who sat on the floor rocking Cornelia back and forth in her arms and moaning. "Oh, my child! My baby, my po' li'l lamb!"

Her hands over her face, Cornelia had buried her head on Dilcy's bosom and was giving muffled little groans. Eleanor reached to take her and Cornelia's hands slipped down, and as Eleanor's arms went around the child's tense little body she heard her own voice come out of her throat with a sound hardly less frantic than Cornelia's first screams.

"It's her eyes!" she cried out. "Oh my God, it's her beautiful eyes!"

There was an instant of silence, broken only by Cornelia's moans and Philip's frightened sobs. The Negroes stood frozen. Eleanor stared at the tiny drop of blood creeping from beneath Cornelia's left eyelid. For the moment she was as though paralyzed. What had happened she did not know nor had she voice to inquire; she simply sat gazing, her mouth half open and her arms rigid around Cornelia, and her mind stupidly repeating, her eyes, her eyes, her yes.

Then all of a sudden everybody was moving again. The Negroes were talking, soothing Philip, offering to help Cornelia, asking each other what had happened to her. Cameo bent to pick up something from the floor and Eleanor heard him exclaim, "Why I declare, it's Mr. Kester's knife."

Eleanor jerked up her head. Kester's knife—the words struck her like an accusation. She remembered leaving it on the table last night, after years of warning the servants never, never to put sharp instruments where the children could reach them. Her face evidently betrayed her horror, for Cameo bent over her.

"You better let me tote her upstairs, miss," he said.

247

Without waiting for permission he lifted Cornelia and as he stood up he went on sternly: "You Bessie, you get right out and phone Dr. Purcell Can't you see de missis got such a shock she can't do nothin'?"

Eleanor got to her feet. "Thank you, Cameo," she said faintly, and with a great effort she recalled her stunned intelligence and began to give orders. "Call Dr. Purcell, Bessie. Say Miss Cornelia fell on a knife and it went into her eye. Tell him to come over at once and ask if there's anything we can do for her before he gets here. Dilcy, take care of the baby. Bring Miss Cornelia up to my room, Cameo. And will the rest of you for heaven's sake be quiet!"

She followed Cameo upstairs, and when he had laid Cornelia on the bed Eleanor bent over her. Cornelia was whimpering, her hands held over her eyes with such force that it was hard for Eleanor to bring them down. Cornelia writhed under her touch. Both her eyes were shut tight, and Eleanor was surprised that the only evidence of her injury was still no more than that single small drop of blood. Hot packs, Eleanor wondered, or cold packs, or what? She did not know. Bessie came in.

"De doctor say he be right over, miss. He's leavin' dis minute."

Eleanor sprang up. "What can we do for her?"

"He say don't do a single thing till he gets here."

"Oh." Eleanor sat down by the bed again, putting her arm around Cornelia and trying to speak soothingly, but her voice was small with terror. It was several minutes before she realized that Cornelia's moans had become an articulate plea. She leaned closer to listen "Yes darling? What did you say?"

"Tell father to come home," Cornelia was begging. "I want father."

Eleanor was holding her, keeping Cornelia's hand away from her eyes. "All right, dear," she answered gently. "I'll get him as soon as I can."

"Can't you get him now? Can't you phone the place where he is?"

"Yes. I'll phone him. Do you promise not to touch your eyes while I'm phoning?"

Cornelia nodded.

"Very well. I'll call this minute."

She released Cornelia and turned to the bedside telephone.

248

Kester was at the government cotton station. Eleanor called the long distance operator and asked for the office.

A switchboard operator answered. Eleanor gave her name and asked for Kester. Mr. Larne had gone out to the experimental field the operator answered; she would have him return the call when the men came in at noon.

Behind Eleanor's back Cornelia was asking, "Have you got him? Can I talk to him?"

"Not yet, dear," said Eleanor, and to the telephone she added, "This is a matter of vital importance. Send for Mr. Larne. I'll hold the line."

"Just a minute. I'll see if I can find him."

She waited. It was a long time before she heard anything else. But at last Kester's voice came over the wire.

"Hello? Eleanor?"

It had been two months since she had heard him speak. As his words reached her their sound reminded her of how well she would have known his voice anywhere, even if his silence had lasted twenty years instead of two months. He sounded both surprised and puzzled at her summons. She tried to answer clearly. "Kester Cornelia has been hurt. She—"

"Cornelia! What did she do? How serious is it?"

"I don't know yet. It's her eyes."

"Good God!"

"She wants to talk to you."

"When did it happen?"

"Just a few minutes ago."

"Have you got a doctor?"

"I've called Bob Purcell. He isn't here yet."

"Bob Purcell? That pill-packer! What does he know about eyes? Take her to New Orleans. I'll go down right away and have a specialist waiting when you get there. How soon can you leave?"

"As soon as the doctor has seen her."

"Do you have to wait?"

"He'll be here any minute, and she's in a lot of pain."

She heard Kester give a wordless sound like a shudder made audible. Eleanor fastened her teeth on her lip to steady herself.

"She wants to talk to you, Kester," she said after an instant. "Cornelia, here's father."

She laid the telephone by Cornelia and held the receiver so Cornelia could hear. Kester spoke, but she could not distinguish his words. Cornelia said, "Why can't you come now? Do I have to go to New Orleans?"

They talked until Eleanor heard Bob Purcell running up the staircase. As he came in she picked up the phone. "Kester, Bob is here. You and Cornelia will have to stop."

"I'll drive down to New Orleans this minute," Kester said quickly. "There's a train about ten, isn't there?—you take that and I'll meet you at the station."

"All right." Eleanor put back the receiver and turned around.

Bob was already bending over Cornelia, who was crying out again, whether in pain or fright Eleanor had no way of knowing.

"I've just talked to Kester," Eleanor said. "He's on his way to New Orleans to get a specialist. Can you come down with Cornelia and me?"

Bob glanced over his shoulder. "Yes, I'll be glad to. But first let me take a look at her." Cornelia shrank away from him and he looked up again. "Eleanor, there's no time for me to be gentle. She can't understand that I've got to do this. You'll have to hold her still so I can look into her eyes."

"Are you going to hurt her?" Eleanor asked, then without waiting for an answer she said, "Very well, I'll hold her," and sat on the bed, drew Cornelia's arms down and held her head rigid. She shut her own eyes and turned her head away. It seemed a long time that she had to sit there, letting Bob be as cruel as he had to be, and when at last she heard him say, "That's all, you can let her rest now," Eleanor found that her muscles were painful with tension. Bob picked up Cornelia and laid her down in bed, drawing the covers over her. He had put shields over her eyes and fixed them with a bandage, and she was growing quiet under a sedative. Eleanor looked at her, and reached up to push her own hair off her face. Now that Cornelia was temporarily relieved she was remembering for the first time that she had not so much as washed her face or put a comb to her hair that morning.

"You're very brave," said Bob. "Not every mother could have done that so quietly."

For a moment Eleanor did not reply. She did not feel brave. She felt as if it might have been a relief to faint and have a few minutes of blankness.

"Let me talk to you," she begged.

"Come in here," said Bob. They went into the next room. Eleanor asked,

"Bob, what has she done?"

"It's her left eye," said Bob. "She has cut the sclera at the margin of the cornea—does that make sense to you?"

Eleanor shook her head.

"The sclera is the white part of the eye. The cornea is the clear window in front of the iris."

"How dangerous is it?"

He hesitated.

"Bob, I want to know!"

"It's almost impossible to foretell, Eleanor. Sometimes eyes have astonishing powers of healing. Now if you'll get dressed and have somebody pack a grip for you, I'll attend to everything else."

He smiled with what looked like professional optimism, and added that he was going to order breakfast sent up to her. His gentleness struck her with deeper fear than Cornelia's screams.

3

Bob engaged a drawing-room on the train, and when Cornelia had been put to bed, still quiet under the sedative he had given her, he sat by Eleanor on the seat near the window. Eleanor looked out at the cypress swamp through which they were passing. It was a cool silver landscape, thick with clouds that now and again broke into showers over the gray trees and their draperies of gray moss. She thought of the day when she and Kester had first driven into a cypress swamp together, and had sat watching the rain while he had shown her beauty where she had never seen it before. That had been during the enchanted winter when she was first beginning to be aware of her love for him. Their love had been so rich and tender once, a love full of splendid possibilities that they had let slip by them unrealized until now the citadel they might have built for their marriage was a pile of ruins and they had to face each other across the body of this tortured child.

She must have trembled visibly, for Bob spoke to her, and it was not until she heard his voice that she realized how silent she had been.

"This isn't necessarily tragic, Eleanor," he advised her.

"I was thinking of Kester," she returned faintly. "He loves her so."

Bob did not answer, for he could give her no comfort there and was too wise to offer anything less, but he reached over and took her hand in a simple gesture of friendliness. Watching Cornelia's tumbled dark hair shake on the pillow with the motion of the train, Eleanor wondered how much mutilation Cornelia's parents had wrought upon her by their failure to control their own lives. Nobody would ever hold out to them anything but sympathy for an undeserved accident. But as the train went through the dripping cypress swamp Eleanor's own memory was setting facts in order and mercilessly drawing its conclusion, that if she had kept her temper Kester would not have left Ardeith, if he had kept his she would not have found his knife in Isabel's room. If they had behaved with a decent sense of responsibility toward each other and toward the children they had no right to have until they were ready to stop being children themselves, this would not have happened.

How strange it was, Eleanor thought as she watched the trees glide past, you were told the accumulated wisdom of generations who had suffered to acquire their knowledge, and you simply did not believe it. Those difficult rules might be right for other people, but as for yourself, you were going to get what you wanted. You were the center of your own universe and intended to have supremacy in it. She looked at Cornelia's bandaged eyes, and her fists clenched in the cushion of the seat as she remembered. "He that is slow to anger is better than the mighty; and he that ruleth his spirit, than he that taketh a city."

As the train drew into the station she saw Kester from the window. His face was grim, the mouth a thin line and the forehead creased with his search among the alighting passengers. The sight of his anxiety would have told her if she had not known it before how much he loved Cornelia. Bob picked up Cornelia in his arms and motioned Eleanor to go ahead of him. When she stepped down from the train Kester sprang forward to meet her.

"Where is she, Eleanor?"

He spoke as though there were no other subject of concern between them, and she was glad of it; everything else they had to say to each other could wait. Eleanor answered,

"Here she is. Bob is carrying her."

"Give her to me," said Kester. He took Cornelia in his

252

arms, wincing visibly at the sight of the bandage over her eyes. "There's an ambulance waiting," he told them. "Come this way." Carrying Cornelia, who had stirred and then quieted again, he went on talking as he led them through the station. "Dr. Renshaw and his assistant are at the hospital. I'm told he's one of the best eye-specialists in the country. When you've talked to him Bob, tell me what he says."

Bob promised that he would. They got into the ambulance, where a nurse was ready to make Cornelia as comfortable as possible on the little cot at one side. The other three of them sat opposite, Eleanor between Kester and Bob. They said very little. Kester kept his gaze on Cornelia as though his eagerness could command her to get well.

Eleanor had never seen him look so grave or so frightened. She hoped she could prevent Kester's discovering that any action of his had helped bring this about. Cornelia's danger was anguish enough for him without her adding to it, and it was enough for herself too.

When they reached the hospital Eleanor could not help feeling a certain surprise at the thoroughness with which Kester had attended to all the details of preparation, and she realized then that she had been unconsciously expecting to have to do all this herself. But there was nothing left for her to do. The doctor was ready. A room had been prepared for Cornelia and another room where she and Kester could wait in private. Bob went at once to confer with the specialist. Cornelia was caught up in the silent white efficiency of the hospital and the doors closed on her. Kester and Eleanor were left alone.

They were in a hospital waiting-room, furnished with a table, several chairs and a sofa. There had evidently been an attempt to make the room pleasant by bright curtains at the window and a fern growing in a pot on the table, but in spite of that it had the bare coldness of a room used day after day by occupants who did nothing here but sit or pace, waiting for news and dreading what it would be when it came. Eleanor looked around, wondering how much anonymous agony this room had held before today. In front of her was an armchair, the varnish on its arms stained by the cold sweat from a succession of gripping hands. She turned away from it and sat down on another chair drawing off her gloves, and as she did so she found that there were little drops on her own palms.

Kester set her suitcase in a corner. He began to walk up

and down. He went to the end of the room and back again, then said,

"I haven't notified your family or mine. I thought I wouldn't till later on. Relatives get in the way so."

"Yes," she agreed, "they do."

Kester took another turn. Coming back, he stopped in front of her. "Eleanor, tell me about it! What happened?"

"It was early this morning," said Eleanor. "I was asleep." Her hands were holding each other tight on her lap. "Cornelia and Philip had some kind of scuffle over a knife. She fell and it went into her eye."

"What did Bob say?"

"Nothing. I mean, nothing definite. He said you couldn't tell at once."

"Her eyes," said Kester. "Of all things—her eyes."

"Kester, it's only one of them," she said banally.

"I wonder if the cut will show," he said. "She has such beautiful eyes." He sat down in the armchair, and without noticing them closed his hands over the marks on either side of him. There was a pause. As long as there had been necessary activity to occupy them, both he and Eleanor had been supported by it, but now that they could do nothing but wait they were sick with their own helplessness. At length Kester asked, "Who could have left a dangerous instrument where the children could pick it up?"

"I did," said Eleanor. "It was my fault."

"You?"

She nodded. "It was a knife I was using last night. I was tired and sleepy and I forgot about it. I left it lying on the parlor table."

Kester took a short breath. As though glad to have something on which to vent his alarm, he exclaimed, "What a damnably stupid thing to do!"

"Yes, it was," said Eleanor.

The door opened and a young woman came in. She had a French face, sleek black hair, and long hands in which she carried a notebook. "Mrs. Larne?" she said briskly.

"Yes."

"I am Amélie Crouzet, Dr. Renshaw's assistant. Will you tell me, please, just how the accident occurred?"

"How is she?" Kester exclaimed.

"Dr. Renshaw is with her, Mr. Larne. She's not in pain, if

254

that's what you mean. I understand you were not at home this morning?"

"No," said Kester, "I wasn't at home."

He set a chair for Miss Crouzet. Notebook on knee, she addressed Eleanor again. Eleanor told her the children had quarreled over a knife After scribbling notes for a moment Miss Crouzet took something wrapped in surgical gauze from the pocket of her white uniform. "Is this—"

"Kester, would you get me a glass of ice water?" Eleanor asked suddenly. "They keep it so hot in here."

"Yes, certainly." said Kester. As he went out Eleanor turned back to Miss Crouzet. who continued,

"Is this the knife that cut her? Dr. Purcell says one of the servants gave it to him." She opened the packet of gauze and held out Kester's knife.

"Yes," said Eleanor.

"The blade was clean, evidently," Miss Crouzet observed.

"I suppose so. Of course it wasn't surgically clean."

"I understand. Thank you." Miss Crouzet got up with a competent rattle of starched skirts.

"Just a minute." said Eleanor. "Miss Crouzet, if you can help it, don't show that knife to my husband. You see, it's his —it has his name on the handle—it will simply add to what he's bearing now if he finds he left it lying around."

Miss Crouzet smiled slightly, glancing at the door through which Kester had gone for the ice water. "Very well. Mrs. Larne. I'll do my best." She waited until Kester returned with the glass of water but in reply to his eager queries about Cornelia all she could say was, "I can't answer yet. We'll let you know as soon as there's anything definite to tell you, of course."

When she had gone out Eleanor drank the water. She set the empty glass on the table. Kester stood by the window looking down into the street. After several minutes he turned around and came across the room to her.

"Can't you even speak to me?" he asked. "Don't you know I love her as much as you do?"

"Yes, I know!" she exclaimed penitently. "Forgive me."

As she spoke she shivered and covered her face. Kester put his arm around her shoulders and drew her to lean against him. Eleanor felt herself relaxing as though she were holding to a pillar. She thought of what joy they had had of each other once, and with what carelessness they had pulled it

255

down around them, and wondered if they were ever going to be given a chance to rebuild it. There had been so much she wanted to say to Kester. but at this moment she had not strength to begin it. The ground where they had met was solid but very narrow, simply their knowledge that no one shared their relationship to their child but themselves. But for the present neither of them could go any further. They had to wait, and they waited together but except for occasional jerky speeches that were no more than uncontrollable expressions of their suspense they did not say anything more until Miss Crouzet came in to tell them they could speak to Dr. Renshaw.

4

But even that brought them no relief, for all they learned was that not even the most expert doctor could prophesy the exact future of a cut in a child's eye. Through the afternoon they alternately sat with Cornelia and returned to their room to pace the floor in torments of uncertainty.

Eleanor was so unnerved that she was nearly as helpless as Cornelia. The emotional strain she had been undergoing since her last quarrel with Kester had left her very little strength to cope with such a crisis as this. Except for the brief periods when they would let her stay with Cornelia she spent most of the afternoon making purposeless movements such as walking around the floor or tying and untying knots in her handkerchief.

Without remarking on her distracted state, Kester quietly took upon himself the task of attending to the undramatic details accompanying the major catastrophe. He finally notified their respective families, received them when they came to the hospital. and withdrew so Eleanor could have an uninterrupted hour with her parents. Molly offered to bring little Philip down to New Orleans so he would not be left entirely to the care of servants, and when Eleanor told him about it Kester went off at once to wire Dilcy to get ready for the trip. He answered telephone calls and made no comment as he accepted the flowers and picture-books that began to arrive from well-meaning acquaintances who had not taken the trouble to ascertain that Cornelia could not look at them. All the rest of the time he stayed with Cornelia as much as he was permitted, and told her funny stories that made her forget how uncomfortable she was. Eleanor watched him with a grateful admiration that she was too overwrought to express. It occurred to her that this was perhaps the first time in his life that Kester had been called upon to meet a situation that demanded his ultimate resources.

Shortly before dark he came back into their waiting-room, where Eleanor sat on the sofa twisting the corner of a sympathetic telegram. The nurse had said they could speak to Cornelia again before she went to sleep, and Kester had gone downstairs while they waited for the summons.

"The room across the hall from Cornelia's is vacant," he said to her as he entered. "I've arranged for you to have it—they say we can both stay here unless they have to use the rooms for patients."

"That was good of you," she said. She had not thought of leaving, but neither had she remembered that in a hospital such arrangements were sometimes difficult to make. "Where are you going to stay?" she asked.

"They'll put up a cot for me in here," said Kester. "Is that another wire we'll have to answer?"

"Yes, from Neal and Clara Sheramy. Put it with the others." Eleanor handed it to him, wondering if the hospital clerk had made any protests against allowing them two rooms tonight instead of one. She was glad Kester had managed to avoid any direct reference to the fact that there was very little left of their marriage but its legal existence.

The nurse came to tell them they could see Cornelia now. They went to her room.

Cornelia turned her head as the door opened. "Is that mother and father?"

"Yes, both of us," said Eleanor. They sat down, one of them on each side of her bed, and she reached to take their hands to assure herself of their presence.

"I wish I could see you," she said to Kester. "How soon will they let me see you?"

"Very soon, I hope. As soon as your eye gets better."

"I don't know why they won't unwrap my eyes for just a minute. I haven't seen you in so long."

"I don't look a bit different."

"Are you going to be here every day?" asked Cornelia.

"Every single day."

"You aren't going away again?"

257

"Of course not."

Cornelia smiled contentedly. "Mother, can I have anything I want to eat tomorrow?"

"Why yes. I think so," Eleanor said.

"Chocolate ice cream?"

"I'm sure you can have that. I'll tell them you want it."

A moment later the nurse touched Kester's shoulder and pointed to the clock in her hand. He nodded. They told Cornelia good night promising they would come back if she woke and wanted them, and went outside.

Kester brought Eleanor's suitcase to the door of her room.

"Tomorrow I'm going to ask if she can't have a phonograph," he remarked. "That should help keep her happy."

"I don't see any reason why she couldn't have it. The nurse will keep the door closed when she plays it."

"I'll find out," said Kester. He opened the door and set down the suitcase and after what seemed like an instant's hesitation he followed her inside. "Eleanor, you needn't be so afraid of me," he said simply. "Neither of us is fit for anything now but to watch Cornelia. We can talk about ourselves later."

"Yes, please!" she exclaimed.

"I just wanted you to know I understood that," said Kester. "Good night."

"Good night."

He left her. As the door closed Eleanor crumpled up on the bed and put her arms around the pillow, trembling with weariness and an overwhelming sense of defeat, and wondering if behind Kester's gentle courtesy there lay a loneliness like hers.

5

During the weeks that followed Kester never made an attempt to cross the barrier between them. He was helpful, sympathetic, considerate, but his whole manner made it plain that he was not going to ask any expression of intimacy unless she showed him that she desired it. Their hours of soothing Cornelia and devising amusement for her left them little time for clarifying their own situation even if Eleanor had felt equal to it, and she had to acknowledge to herself that she was not equal to it. Her anxiety regarding Cornelia made her feel bankrupt of courage.

But when she went to her room at night Eleanor sometimes sat for a long time with her head in her hands, wondering whether Kester would tell her the truth if she asked him if he detested her as much as Isabel Valcour had said he did, and deciding again and again that he would not. He was himself too distressed, and had too much knowledge of how she felt. "When this is over," she told herself. "It can't be much longer." But she trembled with a suspense that had nothing to do with Cornelia, for now that she was seeing Kester again every day she knew more surely than ever that if she had destroyed his love for her it would be the most dreadful knowledge she would ever have had to face.

At first Dr. Renshaw seemed to be optimistic. Then one evening in January Eleanor came in from a visit to her parents to find that Kester had been summoned to the doctor's office downtown for a conference that had already lasted more than two hours.

She tried to find Miss Crouzet to ask the reason, but was told Miss Crouzet was with Cornelia, and she herself was not allowed to enter. Eleanor went into the waiting-room and walked up and down in an agony of impatience until Kester appeared.

She spoke to him in alarm as he came in. Kester's face had a grayish whiteness. He hardly seemed to hear her, or even to notice that she was there. Eleanor rushed to him and gripped his arm with both hands.

"Kester! What's happened?"

He looked at her vaguely, brushing his hand across his eyes as though any sort of reply was difficult. "They say we can see her in a few minutes," he said.

"But what's the trouble?"

Kester drew a quick breath. "The doctor is scared. They—" He stopped as though not knowing how to say it.

"Tell me, Kester, for heaven's sake!"

"Did you ever hear of a thing called sympathetic ophthalmia?" he asked.

Eleanor shook her head. She cried, "Does that mean—*both* eyes?"

"Yes." He began to speak with resolute calmness. "It seems that the two eyes aren't independent units. When one of them

259

has been injured, sometimes the other eye becomes affected. Nobody in the world knows how to foresee it."

"What does it mean? Not—" She could not go any further. Her throat seemed to have closed over an impossible word.

"Unless they can stop it," said Kester.

Eleanor's hands dropped. For a moment there was a blank silence between them. Then she demanded,

"Isn't there anybody in the world—Kester, there must be somebody!"

"That's what he wanted to ask me. Dr. Renshaw is one of the finest ophthalmologists in America. But there are others who might be able to help him if they could get here immediately—"

"Why hasn't he sent for them? If there's even a chance anybody will do any good—why hasn't he sent for them?"

"I'm trying to tell you. He's on the telephone now, long-distancing a man in Chicago and one in Baltimore. What he wanted to ask me was whether we could afford it."

"Was that all?" Eleanor exclaimed. "Did you tell him it didn't matter what the consultation would cost? That we could afford anything she needed?"

"Yes," said Kester. "I told him that." He put his hand on her shoulder. She looked up at him. "I'm sorry, Eleanor," he said earnestly.

Too dazed to comprehend at once, she echoed, "Sorry? For what?"

"Don't you know for what?" he returned sharply. "For calling you nigger-rich."

He released her. Eleanor shook her head slowly, for a moment surprised that he should have recalled anything so trivial in such a crisis. Then she said,

"Oh, that. It's not important. I suppose," she added hesitantly, "we could work it back—to where I'd say what I've been thinking since—that you were right—I did get money mad—and I didn't foresee this."

Kester was looking at her intently. What he might have said had there been time enough she could not tell, for Cornelia's nurse came into the room. They wheeled abruptly to face her. She told them they could see Cornelia now.

Cornelia was evidently not in pain. They took their places on either side of the bed, and with the eager gesture so familiar to them now she reached to hold their hands. She told them she had been listening to her phonograph.

Eleanor forced herself to emulate the cheerful manner with which Kester was listening to her and answering. But Cornelia's grasp on her own hand gave her tremors of fear. She could almost hear the tap of sticks in the street and see fingers groping across pages of raised dots. In the days when she and Kester were still making plans together they had talked of so much they wanted Cornelia to have, so many innocent, happy things; school, parties, beautiful dresses, and she was going to come down the spiral staircase in a bridal veil.

"Mother, you're hurting me," said Cornelia. "Don't squeeze my hand so tight."

"I'm sorry, darling."

They stayed with her until she had fallen asleep. When they tiptoed out into the corridor they saw Miss Crouzet waiting for them. She spoke to Kester.

"Dr. Stanley is chartering a special plane to bring him down from Chicago, as you suggested," she said. "He and Dr. Field should both be here by tomorrow."

"Thank you," said Kester. "There's nothing more you can tell us?"

"Not yet, Mr. Larne."

Eleanor turned around abruptly and almost ran across the corridor into her own room. She dropped into a chair and pressed her fist over her mouth to hold back what she had suddenly been afraid was going to be an outburst of terror. When she had forced herself to be calmer, she thought she could at least be thankful that she had not flung herself upon Kester, making him offer any pretense of an affection he might not feel.

It was not until halfway through the night, when exhaustion was finally putting her to sleep, that she remembered Kester's making his first reference to their quarrel the night he had left Ardeith and saying he was sorry. "But that might have been only his native generosity," she thought. "He's sorry for me."

The next day she did not remind him of it, and they met the doctors with such a barricade of silence between them that Miss Crouzet praised them for their self-control, saying, "I've never seen parents face danger to a child as bravely as you two are facing it."

Eleanor felt astonished that even a stranger could not see that behind their frozen faces she and Kester were half frantic with apprehension and did not dare ask each other for sympathy.

6

The doctors came and went, grave, low-voiced specialists who held long conferences and reappeared to say only, "We are doing the best we can." Eleanor could hardly have told how she passed the days. She sat with Cornelia, she tried to find escape in the books her father brought her, she received bills and made out checks, she wrote notes of thanks for the flowers that continued to come. None of it made sufficient impression on her consciousness to blot even for a little while the suspense that tortured her, or a new growing feeling of guilt as she began to realize that though she had been married to Kester eight years she had never appreciated what reserves of courage he possessed.

She was almost reverent as she observed his fortitude. She watched him: Kester standing by with Cornelia's hand in his while the doctors made all sorts of terrible examinations, getting little mists of cold sweat on his forehead at the sight of them but never flinching; Kester holding Cornelia asleep in his arms till his muscles were dead from exhaustion but not willing to move lest she wake up; and then Kester bending over Eleanor herself when she doubled up into knots and felt unable to endure it one more day, speaking to her quietly and simply, and making her pretend a valor she did not have. Though she and Kester were rarely alone together, and when they were they spoke of almost nothing but Cornelia, Eleanor had never realized it was possible for her to feel such a sense of dependence as she felt now. The difference between her power and his was that between the strength to make an onslaught and that required to withstand a siege. She began to understand how ignorant she had been when she assumed that only the aggressors were of much value in the world, and she began also to know how it was that for all their mannerisms Kester's people had survived and maintained their way of life through so many hazardous years.

As she came to understand this, her memory began to hand back to her with relentless accusation phrases that she did not even know she had heard because she had been too angry to give them conscious attention. "Don't you know Kester wants to be needed? . . . You never gave him anything he wanted. The little triumphs, the little applauding whispers. . . . No matter what the Larne men were like, the women who loved them made them feel like heroes. . . . Kester is coming to me because I can give him back his faith in himself." A hundred times she was on the verge of crying out, "Kester, forgive me! Can't I have a chance to prove to you I've learned something?" But she did not, because she had no way of being sure Kester would want to hear it.

Kester did not know it then, but Eleanor always believed it was his strength and not her own that saved her from collapse through the period that ended one February morning when she heard a knock at her door, and before she could answer it Kester burst in, exclaiming,

"Eleanor! They say she's better!"

For an instant Eleanor was as though stunned. Her joy was too great for her to comprehend it at once. She gasped, "They say—?"

"Dr. Renshaw. He's just told me they believe they've arrested the ophthalmia." He waited a moment, then persisted, pushing the knowledge into her mind, "Don't you understand? She can see!"

Eleanor started toward the door, with an impulse to rush into Cornelia's room, but as she took a step her knees buckled under her and she found that she was kneeling on the floor, her face hidden on the seat of a chair, and she was shaking with a storm of sobs that told her, even more than she had realized, what these weeks of tension had cost.

Kester was too wise to try to quiet her. He stood with his hand on her head, waiting until her reaction had spent itself. When at last she could look up his first gesture was the homely one of giving her his handkerchief to replace her own, soaked to worthlessness by her tears.

Eleanor caught her breath and tried to dry her eyes. Kester helped her to her feet.

"Can't I go to her?" she urged breathlessly. "Can't I speak to her?"

"Not like that," said Kester. He shook his head. "Eleanor, try to listen. She doesn't see as well as we do. She never will. But she can see. And she doesn't know she's been in danger of not seeing at all. It might be disastrous to get her excited now."

Eleanor hesitated unwillingly, then she sat down. "How can you be so reasonable?" she murmured.

"I'm not. I feel the same way you do." He smiled faintly. "I'm just repeating what the doctor had to say to me."

Eleanor was nervously making little creases in the fabric of her skirt. She saw herself doing it, and resolutely quieted her hands. "How soon can we go to her?" she asked.

"In about an hour. They've been making some tests. Miss Crouzet will call us." He put his hand on her shoulder. "Try to relax, won't you?"

She promised that she would, and that she would say nothing to let Cornelia guess that this day was anything but one more in the process of an orderly recovery, and Kester left her. But she found relaxation impossible. Her sudden relief had brought with it a flood of energy. For the sake of giving it release while she waited to see Cornelia she telephoned the news to her parents, wrote Wyatt a letter about the plantation, and finally, her hands still trembling with happiness, she looked up an address in the telephone book and sent a check to the Braille Institute, a thank-offering that Cornelia would not need the books it would buy.

7

Day by day Cornelia reported her progress. "This morning I told a red ball from a green one. The doctor said that was good."

When they attempted to express their gratitude, Dr. Renshaw talked to them candidly. Cornelia could see, but her eyesight was not and never would be faultless. Though the ophthalmia had been arrested in time to provide that she could lead a normal life, she would have to wear strong glasses for reading and they would be wise to turn her attention as much as possible to music and other interests that put no strain on the eyes.

Hearing him, Eleanor rested her chin on her hand and looked past him to the regular buttons down the front of Miss Crouzet's white dress. She was letting Kester carry their side of the conversation. because her own conscience was returning an accusing echo to every one of the doctor's crisp advisory sentences.

"It isn't really tragic. But she's hurt. To the end of her life she'll carry a scar of our battle. I wonder if Kester knows it's our fault. Unless he does we'll never have a chance to start again. Oh God in heaven, the doctor says we should teach her music! Music won't save her from what I'm bearing now. Help me to teach her understanding of people who aren't like herself. Help me to save my children from pride in their own virtues. Blessed are the meek—blessed are the poor in spirit— blessed are the merciful. I never believed that until now."

To her astonishment she heard Kester asking, "Dr. Renshaw, will it hurt her appearance?"

Eleanor jerked up her head. Since the accident had happened it had not occurred to her to notice whether or not Cornelia was pretty. Only Kester, she realized with a sudden faint amusement, would have thought to ask such a question. And maybe, after all, it was important.

Dr. Renshaw had become reassuring. Certainly not, that is, unless one thought to make a close examination, when a very small irregularity of one iris might be discerned. But Miss Crouzet, who had sat with professional imperturbability through the conversation, startled them all by suddenly beginning to laugh.

They turned to her with inquiring surprise. "How can you ask?" she exclaimed to Kester. "Mr. Larne, have you *looked* at her?"

"What on earth do you mean?" Kester demanded.

She shook her head, still laughing. "No, I suppose you wouldn't have noticed. You've been too excited. Why don't you both go in now? The shields are off for the present."

Kester glanced at Eleanor. She sprang up, and leaving the doctor where he was they hurried to Cornelia's room. She was sitting up, listening to a story the nurse was reading aloud.

"Hello," she greeted them. "Wait till she finishes."

They took chairs facing her. The nurse went on reading a thrilling narrative about queens and goblins. In response to Miss Crouzet's words, Kester and Eleanor looked at Cornelia, and after a moment they looked at each other, incredulously, and turned back to stare at Cornelia again. Eleanor involuntarily leaned nearer to make sure she was not mistaken.

Cornelia was the most beautiful child she had ever seen. Her eyes had always been large and dark, but Eleanor was not looking directly at them. For the first time she was seeing Cornelia's eyelashes.

She had never before seen lashes like that. They were a quarter of an inch long, and edged her lids like a heavy fringe of black silk. Cornelia had always been a pretty little girl, but with those eyelashes she had the incredible beauty of a portrait idealized by some romantic artist.

Eleanor felt Kester's hand close on her wrist. "We'll be back in a minute," he was saying to Cornelia. "We want to find out something from Miss Crouzet."

They saw her sitting in the corridor. She was apologetic. Perhaps she should have told them. But when you worked around eyes every day of your life you forgot other people didn't know what you took for granted yourself. Hadn't they ever heard that an injury to the eyes often brought a particularly rich supply of blood to the eyelids, stimulating the lashes to such luxuriance as ordinary eyelashes never attained? Yes, it might last indefinitely. It probably would.

They had not known it. It had never occurred to them that Cornelia's handicap would bring such an ironic compensation.

Chapter Fourteen

1

When they saw Cornelia again she was being put to bed, protesting that she wasn't sleepy and interrupting her protests with yawns. The nurse told them they could sit with her until she went to sleep, and they took their places on either side of her bed. She was complaining that she was tired of the hospital. They were glad to hear it. For so long Cornelia had been too ill to care where she was.

"How soon can I go home?" she asked.

"In a week or two," Kester promised.

Cornelia screwed up her face. In her calendar a week or two was a long time. "I sure do miss being home. What's everybody doing there?"

"About what they were doing when you left," Eleanor told her. "Mamie is cooking, and Dilcy is missing you more than you miss her."

"Is Philip there?"

"No, he's still at grandpa Upjohn's. But he'll go home with us."

"Won't it be fun, everybody being there like we used to be!

266

You and me and father and Philip and everybody. Is the cotton blooming?"

"No, it isn't even planted yet. They're plowing now."

"I like it when the cotton blooms. In the summertime, when we can play outdoors and have watermelons, and the whole plantation looks so pretty. Mother, is it warm outdoors?"

"It's getting warmer every day."

"I think I ought to have some new dresses. Couldn't I get some new ones?"

"I'll take you shopping as soon as you're well enough."

"That'll be fine. I bet I'm too tall for all my clothes. I bet you're going to have to buy me everything new." Cornelia spoke complacently. "I'll have everything new when I go back to school. Father, you ought to hear me read."

"Can you read, really?" Kester asked.

"I sure can." Cornelia chuckled sleepily. "I can read everything in the first part of my primer."

"You've learned very fast."

"I'm smart at school. Can't I read in my book, mother?"

"You read very well," Eleanor agreed.

"You'll be surprised when I show you," Cornelia said, speaking to Kester again. "I can read *good*. I could read your name on that knife."

"On what knife?"

"The knife that hurt my eye. I showed it to Philip. It had 'Kester Larne' printed right on the handle."

"But my knife wasn't—"

"Did you tell father about that big word in your lesson one day?" Eleanor asked. "Don't you remember—bridge, I think it was, and you were the only one in the class who knew it right away?"

"That isn't as big a word as Kester. Kester is a really big word, but I knew what it was as soon as I'd picked up the knife."

"But my knife wasn't there, Cornelia!" he protested. "I had it with me."

"No you didn't. It was right there on the table. I was going to cut out the elephant's tusks for Philip, and I needed something with a point and then he wanted to do it—" Cornelia interrupted herself with a yawn.

"Hadn't we better leave her now?" Eleanor asked, though

267

she was afraid Cornelia had already prompted Kester to ask the questions she had hoped she would not have to answer.

"She isn't asleep yet," Kester objected. There was a puzzled frown between his eyebrows. "But Cornelia, I'm sure—"

"I told him he was too little," Cornelia went on sleepily. "He always wants to do everything. If he hadn't tried to take it—" she yawned again—"I wouldn't have got hurt."

She was too drowsy to talk any more. When they spoke to her again she only mumbled, and in a moment more she was sound asleep. Eleanor slipped her hand out of Cornelia's and drew the cover over her. Kester was frowning in evident perplexity. Eleanor pretended not to notice. She summoned the nurse, and leaving her with Cornelia they tiptoed back to their waiting-room.

As they went in she said in what she tried to make an encouraging voice, "She seems comfortable, doesn't she? I hope she'll sleep all night."

"She doesn't know her eyes will never be quite well," said Kester. "Eleanor, you didn't tell me it was my knife she cut herself with."

"Didn't I?"

"How did it get there, I wonder?" he persisted. "I thought I'd lost it."

"It doesn't matter," she exclaimed. "Isn't it enough that she's harmed without our torturing ourselves with going over every single detail of it again? Don't talk about it!"

"But I don't understand," said Kester. "I had that knife when I left Ardeith. I know I had, because I remember using it after that, several times. Who brought it back?"

"Oh, it doesn't matter!" she cried again. She wanted to say something else, anything that would turn his attention from the instrument of their damage. But she could think of nothing else to say.

"You said she hurt herself with a knife you had left on the parlor table. Where did you find it?"

"Oh—lying around somewhere."

"Lying around," Kester repeated. He sat down and rested his forehead on his hands. "Why don't I take care of things!" he exclaimed, speaking more to himself than to her. "That's the way I am. I've been missing that knife, wondering where I'd put it."

She sat twisting her handkerchief into knots again. "Stop blaming yourself!" she urged him.

But with masochistic intensity Kester turned the subject over, unable to let it go. "Why didn't I look for it? I meant to look for it. I missed it one day not long ago."

He considered, holding his head in his hands. She thought she would have given anything she owned to keep him from pushing his knowledge any further. But he went on, speaking to the floor.

"I was using it one evening. Opening a bottle of Bourbon. I used it to peel off the tinny stuff around the cork. I must have laid it down—"

As he spoke the last phrase his head jerked upright. He sprang to his feet, reaching her in two steps.

"Eleanor, how did you get that knife?"

His question struck down the remnant of the wall she had tried to hold up for his defense. Eleanor shook her head, silently begging him not to make her answer. Kester gripped her shoulders.

"Tell me."

Her reply rushed out of her in uneven little sentences. "I found it that night in Isabel Valcour's bedroom. I had to take shelter there from the rain. I brought it home."

She stopped, out of breath as though her quick words had been a long exhortation. She turned away her head, with a little choking sob in her throat as she exclaimed,

"Why did you have to ruin the only generous thing I ever tried to do for you?"

Kester released her. He walked away from her and went to the window, where he stood looking down into the street. The silence between them lasted a long time. His hands in his coat pockets, Kester was staring at the window, not moving at all. At last Eleanor stood up. She went over to him, and standing slightly behind and to one side of him she begged,

"Kester, say something to me."

Without turning around he answered, "I don't know whether I'll ever get a chance to say anything else to you. So I'd like to tell you I know just the kind of person I am. I suppose people like me are born to destroy themselves."

Eleanor wet her lips. Her mouth felt so dry she had difficulty in speaking. "Would it do you any good," she asked, "if I told you I felt the same way about myself?"

Still looking away from her, he shook his head. Eleanor stood where she was. "What havoc we've wrought!" said

Kester. A moment later she heard him ask, "Do you want me to go?"

"No!" she cried. As she said it she felt her spine stiffen. She had just realized that Kester, not so much speaking to her as giving words to a thought that would not be quiet, had said, "What havoc we've wrought." *We.* If he understood as she did that neither of them was blameless for what had happened they could meet squarely before it. She said, "Kester, please look at me."

He turned slowly. Their eyes met.

"I tried not to tell you about your knife," said Eleanor, "but maybe it's just as well that you made me do it. Because now we can be quite honest with each other. Isabel Valcour asked me that night if I'd divorce you."

"She did!" He was evidently astonished.

"Yes. I wouldn't answer her. I told her if you ever asked me I'd answer you. You wouldn't speak of this during the time since we came here, of course. You were too sorry for me. I've been behaving like a nervous wreck. I suppose you thought it was all because of Cornelia. It wasn't—I've been worried sick about her, but that's not everything. If you think I can stand this much longer, seeing you every day and not knowing what you think of me—"

When she stopped, with a jerk in her voice, Kester returned steadily,

"I asked you if you wanted me to go."

"Do you want to?" Eleanor demanded. She held the side of the window tight with one hand. "There's no use in my trying to pretend I think I'm the only one of us who's been injured," she went on. "I'm beginning to understand that you didn't leave Ardeith because of anything I said to you that last evening—though I'd give half my life to take back what I said about 'my plantation'—that was just the climax of what I'd been doing to you for years. I'd been taking away your self-respect till you got tired of fighting me. That's the most terrible confession I've ever made. But I told you, so you could be sure I know as much about myself as you know about me. Now do you want to go?"

He had listened to her with a growing amazement. "How did you know that?" he asked slowly. "I've only begun to say it even to myself."

"Please answer me!" she cried.

He spoke steadily, his eyes on her. "No, I don't want to go. Not if you want me to stay."

Eleanor caught her breath. She half put out her hands to him, then quickly drew them back. "Are you saying that because of Cornelia? Say what you would have said the day before I telephoned you."

"Do you want me back?" he asked.

"Yes, I love you. I never knew how much I loved you until I thought you might be gone for good. But I don't want you for the children's sake or because you have a sense of duty or for any reason except that you love me. Did you love me the day before I telephoned?"

"I loved you that day," said Kester, "and the day before that. I've always loved you. But until this minute I didn't know you had shed any scrap of that unbearable arrogance of yours—yes, I'm being cruel, Eleanor, but I'm being as honest as you said you wanted."

"I do want it! I love you too much to want anything else. I've borne all the suspense I can stand."

"Why haven't you said so before?" Kester exclaimed.

"How could I?"

"I wrote you where to find me."

"Four lines like a business letter. After you had walked out of your own accord—"

"You had practically asked me to."

"I didn't know what I was saying. I'm a fiend when I'm angry. I can't be cold and superior like you. Did you tell her you wanted a divorce?"

"I never mentioned your name to her in any connection whatever. Did you think I would?"

"I didn't know what to think! Why would she tell me that unless she had reason to believe it?"

"I was beginning to think there was nothing else to do," replied Kester. "I never said so, but I suppose it was apparent. I wasn't anything you wanted me to be."

"And I wasn't anything you wanted me to be! Kester, do you love me?"

"I love you more than anything else on earth. I've tried not to. I've tried to get myself reconciled to knowing you were done with me. I had never given you anything. I wasn't virtuous and invincible like your father, and you were judging me by him every day of your life."

"Was I?" she asked in astonishment.

271

"Didn't you know you were?"

"No, I never thought of that."

"You kept pushing me into a mold I couldn't fit," said Kester, "until I wanted nothing but to be free of it. I did try to be free of it. It was no use. I kept remembering you. But you—"

"Oh, say it!" she exclaimed when she saw him hesitate. "If you don't you never will."

"You didn't like me," said Kester. You got along perfectly well without me. You didn't need me."

"That's what I've done to you. I've made you believe it."

"You had said so."

"I thought I didn't need you. I liked to believe I was strong and self-sufficient. I liked to believe I could do anything I wanted to without help. But when you weren't there and I thought you were never coming back, if you could have known how lonely I felt, how lost and defenseless—Kester, did you say you kept remembering me? Even when you didn't want to?"

"More then than ever. I tried so hard to forget you that I was always aware of you. I kept remembering you—the way you stand and walk, your hands on the typewriter, a hundred little details of you I'd never thought of before. I kept remembering everything that's happened to us."

"So much has happened to us!" she exclaimed.

He gave a faint smile of reminiscence. "I thought about all of it."

"Do you remember the party we gave when the cotton market was falling?"

"Of course. Remember the day we got the telegram saying cotton couldn't be sold anywhere in the world?"

"The dreadful clothes we had to wear that year? No toothpaste and nothing to eat but what grew in the garden?"

"That abominable man you brought up to buy the furniture?"

"The way he kept calling your family portraits Aunt Minnie—" Eleanor bit her lip. "I'm sorry. I didn't mean to be sentimental. We could go on like this till we were both in tears and it wouldn't get us anywhere."

"Oh, wouldn't it!" Kester retorted. "You goose. You dear indescribable idiot. What makes you so afraid of yourself? What makes you so afraid of me?" He put his arms around her and drew her to him. For a moment she yielded, then she found that by no conscious volition of her own her arms were around him too, and she and Kester were holding each other with a joy she had thought she was never going to feel again, a sense of having belonged to each other since the beginning of time.

After awhile she moved her head backward and looked up at him. "I love you so!" she said. There seemed nothing else worth any use of words.

"To think I ever imagined I could do without you," said Kester. "Eleanor, have you forgiven me for being the fool I've been?"

She nodded. "Am I forgiven too?"

"Oh my darling, stop it. Nothing seems important except that I know I'll never lose you again."

"You never will." She went on seriously. "That's not just because we love each other, Kester. We've always loved each other. But I think it's because we know now how hard it is to win this and how easy it is to risk losing it. And how terribly precious it is!" She put her head on his shoulder again. They were silent for some time, then Eleanor said, "I'd like to ask you something else."

"Go ahead."

"Did she suggest that you go to work at the cotton station?"

"Why yes."

"Did she remind you of how much you knew about fertilizers and pest control and tell you how glad they'd be to get a man of your experience?"

"How did you know?"

"I'm wiser than I used to be. I haven't learned very much, but at least I know I don't know everything." She laid her head on his shoulder again, and with a beloved gesture that she remembered he pushed her hair back from her temple and kissed it. "You thought I didn't need you!" Eleanor whispered.

As she said it she had a strange sense of peace. She wondered if even now Kester knew how defeated she had felt until he put his arms around her.

2

The doctor gave Cornelia glasses that cleared her sight, but he advised that to save any possible taxing of her eyes she be sent to a special school where instruction was more oral than visual. Cornelia made no objection to having the glasses fitted, for she was so used to examinations of her eyes that she regarded such proceedings as part of the ordinary routine of life, but she protested volubly when Eleanor pinned a leather case containing the glasses to her dress and told her she must never be without them.

"Spectacles are for old ladies!" she exclaimed in disgusted bewilderment. At last, to her parents' insistence, she agreed, "Well, I'll keep them pinned to my dress a *little* while, till I can see the way I used to."

Neither Kester nor Eleanor could bear yet to tell her that she would never see the way she used to. Though the case was always attached to her dress Cornelia usually ignored it, and for the present they did not require her to do otherwise. But when they took her home they observed that except at close range she could not tell Mamie from Dilcy, and when Violet Purcell came to call, Cornelia, glancing from the window, said, "There's a lady coming up the steps, mother," and not until Violet came in and crossed the room to welcome her back did she exclaim "Why hello, Miss Violet!"

But her handicap was not as great as they had feared, for Cornelia, apparently hardly realizing that she did so, made clever adjustments. They had not been at home a month before Kester and Eleanor discovered that while it was possible to speak in undertones before Philip and not attract his attention, they dared not say anything in Cornelia's presence unless it was meant for her hearing. Evidently Cornelia had been sharpening her ears during her winter in darkness until now she listened as instinctively as most people looked. Her habit of listening supplemented her vision remarkably well. They were surprised and delighted to observe it.

According to promise, Eleanor took her shopping. Cornelia reveled in her new clothes, and smiled when acquaintances and strangers alike exclaimed "What a beautiful little girl!" To the frequent "Where did you *get* those eyelashes?" she replied in some astonishment, "They grew on me," which

Eleanor thought a more intelligent answer than the query deserved. Fearing that Cornelia was going to be made a very vain little person, she tried to shield her from too many compliments, but there was little she could do about it. Cornelia was undeniably exquisite, and so far at least she accepted remarks on her own beauty as she did those on the beauty of the oak avenue, as reasonable observations about a fact nobody ever thought to question.

But sometimes her parents almost wished Cornelia were not so acute, for she was quick to realize that nobody had said anything about her going back to school. Insisting that her eyes were almost well, Cornelia wanted to know how soon she could go back. She liked school, and complained that all the others would learn to read better than she did. Eleanor would have been willing to postpone indefinitely the painful task of telling Cornelia her eyes would never recover completely. But with his new grim quietness Kester said she had to be told, and one day without warning he told her.

It was a summer afternoon. Kester and Eleanor were in the library discussing the merits of the school upstate where they had decided to send her, and as she went through the hall unnoticed by them Cornelia's eager ears caught the word "school." She came in, saying she wanted to go back.

"You can't now," Eleanor answered her with determined cheerfulness. "School is out—it's summer."

"Oh," said Cornelia. She drew up a footstool and sat down upon it. "Then in the fall I can go back?" she asked. "My eyes will be cleared up by then?"

Over her head Eleanor and Kester exchanged glances. Kester straightened himself in his chair. He addressed her in a matter-of-fact tone.

"Cornelia, this fall you're going to a new school. This one is up the river."

"Up the river? But why must I go to a new place?"

"This is a special school. While you're there you'll learn a lot of things most boys and girls don't ever learn."

"Special? But I like my school!" Cornelia protested. "I want to be with all the children I know!"

But Kester went on, telling her in more detail that at the new school she would acquire accomplishments that would put her friends to shame. He made the prospect sound inviting, and as Cornelia heard him she gradually began to like it, while Eleanor for the hundredth time was admiring his

275

bravery and tact. "You'll have a fine time there," Kester continued. "You'll learn to typewrite without looking at the keys—"

"Like mother?"

"Maybe even faster than she can. And you'll learn to play the piano—"

Cornelia was still puzzled. "But even learning all that why can't I stay at home. like other people?"

Eleanor bit her lip hard, but Kester's answer was unhesitating. "Because your eyes aren't like other people's, Cornelia."

"But aren't they going to be?" she cried.

"No."

Cornelia started; she turned her head to look at him. Her glasses were in their case. She put them on, looking at him again through their lenses, and then slowly she took them off again. She asked in a hurt surprise, "You mean—my eyes aren't going to clear up? Not ever?"

"Not ever," said Kester.

Cornelia opened her eyes wide and stared around the room; she narrowed them. trying to look through her long lashes. Her eyes filled with tears, which she tried to blink back. One tear toppled over the edge and she lifted her hand quickly to brush it away. She rested her chin on her hand. For a long time she sat quite still.

Kester reached out and put his hand over Eleanor's. Not daring to move or speak, they waited tensely. It was as though they had stumbled upon a scene too private to be fit for observation and now could not withdraw, so that all they could do with decency was try to make themselves as little obvious as possible. Cornelia's experience of life was tiny. They did not know how much she remembered of what she used to see nor how sharp a contrast she felt between her previous situation and her present one. With the flexibility of childhood she had already to a great extent adapted herself to the change. The main difficulty she was facing now was that of being different from other people, though how clearly she was comprehending this they could not tell. But they both felt that they were seeing her, not yet seven years old, take the first step in the hard transition between being a child and an adult. At last Cornelia swallowed, drew a long breath, and turned to them.

"I thought—" she began, and her voice broke with the effort to make words. Her mouth quivered, and she turned helplessly to Kester. He picked her up. Cornelia flung her arms about his neck and buried her face. Kester held her tenderly, speaking to her in undertones until she grew quiet and lifted her head. Eleanor gave her a handkerchief, and when Cornelia had dabbed her face dry she sat curled up on Kester's knees, folding the corner of the handkerchief with concentrated attention. At last she looked up.

"I can see *pretty* good!" she said to them defiantly.

Eleanor had such a pain in her throat that she could not speak. But Kester said,

"Why yes, you can. And by the time you've learned to swim and dive and dance folks will hardly notice that your eyes aren't quite as good as theirs."

"I can do all that?" Cornelia asked anxiously.

"Of course you can."

"Like other girls?"

"Like other girls."

Cornelia thought a moment, then scrambled down from his knees. "Can I go up there soon? Do they have school in the summertime?"

"You can go next month."

She put up her hand to brush back a lock of her tumbled hair. "I can see all right," she insisted. "I can see everything. I can see the door."

As though to prove it she walked to the door and put her hand on the knob. Eleanor stood up. "Where are you going?" she asked. It was hard to keep her voice level.

"No place. Just upstairs. To tell Philip what a good school I'm going to." She glanced back over her shoulder. "I can see all *right!*" she exclaimed. and slammed the door behind her.

Eleanor sat on Kester's knees where Cornelia had been and hid her face against him as Cornelia had done, and he held her as gently as he had held Cornelia. She was not shedding tears, but she clung to him for comfort. At length, when she raised her head, Kester said to her,

"Cornelia is very like you."

"Yes," said Eleanor, "she defies life. I've been observing that lately. But she's like you too. She's gallant. She's going to boast to Philip about the superior advantages of that school until by suppertime he'll want to go with her."

"Don't ever mention her eyes unless you have to," Kester urged. "She doesn't want to talk about them. I'm glad of that. She'll never whine."

Eleanor nodded. "I believe she has a chance to be happy. She's beautiful, she's clever, she's courageous."

"I've been thinking," said Kester. "Her eyes aren't strong, but we've never been intellectuals anyway. She's not likely to want to be a profound student. And she won't need glasses for dancing—Eleanor, imagine that devastating child ten years from now at a Mardi Gras ball in New Orleans!"

She laughed at the picture, and then grew serious again. "I want her to be more than beautiful, Kester. I want her to be wise. To be generous. Do you think we can make her so?"

"At least," he returned, "we have more knowledge than we used to have."

"I hope so. Yes, I'm sure of it."

Kester added, "I have an idea that she's going to be a better person than either of us."

Eleanor smiled suddenly. "Kester, has it occurred to you that she ought to be? You and I—we're so intensely what we *are*. Your parents are very much like each other and so are mine. But our children have two inheritances. They'll blend that fine, impractical idealism of your people with the savage strength of mine. You're right. They can be better than either of us."

"If we can teach them tolerance instead of pride," Kester said.

Eleanor slipped off his knees. She went to the window and stood looking down the two long lines of oaks that had rustled above the heads of many generations.

"Why couldn't we let each other alone?" she asked in a low voice. "We fell in love because we were so different. Then all we did was twist and pull at each other, trying to make changes that couldn't be made—"

"I know. Why should anyone do that? Why is it that we can't think of any higher destiny for the people we love than that they become just like ourselves?"

She shook her head. Through the window a warm drift of wind blew in from the cottonfields. Eleanor remembered the night when she had walked along the river toward Isabel Valcour's home. She had been so desolate that night. Today was very different. Today she felt a spiritual security that was both an anchor and a guide.

"Kester," she asked, "what has become of Isabel Valcour?"

"She's gone away," said Kester. "To New York, I think."

"Why?"

"Possibly because I suggested it."

"When did you see her?" she asked, turning around.

"I didn't. She wrote to me several times while we were in New Orleans. At first I didn't answer, then after you and I had that frank talk of ours I sent her a rather long letter."

"What did you say to her?"

"None of your business," he returned with a faint smile.

"Why not?"

"Because it's not. After all, she was in love with me, you know."

"She wasn't."

Kester gave a little sigh, but there were humorous crinkles around his eyes. "I suppose men and women have been arguing about these things since the fall of Jericho. Since she's gone, since I don't give a damn whether or not she ever comes back, what difference does it make?"

Eleanor tied a loop in the cord that held back the curtain. For some time she said no more. She was thinking that in spite of what Kester said she would be very glad to hear that Isabel had starved to death in a garret, but she was sure life held for her no such prospect. Isabel had spoken of a millionaire she could marry if she chose. Though she had only half believed her at the moment, Eleanor reflected that she had probably been telling the truth. With her powers of enchantment unimpaired, now that she had no more hope of Kester, Isabel had almost certainly gone away to take up another bejeweled existence. Eleanor glanced around again at Kester, and as their eyes met she found suddenly that she did not care at all what happened to Isabel Valcour. She said,

"Very well. Now I'm never going to mention her name to you again as long as I live."

"Thank you," said Kester. "Thank you very much."

He came over to the window and put his arm around her shoulders. Looking up at his handsome profile Eleanor thought of the time when he had first enraptured her imagination, and of the bright beginning of their marriage, and marveled at how little one learned from happiness.

As she remembered it, that time seemed remote, and she and Kester seemed almost incredibly young and arrogant. They had been so sure they did not need to learn anything. They had rushed into marriage across a barrier that intolerant generations had been building for a hundred and fifty years, they had laughed when warned of its existence and then blamed each other when they had found that laughter did not blow it down. It was all very well to say that such different philosophies as theirs never should have come into existence in a country supposedly based on equality of privilege. Quarreling with dead grandfathers was easy, and useless; they might as well have faced the fact that Kester reverenced the manner of life while she reverenced its means, and that such divergent standards could be reconciled only by humility. But they had not learned humility, and so instead of being indulgent they had been wrathful.

Nothing could give them back those turbulent years. But there were probably a great many years ahead of them, in which they could attain and give to their children the peace of self-mastery. Eleanor looked out at the moss-hung trees, thinking of the long lines of her people and Kester's who had lived in this country, and wondered if each of those generations had had to pay the price of its own understanding. She and Kester were too battered by conflict ever to recapture the thoughtless delight they used to have. But as she thought of that Kester turned his head suddenly and smiled at her, and Eleanor felt closer to him than she had ever been before. Their faults had not undergone any miraculous reversal, and they knew enough not to expect the coming years to be either easy or simple, but whatever happened, they would face it without doubt of each other. She smiled back at him with a quiet assurance, because, though they had come down from their shining pinnacles, the descent had taught them the beginning of wisdom.